PROOF
POSITIVE

PHILLIP MARGOLIN

PROOF POSITIVE

**Doubleday Large Print
Home Library Edition**

HarperCollins*Publishers*

This Large Print Edition, prepared especially for Doubleday Large Print Home Library, contains the complete, unabridged text of the original Publisher's Edition.

ISBN-13: 978-0-7394-7027-5

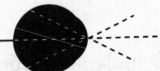

**This Large Print Book carries the
Seal of Approval of N.A.V.H.**

FOR MY DAUGHTER, AMI,
AND HER FIANCÉ, ANDY—
HAVE A WONDERFUL
LIFE TOGETHER

PROLOGUE

DOUG WEAVER HAD EXPERIENCED his fair share of bad days during his legal career, but the day Oregon executed Raymond Hayes was one of the worst. Doug tried to convince himself that watching someone die from a lethal injection wasn't like seeing someone stabbed to death or crushed by a train, but that only helped him deal with what he would see. It didn't ease his guilt. Deep down, he believed that Raymond Hayes was going to die because he had screwed up.

The fact that Doug liked his client made it even more difficult. Bonding wasn't unusual during a death case where the attorney and his client were thrown together for months or years at a time. Sometimes during a visit at the penitentiary, when they were talking about NASCAR races or football games, Doug would almost forget why Ray had needed representation. There were even moments when he thought, There but for the grace of God go I. The slightly overweight attorney with the receding hairline did bear a faint resemblance to his chubby, balding client. Both men were also in their early thirties and they'd grown up in small towns. But that was where the similarities ended. Doug was a lot smarter than the majority of his high school classmates, while Ray had barely graduated. After high school, Doug had gone to college and Ray had stayed home, working the farm for his ailing, widowed mother before selling out and moving with her to the cottage in Portland where she had been brutally murdered.

The last time Doug had made the fifty-mile drive from Portland to the Oregon State Penitentiary it had been to tell Raymond that the justices of the United States Supreme Court had voted against taking up his case.

"Does that mean I'm going to die?" Ray

had asked in that lazy drawl that sometimes made you wonder if he was even slower than his below-average intelligence test scores suggested.

The question had caught Doug off guard. It took a shifting of mental gears to accept the notion that a denial of a writ of certiorari in Ray's case was the legal equivalent of shooting his client between the eyes.

"Well," Doug had stammered as he tried to think of a tactful way of answering the question.

Ray had just smiled. He'd been seeing Father McCord a lot, and Jesus was now a big part of his life.

"It's okay, Doug," his client had assured him. "I'm not afraid to meet my Lord and Savior."

Doug wasn't so sure that there was a place in Heaven for a son who had beaten his seventy-two-year-old mother to death with a hammer so he could steal her diamond wedding ring and forty-three dollars, but he kept the thought to himself. If Ray was convinced that he was straight with the Lord, Doug wasn't going to play devil's advocate.

"My life ain't been so great," Ray had said. "I hope I'm a better person in Heaven."

"You will be," Doug had assured him.

Ray had studied his attorney with a sad, compassionate eye. "You still think I killed Mom, don't you?"

Doug had never told Ray that he didn't believe his protestations of innocence, but he guessed that somewhere along the way he'd slipped up and revealed his true feelings.

"I really don't know, one way or the other, Ray," Doug had hedged.

Ray had just smiled. "It's okay," Ray said. "I know you think I lied to you. I appreciate how hard you worked for me, even though you thought I done it. But I didn't kill Mom. It's the way I always said it. So I know I'll go to Heaven and stand by the side of Jesus."

Doug had handled other capital cases, but only Ray had been sentenced to death. Very few Oregon inmates had been executed since the reinstatement of the death penalty in 1984. Doug hated the fact that he would be one of the few attorneys in the state who could say he'd witnessed the execution of a client.

During the week leading up to the execution, Doug didn't sleep well and felt tired and cranky. Anxiety caused his mind to wander at the office and made it difficult to get any work done. He had been drinking more than usual, too, and that was always a bad sign.

Doug had never questioned Ray's guilt, but his inability to stave off death ate at him. He was constantly second-guessing decisions he'd made, especially the decision to persuade Ray to plead guilty. It wasn't as if his strategy was unreasonable. He'd consulted several lawyers who handled death cases, and most had agreed with his plan. The older, experienced attorneys had convinced him that winning a death case meant keeping your client alive. The evidence against Ray was incredibly strong, and Doug had gambled that Ray's acceptance of guilt and his spotless record would sway the jury in favor of life in the sentencing phase of the trial. He had been horribly, horribly wrong.

Doug worked on the day of the execution, but he didn't accomplish much. Before leaving for the prison, he ate a light dinner; put on his best suit, a clean white shirt, and his nicest tie; and even shined his shoes. He wanted a drink badly, but he limited himself to one glass of scotch. Doug was going to be sober at the execution. He figured he owed Ray that.

The day had been out of sync with Doug's

mood and the seriousness of the event he was about to witness. Dark clouds should have blocked the sun. There should have been lightning strikes, heavy rain, and a sky filled with ravens. Instead, spring was in the air, gaily colored flowers were in bloom, and nary a cloud hung over the interstate. Doug found the weather profoundly depressing, and he was grateful when the sunset cast shadows over the landscape.

At nine-thirty p.m., Doug parked in a lot several miles from the prison. The location of the lot had been shrouded in secrecy to keep all but a select group of reporters from finding the witnesses, who were to be shuttled to the penitentiary. Ray and his mother were the last of a small family, so, thankfully, there were no relatives waiting. Doug noticed a group of government officials standing off to one side. Among them were Amaya Lathrop, the assistant attorney general who had persuaded the appellate courts to affirm the sentence of death; and Martin Poe, a career prosecutor in the Multnomah County District Attorney's Office, who had obtained the death sentence at trial. Jake Teeny, the deputy DA who'd second-chaired the case, had moved back East two years ago. Lathrop had always seen the case as a debate about issues of constitutional law far removed from the gore through which Doug and the prosecutors had waded in the courtroom, so Doug wasn't surprised that the AG nodded in his direction, while Poe studiously avoided looking at him.

Marge Cross drove up moments after Doug parked. She was a short, chunky brunette with the courtroom demeanor of a pit bull, who had been single and fresh from a clerkship at the Oregon Supreme Court when she second-chaired Raymond's case. Marge had been dead set against the guilty plea, but she'd never criticized Doug after the verdict of death, and had second-chaired two other cases with him after *Hayes*. The attorneys had talked about driving to the prison together, but Marge's two-year-old daughter had come down with the flu and Marge had had to stay with her until her husband finished teaching a class at Portland Community College.

"I see Poe has come to gloat," she said bitterly.

"I don't think he's gloating, Marge. He's not that low."

Marge shrugged. "You're entitled to your opinion. But he and Teeny were snickering all through the trial and I heard they celebrated with some of the other Neanderthals from the office after the sentencing hearing."

Doug didn't bother to argue. Marge was very political. She saw every case as a battle against the forces of fascism. Motherhood had not softened her. Doug—oddly, for a lawyer—didn't really like conflict. He got along with the DAs, as a rule, and thought of the prosecutors as men and women doing a tough job to the best of their ability.

"Hooper's here," Marge said in a tone even more scathing than the one she'd used when she was referring to Poe. Doug spotted Steve Hooper, the lead detective on Ray's case, talking to a state trooper near the van that would take them to the prison. The detective was a linebacker in street clothes, with wide bunched shoulders, a thick neck, and the hint of a gut. His head was covered with a thatch of jet-black hair, and a shaggy mustache drooped over his upper lip. The only thing small about the detective were his close-set eyes and his pug nose, which looked out of place on such a broad face.

Hooper was an aggressive cop who believed that he was never wrong. Marge called him "the Fuehrer," and Doug found it hard to disagree. Hooper had certainly used gestapo tactics when he arrested Ray, and Doug was certain that he had lied about certain incriminating statements that Ray was supposed to have made before the detective switched on his tape recorder in the interrogation room. Ray swore he never made the statements, but there was no way to prove that Hooper had falsified his report.

"Did you talk to Ray?" Marge asked.

"By phone just before I left the office."

"How's he doing?"

"He sounded calm. Spoke about going to a better place, standing by the side of the Lord. I'm glad he found religion. It's helping him accept . . . what's going to happen."

Doug licked his lips. He found it hard to talk about the execution.

"Listen up, people," shouted Thad Spencer, the community relations representative of the Department of Corrections. "We'll be heading out in a minute. Just a reminder. There will be medical people standing by in the viewing room in case any of you need help, and there's no talking permitted after you enter the viewing room. Any questions?"

Spencer fielded a few from the reporters, but the attorneys were quiet and somber. After the last question, Spencer herded the witnesses into a van. They took backstreets all the way to the penitentiary. Along the route, they passed police cars at several locations. They were there to deal with the protesters who were chanting outside the prison. Doug noticed that the police officers stopped talking and stared into the van as they drove by.

The van passed Cyclone fencing and razor wire on the way into the penitentiary.

"I saw some old newsreels of East Berlin in the 1960s," Marge said. "There's an uncanny resemblance. Makes you wonder if we're still in America."

Doug didn't respond. He wasn't feeling well, and he was thankful that there would be medics in the viewing room. He didn't think he'd throw up or pass out, but he couldn't be sure.

Inside the prison, Doug went through a metal detector and had his hand stamped. Then everyone waited in a comfortable office where coffee and fruit had been provided. Doug didn't touch either. Amaya Lathrop, the assistant AG, walked over and offered that it must be really tough for him to have to see the execution. She was so genuinely sympathetic that Marge loosened up. Soon she and Doug were talking to Martin Poe, who turned out to be as nervous as everyone else. It soon became clear that no one but Steve Hooper was feeling particularly good about what was going to happen. The detective sat by himself, looking relaxed and happy as he snacked, balancing a plate loaded with fruit on his lap. Adding to the general unease was the chanting of the demonstrators on State Street, loud enough to be heard inside the office.

At eleven-thirty, Thad Spencer led the witnesses to the death chamber at the rear of the prison. Each time they were moved to a new location, Doug's tension level skyrocketed, and he regretted his decision to come to the prison sober. As they walked down the silent corridors, he felt light-headed and worried again about fainting. Talking would have helped, but everyone was so uptight that Doug was afraid a single word would sound like the crash of a thousand accidentally dropped dinner plates. He couldn't think of anything to say anyway.

By the time the witnesses were led into the death chamber, it was a little after midnight.

The viewing area was claustrophobically small, about eight by twelve. The witnesses stood on a raised platform. In front of them was a window veiled by a curtain. The silence was broken only by the sound the reporters made when their pencils scratched across their notepads.

At twelve-twenty, the curtain lifted. Ray was strapped to a gurney. Intravenous tubes had been inserted in his veins. They were attached to glass tubes that protruded from the wall. The tubes would supply the lethal chemicals that would end Raymond Hayes's life. Behind the wall—unseen—was the executioner.

From his spot on the platform, Doug could look down on his client. Ray seemed a little nervous but calmer than Doug had expected. The superintendent of the penitentiary was standing next to the gurney. He laid a comforting hand on Ray's shoulder. Ray turned his head, scanned the room, and fixed on Doug. A microphone in the death chamber must have been activated, because Doug could hear Ray clearly when he spoke.

"Superintendent Keene told me you ain't allowed to talk, so I understand if you don't answer," his client said. "Thanks for coming,

Doug. You being here comforts me. You too, Marge."

Doug heard Marge's sharp intake of breath.

"Well, these are my last words, so I want to make them good."

He fixed on Martin Poe.

"I am innocent, Mr. Poe, but don't worry. I know you think I killed my mom and that you were only doing your job. I forgive you and God will forgive you, so find peace in your heart."

Ray choked up for a second and had to stop. As hard as he was fighting, he could not stop a tear from trickling down his cheek.

"Mom knows I didn't do her no harm and she'll be able to tell me so right soon. God bless all of you."

Ray nodded to the superintendent. The superintendent nodded back and left the room. Ray closed his eyes and breathed deeply a few times; then all activity stopped. His right eye was completely closed but, bizarrely, his left lid was slightly open, allowing the institutional light to reflect in his dark pupil. Doug could see that no one was in there anymore. He sighed and fought back tears. Poor Ray, he thought. He'd been put down like a dog.

* * *

No one said anything during the walk back to the van. Doug guessed that no one could think of anything to say that wouldn't sound forced, trite, or false. As soon as they were in the lot, Marge took Doug's hand and gave it a squeeze.

"You did all you could, Doug. No one could have done more. If you ever start thinking that you failed Ray, remember that he didn't think so. And also remember that no matter what he said just now he did kill his mother in a horrible way. I think it's wonderful that he found God but he was a guilty man no matter what type of man he was when he died."

Doug nodded, afraid to speak. Marge touched his shoulder. "See you in town," she said. Then she walked to her car.

Doug paused for a minute. The air was warm, and the night sky was clear and covered with stars. It would be nice to think that Ray was one of them, but he didn't have much hope. The sound of several engines starting up snapped him out of his reverie. He got into his car and was shocked to discover that it was only a little after one-thirty. He thought for sure that he'd missed an entire night. Doug took a few deep breaths, jammed a Rolling Stones CD into the stereo, cranked up the volume until it was so loud that he could not think, and headed home. As he drove out of the lot, he noticed Steve Hooper standing beside his car, speaking into a cell phone.

When the phone rang, the clock on the mantel read 1:36. Bernard Cashman had been expecting the call, and he picked up on the first ring.

"He's dead," Steve Hooper said.

"Thank you for telling me."

"We couldn't have done it without you, Bernie."

Cashman's chest swelled with pride. "It was a team effort, Steve. I just played a small part."

"Hey, you don't have to be modest with me. You're the best lab guy I've ever worked with. It was the print on the hammer that nailed Hayes, no pun intended."

"Are you calling from the prison?"

"I'm at my car. We just got out."

"You must be exhausted. Go home and get a good night's rest."

"I'll sleep like a baby knowing that scumbag is six feet under. Nice work, and I'm not just saying that."

"I appreciate it. Thanks again for the call."

Cashman hung up the phone and enjoyed the moment. Then he stood. He was in his late thirties, a tall man with a lean face and a dignified bearing, who kept himself trim and fit with workouts in the gym and long runs. His ash-blond hair was expertly cut, and his manicured beard and mustache gave him the look of an eighteenth-century count. When he moved, it was with the grace of a duelist. His melodic baritone would find a home in the finest choir and was hypnotic in a courtroom.

Cashman went into the kitchen and uncorked a bottle of La Grande Dame 1979 that he'd kept chilled in a bucket of ice. The champagne was outrageously expensive, but only the best was suitable for an occasion like this. Bernard Cashman's testimony had put three men on death row, but Raymond Hayes was the first to be executed.

Next the forensic expert prepared blini, on which he spread crème fraîche and fine beluga caviar. There was a ban on the Caspian Sea delicacy, because the Russian Mafia was overfishing the sturgeon that produced it, but Cashman had connections that were willing to bend the law when gourmet cuisine was at stake.

Cashman filled a slender glass flute with the sparkling, golden champagne and sipped. He sighed, then bit into a blini. A delicate globule of roe burst on his tongue, and the explosion of flavor was exquisite. The criminalist closed his eyes and smiled with satisfaction. What a perfect moment!

Open on the kitchen table was a scrapbook in which Cashman kept a record of his courtroom triumphs. The section devoted to Raymond Hayes was filled with articles detailing the guilty plea and sentencing. Tomorrow, he would cut out the article about Hayes's execution and paste it in.

Cashman finished his glass of champagne and ate the rest of the caviar. He wished there were others here to celebrate with him, but he knew many people would find his celebration inappropriate, peculiar, or both. They were entitled to their opinions, but he did not believe that it was wrong to rejoice when justice was done.

PART ONE
THE MADMAN

1

IF YOU LOOKED UP THE WORD "pathetic" in the dictionary, you might find a picture of Vincent Ballard. Ballard had not always been pathetic. At one point in his life, he had been considered brilliant and dynamic. That era had coincided with the dot-com bubble, when Vincent was making more money than he could count as a partner in an Internet start-up that could not miss. In those days, Vincent rode the tiger; hell, he had tamed the tiger and turned it into a pussycat.

Before he became rich, people described Vincent, with his Coke-bottle glasses, acne, and unkempt hair, as a skinny nerd who couldn't get even ugly girls to give him a second look. By the nineties, Vincent was wearing contact lenses and handmade suits from London, collecting sports cars like baseball cards, and kicking one centerfold-quality babe out of his bed as soon as another luscious cutie made his cocaine-powered dick rise.

Then the bubble burst. Overnight, Vincent's stock options didn't add up to the price of a Starbucks latte. But, hey, no problem. Vincent wasn't worried. He was so high all the time that reality had become irrelevant. Was he not *the* brilliant, sexy Vincent Ballard, brain and stud extraordinaire? So what if his company went under? He'd get a new idea and soon he'd be rolling again. There was only one problem; drugs had messed up Vincent's mind so badly that the idea part of his brain was now as limp as his dick.

Drug habits are expensive. Vincent sold the sports cars and his collection of fine wines. He downsized from his two-million-dollar home to a one-bedroom apartment in Portland's fashionable Pearl District. Five years after his company went under, he couldn't make the rent anymore. Now he lived in a residential motel in a single room that smelled like beer, stale pizza, and garbage; and he worked at minimum-wage jobs when he could scam the drug tests.

A few months before he met Juan Ruiz, Vincent had been busted for possession and given probation on the condition that he enroll in a county drug program. Vincent had graduated summa cum laude and was as clean as a whistle. His probation officer had even helped him land a halfway decent job at a software company.

Vincent had kicked the habit several times before. During the early days of cleanliness, he was always euphoric. This time was no different. Vincent *knew* that soon he would be back in the land of Armani and Porsche. Then he had the predictable clash with his supervisor, which led to his early exit from employment, followed by depression and the inevitable reunion with Mr. H.

A few weeks after he started using again, Vincent's connection was arrested. Vincent badly needed a fix, and he learned through the junkie grapevine about a new source for the Mexican black-tar heroin he craved. Juan Ruiz was dealing in Old Town. Since he was selling and Vincent was buying, Ruiz was higher up the food chain than his customer, but not by much. When Vincent spotted Ruiz, the emaciated pusher was dancing from foot to foot to cope with the cold and damp, and his eyes were continually shifting as he scanned the dark, deserted streets for cops.

"Are you Juan?" Vincent asked nervously. He was twitchy and needed his fix.

"What you want, bro?"

"Toby told me your stuff is good."

"My shit is the best," Ruiz said. "Show me some money and you can see for yourself."

Vincent pulled out a handful of crumpled bills, and Ruiz spit out a balloon. If Vincent had been a cop, he would have swallowed it.

"Where you been buying?" Juan asked as he counted the bills.

"Around, you know."

All junkies are paranoid, so Vincent was intentionally vague.

"Well, you buy from me and I'll treat you right. Our shit's cheaper, too," he added, holding out two bills.

"What's this?"

"A rebate, amigo. There's a new man in town. He wants to treat you right. We got the best shit and the cheapest. You come to me. Don't go to no other dealers. Spread the word."

A light went on in one of the few areas of Vincent's brain that were still working. Martin Breach ran the drug business in Portland, but rumor had it that a Colombian cartel was trying to cut into his territory. Breach was not known for being a good sport or a gracious loser, and the word on the street was that he was giving drugs and money to anyone providing information about dealers who were working for Felix Dorado, the cartel's front man.

Back at the motel, Vincent shot up. First things first. But what goes up must come down. Vincent knew that he'd need to score again soon, but he couldn't afford another hit. When he was able to get out of bed, he walked up the street to Lombardi's. The bar stank of sweat and cheap beer, and catered to people like Vincent. Martin Breach owned it.

Twenty minutes after Vincent convinced the bartender that he had some information Mr. Breach would be interested in hearing, the door opened, and two men walked over to the wooden booth where the bartender had told Vincent to wait. Vincent had once been a businessman, and this was business. He slicked down his hair as best he could, squared his shoulders, and stood up.

"Vincent Ballard," he said, offering his hand. Neither man took it. After a few seconds, Vincent felt ridiculous, and his hand dropped to his side.

"Sit down," Charlie LaRosa said as he slid in across from Ballard. LaRosa had a square face with dark, flat eyes that made him look very intimidating, so Vincent was surprised by how gentle he sounded.

Vincent sat on the bench, and the other man squeezed in beside him, forcing Vincent against the wall and cutting off all avenues of escape. The man smelled of aftershave and had thick, greasy hair and long sideburns. Vincent's head was even with his chin. Dark stubble highlighted a pale, jagged scar. This man never spoke during the time they were together.

"So, Vincent, how you doing?" Charlie inquired politely.

"Okay," Ballard answered, trying hard to keep a tremor out of his voice.

"Good, good. So, I understand you have something to tell me."

Once upon a time, Vincent had been a big shot who sat at polished mahogany conference tables, listening to his lawyers conduct negotiations involving millions of dollars. He had picked up a thing or two, and he knew that he shouldn't give away anything before he got something. Vincent licked his lips.

"Yeah, yeah, I do, but I want to know what's in it for me."

Charlie smiled and extended a ham-size hand. When he opened his fist, three dime-bags were resting in his palm. Vincent made a grab for them, but the fist closed and Vincent's fingers hovered above a set of scarred knuckles.

"So, Vincent?" Charlie asked.

Vincent told LaRosa about buying the dime bag from Juan Ruiz, about his rebate, and about Juan's sales pitch for better, cheaper dope. The man's expression didn't change. As soon as Vincent was done, he stood.

"Let's go for a ride and meet your friend," he said.

"He's not my friend."

"Good. Then you won't mind finding him for us."

Charlie nodded, and a hand circled Vincent's biceps. When the man beside him stood, Vincent's body rose with him. He didn't waste his breath protesting, but he did ask for his dope, which was more important to him than his life.

LaRosa patted Vincent on the shoulder.

"Don't worry. You done the right thing and I'm going to take care of you. But I have to make sure you aren't yanking my chain." He smiled. "Point out this fuckhead to us and the dope is yours. There might even be a bonus for you."

Vincent resigned himself to waiting for his fix. He'd hold it together, finger the dealer, and go to heaven. He was okay, for now anyway. The shakes wouldn't come for a while.

The men drove Vincent around Old Town in a dark blue Lincoln Continental until they spotted Juan Ruiz next to a chain-link fence on the periphery of a construction site. Vincent hadn't noticed Juan's minders when he made his buy the day before, but LaRosa spotted the gunmen lurking in the shadows when they drove by. As soon as they were parked around the corner, he took out his cell phone.

"I found that gift you're looking for," he said. "Nice ring. There's a pair of pearl earrings, too. We should meet. You know that Chinese joint over in Old Town?"

LaRosa listened for a moment. "Fifteen minutes. Have the Ratman buy the present.

I look too prosperous. I'm afraid they'd jack up the price."

"So, are we all done?" Vincent asked anxiously as soon as LaRosa cut the connection.

"We're done when I say we're done."

Ratman's real name was Henry Tedesco and he had been born in Ireland. Tedesco was tall and skinny. His eyes protruded from a face ravaged by acne when he was a kid. A long, thin nose and overbite made him resemble a rodent. There was a debate over whether he looked more like a weasel than a rat, but no one offered an opinion when Henry was around.

The true reason for Henry's emigration was a mystery, and Henry never spoke about it, but he was rumored to have been an IRA assassin before coming to America. Some people believed that Henry had fled Ireland because he had botched an attempt on a British MP. Others had heard that he had revealed an IRA arms cache to the British. What they did know for certain was that he was a distant relative of Martin Breach, who had supposedly squared Henry's problem with whoever was after him. Now Henry did special jobs for Martin.

Ratman was ideal for this job. He looked like a junkie. Juan Ruiz hadn't suspected a thing when Henry sidled up to him, making sure that Ruiz was between him and his protectors so Juan's minders wouldn't spot the gun he jammed into Ruiz's belly.

"Make one move or say anything and I'll shoot you in the gut. You'll die screaming," Henry said.

"You're making a big mistake," Ruiz said.

"You made the mistake when you started selling in Martin Breach's territory," Ratman said just as the Lincoln screeched to a halt behind him. The doors flew open. Henry shoved Ruiz inside and slammed the door before Ruiz's protection realized what was happening. The car was rounding the corner before the gunmen could get off a shot.

Before meeting Henry Tedesco, Charlie LaRosa had taken Vincent to a deserted warehouse in an industrial park on the Columbia River. He'd had the key to a padlock that secured the gate in a chain-link fence and the key to a door that lay in the shadows on the side of the building facing the river. The man who never spoke waited behind the wheel of the Lincoln while Charlie escorted

Vincent inside. Three men had been waiting for them. Two of the men stayed in the shadows. The third was Arthur Wayne Prochaska, Martin Breach's right-hand man.

Prochaska was a giant with thick lips, a broad nose, pencil-thin eyebrows, and a bald, bullet-shaped head that he had used to stun debtors in the old days, when he and Martin Breach were leg-breakers for the mob. Nowadays, Martin ran the mob and Art managed a couple of bars and considered himself an entrepreneur, except for those rare occasions when Martin wanted the only man he could trust to take care of a different kind of business.

By the time they arrived at the warehouse, Vincent had been sweating profusely and fidgeting. After listening to LaRosa, Prochaska let Vincent shoot up. When Ratman pushed Ruiz into the warehouse an hour later, Vincent was in a pleasant mood.

Ruiz stumbled forward, and LaRosa threw him onto a chair.

"I'm going to ask you questions," Prochaska said as Ratman used duct tape to secure Juan to the chair. "You'll give me truthful answers."

Prochaska was holding a ball-peen hammer, which looked like a toy in his massive hand. He tapped Ruiz on the knee hard enough to make him flinch.

"You don't give me truthful answers and I'll break your right knee and ask you again. Then I'll do the left knee, your shins, et cetera. You got the picture?"

Ruiz nodded. His eyes were wide with fear, and he was on the verge of tears. Juan wasn't tough and he had not signed up for something like this.

"I help you," he said. "You ask me. I help you."

"Good. You're being smart," Prochaska said. "Your name is Juan, right?"

"Yes, sir, Juan Ruiz."

"See, that was easy. You gave me a straight answer and I didn't hurt you. So, Juan, who you working for?"

"Felix," Juan answered, eager to please and grateful that Art hadn't hurt him.

"What's Felix's last name?"

"Dorado. I can tell you where he lives."

"That won't be necessary, Juan. I know where he lives. What I don't know is how many pieces of shit like you he has dealing where they ain't supposed to and where they're selling. But I'll know that as soon as you tell me."

2

DOUG WEAVER WAS ON HIS WAY TO the Justice Center jail to interview a new, court-appointed client when the light on the corner of Fourth and Yamhill changed to red. The case sounded dull, and Doug wasn't thinking about it as he waited for the light to change. Doug was thinking about the dinner invitation he'd received from his wife, Karen, just before he left his office. He and Karen were separated, and this was a rare communication. The fact that she actually wanted to meet him face-to-face made him nervous and highly suspicious.

Karen was a rising star in the Portland

branch of an investment banking firm. She made a lot more money than he did, and Doug's failure to "pull his own weight" had been a major problem in the marriage. Doug's life had not changed much when Karen moved out two months ago. She traveled a lot and worked late when she was in Portland, so they didn't see much of each other, and they hadn't had sex regularly for a long time. Doug was certain that Karen was having an affair but he didn't have the energy to work at confirming his suspicions. It was hard for him to condemn Karen, anyway, because he felt guilty about the reasons for the breakup. He had convinced himself that he would probably have walked out, too, if Karen had been drinking as much as he was and had not lived up to the expectations with which both of them had started their marriage.

Thinking about his failed marriage depressed Doug. Fortunately, the Justice Center came into view and he turned his thoughts to his new case. All he knew about it was that Jacob Cohen—a homeless man—had spent time in prison for attempted rape. Convicted sex offenders had to register when they were paroled, and Cohen had been arrested for failing to register. A conviction could send him back to prison.

Doug hauled his briefcase up the Justice Center's broad steps. The sixteen-story concrete-and-glass building was separated from the Multnomah County Courthouse by a park. In addition to the Central Precinct of the Portland Police Bureau, the Justice Center was home to a branch of the Multnomah County District Attorney's Office, several courtrooms, State Parole and Probation, and the Multnomah County jail, where Doug's client was currently residing. The jail occupied the fourth through tenth floors of the building, but the reception area was on the second floor. To reach it, Doug walked through the center's vaulted lobby, past the curving stairs that led to the courtrooms on the third floor, and through a pair of glass doors.

The sheriff's deputy who was manning the reception desk checked Doug's ID, searched his briefcase, and motioned him toward a metal detector that stood between Doug and the jail elevator. He passed through without setting off an alarm, and the guard walked him to the elevator and keyed him up to the floor where Cohen was being held.

After a short ride, Doug found himself in

a narrow hall with a thick metal door at one end. Next to the door, affixed to the pastel-yellow concrete wall, was an intercom, which he used to announce his presence. Moments later, a massive African-American jail guard peered at Doug through a plate of glass in the upper half of the door, then spoke into a walkie-talkie. Electronic locks snapped, and the guard ushered Doug into another narrow corridor, which ran in front of the three contact-visiting rooms, where prisoners had face-to-face meetings with their attorneys. Doug could see into the rooms through large windows outfitted with thick, shatterproof glass.

Waiting for him in the room farthest from the elevators was an emaciated prisoner with deranged hair, wild eyes, and a complexion that was one step removed from albino. Dressed in a shapeless orange jumpsuit, he sat in one of two molded plastic chairs that stood on either side of a round, Formica-topped table that was bolted to the floor, although "sat" did not quite describe what he was doing. His body was twisted on the chair, his knees were drawn up to his chest, and he looked like someone preparing to flee.

"You watch yourself with this one," the

guard said. "He isn't playing with a full deck."

"I'll be okay, but thanks," Doug said. The prisoner's obvious insanity was unsettling, but Doug didn't want the guard to know that he was nervous.

"Hey, I don't want to have to waste my day filling out reports," the guard answered with a smile. Then he opened the door to the contact room and stepped aside. Cohen's eyes fixed on Doug. The guard pointed to a black button that stuck out of an intercom affixed to the yellow wall.

"Press that when you're through or," he looked directly at Jacob Cohen, "if you need help. I'll come and get you." Then, before closing the door, he pointed at the prisoner. "And you, behave yourself, you hear?"

Jacob Cohen glared at the guard but stayed mute. As soon as the door closed, his sunken eyes shifted back to his visitor.

"Hello, Mr. Cohen. I'm . . ."

"Cohen is not here."

"You're not Jacob Cohen?" Doug asked, confused by the prisoner's answer. Of course, it wouldn't be the first time that the jail had screwed up and brought the wrong person for an initial interview.

"Cohen is not here."

"Okay, who are you?"

"John Doe." He smiled strangely. "I'm nameless and faceless. They've given me a number."

Doug was too tired for this bullshit, so he decided to ignore the weirdness and play it straight.

"Okay, Mr. Doe. My name is Doug Weaver and I've been appointed to be your lawyer."

A self-satisfied smile spread across Cohen's face. He dropped his feet to the floor, crossed his arms across his chest, and leaned back in his chair, suddenly at ease.

"Do you think I'm stupid? Who controls the court? They do. I'm no fool. I see right through you."

"By 'they' do you mean the government?"

Cohen just smiled, and Doug felt drained, even though the interview had barely started. It was a case like Cohen's that brought home how unsuccessful he was. A big-time criminal lawyer wouldn't be stuck handling a court-appointed failure-to-register case. But Doug wasn't earning enough to be able to turn down even a low-paying court appointment.

"Well," Doug said halfheartedly, "if you do mean the government, you're half right. I will be paid by the state because I'm taking this case on as a court appointment. But I don't work for the government. I'm in private practice." He laid one of his business cards on the table and sat down. "I specialize in criminal defense, Mr. . . . Doe and you're charged with a crime."

"A so-called crime," Cohen corrected, "manufactured from thin air by that slut and her minions."

"The DA is saying that you failed to register as a sex offender."

Cohen was suddenly AWOL mentally, his focus clearly turned inward.

"If she profane herself by playing the whore she shall be burnt with fire. Leviticus 21:9," he muttered.

Doug forged on. "Mr. Doe, when you were released from prison, were you told that you had to register as a convicted sex offender?"

"Oh, they told me, and I tried, but they conspired against me. 'And he saith unto me, the waters, which thou sawest, where the whore sitteth, are peoples, and multitudes, and nations, and tongues. And the ten horns which thou sawest upon the beast, these shall hate the whore, and shall make her desolate and naked, and shall eat her flesh, and burn her with fire.' Book of Revelation 17:15–16."

"So you knew that you had to register and you're telling me that you tried to register, but you think government conspirators made it look like you didn't try."

"You work for them, so you should know what they did."

Doug sighed. "I guess you wouldn't believe me if I told you that I usually work against the government."

Cohen smiled his weird smile and said nothing.

"Well, I do. The court-appointment system was set up to provide lawyers to people who don't have the money to hire counsel. We're paid by the state, but I'm not an employee of the state and I'll work like hell to defeat the state so you can stay out of prison. But I don't suppose you believe that?"

"I believe that lies come easily to your lips."

"Let's pretend that I'm not lying and that I'm really on your side. Or, better yet, let's pretend that you're the lawyer and you're giving your closing argument. What would you tell the jury about these charges?"

"Ah, the jury. A jury of my peers." Cohen

laughed. "I've met them before. They saw and heard the woman sitting on her scarlet-colored beast, full of names of blasphemy, having seven heads and ten horns, the mother of harlots and abominations of the earth. And they saw and heard me. And they chose."

His head nodded up and down. Then he looked at Doug.

"They can control them, so it wouldn't matter what I said."

"We're pretending here, so just tell me your story."

Cohen laughed. "Why not? I have nothing better to do. I was living in my car. It's not really mine. I found it in a lot, abandoned, so I slept there. I didn't at first. Two years ago, when I got out of prison, I was staying in a hotel and I had a job, but I lost the job and I couldn't pay my rent, so I moved to the lot." He flashed his weird smile. "No rent in my lot, no rent in my car."

"What did you do about a mailing address?"

"I had my mail sent to the parole office. They're supposed to keep it for me. But I don't get all of my mail. I think they take it."

"The police report says that you were supposed to register every year within ten days of your birthday and you didn't do that this year. A detective tried to find you at the address you listed as your home on your last form and concluded that it was a false home address."

Suddenly Cohen looked spent and defeated. "I don't want to go back there," he said.

"To prison?"

He nodded. "I am tormented." His hands gripped and tore at his frenetic, Brillo locks. "It's hell on Earth." Then he grew quiet, and Doug thought he heard his client say, "But it's what I deserve."

Doug suddenly saw through the facade. Jacob Cohen was definitely crazy, but he was also terrified and lost in a world that overwhelmed him. Doug's heart went out to his new client.

"I'm going to work hard for you. Believe me. I am on your side and I will try to help you."

He wasn't certain that Cohen had heard him, because Cohen's head was down, he was staring at the floor, and he was muttering so quietly that Doug could not make out what his client was saying.

Karen was waiting in a booth when Doug walked into South Park. She was a small woman with a narrow waist, large breasts, and straight auburn hair. She wore steel-rimmed glasses because she believed they made her look more serious, and she always dressed for success. Tonight, she was wearing a severe navy blue pantsuit. Doug tried a smile, and his anxiety increased when his wife didn't return it.

"Glad you could make it," Karen said, sounding like an investment banker greeting a potential client.

"You look good," Doug said as he slid into the booth. He figured that a compliment might lighten the heavy atmosphere. And the truth was Karen did look good. She had always looked good, and she looked her best naked, but Doug didn't want to go there, because it would be a sharp and painful reminder of what he'd been missing since their marriage had turned sour.

"Thank you," Karen answered with enough formality to let Doug know that he wasn't going to like what she was going to tell him. "Do you feel like a cocktail? I've ordered already."

Doug was shocked that Karen was offering him alcohol knowing the effect it had on him, but he decided that he would probably be able to handle what he was about to hear much better if he wasn't completely sober.

"Why not? I've had a rough day. I can use a stiff drink."

Karen signaled the waiter, and Doug placed his order.

"What happened today?" Karen asked when the waiter left. Doug didn't think that Karen was the least bit interested in his day. He thought that she wanted him to talk so she could build up the courage to tell him what she wanted to say.

"I had to go to the jail to interview a new client, a court appointment. He's a doozy."

Over their cocktails, Doug told Karen about his strange encounter with Jacob Cohen. As the alcohol kicked in, Doug began to feel warm, light-headed, and relaxed.

"Are you going to use an insanity defense?" Karen asked.

"The insanity defense is popular on TV but it's rarely used in real life. If a defendant is really crazy it's so obvious most of the time that a prosecutor can see it too and the case is usually resolved by a plea involving psychiatric care."

"Do you think Cohen is faking?"

"No, I think Cohen's the real deal, a genuine nutcase. If my shrink agrees I'll show his report to the DA."

So far, Karen had maneuvered Doug into doing all of the talking. He decided that it was time for her to tell him why she'd asked him to dinner.

"So, what's up with you?" Doug asked.

The question seemed to startle Karen.

"You did ask me to meet you here," Doug said. "I assume you have something to tell me."

"I do." Karen paused. "I got a promotion. They told me, this morning."

"That's terrific," Doug said, faking his enthusiasm and forcing a big smile. The smile faded when he saw the look on Karen's face.

"I'm moving to New York. I'm going to be working out of our national headquarters in Manhattan."

"Oh."

"I'm leaving next week. I . . . I did think about turning them down, but this is very important for my career."

"I see."

Karen sighed. "Oh, hell, Doug, I don't want to lie to you. I didn't think about the offer for one second. I jumped at it. Our marriage isn't . . ." She let out a breath. When she spoke again, she sounded sad. "It's an utter failure, Doug. You know that. This move will give us both a fresh start. If I stay in town you're going to think we have a chance of getting back together. But we don't. We just didn't make it."

Doug couldn't breathe. He was afraid that he'd start to cry if he tried to speak. Karen's decision to move three thousand miles from him made it crystal-clear that he had lost her forever. Then, for a brief moment, he fooled himself into thinking that she was just waiting for him to fight for her. Only he didn't have the self-confidence or the energy for such a fight, and that, more than anything else, was probably why she was leaving him.

"I've hired an attorney," Doug heard Karen say. "Ben Altman. He's preparing the divorce petition. I hope we can handle this amicably."

Doug nodded, not trusting himself to speak.

"The division of assets shouldn't be difficult. We can talk about it after you hire a lawyer."

"Okay," Doug managed.

Karen looked away again. "This isn't easy

for me, Doug. I really care for you. I hope you can stop drinking and pull yourself together. Raymond Hayes was not your fault. You've got to . . ."

She stopped and took a deep breath.

"You're right, Karen. I knew you'd want to . . . I'm not surprised. I guess I just hoped that we could work everything out, but I know I'm not what . . . that the marriage was not what you wanted. I hope you get what you do want in New York. I hope everything goes great for you."

Doug spotted the waiter and signaled him over.

"Could you give me the check, please," he said.

"I'll get this," Karen said when the waiter walked away.

"No, Karen. I can handle it. I hope you don't mind my leaving. I don't have much of an appetite."

Karen didn't say anything. She dipped her chin and Doug couldn't see her eyes. But in the moment before she hid them, he thought he saw the beginning of a tear. He hoped that he wasn't imagining it.

3

FELIX DORADO WAS FINISHING HIS breakfast in Little Havana, a Cuban restaurant in southeast Portland, when Pablo Herrera, his lieutenant, walked in, followed by Reuben Corrales, a huge, frightened man with massive arms, tree-trunk legs, and a bloated face. Felix ate breakfast at Little Havana almost every day, because he loved the ham *croquetas*, smoky creamed ham shaped in finger rolls, which were lightly breaded and then fried. They weren't as delicious as his mother's, but they were good enough to make him nostalgic about his childhood in Cuba and the thick-waisted, heavy-breasted woman who had filled his early years with love and heavenly cooking before Castro's thugs had murdered her and his father.

Felix was five-nine, with a dark complexion, soft brown eyes, and a thin, neatly trimmed mustache. After fleeing Cuba as a teenager, he had traveled through South America until he found a home with Javier Ramirez's cartel in Colombia. Over the years, Ramirez had come to trust Felix enough to make him his point man in Portland, where his mission was to take over the drug trade from Martin Breach.

Felix sipped from the large, deep coffee cup that held his *café con leche* as Pablo walked toward the table that the restaurant reserved for his boss. It was at the back, surrounded by bodyguards, making it harder for people to shoot Felix. As soon as he reached the table, Pablo pushed forward the thick-necked, steroid-pumped giant.

"Tell him," Pablo commanded.

Corrales was six inches taller than Dorado and twice as wide, but he trembled and cast his eyes down toward the floor.

"We lost Juan," he mumbled.

Felix looked confused.

"This moron was guarding Juan Ruiz, one of our dealers," Pablo explained to Felix.

"Tell him, you *hijo de puta*," Pablo ordered Corrales, his voice low and threatening.

"They took him. We were out all night looking, *jefe,* but we couldn't find him."

Felix took another sip of his *café con leche*, then put down his coffee cup. He did not show any outward signs of anger or concern. It was his self-control that made him dangerous, because he seemed the same whether he was eating contentedly or sliding a stiletto into an unprotected stomach.

"If this fool doesn't explain what happened in clear, complete sentences, cut out his tongue," Dorado told Herrera.

"We were protecting Juan," Corrales answered rapidly. "This guy came up. He was skinny, like a junkie. That's why we didn't pay him no mind. Then a car came up fast and the skinny guy pushed Juan in the back. They was gone before we could do anything. It wasn't our fault."

"Pedro Lozano hasn't reported in, either," Herrera said, "and the guys we had guarding him also disappeared."

Felix's skin darkened, his eyes narrowed, and he swore softly in Spanish.

"It's that fucker Breach," he said. "He's making his move."

"That's what I thought. Word is that he's giving dope and money to anyone who points out our dealers. One of our people was in Lombardi's yesterday. He saw Charlie LaRosa and another of Breach's men talking to a junkie named Vincent Ballard. This was about an hour before Juan was snatched."

"Have someone talk to Ballard, see what he knows," Felix said.

"Done," Herrera answered. "And we should take out some of Breach's dealers tonight for payback."

Dorado was about to reply when the waitress walked up with a gift-wrapped box secured on top with a festive red bow.

"A man left this," she said cheerfully. "He said it was a present and to wait to give it to you until you were finished with breakfast."

Felix's eyes widened with fear, and he shrank back in his seat. Herrera grabbed the package, rushed out the back door into the alley, and flung the box into the deep metal dumpster. Dorado and his bodyguards were peering down the hall anxiously when Herrera dove back inside.

"You think it's a bomb?" Herrera asked

when several minutes had passed without an explosion.

"Send this idiot to check," Dorado ordered, flicking a thumb toward the bodybuilder who had lost Juan Ruiz.

"But, *jefe*," Corrales stuttered.

"Check the box," Pablo ordered.

Corrales swallowed and walked down the corridor like a convict on the way to his execution. The door to the alley slammed behind him. Minutes passed without a big bang. Then the door opened and Corrales reappeared, carrying the box as far from his body as his muscle-bound arms would allow. The bodybuilder's face was ashy gray, and he had averted his eyes, which were wide with fear, so he didn't have to look at the contents of the box. He stopped a few steps from his boss and tilted the package so Dorado could see the present that Martin Breach had sent him. Dorado's normally nut-brown skin turned pasty, and he pulled back. Inside the box was Pedro Lozano's head.

4

THE MORNING AFTER HIS ABORTED dinner with Karen, Doug Weaver woke up at nine o'clock more exhausted than he'd been when he passed out from drinking at two a.m. He dragged himself into the bathroom and splashed water on his face. Then he slapped his cheeks to get his adrenaline going. Nothing worked. Doug felt as if there were grains of sand in his eyes, and every thought seemed to take forever to get from the back to the front of his brain.

After a breakfast of black coffee and unbuttered toast, Doug called Jerry Cochran, the attorney who had represented Jacob in the case that had sent him to prison. He knew Cochran from Oregon Criminal Defense Lawyers Association conferences and had seen him around the courthouse. Cochran's secretary said he'd be able to give Doug a few minutes at ten.

Jacob Cohen's former lawyer was sharing space with several other sole practitioners in a suite on the third floor of a ten-story building in midtown. Doug's office was on the outskirts of downtown Portland, near the freeway. Doug parked in his office lot at 9:45 and decided to walk to his meeting in hopes that the exercise would help dispel his hangover, but the crosstown walk felt like a trek up Mount Everest. A few blocks from Cochran's office, Doug realized that he was near the place Jacob had listed on his last registration form as his mailing address. Doug detoured a few blocks and discovered that the address was not a residence. It was an office building. But one of the offices was Parole and Probation. Doug checked his notes. The address for Parole and Probation was the address that Cohen had said he'd put on the form because he was living in a car in a vacant lot. Doug bet that someone in the office had seen the letter with the registration form but hadn't known that Jacob was using the office for his mail and had returned it. He thought about going up to the office and asking around, but he was running late for his appointment with Jerry Cochran, so he rushed over to Cochran's office.

Doug gave the receptionist his name and thumbed through a copy of *Sports Illustrated* while Cochran finished a phone call. Ten minutes later, a chubby, pear-shaped man with a receding hairline appeared in the waiting area. Doug flipped the magazine onto the end table and stood up.

"Hi, Doug, what's up?"

"We have a client in common, Jacob Cohen."

"Don't tell me he's gotten himself in more trouble."

"Looks like it."

"Come on back. Do you want some coffee?"

"That sounds great."

Cochran's medium-size office was at the back of the suite and across the street from a department store. The lawyer's desk was cluttered, and there were files scattered across his credenza. Cochran was as messy as his surroundings. He'd thrown his suit jacket over the back of a chair instead of hanging it up; the top button of his shirt was undone, exposing the top of his undershirt; and his shirttail was out. Doug noticed a nick on his cheek where he'd cut himself while shaving.

"What did Jacob do now?" Cochran asked when he was settled in his chair.

"When he was paroled, he was supposed to register as a sex offender. The DA says he didn't."

"I'm not surprised. I don't think registration is required on Jacob's planet. So, what do you want to know?"

"Why don't you tell me about the case you handled?"

"It was for assault on and the attempted rape of a prostitute named Janny Rae Rowland, a real piece of work. Jacob was living in a vacant lot over by Queen Anne and Hobart."

"He was back there when he was arrested."

"It wouldn't surprise me. The area is loaded with bars, pawnshops, and vacant stores. It's a haven for drug dealers, low-end prostitutes, and criminals of all types. The lot is big. The side on Hobart is across from a warehouse, but the lot fronts on Queen Anne, where a lot of prostitutes work. Janny Rae had staked out the strip of sidewalk on Queen Anne as her territory."

Cochran paused. "Have you met Jacob yet?"

"I was up at the jail, yesterday."

"Okay, then you probably know that he's really got a thing for women. As far as he's concerned, they're all the spawn of the devil. Anyway, the cops patrol that area all the time and they saw Janny Rae wrestling on the sidewalk with Jacob. From what I gather, it was hard to say who was getting the worst of it. The cops questioned them separately. Janny Rae said that Jacob had propositioned her. According to her, she told him how much a little action would cost and Jacob told her he was broke. She said she didn't give out freebies and that's when, according to Janny Rae, Jacob tried to rape her."

"What did Cohen say?"

"Nothing coherent at the scene. The cops said that Jacob was screaming about whores and harlots and quoting the Bible, which I find highly credible. Since Janny Rae was making sense and there were no witnesses, they busted Jacob."

"Were you ever able to get Jacob's side of the story?"

"Yeah, he calmed down enough during one of my visits to the jail to give me his version of what happened. Jacob told me that he wouldn't tolerate a whore befouling his home, so every time Janny Rae tried to solicit a customer he would run up and start spouting Bible verses at the john at the top of his lungs. Jacob claims that Janny Rae attacked him after he ran off a few customers."

"What happened at trial?"

"What you'd expect. When Janny Rae came to court, the DA had her looking like a member of the garden club. I dressed Jacob in a suit but he still looked like a lunatic. I got him through direct with minimal references to the failings of the gentler sex, but he spent cross-examination quoting the Bible about the defects of women, which wasn't so good for our side, since eight of the jurors were female. It only took the jury half an hour to find him guilty. The judge wasn't too tough on him at sentencing. I don't think he

"That's the one."

"Do you think there would be anything wrong if I contacted them?"

"I'd clear it with your client first. You're going to have enough trouble winning his trust. If you go behind his back and he finds out . . ."

Cochran shrugged.

"You're right." Doug stood up. "I'll ask him for permission."

"Do you think you can help him?" Cochran asked.

"Probably not. The state's case is a cinch to prove. I'm not even certain it would help if we did prove he's crazy. The law says that it's his responsibility to register and he didn't."

"That's too bad. Jacob is totally nuts but he also seemed pretty helpless. I really didn't buy Rowland's story and I felt bad for Jacob when he was convicted. I imagine prison must have been tough on him."

"From some stuff he said, I think he had a very hard time."

Cochran shook his head. "Poor bastard. Well, all you can do is try your best."

"Yeah," Doug answered. "Thanks for taking the time to see me."

Jerry Cochran walked Doug to the recep-

tion area and Doug walked over to the elevators. While he waited for the car to come, he
thought about Jacob's parents. Doug wasn't
Jewish but he'd heard of Rabbi Cohen. The
rabbi had been active in community affairs
for a long time, and his name was frequently
mentioned in the newspaper in connection
with civil-rights issues, antiwar protests, and
other political topics. He was certain that the
rabbi could help Jacob's case, but Jerry Cochran was right. If Jacob forbade him to contact his parents, Doug would have to honor
his client's wishes. He decided to go to the
jail and see if he could persuade Jacob to
change his mind.

Jacob had been adamant that Solomon and
Valerie Cohen were not his parents. When
Doug suggested that there shouldn't be
a problem with him talking to the Cohens,
since Jacob was not related to them, Jacob
had gone ballistic, spouting Bible verses
about Judas Iscariot and other famous trai-
tors until Doug promised that he wouldn't
speak to the rabbi, just to get his client to
shut up. When Doug left the jail, he had a
splitting headache.

It wasn't lunchtime yet, so Doug decided

to go to the DA's office and touch base with the prosecutor who was handling Jacob's case. If he was lucky, the prosecutor would be reasonable and he could negotiate a deal that would keep Jacob out of prison.

When Doug asked the receptionist for the name of the deputy handling Jacob's case, she called the trial assistant in the sex crimes unit.

"Hannah Graves is handling that matter," the receptionist said. "I'll see if she's available."

Doug's hopes dimmed. He had never tried a case against Graves, but she had a horrible reputation in the defense bar. Ten minutes later, Graves marched down the hall, a self-satisfied smile plastered on her face.

"Hi, Doug," Graves said cheerfully, holding out her hand. "I don't remember having a case against you."

"This is the first time."

"I did sit in on a little of the Raymond Hayes case," Graves said.

Doug's stomach rolled. He wondered if Graves had mentioned Ray's case to unsettle him or if she was just insensitive.

"Tough break," Graves added without an iota of sincerity. The prosecutor held open the low gate that barred entry to the rest of the DA's office. "Come on back."

Doug followed Graves down a narrow hall that ended in a large open area. The offices of the deputies with seniority lined the walls. Filling the center of the room were cubicles for the newer deputies and support personnel, a conference room, and other workstations.

Hannah had an office along an interior wall. It was narrow and cluttered with case files. A bookshelf with a copy of the criminal code sections of the Oregon Revised Statutes, criminal law texts, and the advance sheets of the Oregon Supreme Court and Court of Appeals took up most of one wall. The only decorations were Graves's college and law school diplomas. There were no family photos, framed prints, or personal items in evidence.

"So, you're representing Jacob Cohen," she said when they were seated. "I'm not surprised your boy is back in trouble. In fact, I was certain we'd meet again."

"Were you the DA in the attempted rape case?"

"Yup."

"Well, this is just a failure-to-register situation and Jacob has a good explanation."

"I'm sure he does, but I want you to know up front that I'm not going to cut a deal with you."

"Why not?" Doug asked, surprised by Hannah's hard line.

Graves leaned back in her chair and played with a pencil she had picked up from her blotter.

"Jacob Cohen is a violent, unpredictable maniac who hates women. There are no women in the Oregon State Penitentiary. When Cohen is locked up the women of this state are safer. So I'm going to do my best to send him back to prison."

"But he may not be guilty."

"I've seen the registration form that was sent to your client. It's blank. That means he didn't register. If he didn't register he's guilty."

"Jacob was living in a vacant lot," Doug said patiently. "He didn't have a mailing address so he had his mail sent to the building that houses the Office of Parole and Probation. Jacob never got the letter with his form. Someone at the office must have returned it."

"Who?" Graves challenged.

"I don't know yet."

"So Cohen's story is uncorroborated." Graves twirled the pencil around her fingers as she leaned back. "And even if he didn't get the letter, so what? The statute says that he has a duty to register. It's his problem, not the responsibility of the U.S. mail or the parole office."

Graves smirked. "Of course, your client makes an excellent witness. Maybe the jurors will feel sorry for him. Perhaps he can convince them that he's the victim of a vast feminist conspiracy. He tried at his rape trial, but he'll probably get better with practice."

Doug saw that he wasn't getting anywhere, so he stood up.

"Thanks for seeing me. I guess we'll have to settle this in court."

Hannah didn't get up. She smiled smugly. "Most definitely. I'll be looking forward to it."

PART TWO
THE GANGSTER

5

THE PHONE ON BERNARD CASH-man's night table rang at 2:39 a.m. Seconds after he answered the call, he was striding into his bathroom, fully alert. There was no regret at missing sleep. The forensic scientist loved getting a call in the middle of the night. It signaled that a new crime scene waited, providing him with an opportunity to seek justice for another victim.

Cashman turned on the coffeemaker he kept by the bathroom sink. A fresh pot of an exotic blend made especially for him by a gourmet food store in Hillsdale would be brewed by the time he was ready to leave.

After a brisk shower, he dressed in a T-shirt, fatigue pants with lots of pockets, and hiking boots. When he'd filled his thermos, he ran downstairs, where he slipped into a windbreaker and tucked his ash-blond locks under a Seattle Mariners baseball cap, to prevent his hair from contaminating the crime scene. Contamination by police, emergency personnel, civilians, and even experts from the crime lab was always a major concern.

The crime lab provided Cashman with a three-quarter-ton Ford pickup. His shovels, axes, metal detector, vacuum cleaner, and other equipment rested on a metal platform on rollers in the back of the truck called a joy bed. The joy bed slid back and forth to make it easy to get out the equipment, and a canopy covered the flatbed and kept everything dry. When Cashman drove off, he was in a terrific mood. He did not think of forensics as a job; it was a calling, a means of righting the injustices of a decadent world. It had been a long time since the dead had repulsed him. For Cashman, the blood, the gore, and the odors were clues that helped him solve the puzzle that each crime presented.

A little before three-thirty a.m., Cashman parked away from the hustle and bustle in the parking lot of the Continental Motel. It only took him a moment to spot Mary Clark, the other forensic expert who had been dispatched to the crime scene. Mary was a plain, slightly overweight woman with a pleasant smile and bright blue eyes. She tended to be the optimist in any gathering. Her garb was similar to Cashman's, and her strawberry-blond tresses were tucked under a Portland Trail Blazers cap.

Mary was talking to a homicide detective, Billie Brewster, a slender African-American woman with close-cropped hair, wearing a blazer over a black T-shirt and jeans. The criminalist and the detective were standing in the middle of the lot, surrounded by uniformed officers who swarmed around them, manning crowd-control barriers, directing traffic, clearing a path for the investigators, and establishing limits beyond which the media could not go. Yellow crime-scene tape had been strung from the wall and wrapped around the beams on the walkway that supported the second-floor landing. On the edge of the lot, an ambulance was preparing to leave now that the EMTs had confirmed that the corpse in room 109 was beyond help. Behind Brewster was an open door. Inside, an occasional flash proved that a technician was documenting the crime scene.

Cashman found the officer in charge of the security log, which contained the names of everyone at the scene and the time everyone had signed in and out. He added his name to the list and joined Brewster and his colleague.

"Hi, Bernie," the detective said as soon as Cashman joined the women.

Cashman nodded. "What have we got?"

"A white male, name of Vincent Ballard. Driver's license puts his age at thirty-five but he looks about one hundred and two. He's got enough tracks on his arms to run an Amtrak train."

"An OD?" Cashman asked.

"If it was that simple I'd be home in bed. No, our boy got popped in the back of the head, twice. By the way, when I did my initial walk-through I spotted a cartridge case under the edge of the bed on the window side."

"Did you touch it?" Cashman asked.

Brewster cocked her head to one side and gave the criminalist the evil eye.

Cashman laughed. "Don't get mad at me, Billie. I had to ask. What about the people who found the victim or the first cops on the scene? Did they touch or move anything?"

"Carl Maggert, Ballard's neighbor, found the body. The victim's radio was blasting hip-hop. I'm guessing whoever greased him turned up the volume to cover the sound of the shots. Anyway, Maggert put up with the noise for half an hour before pounding on Ballard's door to get him to turn down the volume so he could sleep. When Ballard didn't answer, Maggert opened the door. It was unlocked. He said that the light was off but there was enough light outside to let him see that Ballard was lying on the floor. That's when he went to the office and told the clerk."

"He didn't go inside?"

Brewster consulted her notebook. "Maybe a step or two. He's not sure. The clerk went into the room and turned on the light. When he saw the blood he went back to the office and called 911. I've had Maggert and the clerk printed and we've taken some hairs and a saliva swab for elimination purposes.

"Mitchell and Chang were the first responders. Chang checked for a pulse, then got out. Mitchell stayed outside to keep away the rubberneckers. I've got them canvassing for witnesses but no luck so far. This isn't the type of place where anyone is going to come forward anyway. I'll bet most of the tenants have records or don't have green cards."

"Any idea whodunit?" Clark asked.

"We found a kit for shooting up in a dresser drawer but we haven't found any drugs so far. Robbery may have been the motive. But there could be something more sinister at work here. My first reaction when I saw the body was that it was an execution. Word on the street is that a Colombian cartel is trying to move in on Martin Breach's territory. Their front man is Felix Dorado. In the past week, we've had two dealers turn up dead. If this guy was working for Breach, then Dorado is a good person to look at. If he was selling for Dorado, Art Prochaska or someone who works for him may be our man. Prochaska does Breach's heavy lifting."

"Has the ME been here yet?" Cashman asked.

"She's on the way."

The technician who had been photographing the motel room told Brewster that he was finished. Cashman and Clark put on latex gloves and dust-filter masks to prevent their prints and saliva from contaminating the crime scene, then slipped Tyvex paper booties over their hiking boots.

"We better get to work," Bernie said. "Tell us what to expect in there, Billie."

"The place is really small. There's a bathroom and the motel room. That's it. It's a real pigsty, too, so watch where you step."

As soon as he and Clark entered the room, Cashman saw Vincent Ballard sprawled facedown on the floor, disposed of as unceremoniously as the unwashed laundry the victim had dumped on the floor beside his bed. Even through the mask Cashman could detect the fetid smell of the dead man's evacuated bowels mixed with the odor of rotting food. He let his eyes roam the room. There were several slabs of greasy pizza in an open box on the dresser next to a TV, a small writing desk in one corner of the room, and a laptop computer resting on the blotter next to the phone. It struck Cashman as odd that a junkie would still own a laptop, something he assumed would be sold for drugs by a person in circumstances desperate enough to force him to live in a motel like the Continental. It also occurred to him that someone who would kill Ballard for his drugs would probably take his laptop. Cashman photographed the top of the dresser. He would bag the pizza on the off chance that Ballard's killer had been hungry enough to leave his DNA on a slice. He'd also cart off the computer and have one of the experts at the lab go over the hard drive for clues.

Cashman turned his attention to the bed. An open can of beer stood on the night table. The bed was unmade. The blankets were crumpled and had been pulled aside, exposing rumpled, stained sheets. Cashman remembered that Maggert, the neighbor, had said that the light was off when he opened the door. Maybe Ballard's killer or killers had broken into the room while Ballard was sleeping. Cashman squatted down so he was even with the lock on the door. It didn't look as though the lock had been forced, but he photographed it anyway and checked for tool marks. Cashman bet that no one staying in this motel left the room door unlocked at night. If Ballard's door wasn't forced, the killer had probably talked his way in. Ballard would have tossed the blanket aside when he got up to go to the door.

Mary Clark was on her knees on the other side of the bed, taking a picture of the location of the cartridge case that Detective

Brewster had spotted. Cashman photographed the top of the night table, then placed the beer can in a plastic evidence bag. He would print it later. While Clark was putting the shell casing in another bag, he squatted next to the body. It looked as if Ballard had been forced to kneel. There was gunpowder residue sprinkled across a wound behind his ear, and more residue surrounded another wound in the back of his head. The vic had probably pitched forward after the first shot, and the killer bent forward to deliver the coup de grâce. An execution, just as Brewster had guessed. Cashman would bet on it.

The right side of Ballard's face was exposed. Cashman studied it. The killer had sealed Ballard's mouth with gray duct tape so no one would hear his screams. His eyes were swollen shut, and dried blood had crusted on pale skin that was even paler in death. The medical examiner would make it official, but it was obvious that Ballard had been beaten before he'd been shot. A brutal man had done this, a violent man like Art Prochaska.

Almost six years ago, Prochaska's testimony had been used to destroy the reputation of a Portland police detective. The result was the suppression of evidence against an accused serial killer. Cashman had overheard several officers and detectives curse Prochaska, and he'd learned a lot about Martin Breach's lieutenant. He was a vicious killer who inflicted pain without mercy; a vile creature who committed many terrible crimes. If Prochaska was responsible for this murder, Cashman would see that he paid for it.

6

JUDGE IVAN ROBARD PRESIDED OVER one of the most elegant courtrooms in the Multnomah County Courthouse, and felt that this was just. Marble columns supported the high ceilings, and oil paintings of the stern-faced judges who had preceded him frowned down on the supplicants who stood beneath his carved-wood dais. It was from this pulpit that Judge Robard nodded majestically, like a sultan of the Ottoman Empire, toward the prosecution table, indicating to Hannah Graves that she had his permission to give her closing argument.

Amanda Jaffe got along with most of the assistant district attorneys in Multnomah County, but she really disliked Hannah Graves. The DA was as thin as an anorexic, but Amanda suspected that meanness, not dieting or exercise, kept the weight away. What self-respecting calorie would want to bond with someone as nasty as Hannah Graves?

There was a smirk on the prosecutor's face when she strolled to the jury box for her closing argument in *State of Oregon v. Bobby Lee Hartfield*. Bobby Lee didn't see it, because he was staring at the top of the counsel table, embarrassed to be back in court and more embarrassed by the circumstances that had brought him there. Amanda had laid those circumstances out for Graves at a pretrial conference, during which she had offered to plead her lumbering, slow-witted client to the misdemeanor crime of trespass. Graves had laughed at the suggestion and demanded a plea to burglary, a felony that would send Bobby Lee to the penitentiary. When Amanda explained patiently why the facts of the case would not support the charge, Graves had flashed a patronizing smile and told Amanda that she could try selling her story to a jury.

During the trial, one thing had surprised Amanda and made her rethink her negative view of the prosecutor. Amanda had been forced to put Bobby Lee on the stand so he could tell his story. Normally, a DA cannot introduce evidence of a defendant's prior convictions, but when a defendant testifies, a prosecutor can introduce the judgment rolls on the theory that they are evidence a juror can use to determine the witness's credibility.

The year after he graduated from high school, Amanda's twenty-five-year-old client had been fired from a hardware store for coming to work drunk. A week after he was canned, an intoxicated Bobby Lee had used a key he had forgotten to return to break into the store at night. Bobby hadn't taken much, but he had left the key with his fingerprints in the backdoor lock. Bobby had pleaded guilty to a burglary charge and had successfully served a sentence of probation. Given that the charge against Bobby was burglary, Amanda had fully expected the vindictive DA to tell the jury about the hardware-store burglary, but Hannah had shocked Amanda by not introducing the record of Bobby Lee's prior conviction to impeach him during cross-examination.

"Ladies and gentlemen," Graves said, "I want to thank you for your patience. I'm guessing that it took a lot to sit through the defendant's self-serving sob story. And what a pathetic attempt he made to weasel out of the predicament he created for himself.

"The evidence is so clear that I won't waste much more of your time. The defendant is charged with burglary. The judge will instruct you that a defendant commits that crime when he enters a house with the intention to commit a crime therein. Now there is no question that the defendant entered his father-in-law's home, although that's an understatement. He didn't just enter. He dove headfirst through the screen on Claude Smith's bedroom window.

"And did he intend to commit a crime when he broke in? What do you think he would have done to his wife after wrestling her father to the ground and chasing her into the living room, if she didn't shoot him? Thank God, Cora Hartfield picked up her father's gun during his struggle with her drunk and enraged husband. If she had been unarmed, the charge against Bobby Lee Hartfield would probably be assault in the first degree or," and here she paused to stare venomously at Amanda's client, "murder."

Although she had promised to be short, Hannah Graves ranted on for twenty more minutes, her voice rising as she became more and more self-righteous. Amanda let her rave, pleased to see that the eyes of the jurors, which had been riveted on the prosecutor when she started, were glazing over as Hannah went on and on and on.

Finally, Graves concluded, and Judge Robard told Amanda that she could present the defendant's argument. Amanda stood, and her long black hair fell across her broad, muscular shoulders. Years of competitive swimming had given Amanda an imposing figure that was too full to grace the covers of today's fashion magazines but always attracted male attention when she entered a room. She stopped a few steps from the rail of the jury box and looked at the jurors with her clear blue eyes. When Amanda smiled, two of the jurors smiled back, but most kept a poker face, unwilling to show how they were going to vote.

"The prosecutor told you some of what happened on the night in June when Bobby Lee Hartfield almost lost his life, but she conveniently forgot the most important piece of evidence that was introduced in this case: the fact that Bobby Lee Hartfield is madly and passionately in love with his wife, Cora Hartfield.

"On the warm summer evening of June fifth, after a meal at her parents' house, Cora refused to let Bobby Lee drive her home and told him that she was staying at her parents' house until he sobered up. Now, Cora was right to refuse to drive home with Bobby. He has a drinking problem and he shouldn't have been behind the wheel of a car that night, but Bobby wouldn't admit that she was right and he stormed out of his in-laws' house and drove home. Sitting in the dark, he continued to drink and grew more and more despondent. He called Cora several times to beg her to come home, but she was so mad that she told her father, who answered the phone, that she didn't want to talk to Bobby.

"You heard the testimony of Claude Smith, Bobby's father-in-law, about those phone calls. Did Bobby tell Mr. Smith that he wanted to beat his wife or murder her? No, he did not. He told Mr. Smith, often while sobbing, that he loved Cora and missed her. Mr. Smith told Bobby that Cora loved him too and that he should sober up and drive over in the morning, when he was certain that the couple could patch things up.

"You also heard the testimony of Bobby's old girlfriend Ronnie Bosco, who told you how Bobby called her at a little before two in the morning for advice on how to get his wife to come home. She said that he sounded highly intoxicated and cried through most of the conversation.

"Shortly after he hung up on Ms. Bosco, Bobby drove back to the Smiths'. At the hospital, shortly before the doctors operated on him, a blood test showed that Bobby had an alcohol level of .27, way beyond .08, the level at which an Oregon citizen is deemed to be under the influence. In this highly intoxicated condition, Bobby pounded on the front door of the Smith home. Mr. Smith called to him through the screen over the open bedroom window and asked him not to wake the neighbors. Did Bobby threaten to kill Mr. Smith? He did not. He apologized for causing trouble and told Mr. Smith how lonely he was and how much he loved his daughter.

"Mr. Smith urged Bobby to go home and sleep off his drunk, but Bobby said he loved Cora so much he could not stand to be separated from her. Then he said he was coming in and he dived through the screen and tumbled into the Smiths' bedroom.

"Mrs. Smith and Cora huddled in the doorway. Mr. Smith stood in front of them. He was holding a pistol and he testified that his hand was shaking so badly that he was afraid it would go off. Bobby looked up at Mr. Smith, shocked to see the pistol. 'Are you going to shoot me, Dad?' he asked, and Mr. Smith said no. But he also told Bobby to leave. Bobby stood on shaking legs and said he would not leave without his wife. Then he spotted Cora and lunged toward her. Mr. Smith dropped the gun and got in Bobby's way. As they wrestled on the bedroom floor, Cora grabbed the pistol and ran into the living room.

"Do you remember what happened next? It's the key to this case. Bobby threw off his father-in-law and staggered after Cora. He walked into the living room. Cora, terrified, was braced against the couch, the pistol stretched out toward the doorway. As soon as Bobby stepped into the room, she fired.

"Now, you heard Cora Hartfield's tear-drenched testimony. What were Bobby Lee's last words, spoken just before he crumpled to the floor, thinking that he was going to die? Cora testified that Bobby Lee sank to his knees, looked into her eyes, and said, 'Honey, I love you.' "

Amanda paused. Two of the jurors pulled out handkerchiefs and dabbed at their eyes.

"Ladies and gentlemen, the prosecutor is correct. The judge is going to instruct you that you can convict Bobby Lee Hartfield of burglary only if you find that he entered the Smith home with the intent to commit a crime therein. We do not dispute that the state has proved beyond a reasonable doubt that Bobby Lee entered the Smiths' home without their consent, but I have searched the law books and statutes of this state, I have looked high and low, and nowhere have I found any Oregon law that makes love a crime."

The jury was back in twenty-five minutes. Hannah Graves smirked at Amanda, and that smug look stayed plastered on her face for a few moments after the jury foreperson pronounced Bobby Ray Hartfield unanimously "not guilty."

As soon as the judge dismissed the jury, Cora and her parents rushed up to tell Amanda what a great job she'd done. Amanda told them to hold on for a minute so she could catch the DA before she left the courtroom.

"Hannah," Amanda said.

"What?" Graves asked angrily as she gathered up her law books and paperwork.

"I wanted to thank you for trying a clean case."

Graves looked confused. "What are you talking about?"

"Bobby's prior conviction for burglary. I wanted to thank you for not using it and letting the jury decide the case on the facts."

A horrified expression twisted Hannah's features. She shuffled through a stack of papers she was holding. When she found her certified copy of the judgment roll of Hartfield's burglary conviction, she stared at it for a second. Then she muttered, "Shit, shit, shit," and stormed out of the courtroom.

It was almost six by the time Amanda finished up at the courthouse, and close to seven when she left her office in downtown Portland. She picked up an order of sushi to go from the Japanese restaurant on the corner and walked to the trolley stop on Tenth Avenue. The biting wind should have chilled her, but Amanda was too exhausted to notice.

The trolley rumbled across Burnside and into the Pearl District, where Amanda lived in a 1,200-square-foot loft in a converted red-brick warehouse. There were two art galleries on the ground floor, and any number of good restaurants and coffeehouses in the surrounding blocks. The condo had hardwood floors, high ceilings, and oversize windows that let in plenty of light and gave her a view of Mount Saint Helens and the Columbia River. The volcano was dome-building, and she could see smoke drifting up from the crater on clear days.

Amanda put water on for tea. The kettle was whistling by the time she changed into her sweats. She had been too busy to read the paper in the morning, so she went through it while she ate. When she turned to the TV listings, she noticed that Turner Classic Movies was showing a picture rated four stars that she hadn't seen before. She checked the kitchen clock. The film was going to start in half an hour.

It would have been nice to watch the movie with someone else, but she'd broken up with Toby Brooks two weeks ago, when it became clear that their relationship was going nowhere. Amanda felt sad about the breakup, but she wasn't devastated. That was good; still, she would have preferred dining tonight with someone who cared to eat takeout sushi at her kitchen table. Sometimes she wondered if she'd ever find someone with whom she could share her life.

It was at times like this that Amanda wished her mother were alive, so she could talk to her. But Samantha Jaffe had died giving birth, and Amanda's father, Frank Jaffe, had raised her. Her dad was very smart, but some problems needed a woman's point of view.

Frank was a great father. He was also one of the best criminal-defense lawyers in the country. Ever since Amanda had been old enough to understand what her father did for a living, she had been seduced by the mystery and adventure of criminal law. While other girls were mooning over teen idols, she mooned over Perry Mason and read every legal thriller she could get her hands on. After a stellar academic career in law school, Amanda had accepted an offer to clerk for a federal judge on the United States Court of Appeal for the Ninth Circuit in San Francisco. Many of the top San Francisco firms had courted her, and her judge believed that she had an excellent chance of clerking at the United States Supreme Court, but Amanda could no longer resist the pull of criminal practice, and there was really only one place that she wanted to work. As soon as her clerkship ended, Amanda became an associate at Jaffe, Katz, Lehane, and Brindisi. Four years after starting at the firm, Amanda had made a name for herself in the notorious *Cardoni* case. Last year, she had made headlines again, when she had almost lost her life while defending Jon Dupre in a case that involved some of the most powerful men in the state and a conspiracy that stretched all the way to Washington, D.C. Amanda had a national reputation and was a partner in the firm. The cases poured in and she was making more money than she thought possible, but her personal life wasn't going nearly as well.

The film started, and Amanda carried her tea to her lounger. After a while, she lost herself in the movie. It was a silly comedy; just what she needed. She forgot how restless and lonely she was feeling until she turned out the lights two hours later and crawled into bed.

7

DOUG WEAVER SAT UP IN BED. HE was sweating, and his heart was beating rapidly. For a moment, he was not certain if he was home or in the death chamber at the Oregon State Penitentiary, staring down at Raymond Hayes's corpse. Then he saw the blurry red numbers on the clock on his nightstand and he knew that he'd had the nightmare again.

Doug swung his legs over the side of the bed and bent over to catch his breath. His neck and chest were damp. He was exhausted, but he knew that he wouldn't be able to get back to sleep for a while. He was never able to relax right after the dream. When a few minutes passed, Doug's breathing started to slow, and he stood unsteadily. Almost a year had passed since Raymond's execution, and he had not slept well. Many evenings, before he could drop off, he would think about the sentencing hearing and what he could have done differently. Marge Cross had assured him that he had done everything he could and she'd chastised him for punishing himself with hindsight, but in Weaver's nightmare, Ray said something else.

In the dream, only Ray and Doug were at the execution. Ray was strapped down on the gurney, and Doug was standing over him in the death chamber. Ray was as Doug had last seen him: his right eye closed and the left partly open, light reflecting off his dead, black pupil. What was different were Raymond's lips, which parted and mouthed words Weaver could not understand unless he bent close to his client's corpse.

"Save me," Hayes whispered in the dream, and in the dream Doug snapped back, terrified.

Weaver always woke up after hearing the pathetic plea for help that he could never fulfill.

Doug wore contacts, but he kept eyeglasses on his nightstand for circumstances such as this. With his glasses on, he could see the clock clearly. It was 3:45. He had a court appearance at nine and he hadn't fallen asleep until after midnight. He would be a wreck in the morning—his head would ache and his eyes would be raw and red. Most days were like that now.

Doug had let Karen stay in their house when she told him that she wanted to separate. He was renting a small Cape Cod in southeast Portland. It was all he could afford, since his practice wasn't going very well. It wasn't that he was a bad lawyer. If he were objective about his abilities, Douglas Weaver would conclude that he was better than most. He seldom screwed up, and there were occasional instances of brilliance. The problem was that Raymond's execution had taken the heart out of him.

Why did he go on, then? He had asked himself that question on several occasions, especially when he was depressed after a loss. The answer was always the same. Doug was a believer. He had wanted to be a lawyer all his life, and the origins of that desire were located in a youthful, exuberant belief in the law as a protector of the little person. Doug had always been a little person, the object of bullies, never a member of the in crowd, the poor, pathetic soul who hid his love for the most popular girls in high school because he knew it would never be returned. Armed with the might of the law, Doug believed that he could help those without the power to help themselves. Reality had been a cruel teacher, but deep down, he still held on to his belief that he could make a difference.

Doug's bedroom opened on a small living room. There was no wall between the living room and the kitchen. He turned on the kitchen light and poured himself a glass of cheap scotch from a bottle that was almost empty. Doug added ice to the glass and sat at the kitchen table. He took a strong taste, then held the glass to his forehead. The cold felt good, and the burn of the liquor distracted him for a moment. He put down the glass, rested his elbows on the table, and held his head in his hands. He was all messed up and he didn't know what to do. Each day he had to drag himself to his office. He called himself an attorney, but sometimes he felt like a fraud. What if Ray had really been innocent? Doug had talked Ray into pleading guilty, coerced him. Now he felt sick with doubt. Maybe he should quit his practice, but what else could he do? He was too old to start over in a new profession—assuming that he could even think of something else he wanted to do. He came to the same conclusion whenever he had this argument with himself. He would muddle through and hope that he didn't hurt anyone else. He had to earn a living; he had to pay rent and feed himself. And there was one other thing that kept him going: the hope that someday he would redeem himself.

8

THE DETECTIVE DIVISION OF THE Portland Police Bureau Central Precinct was a wide-open space that stretched along one side of the thirteenth floor of the Justice Center. Each detective had a cubicle separated from the other working spaces by a chest-high divider. Billie Brewster's cubicle contained a gunmetal gray desk, an ergonomically designed chair she had purchased with her own money to try to save her back, and the desk chair she had been issued, which was now used to hold case files. Hanging on one of the walls was a psychedelic poster of Jimi Hendrix that Billie had owned since middle school and had brought to work to serve as a reminder that there was more to life than abused children and dead bodies.

The only other personal items in the cubicle were photographs of Billie's mother and her brother, Sherman Brewster. Sherman, who was serving serious time in the Oregon State Penitentiary, was a constant source of sorrow to Billie. When she was sixteen, their father had deserted the family, and her mother had been forced to work at two jobs to make ends meet, leaving Billie to raise Sherman. She had tried her best, but she had lost the battle to keep him straight when he joined a gang. Even though no one else blamed her, Billie could not help feeling responsible for Sherman's failures.

The detective had just finished a fifteen-minute call from an Idaho state trooper who was investigating a Boise case with Portland ties when Bernard Cashman called from the crime lab.

"Hey, Bernie, what have you got?" Brewster asked, leaning back in her chair.

"For you, only the best."

"Speak."

"Our special of the day is a beautiful thumbprint belonging to Arthur Wayne Prochaska."

Brewster sat up straight. "Where was it?"

"On the beer can on the nightstand in Vincent Ballard's motel room."

"You're shitting me?"

"Would I lie to a fellow Hendrix aficionado?"

"That is fucking great! Look, I need a report I can attach to a search warrant affidavit. If you can put Ballard's murder on Prochaska you'll have made my year."

"You'll have the report ASAP and anything else I come up with as soon as I get it."

Cashman was the best. When Brewster hung up the phone, she was one happy woman. Now all she had to do was persuade a judge to issue a search warrant for Prochaska's home and hope that she could find more evidence connecting the evil son of a bitch to Vincent Ballard's murder.

Art Prochaska and Martin Breach had been violent offenders since they extorted lunch money from the weaker kids in elementary school, but breaking legs for loan sharks had provided their entry into organized crime. The combination of a genius IQ and no conscience had catapulted Breach to the top of his chosen profession, and he had brought Art with him every step of the way. Prochaska was the only person in the world Breach trusted.

Art was now worth several million dollars, most of which was stashed in a Swiss bank account that Martin Breach had set up for him. But, following Martin's example, Prochaska lived modestly in a ranch house in a middle-class Portland suburb. He paid taxes on the reported profits of the bars he managed, and his only ostentatious possession was a cherry-red Cadillac that he parked in his garage so as not to attract the attention of his neighbors. At eight o'clock at night, those neighbors were drawn to their front windows by the flashing bubble lights on the police cars that were parked in Prochaska's driveway and in front of his house.

Billie Brewster led a contingent of uniformed police officers up a slate path to the front door. Zeke Forbus, her heavyset partner, rang the doorbell and slammed a lion's-head knocker against the door while shouting, "Open up, police." When an anxious face peered through a break in the living room curtains, Brewster flashed her badge. Moments later, the door was opened by Prochaska's current girlfriend, Maxine Hinkle, a performer at the Jungle Club, a strip joint that Martin Breach owned.

Billie identified herself and showed Maxine the search warrant.

"I don't know if I can let you in without asking Artie," Maxine said.

"Miss Hinkle, this warrant gives us the right to enter Mr. Prochaska's house with or without his permission," Billie said politely. "You don't want to get in trouble, do you?"

"No," Maxine answered quickly, alarmed by the possibility.

"And we don't want you to get in trouble for resisting a lawful court order," Brewster continued in a reasonable tone. "So I'll tell you what. Why don't you call Mr. Prochaska and tell him we're here and what we're doing. I'll even speak to him if that will make you feel better. But I'm going to do that from inside this house, because the judge says I can. So, please step aside."

Maxine did as she was told, and Billie assigned an officer to watch her. Then she gave the other officers their assignments while Forbus looked around. The house was neat and decorated in good taste, like something out of *House & Garden*.

"Not the kind of place I expected a goon

like Prochaska would be living in," he told Billie.

"Maybe he's trying to get in touch with his feminine side," she cracked.

Forbus snorted. "Let's see if we can find anything that'll tie this scumbag to the Ballard murder. I'll take the ground floor."

Billie suspected that Forbus had volunteered to search the ground floor so he wouldn't have to climb the stairs. With the weight he already carried, and his atrocious eating habits, Billie figured her partner had less than a fifty-fifty chance of making it to retirement without having a major coronary.

The bedroom was messier than the rest of the house, but the furniture, the rug, and the drapes looked as if they had been selected by an interior decorator. Billie went through Prochaska's dresser and nightstands without finding anything unusual, but she hit pay dirt when she pulled over a chair and searched the top shelf in the bedroom's walk-in closet. At first, all she could see were an extra blanket and pillow. When she moved them aside, she saw something else: a shiny 9-mm Glock and a box of 9-mm Remington ammunition. As they came into view, Billie's lips curled into a triumphant smile.

9

FRANK JAFFE WAS A BIG MAN WITH a ruddy complexion and gray-streaked curly black hair. He looked more like a heavyweight boxer who'd had his share of tough fights than one of America's top criminal-defense attorneys. Tonight, he felt like Sisyphus, the ancient king of Corinth who was condemned by the gods to roll a heavy boulder up a steep hill in Hades only to have it roll down again each time he reached the top. Frank's hell was a courtroom in Medford, a small city near the California border, where he had spent the past week trying a grueling meth case. Just when it seemed that he'd snatched victory from the jaws of defeat, George Featherstone, the prosecutor, gave an emotional closing argument in which he revealed that the defendant had been convicted for sexually abusing a minor.

Prior to trial, the judge had forbidden Featherstone to breathe a word of the conviction on the grounds that the jury would not be able to give Frank's client a fair trial if they learned he was a child molester. As soon as the words were out of Featherstone's mouth, Frank had gritted his teeth and moved for a mistrial. The judge had no choice but to grant Frank's motion. Now Frank was condemned to return to Medford in two months to try the case all over again. This had put him in a terrible mood during the five-hour trip back to Portland, and he was still in a bad mood at nine that night when a car pulled into his driveway.

Frank lived by himself in the Victorian home in the West Hills where he'd raised his daughter and law partner, Amanda. By the time he got back from Medford, he barely had the energy to fix a dinner of scrambled eggs and toast before retiring to his den to watch television in the hope that it would take his mind off the drug case. When the car door slammed, he was in his shirtsleeves and stocking feet, nursing a glass of bourbon and watching the current governor of California battle aliens. Frank swore softly and set his glass on the coffee table. He swore even more forcefully when he looked through the window and recognized the burly man who was walking up the driveway.

"Evening, Charlie," Frank said, opening the door before his visitor had a chance to knock.

"Evening, Mr. Jaffe," answered Charlie LaRosa. "Sorry to disturb you."

Charlie LaRosa performed a variety of tasks for Martin Breach, most of which were prohibited by the penal code. Frank had beaten two assault charges for LaRosa.

"What is it this time?" Frank asked wearily.

"Hey, no, I'm doing fine, staying out of trouble. This is for Marty. He sent me to get you."

"Tell Martin I'll see him in the morning. I just drove up from Medford and I'm wasted."

Charlie's nervous look meant that Breach had ordered him to bring Frank back with him.

"It's Artie, Mr. Jaffe. He's in jail. It's serious. Marty said to say as serious as your daughter's problem was."

Amanda had crossed some very powerful men while representing Jon Dupre, a pimp and accused murderer. They had put out a hit on her, and Frank had gone to Martin Breach for help. He'd come through for the Jaffes. Now Breach was calling in a favor, and Frank couldn't refuse. His shoulders sagged, and he resigned himself to a long evening.

The Jungle Club was a square pink-and-green concrete box that sat in the middle of a parking lot on a corner of a busy intersection on Columbia Boulevard. A neon sign featuring a naked woman and flashing letters that spelled GIRLS, GIRLS, GIRLS left no doubt as to what awaited patrons inside. There were a few open spots in the front lot, but Charlie ignored them and parked in a reserved space in the rear of the building. The music from the club was so loud that Frank could feel vibrations in his body when he got out of the car. As soon as the back door opened, he was hit by a wave of sound that almost knocked him over. Martin Breach had the office of the Jungle Club swept for bugs every day, but he was paranoid about surveillance and liked his dancers to disrobe to the loudest music possible, on the theory that it would make the life of any DEA, FBI, or PPB eavesdroppers more difficult.

Frank took a few steps down a narrow hallway and waited while Charlie chatted with the massive bodyguard stationed outside the door to Martin Breach's office. The bodyguard knocked, then opened the door, and Charlie LaRosa ducked inside.

"Go on in, Mr. Jaffe," Charlie said a moment later.

Martin Breach, Portland's most violent citizen, was almost six feet tall, but his stubby legs and chunky upper body made him seem shorter. Thinning sandy hair, drab brown eyes, and a pale complexion gave him the look of a failed used-car salesman. His ghastly taste in clothes added to the mistaken impression of ineptitude—the last impression some of his victims ever formed. Tonight he was attired in plaid golf slacks, an aloha shirt, and a Madras sports jacket that had gone out of fashion decades ago.

Martin's tiny office was as unimpressive as its owner. The rickety furniture was secondhand. An out-of-date calendar from a motor-oil company and pictures of strippers decorated the walls. If the IRS was going to run a net worth on Martin, it would have to start someplace other than the Jungle Club.

Breach closed the skin magazine he was reading and gave Frank a genuine smile of welcome before waving at a chair on the other side of his desk.

"Take a load off, Frank," Breach said, speaking so low that Frank barely heard him above the AC/DC track blasting through the paper-thin walls. Frank collapsed in the chair. It swayed under his weight.

"How's my favorite mouthpiece?"

"I'm wiped, Marty. I just drove up from Medford after trying a case for a week."

"Sorry," Martin said, sounding sincere. "I wouldn't have asked you to come over if it wasn't serious."

"Charlie told me that Art is in trouble," Frank said, getting right to the point in the hope that he could wrap up the conversation as soon as possible.

"They busted him for murder and ex-con in possession of a firearm this afternoon. He tried to call you."

"I must have been on the road. Where is he?"

"The Justice Center."

"What do you know about the charges?"

"Not much. The cops searched his house a few days ago and found a gun."

"Did they have a warrant?"

"Yeah. It sounds like everything was done nice and legal."

"We'll see."

Martin smiled. "That's why I want you representing Artie. You're thinking of ways to beat the rap already."

Breach reached behind his desk and swung a battered brown leather briefcase onto the blotter. He swiveled it so it was facing Frank and opened the lid, revealing stacks of soiled, wrinkled cash. The bills on top were hundreds. It was illegal for Frank to accept a fee that was the fruit of an illegal activity, like drug dealing. He started to say something, but Martin held up a hand.

"Don't worry. This dough is as innocent as a newborn babe. You don't think I'd let you get in trouble, do you? Put it in the bank and let them call the feds. You'll be just fine."

Frank held his tongue. He was certain that the money was clean because it had been laundered, but he was also certain that the government would never be able to prove it.

Besides, he owed Martin big. Amanda was the most important person in his life, and she would be dead if Martin hadn't protected her. Art Prochaska was Martin's closest friend and he was in trouble. Frank was going to give him the best defense possible.

"Take this home, count it, then tell me if it's enough. If it ain't, tell me what you need. Nothing's too good for Artie."

Frank found Breach's show of affection touching, and had to remind himself that Breach and Prochaska's friendship had been forged by joint acts of mayhem that would have horrified Hannibal Lecter.

"Hey, I just remembered something. One of the cops asked Artie if he knew a guy named Vincent Ballard." Breach held up a hand. "Don't worry, Artie didn't answer. In fact, he didn't answer none of their questions and the only thing he said was that he wanted a lawyer. But I did some digging and a guy named Vincent Ballard got popped a few days ago in a fleabag motel over on Eighty-second, the Continental."

Frank knew that Martin had cops on his payroll, so he didn't bother to ask how he'd gotten his information.

"Did Art know this guy?" Frank asked.

Breach smiled. "Why don't you ask him? I don't want to put words in Artie's mouth."

"Of course. I must be tired," Frank said, realizing his mistake. Breach was too clever to implicate himself or Prochaska in any way.

"I'd ask if you wanted a beer or something stronger, but I can see you're all in," Martin said. "Charlie will drive you home. Get a good night's sleep and see Artie in the morning. He's expecting you."

Frank picked up the briefcase with the cash. "Nice seeing you again," he said, half meaning it. He couldn't help liking Breach, especially after what he'd done for Amanda. Of course, he didn't kid himself. He knew that Martin was the type of guy who could be your best friend one minute, then cut off your head to get your tie if he was late for an appointment.

"Say hello to Amanda. How's she doing?"

"She's good, Martin. Thanks for asking."

"Hey, I like her, and she ain't ugly like her old man."

Frank smiled and opened the door. "I'll take good care of Art," he assured Breach.

"Do your best."

10

WHEN FRANK JAFFE ENTERED THE contact-visiting room at the jail the next morning, Art Prochaska was seated at the table, looking as relaxed as a meditating monk. Frank couldn't help smiling. It was a pleasure to deal with a client who wasn't a mess after a night in jail. Of course, this client's calm came as no surprise. In Prochaska's world, jail time was part of doing business.

"How you doing, Frank?" Prochaska asked, returning Frank's smile.

"Better than you, Art," Frank answered as

he sat across from his client. He laid a pen and a yellow lined legal pad on the table. "I hear you've got a problem."

"Not me. I didn't do nothing. With you on the job I'll be out of here soon."

"We'll see, Art. You know me, I never promise anything."

Prochaska's grin widened. "But you do deliver, just like the Domino Pizza man."

Frank laughed, then forced himself to become serious.

"Look, Art, I know you've heard this before, but I'm going to give you my lawyer speech before we discuss your case, to make sure you understand what I will and won't do for you, and some of the consequences you might suffer if you break my rules."

"Sure thing, Frank," Prochaska answered, folding his hands on the table like a student on his first day at school. His brow furrowed as he concentrated on what Frank had to say.

"First off, you know that anything you tell me is confidential. In other words, it stays between us, I won't tell anyone unless you say it's okay. You got that?"

Prochaska nodded.

"Okay," Frank continued. "If you tell me something, it should be the truth. I won't get upset if you lie, but I'm going to have to make decisions in your case and I don't want to do something that hurts you because you lied to me."

Prochaska nodded again, but he didn't tell Frank that he wouldn't lie. If Art was guilty, Frank was certain that he'd never hear the truth from his client.

"I have to warn you that I'm an officer of the court as well as your attorney. If you admit the crime you're charged with I can't let you take the stand and deny you committed the murder. If you do lie in court I won't reveal the perjury to the judge or the DA, because of the attorney-client privilege, but I'll resign from the case and you'll have to get a new lawyer. If some of your buddies lie for you, I won't have an attorney-client relationship with them, so I will tell the judge and the DA. You following this?"

"Sure, Frank."

"Okay, so do you know the cops who busted you?"

"Yeah, it was that black lady detective, Brewster, and her partner, Zeke Forbus. You know them?"

"Yeah," Frank said as he wrote the names on his legal pad. "Why did they say they were arresting you?"

Frank always phrased the question this way so his client's answers wouldn't be a confession.

"They think I killed a guy named Vincent Ballard. But I want you to know up front that Marty and I had nothing to do with this guy getting killed, nothing at all."

"Marty said someone by that name was murdered at a motel a few days ago."

"I don't know anything about that."

"Did you know Ballard?"

"I bump into guys all the time at the clubs, but the name don't ring no bells."

Frank thought that the answer sounded evasive. He had looked up the story about the murder on the Internet before coming to the jail, and he told Prochaska the date of the killing.

"Do you remember where you were that evening?" he asked.

"I might have been home with Maxine, but I can't be sure. I'd have to think."

"Who is Maxine?"

"A girl who works at the Jungle Club. We been dating."

A stripper was not going to be the best alibi witness, but Frank didn't tell that to Prochaska.

"I should talk to her before you do," Prochaska said. "If I wasn't with her I don't want to waste your time."

Frank knew that Maxine would be calling him as soon as one of Breach's men told her to establish Prochaska's alibi, but there wasn't anything he could do about it. Prochaska was impervious to lectures about ethics and morality.

"What about the gun beef?" Frank asked. "Martin said you're also in here for ex-con in possession."

"Brewster showed me a gun and ammo she says she found in my closet, a 9-mm Glock."

"Do you think the lab is going to find your prints on that gun?"

Prochaska thought for a moment. "Hey," he asked, "do you think Brewster could have planted the gun?"

"Anything's possible, but she's got a reputation as a straight shooter."

Art nodded. Frank paused. When it was obvious that no answer to his question about the prints would be forthcoming, he told Pro-chaska what he'd found out before walking over to the Justice Center.

"Mike Greene is the DA on your case. He's okay. I tried to talk to him this morning, but he's out with a cold. As soon as he's back I'll get the police reports. You're going to be ar-raigned this afternoon. I'll ask for a bail hear-ing but don't get your hopes up. There's no automatic bail in a murder case like there is in other cases."

"That's okay, Frank. You do your best. If I gotta sit for a while I'll be okay."

Frank handed Prochaska his business card. "I'm going to head back to my office. Call me collect, anytime."

"Okay."

Frank stood up and pushed a black but-ton under a speaker that was attached to the wall near the door. The speaker crackled, and Frank told the guard that he was ready to go. He chatted with Art until the door opened.

"I'll see you in court this afternoon," Frank said before the guard closed the door.

During the elevator ride to the jail waiting area, Frank thought about the difference be-tween representing his average client and representing a professional criminal. Most clients were a bundle of nerves and very demanding. This never upset Frank. He knew that it was incredibly stressful for the average citizen to be charged with a crime. An arrest was humiliating, and it destroyed your reputation even if you were innocent. Being charged with a crime tore you out of your routine and forced you to imagine a life without freedom.

Professionals like Art Prochaska and Martin Breach rarely made demands, and they let Frank do his job. They trusted him and they accepted a conviction without rancor, as long as they were convinced that Frank had been honest with them about their chances and had given one hundred percent. And he got paid. That was another difference. Frank had never been stiffed by the people in Martin Breach's organization because they knew they might need him again.

The downside of representing professional criminals—or most criminals, for that matter—was that they were usually guilty as charged. What kept Frank going was his belief that America had one of the best criminal justice systems ever devised. There was no question that injustices occurred. You only had to read the papers to find the latest story about a prisoner who had been released from death row after a DNA test proved his innocence. But the object of the system was to protect the innocent, and it usually succeeded. The cost of maintaining a system this good was the occasional acquittal of a guilty person. Frank believed that this risk was worth taking. He wouldn't have continued working so hard if he didn't.

11

THE STOCKMAN BUILDING HAD BEEN a fixture in downtown Portland since 1915, and the facade displayed the ornate stone scrollwork that was sadly missing from the modern skyscrapers interspersed among the older buildings in the heart of the city. When Frank Jaffe entered the lobby, his thoughts distracted him, and he didn't bother to glance up at the granite cherubs and gargoyles that peered down at him.

There was a week's worth of phone messages in Frank's slot at the front desk, and he gathered them up and headed down the hall to his office. As a senior partner and one

of the founders of Jaffe, Katz, Lehane, and
Brindisi, Frank rated a large corner office
with a view of the tall green hills that stood
only twenty or so blocks from the west bank
of the Willamette River. The office was decorated with his diplomas and framed news
stories detailing his most famous cases. Law
books and state and federal statutes filled a
floor-to-ceiling bookcase. A long credenza
stuffed with files from his active cases ran
under his window.

Frank dropped the huge sample case
containing the case files from the meth trial
on the floor in front of the credenza. Then,
as he did every morning, he looked at the
framed pictures of Amanda and her mother,
Samantha, which stood on a corner of a
large, scratched and gouged desk that had
been abused by cigarette burns and coffee
stains since he began practicing soon after
his graduation from night law school.

Samantha was the great love of Frank's
life—so great a love that he had remained
single since her death. Raising an infant while
building a law practice had consumed Frank
after his wife died. It had also helped him to
hide from his grief. But the intense sorrow
that Samantha's death had caused was al-

ways just below the surface. Frank's friends tried to fix him up with other women. Occasionally, he would try a date with someone who came highly recommended by people whose judgment he trusted. These women were very nice, and often beautiful and intelligent as well, but they could never be compared to Samantha. Now Amanda was the only woman in Frank's life, and he was incredibly proud of her strength, intelligence, and goodness of heart. He knew that growing up without a mother and living with a father who worked as hard as he did had been tough, but she accepted her life without complaint, and he had been thrilled when she decided to work with him.

Frank pulled himself away from the photographs and was starting to put the files from the Medford meth case into his credenza when Amanda poked her head in the door.

"You're back."

"I got in late last night and didn't want to bother you."

"What happened?" she asked as she walked into the office.

Frank told Amanda about the mistrial.

"You must have been pissed."

"I'm still pissed."

"Do you think Featherstone mentioned the conviction on purpose because he thought you were winning?"

"I wish that was it. I'd have a good chance of getting the charges dismissed." Frank shook his head in disgust. "Featherstone's not the sharpest arrow in the quiver. I think he got worked up during closing and forgot the judge's ruling."

"Are you going to file a double-jeopardy motion anyway?"

"Oh, sure, I have Daniel working on it, but I don't think I'll win. Right now I just want to forget the case for at least a week. In fact, I picked up a new case last night that should help take my mind off it. It's a murder, and guess who the client is."

"I have no idea."

"Art Prochaska."

"No kidding?"

"You're surprised?"

"Not that he'd kill someone, but I am surprised that a pro like Art was caught. How strong is the case?"

"I don't know much about the facts, except that the victim was killed at a motel on Eighty-second. I just got back from the jail. Art says that he doesn't know anything about it. Mike Greene is the DA and he's out with a cold, so I couldn't get any more info."

Amanda's stomach tightened when her father mentioned Mike, but she hid her distress from him.

"Art's arraignment is this afternoon," Frank continued. "Maybe I'll learn more then. So what have you been up to while I was having fun in Medford?"

Amanda told him about Bobby Lee Hartfield's case. When she told him how she'd ended her closing argument Frank cracked up.

"Tell me you're putting me on. Tell me you didn't say 'Nowhere have I found love to be a crime.' "

Amanda grinned. "I said it and I'm proud."

"What utter crap. How am I going to be able to show my face in the courthouse?"

"Hey, whatever wins, right?"

Frank smiled and shook his head.

"How's your schedule?" he asked.

"Pretty loose, why?"

"You feel like helping with Art's case?"

"Sure. What do you want me to do?"

"I don't know yet. We'll talk after I get the police reports."

12

ON THE MORNING OF JACOB COHEN'S trial, Doug Weaver felt none of the jitters he usually felt before going to court. With a case like Cohen's, the pressure was off, because he knew that he had no chance of winning. If Hannah Graves had made any kind of offer, Doug would have jumped on it, but there had been no offer. The prosecutor really believed that Jacob was a dangerous lunatic, and Doug suspected that she relished the idea of clobbering him in court. All that was left for him was a hearty breakfast, strong coffee, and a stiff upper lip.

The Multnomah County Courthouse was

an eight-story gray concrete building that took up an entire block between Fourth and Fifth and Main and Salmon in the heart of downtown Portland. Jacob's case was being heard in the fifth-floor courtroom of the Honorable Anita Rome. No one but the participants cared what happened to Jacob, so the only people sitting in the spectator section were a well-dressed older woman and two elderly men, whom Doug recognized as court watchers, retirees who found trials more entertaining than soap operas. Court watchers sat in on spectacular trials or cases that were tried by their favorite attorneys. These three had adopted Doug after the *Hayes* case, though he had no idea why, since he had performed so miserably in it. Maybe they loved an underdog. Doug guessed that they were the type of people who rooted for baseball teams like the Chicago Cubs, which made a business of disappointing their fans. Whatever the reason for their allegiance, it was nice to know that someone cared about him, so he smiled at them on his way down the aisle. But his smile changed to a look of horror as soon as he saw Jacob Cohen, who was wearing his orange jail jumpsuit instead of the business suit, white shirt, and conservative wine-red tie Doug had gotten for him from a thrift store. Jacob grinned broadly when he saw how upset his lawyer looked.

"Where's your suit?" Doug asked, hoping against hope that Jacob would say a sadistic jail guard had prevented him from wearing it. Then Doug could scream about his client's constitutional rights, and the judge would yell at the guard, and Jacob would stand trial looking like a reasonable facsimile of a normal person.

"I will not garb myself in their robes," Jacob said firmly.

"*I* bought that suit, Jacob. '*They*' had nothing to do with it."

Jacob's smile told Doug that his client wasn't buying what he had to sell. He decided to try reasoning with Cohen.

"Look, Jacob, no one goes to trial in jail clothes. How do you expect the jurors to give you a fair trial if you're sitting here looking like a convict?"

"I *am* a convict. If God wants me to have a fair trial I will have a fair trial no matter what clothes I'm wearing. Jesus said, 'Beware of

false prophets, who come in sheep's clothing, but inwardly are ravenous wolves.' Mat-
thew, 7:15."

Hannah Graves chose this moment to
make her entrance. She was smiling, and
her smile grew twice as large when she saw
the way Jacob was dressed.

"Good morning, Doug," she said cheerily.
"Ready to rumble?"

Doug glared at Hannah, who was enjoying herself way too much.

"We may have to delay jury selection.
There's been a mistake about my client's
suit."

Jacob folded his arms across his chest
and stared straight ahead.

"I am not wearing their suit."

"Well, there you are," Hannah said. "Your
client has a right to stand trial in his jail
clothes. I don't think we should go against
his wishes, do you?"

"This isn't any of your business, so please
butt out," Doug said, furious at himself for
letting the DA get to him and more furious
with his client for making an impossible case
even tougher.

"Sorry, you're right," Hannah said before

laughing and walking over to the prosecution table.

"Jacob, I'm begging you. Please wear the suit. You'll look so much nicer in it."

At that moment, the bailiff commanded everyone to rise, and the Honorable Anita Rome appeared on the dais. The judge was an attractive woman in her midforties who had gone through three husbands and—according to rumor—was currently having a steamy affair with a cop. In court, she hid her sharp blue eyes behind thick unattractive glasses, wore her long black hair in a bun, and concealed her trim figure beneath her black robes. When she socialized, the judge let her hair down, dressed flamboyantly, and wore contacts.

Judge Rome frowned as the bailiff read the name and number of the case into the record. When he was through, she asked the parties if they were ready to proceed.

"Ready for the state," Hannah Graves answered cheerily.

"And you, Mr. Weaver, are you and your client prepared to proceed?" the judge asked as she studied Jacob's attire.

Doug got to his feet. "I noticed that Your Honor is looking at Mr. Cohen's jumpsuit."

"Yes, I am."

"Mr. Cohen has a very nice business suit and a white shirt and tie, but he's chosen to wear his jail clothes. I wonder if Your Honor might talk to him about the problem a jury might have giving him a fair trial if he's wearing jail clothes."

Hannah Graves leaped to her feet. "If I may, Your Honor, I was here when Mr. Cohen voiced a strong desire to go to trial the way he's dressed so as not to mislead the jury about his status as a prisoner. I think this is a laudable attitude and I think the court should honor Mr. Cohen's wishes."

"Thank you for your opinion, counselor," the judge said, casting an icy glance Hannah's way to let the DA know that she was on to her.

"Mr. Cohen," the judge asked, "has Mr. Weaver explained the problems you face going to trial dressed as you are? Do you understand that we want you to have a fair trial and that some jurors might form a negative view of you and be less likely to listen to your case fairly if they know you're in jail?"

Jacob smiled at the judge. When he did not answer her question, the judge turned to Doug.

"Does Mr. Cohen understand what's going on here?"

"Hallelujah!" Jacob said. "Salvation and glory and power belong to our God, for true and just are his judgments. He has condemned the great prostitute who corrupted the earth by her adulteries. He has avenged on her the blood of his servants. And again they shouted 'Hallelujah!' Revelations, 19."

Judge Rome stared at Jacob, and he returned the stare. "Has Mr. Cohen been interviewed by a psychiatrist?" she asked Doug.

"He refuses to speak to any doctor."

Hannah stood. "Perhaps I can assist the court. As Your Honor knows, Mr. Cohen is a convicted sex offender who is charged with failing to register. I handled the attempted rape case that led to his conviction. During the course of the trial, Judge Novak became concerned about Mr. Cohen's mental state because he was constantly quoting verses from the Bible, just as he's doing today. He had a psychiatrist sit in court and observe Mr. Cohen's testimony and in-court behavior."

Hannah handed a stack of papers to the judge and a copy to Doug.

"This is Dr. Terrell's report, which contains his opinion that Mr. Cohen was competent to understand the proceedings and aid in his defense."

"Mr. Cohen, what do you think is going to happen in this courtroom?" the judge asked Jacob after reading the doctor's report.

Jacob pointed at Hannah. "This agent of Beelzebub will put on false witnesses who will accuse me of intentionally failing to register as a sex offender, and the jury, which is controlled by Satan and her minions on Earth, will convict me and I will return to Hell."

"You understand that your lawyer will help you fight these charges?"

"So he says."

"Well, I've known Mr. Weaver for some time, and he has always stood up to the government and fought hard for his clients."

Jacob shrugged. "If God wills that I go free I will go free."

The judge reread the report and thought for a few minutes. When she addressed the lawyers, she looked troubled.

"I'm concerned about Mr. Cohen's mental state, but he does appear to understand the charges and that there will be a trial on them.

I'm going to let the jury selection proceed but I'll be keeping an eye on your client, Mr. Weaver. If I change my mind about his fitness to stand trial I'll abort the proceedings and commit him for observation."

Jury selection went quickly, and Judge Rome told the parties to give their opening statements. Hannah Graves told the jury that Jacob had been convicted of attempted rape, sentenced to the Oregon State Penitentiary, and paroled two years before. She explained that Oregon Revised Statute 181.595 required sex offenders who were paroled to register within ten days after leaving prison, and once a year within ten days of their birthday. She said that she would introduce the testimony of a detective and documentary evidence that would prove beyond a reasonable doubt that the defendant was a convicted sex offender who had been released from prison and had failed to register.

Doug had no facts on his side. This was not unusual when one practiced criminal defense, so, as was his practice when the only hope of winning a case was a miracle, he spent fifteen minutes talking about the great American legal system, our sacred Constitution, and the wonderful protections the Constitution and the legal system afforded innocent men like Jacob Cohen. He also asked the jurors to keep an open mind and lauded them for being good citizens by making personal sacrifices to serve on Jacob's jury.

As soon as Doug sat down, Judge Rome called the noon recess and ordered the prosecutor to call her first witness when court resumed after lunch.

"The state calls Stephen Hooper, Your Honor," Hannah Graves said.

The jurors watched Detective Hooper walk down the aisle and through the bar of the court to take the oath. He was dressed in a tasteful dark suit, his shoes were polished, and he looked as confident as you would expect someone who had testified dozens of times to look.

"Can you please tell the jury your occupation," Hannah Graves said as soon as Hooper was sworn.

"Yes, ma'am. I'm a detective with the Portland Police Bureau."

Graves walked Hooper through his employment history and had him tell the jury about the commendations he had received for his police work.

"Have you been assigned to investigate sex crimes during your career in law enforcement?" Graves asked.

"Many times."

Graves pointed toward the defense table, and all of the jurors stared at Jacob. In fact, they had been casting covert glances at him all day, because Jacob had spent the period of jury selection and opening statements muttering to himself and twisting in his seat like a man being jabbed by a cattle prod. Soon after jury selection had started, the judge had called the lawyers to the bench out of the jurors' hearing for a sidebar to discuss the problem. Doug had gotten Jacob to calm down for a while, but he was low on self-control, and another sidebar had been called just before Hooper was sworn.

"During your sex-crime investigations have you ever met the defendant, Jacob Cohen?" Graves asked.

Jacob pressed his chin against his chest, stared at the tabletop, and placed his hands over his ears. The eyes of three jurors widened, and one made a note.

Doug leaned over to Jacob. "Please take

your hands off your ears, Jacob. I need you listening to Hooper's testimony so we can catch him when he lies. You'll know when he makes up something and I won't. Please help me."

Jacob dropped his hands and leaned forward, fixing his eyes on the detective. Doug exhaled.

"Yes, ma'am. I have encountered the defendant during an investigation of a sex crime," Hooper answered.

"What was the reason for this encounter?"

"I was the lead detective in a case in which the defendant was charged with assault and attempted rape."

"Was the defendant convicted of those charges after a trial in this courthouse?"

"Yes."

Graves stood. "I move to have state's exhibit one—a certified judgment of conviction in the attempted rape and assault cases—introduced into evidence."

"Any objections, Mr. Weaver?" the judge asked.

Doug had seen the document before trial, as part of the discovery the prosecutor had sent to him, and he did not object.

"It will be accepted," Judge Rome said. "Proceed, Miss Graves."

"Detective Hooper, when a convicted sex offender leaves the penitentiary, is he required to register?"

"Yes, ma'am. Within ten days of getting out, he has to fill out a form."

Graves gave Hooper a sheet of paper. "I have just handed state's exhibit two to Detective Hooper. Detective Hooper, would you please identify this document for the record."

"It's a copy of a sex offender registration form that was filled out by the defendant a little over two years ago, right after he got out of the penitentiary."

"What address did the defendant list for his residence?"

"The Hotel Monte Carlo on Burnside in Portland."

Graves offered the registration form into evidence. Doug had no grounds on which to object.

"Detective Hooper, does a sex offender have an obligation to reregister within ten days of his birthday every year whether or not he's changed his residence?"

"Yes."

"Did you check to see if the defendant registered again this year?"

"Yes, ma'am. I've been keeping tabs on Mr. Cohen and . . ."

"Objection," Doug said. "I move to strike what Mr. Hooper said after 'Yes, ma'am' as irrelevant and nonresponsive."

"Sustained.   Detective Hooper, just answer Miss Graves's questions. Don't editorialize."

"What did you learn, Detective Hooper?"

"The defendant was sent a registration form by registered mail but it came back unclaimed."

"What did you do when you saw that?"

"I wanted to be fair, so I checked the form the defendant filled out last year and found a new address."

"So he wasn't staying at the Hotel Monte Carlo?"

"Not according to his form," Hooper said.

Graves introduced the registration form from the previous year as exhibit three.

"Was the registered letter sent to this second address?"

"Yes."

"What did you do next?"

"I went to the address the defendant had

listed as his home on the latest form and found out it's an office building in downtown Portland."

"Are there any apartments in the building?"

"No."

"I'm offering into evidence a copy of the defendant's birth certificate marked state's exhibit four."

"No objection," Doug said.

"Detective Hooper, look at the date of defendant's birth. Did the defendant register this year within ten days of that date?"

"No, ma'am. There is no registration form for this year in his file and the form that was sent to him was returned blank."

Hannah entered the registered letter and the envelope in which it had been sent into evidence and told the judge she had no further questions of the witness.

"Mr. Weaver," the judge said.

"Thank you, Your Honor," Doug said. "Detective Hooper, as I understand it you went to the building at the address Mr. Cohen listed as his home address and found an office building in downtown Portland."

"Yes."

"Did you go inside?"

"Yes."

"Are there many offices in this building?"

"Yes. In fact, it's all offices and no living quarters."

"Is one of the offices State Parole and Probation?"

"I believe it is."

"Would it surprise you to know that Mr. Cohen lost his job and was living in an abandoned car in a vacant lot?"

"No, he was living in a vacant lot when the attempted rape happened and that's where I arrested him on this charge."

"You can't get mail delivered to a vacant lot, can you?"

"Probably not."

"Would it surprise you that Mr. Cohen was having his mail sent to the Parole and Probation office?"

"I wouldn't know anything about that. All I know is that your client has a duty under the statute to register within ten days of his birthday and he didn't."

"Move to strike, Your Honor, as nonresponsive."

"Sustained. Detective Hooper, I've warned you before. Don't make me hold you in contempt."

"I'm sorry, Your Honor."

A thought occurred to Doug just as he was about to press on about what Hooper had done inside the building. He ran through a mental checklist of the evidence that Hannah Graves had introduced.

"Mr. Weaver?" the judge inquired.

Since he had nothing to lose, Doug decided to take a chance. "No further questions, Your Honor."

"You may step down, Detective. Any more witnesses, Miss Graves?"

"No, Your Honor. The state rests."

"Any motions, Mr. Weaver?"

"Yes, Your Honor."

The judge turned to the jurors. "We're going to recess while the lawyers and I discuss some legal matters. The bailiff will take you to the jury room and we'll call you out when we're ready to proceed."

The jurors filed out. Several of them cast a quick glance at Jacob, who was hunched over in his seat, muttering to himself again.

"You may make your motions, Mr. Weaver," the judge said as soon as the jurors were in the jury room.

"I move for a judgment of acquittal, Your Honor."

Hannah Graves rolled her eyes.

"On what grounds?"

"Miss Graves rested without proving an element of the crime."

Hannah's brow furrowed. This was unexpected. She picked up the indictment and stared at it.

"Mr. Cohen is charged with failure to report as a sex offender," Doug said. "The state has charged that he was convicted of a felony sex offense and knowingly failed to report his change of address, but ORS 181.595 states that the reporting requirement applies only to a person who—and I quote—'is discharged, paroled, or released on any form of supervised or conditional release' from certain specified correctional facilities. Miss Graves never introduced any evidence that proved that Mr. Cohen was released from prison because he was discharged, paroled, or released on a form of supervised or conditional release."

Graves was on her feet. "This is ridiculous, Your Honor. The defendant was in prison at the Oregon State Penitentiary. How do you suppose he got out?"

"It's not your job, Your Honor—or the jury's job—to guess why Mr. Cohen is not in prison," Doug answered. "Mr. Cohen's conviction could have been reversed or the governor might have pardoned him. We don't know why he's out, because Miss Graves never proved that he was let out of prison in a status that would require him to register."

"What do you have to say to Mr. Weaver's argument, Miss Graves?" the judge asked, obviously disturbed by Doug's logic.

Graves looked panicky. "May I have a moment?" she requested.

"Certainly," the judge said.

Graves shuffled through her papers, re-reading the documents she'd entered into evidence and the notes she'd used to examine Detective Hooper.

"Your Honor, Mr. Weaver asked Detective Hooper if the State Parole and Probation office was in the building listed on Mr. Cohen's last registration form," Graves said, but her voice shook and she did not sound confident.

"I did, Your Honor," Doug agreed, "but the question and his answer only concerned the location of a government office. The discussion had nothing to do with the question of whether or not Mr. Cohen is on parole."

"But he was getting his mail there," Hannah said. "He was obviously on parole."

"Maybe he has a friend who works at the office who was getting his mail because Mr. Cohen was living in an abandoned car."

"Mr. Weaver has a point," Judge Rome said. "I've been looking at the statute and it does limit the registration requirement to people who have been let out of the penitentiary for specific reasons."

"We can solve this problem by reopening my case," Graves said. She sounded desperate.

"I don't think I can do that," the judge answered. "You've rested. Do you have any other arguments, Miss Graves?"

Graves looked tormented. She shuffled through her papers again, as if hoping that a new document would miraculously appear. After a moment, she shook her head.

"Mr. Weaver, I'm going to grant your motion and dismiss the charges against Mr. Cohen," Judge Rome told Doug. Then she turned her attention to Jacob.

"Mr. Cohen, you were lucky today. Through an error on the part of the prosecution and the excellent work of your attorney, you're going to escape being punished for your clear failure to register. As soon as court is adjourned I urge you to register and to make certain that you keep registering each year. Do you understand me?"

Cohen looked confused.

"Mr. Cohen, do you understand that you're free, that I've dismissed your case?"

"We won, Jacob. We beat them," said Doug, who was as shocked as his client by the victory. "You're free. They'll let you out of jail today."

"We won?" Jacob said in disbelief.

"Yes. God was on your side this time."

Jacob started to tremble. "I won't have to go back there?"

"You're not going back to prison," Doug assured him.

Jacob put his head in his hands and began sobbing uncontrollably. Doug sat next to his client and put his hand on Jacob's shoulder.

"You're going to be okay," he assured him.

"I don't deserve this," Cohen said to no one in particular. "I should be punished for what I've done."

"This wasn't your fault. Someone at the parole office returned the letter. They should have given it to you."

Jacob turned his tear-stained face to Doug. "You think I care about that letter," he said, his voice barely louder than a whisper. "That letter is nothing. I killed them, I killed them all. They died because of me."

Doug was not certain he'd heard Jacob correctly.

"Let's bring the jury in so I can explain what happened and dismiss them," Judge Rome said.

Doug stared at his client, still stunned by his statement. Hannah Graves stared straight ahead, her hands folded and her face unnaturally pale. Obviously, she had not heard Jacob's confession.

As soon as the jurors reassembled in the jury box, Judge Rome explained that the case had been resolved through a legal motion. Then she thanked the jurors for their service and dismissed them. When the jurors were gone, Judge Rome adjourned court, and the guards led Jacob back to the jail. Doug followed his client and watched the guards lead him down the corridor to the jail elevator in the back hall of the courthouse.

"I hope you're proud of yourself."

Doug turned. Hannah Graves and Detective Hooper were standing behind him. They were very angry.

"Look, Hannah . . ."

"No, you look. You think you're so smart now, but let's talk after your client rapes his next victim."

Hannah turned on her heels and stomped off toward the elevator, with Hooper following close behind. Normally, Doug would have blown off Grave's tirade or enjoyed the stiff-necked DA's discomfort, but he couldn't get Jacob's words out of his head. Had Jacob killed someone? Was it more than one person? Had he confessed to something he'd really done, or was his confession the product of one of his delusions? Doug hoped that it was the latter, but he couldn't get over the possibility that he had just been responsible for setting a killer free.

13

ON THE AFTERNOON OF THE DAY
that Doug Weaver was trying *State v. Cohen*,
Frank Jaffe was down the hall, handling the
preliminary hearing in *State v. Prochaska*.
There weren't many spectators at his case,
either. Art Prochaska was notorious among
criminals and in law-enforcement circles,
but he was not a celebrity, and the victim
was a junkie who had died in a cheap motel. This was not the kind of story that made
front-page news. Frank noticed a few court
watchers in the gallery; the reporter for the
Oregonian, who covered the courthouse;
and Charlie LaRosa, who would be report-

ing the day's events to Martin Breach. Frank also spotted Billie Brewster and Bernard Cashman, Mike Greene's witnesses, who were sitting in the back near the door.

"Hey, Billie, Bernie," Frank said.

Billie turned to the forensic expert. "Don't you just hate it when the defense attorney tries to act all nice and sweet?"

"I *am* nice and sweet," Frank said, feigning offense.

"Only when you're planning some devastating cross-examination trickery."

Frank snapped his fingers. "Damn, and I thought I'd put one over on you."

"Not in this lifetime, Bubba," Billie answered with a grin.

Frank laughed and walked toward the front of the courtroom, where Mike Greene was going over his notes. Frank liked Mike but hated trying cases against him. He was so nice and polite that jurors believed everything he said, and he was so fair that he rarely gave a defendant grounds for an appeal. If Mike Greene sent you to prison, you stayed in prison.

Mike was frequently mistaken for a former basketball player, because the curly-haired prosecutor was six-five, but he had stopped playing competitive sports in junior high. His passions were tenor sax, which he played with a jazz quartet in local clubs, and chess. Greene had been married when he worked in the Los Angeles District Attorney's Office, but his wife had cheated on him, and her infidelity and their divorce had been devastating. Mike had quit his job and run away to Europe. When he finally decided that the divorce wasn't his fault, he had called a friend from law school who lived in Portland. The friend had gotten him a job interview with the Multnomah County DA's office. Greene had moved into the capital crimes section quickly, because of his experience in California, and now he was one of the top prosecutors in the office.

"How's your cold?" Frank asked.

Mike looked up and smiled. He and Frank fought hard in court, but they were friendly when they weren't litigating.

"I was sick as a dog for a few days, but I'm much better now. Just an occasional coughing fit. Thanks for asking."

Frank stared at Greene. Something about him was different.

"You shaved off your mustache."

"Yeah," Mike answered shyly.

"You're not going through a midlife crisis, are you?" Frank joked.

"Don't worry. There are no Porsches or gold chains in my immediate future. Not on a DA's salary." Mike hesitated for a second before asking, "How's Amanda?"

"She's doing fine."

The DA's tone of voice hadn't changed when he asked about Amanda, but Frank was sure that she'd hurt Mike when she stopped going out with him. Frank had never asked Amanda why she'd quit dating Greene. He knew better than to make unsolicited comments to his daughter about her social life. Frank knew that Greene was awkward at times, and he wasn't handsome, but he was smart, honest, and down-to-earth, and Frank had been happy when Mike was dating his daughter.

Greene started to say something else, when two guards escorted Art Prochaska into the courtroom.

"Your client's here," Mike said.

Frank put his briefcase and the law books he'd been carrying on the counsel table. The guards brought Art over to Frank and unlocked his handcuffs. Unlike Jacob Cohen, Frank's client had no objection to looking respectable. One of Martin Breach's goons had delivered a suit to Frank's office, which had been hand-tailored for Art during a trip to Hong Kong, where he'd met with several shady Asians who were interested in supplying Breach with heroin. Frank's secretary had brought the suit to the Justice Center that morning. With it on, Prochaska looked like a successful professional wrestler.

Frank motioned to the chair on his left, and Art sat down. While Frank poured a glass of water from a pitcher that the judge's clerk had placed on the counsel table, Art slid up his French cuff and rubbed his wrists where the handcuffs had pinched.

"How are you feeling?" Frank asked.

"Can't complain. Any chance I'll get out today?"

"No. This is a preliminary hearing. The DA is only trying to convince the judge to certify your case for trial. They don't have to prove beyond a reasonable doubt that you murdered Vincent Ballard. It's a much lower standard. It's very rare for a case to be dismissed at a preliminary hearing."

"So why bother if you know we're going to lose?"

"Discovery. I get to hear key witnesses

testify under oath and I can cross-examine them. I'll learn a lot about the state's case and we'll have the recorded testimony of the witnesses to use against them if they say something different at trial."

"Are we going to put on a case?"

"No. I don't want to give the DA the chance to examine our witnesses or learn our strategy."

The bailiff banged his gavel, and everyone stood as the Honorable Arthur Belmont took the bench. Belmont was a short, stoop-shouldered African-American with salt-and-pepper hair, who had made his reputation practicing insurance defense at a large Portland firm. He ran his court with a steady hand, and his sense of humor kept even the most irascible attorneys on an even keel.

"Morning, gentlemen. I understand we have a preliminary hearing today. How many witnesses are you going to call, Mr. Greene?"

The prosecutor stood. "Not that many, Your Honor. Mr. Jaffe has agreed to stipulate to a few witness statements and the medical examiner's findings to speed things up."

"Well, that's good," the judge said.

"The defendant is charged with the murder

of Vincent Ballard at the Continental Motel and with ex-con in possession. I'm leading off with Detective Billie Brewster. She'll tell you how the body was discovered and describe the crime scene. Detective Brewster will also tell you about a search of the defendant's home, which turned up a 9-mm Glock and some 9-mm Remington ammunition. They're the basis for the ex-con-in-possession charge.

"My next witness will be Criminalist Bernard Cashman from the crime lab. He'll tell you how the defendant was linked to the crime. And that's it."

"You're willing to go along with the stipulations, Mr. Jaffe?" the judge asked.

"I am, for purposes of this hearing only."

"Okay. Sounds like this is doable this afternoon."

"I expect so, judge," Greene agreed.

"Call your first witness, then."

Billie Brewster was wearing a black pantsuit that she saved for court and a white, open-necked, man-tailored shirt. After taking the oath, Greene had the detective summarize the witness statements of the neighbor at the Continental Motel who had discovered Vincent Ballard's body, the motel clerk

who had called the police, and the first officers on the scene. Then Brewster described
what she had observed when she arrived at
the crime scene, and she identified Bernard
Cashman and Mary Clark as the forensic scientists who had examined the motel room.

"Detective Brewster, the day after Vincent
Ballard was murdered did you receive a call
from Bernard Cashman?"

"I did."

"What did he tell you?"

"He said that he had found a thumbprint
on a beer can he had taken from the nightstand in Vincent Ballard's room."

"Was Mr. Cashman able to match the
thumbprint to a person?"

"That's what he told me."

"Who was this person?"

Brewster turned toward the defense table
and pointed. "Arthur Wayne Prochaska, the
defendant."

Prochaska met the detective's stare. Neither blinked. Then Mike Greene asked another question, and Brewster turned away.
Prochaska leaned over and whispered to his
attorney.

"That's bullshit. I was never in that room."

Frank put his hand on his client's arm.

"Write down anything you want to discuss. We'll talk before I cross-examine Brewster. I have to concentrate on her testimony now."

As Prochaska started writing, Frank glanced at his client. Prochaska had a reputation as a cold-blooded killer who rarely showed emotion, but he was definitely agitated now.

"Detective Brewster, after Criminalist Cashman called you, did you use his information to secure a search warrant for the defendant's house?"

"Yes."

"Please describe what you did after securing the search warrant."

After Brewster told the judge about the team she had put together and the procedure the team had used when they searched Art Prochaska's house, Greene introduced a judgment roll to prove that Prochaska was a convicted felon.

"Were you aware that Mr. Prochaska was an ex-convict when you searched his home?" Mike Greene asked.

"Yes."

"Is it legal for an ex-convict in Oregon to possess a firearm?"

"No."

"Did you make a discovery, while searching Mr. Prochaska's bedroom, that involved a firearm?"

Brewster told the judge about finding the Glock and the ammunition for it in Prochaska's closet.

"Detective Brewster, did you visit the State Medical Examiner's Office recently?" Greene asked.

"Yes, sir. I was over there when Dr. Grace conducted the autopsy of Mr. Ballard."

"Your Honor, pursuant to stipulation, I'm submitting Dr. Grace's autopsy report, which concludes that Vincent Ballard died as the result of gunshot wounds to the brain."

"It will be received," Judge Belmont said.

Greene picked up a plastic evidence bag and carried it to his witness. In the bag were several small pieces of metal.

"Detective Brewster, will you please identify the contents of this bag for the judge."

Brewster turned to Judge Belmont. "During the autopsy of Vincent Ballard, Dr. Grace opened the victim's skull and found these two bullets inside."

"What caliber are they?"

"Well, they're badly fragmented, but Criminalist Cashman was able to say that the fragments are consistent with the ammunition found in the defendant's home."

"Why are the bullets so banged up?" Greene asked.

"They break up when they bounce off bones in the skull. They're designed that way to cause multiple injuries."

"Did you transport these fragments to the lab and deliver them to Bernard Cashman?"

"Yes."

"I have no further questions for Detective Brewster," Mike Greene said.

Frank conferred with his client, who was adamant about not being in Ballard's motel room but said nothing about the weapon and ammunition that had been found in his closet. Frank could not think of many questions for the detective. He'd read the search warrant affidavit, which appeared to be solid, and Cashman's lab reports. There was one area he wanted to ask about, though.

"Detective Brewster, were Mr. Prochaska's prints found on the bullet fragments that were discovered during the autopsy?" Frank asked.

"No. Criminalist Cashman was of the

opinion that they were too fragmented to be printed."

"Thank you. I have no further questions."

"The state calls Criminalist Bernard Cashman," Greene said.

Frank turned toward the back of the courtroom. When Cashman walked toward the witness stand, Frank could not help smiling. The criminalist always made an entrance, like an actor with the lead in a Broadway play. Frank would not have been surprised if one day the forensic expert appeared in court with an opera cape draped across his shoulders.

"I do," Cashman intoned in his deep baritone as soon as the bailiff asked him if he would tell the truth, the whole truth, and nothing but the truth, so help him God.

"Criminalist Cashman, for the record, how are you employed?"

"I am a forensic scientist with the Oregon State Crime Laboratory."

"Judge Belmont is familiar with the work of forensic experts, so you needn't give him a description of your job, but I would like to put your educational background and work experience in the record," Greene said.

"Of course." Cashman squared his cuffs

and smiled at the judge. "I received an under-graduate degree in chemistry from the University of Oklahoma and a master's degree in forensic science from the City University of New York. I spent three years in Colorado at the state crime laboratory before coming to Oregon. I've been here for ten years."

"Mr. Cashman, were you called to the Continental Motel recently?"

"Yes."

"Why were you summoned there?"

"A gentleman named Vincent Ballard was found dead in his motel room. Mary Clark and I conducted the forensic investigation at the crime scene."

"Would you please give the judge a brief overview of the steps you took to process the scene?"

Cashman told Judge Belmont what he and Mary Clark had done at the motel.

"During your search of the motel room, did you notice a beer can on the night table?" Mike asked when Cashman was through.

"I did."

Greene picked up a card that was white on one side and black on the other, and a plastic evidence bag containing a beer can and a strip of tape. A section of the can was coated with black fingerprint powder. He carried the items over to the witness.

"Would you identify these items for the judge, please?" Greene asked.

"Certainly. Exhibit six is a plastic evidence bag containing the beer can. When I examined the can, I dusted it with fingerprint powder so that the print would be highlighted. Then I removed the print from the can using the tape that is in the bag and I placed the print on the white side of the card—exhibit seven—so it would show up against the white background."

"What did you do next?"

"I ran it through AFIS—the automated fingerprint identification system—to see if the computer could identify a possible match."

"Did the computer match the print to an individual?"

"Well, AFIS doesn't make a match. It lists individuals with the highest probability of being a match. The person listed as most likely to be a match was the defendant. Of course, I compared Mr. Prochaska's prints with the print from the can myself before calling Detective Brewster."

"Do you believe that the print on the beer can was placed there by the defendant, Arthur Wayne Prochaska?" the prosecutor asked.

Cashman smiled at the judge. "Yes, I do. I found sixteen points of agreement between the print on the beer can and Mr. Prochaska's known prints. That is enough for me to testify in court that the print on the can was made by the defendant."

"Criminalist Cashman, were you able to find any other evidence connecting the defendant to the murder of Vincent Ballard?" Greene asked.

"Oh, yes."

"What did you find?"

"The bullet fragments that the medical examiner concluded were the instruments of Mr. Ballard's demise are consistent with ammunition discovered in the defendant's home."

"Are you talking about the 9-mm slugs that Detective Brewster testified about?"

"Yes."

Prochaska had been calm during Cashman's testimony, but his face flushed with anger. He leaned close to Frank.

"I'm being framed, Frank. There's no way those bullets match."

"Don't worry, Art. I'm not going to take Cashman's word for anything. I've got my own expert. He'll double-check all of Cashman's conclusions. If the lab screwed up, we'll know."

"Please tell the court how you determined that the bullets Detective Brewster found in the defendant's closet matched the bullets that killed Vincent Ballard."

"Certainly. You might remember, judge, from your high school or college chemistry class that there are ninety-two known elements listed in the periodic table as being found in nature. If we take a bullet and place it in a source of neutrons—atomic particles—the material will absorb the neutrons and become radioactive. More than fifty of the known elements will emit gamma rays when they become radioactive, and we have instruments that will measure how many of these gamma rays are given off by the element and their specific energy."

Frank was always impressed by Cashman's delivery. He sounded more like a lecturer at a university than a cop from the crime lab.

"How did you make this measurement, Criminalist Cashman?" Mike Greene asked.

"We have an arrangement with Reed College, which has a nuclear reactor. In this case, I took a small fragment from one of the bullets found in a box in the defendant's home . . ."

"How small?" the prosecutor asked.

"Oh, I don't need much, just a sliver."

"Go on."

"I shaved off this sliver and took another small fragment from one of the bullets found in the deceased and asked the head of the reactor facility to place the two fragments in the reactor, our source of neutrons. The fragments were placed in vials that had been precleaned to remove impurities that might contaminate the fragments and were lowered into the reactor.

"When the material became radioactive it was removed from the reactor and taken to an area where there is a counter—a machine that will detect gamma rays and measure their energy. We analyzed this data to find out which elements were present and how much of each one was present in each fragment. Then we compared the findings to determine the degree of similarity in the fragments. I might add that one advantage of doing this analysis with bullets is that lead—one of the major components of a bullet—will not become radioactive, so it's easier to see what other elements are in the bullet fragments and if these elements and their energies are similar."

"And what did you find?" Greene asked.

"I discovered that the elements antimony, arsenic, and copper were present in both samples in the same amounts."

"What did you conclude from this?"

"I concluded that the bullet that killed Vincent Ballard was consistent with the bullets that were found in the defendant's closet and most probably both bullets were produced in the same batch."

"No further questions," Mike Greene said.

Frank had been given all of Cashman's reports, including the printouts made at the nuclear reactor. He was personally at sea when it came to the science Cashman used to support his conclusions and could not think of any questions to ask the criminalist about the tests he had conducted. Frank would consult with his own experts and bring out flaws in Cashman's testimony in front of a jury at trial. But he did have a few questions that he wanted to ask the criminalist.

"Mr. Cashman, the batch of bullets that produced the ammunition found in Mr. Prochaska's closet and the bullets that killed Mr. Ballard is very large, isn't it?"

"Yes."

"We're talking about thousands of bullets that are distributed all over the country, aren't we?"

"Yes."

"So you're not saying that your test shows that the bullets that killed Mr. Ballard came from the box found in Mr. Prochaska's house."

"They could have," Cashman answered, "but I could not testify that they did."

"All these bullets were just from this huge batch?"

"That's correct."

"Now, Mr. Cashman, were you able to find striations on the bullets that killed Vincent Ballard that were created when the bullets were fired?"

"Yes. The bullets were badly fragmented but I did find striations on the base area."

"Did you conduct a ballistics test to see if the gun that was found in Mr. Prochaska's home fired the bullets that killed Vincent Ballard?"

"Yes."

"What was your conclusion?"

"It's my opinion that the 9-mm Glock that was discovered during the search of the defendant's home did not fire the bullets that killed Mr. Ballard."

"Thank you, Mr. Cashman. I have no further questions."

As soon as the courtroom door closed behind Bernard Cashman, he let loose the smile he'd been suppressing. He almost felt sorry for Frank Jaffe, but not quite. Most defense attorneys were powerless when he testified. They didn't have the scientific knowledge to challenge his expertise. Cashman knew that Jaffe would consult with a private forensic scientist before trial, but it wouldn't do him any good.

Cashman's chest swelled as he relished the power he wielded. He was the instrument of justice that would send Arthur Wayne Prochaska to the death chamber for the murder of Vincent Ballard. Michael Greene would prosecute the case, the jury would render the verdict, and Judge Belmont would impose the sentence, but none of this could happen without his evidence. Bernard Cashman knew that he was the key. Others would get the credit, but this never bothered him. He was perfectly happy laboring for justice in near anonymity, an avenger of the dead and the defenseless.

As Cashman headed to the elevators, a prisoner in an orange jumpsuit rounded the corner on the way to the jail elevator. When they passed each other, Bernie could not help staring. The prisoner's frizzy, uncombed hair stood out in all directions, and his head was twitching from side to side. Cashman's immediate impression was that the man was insane, and it was reinforced by the fact that the prisoner was mumbling angrily to himself, seemingly oblivious of his surroundings.

Cashman turned the corner and immediately lost interest in the madman. Ahead of him, Hannah Graves was berating Doug Weaver while Steve Hooper looked on, his face flushed with anger. Cashman knew the defense attorney from *State v. Hayes* and a few other cases in which he had been one of the state's witnesses. Doug's face was flushed with embarrassment and he looked as though he wanted to crawl into a hole.

"You think you're so smart now, but let's talk after your client rapes his next victim,"

Cashman heard Graves say. Then the DA and the detective turned on their heels and walked away. Cashman walked up to the defense attorney.

"What was that about?" the forensic expert asked.

Doug whirled toward him, startled. "Gosh, Bernie, I didn't hear you come up."

"Sorry. I guess you were distracted by Ms. Graves. May I assume that you just bested her in court?"

"Yeah," Doug answered, sounding strangely subdued for a victorious defense attorney. "I just won a case that should never have gone to trial. Graves should have resolved it with a plea. But she was so sure of herself that she screwed up in court and she's mad at me when she should be accepting responsibility for her own incompetence."

Doug stopped. "I shouldn't have said that about her being incompetent. Forget you heard that, Bernie."

Cashman smiled. "Between us, Doug, Graves is not the brightest DA with whom I've worked."

"Who isn't?" asked Amanda Jaffe, who had just rounded the corner on the way to the courtroom where *Prochaska* was being heard.

"Amanda," said Cashman. He had testified in several cases that Amanda had defended and believed her to be a worthy adversary. "Do you know Doug Weaver?"

"Sure. We ate lunch together at that CLE last year."

Doug was a little in awe of Amanda, who was the success he wished he could be. He appreciated the fact that she had not mentioned that Doug had been a student at the continuing legal education seminar while she had been lecturing on the latest trends in search-and-seizure law.

"Nice seeing you again," Doug said.

"We were talking about Hannah Graves," Cashman said. "Doug just beat her in court and she didn't take it well."

"She never does," Amanda said. "I won a case from her recently and she stormed out of the courtroom like a two-year-old. Hannah needs to lighten up."

"I heard her say something about a rape," Cashman said. "Is that what the charge was?"

"No. It was failure to register as a sex offender."

Doug gave Amanda and Cashman an abbreviated version of the facts and what had happened at trial. Shortly after Doug started, the criminalist realized that Doug's client was the disturbed prisoner he had passed in the hall.

"Good going," Amanda said when Doug was through.

"Do you think your client is dangerous?" Cashman asked.

Doug hesitated. What did he really believe about Jacob? Did he have any way of judging a person who was as mentally ill as his client?

"Not really," he decided to answer. "I'm not even certain Jacob committed the attempted rape in the first place. I talked to his last attorney and Jacob's version of the facts sounds as plausible as the version his accuser gave. The problem is that Jacob makes a horrible impression in front of a jury because he's seriously mentally ill. He lives in an abandoned car in a vacant lot on Queen Anne and Hobart and he refuses to accept help from anyone. He thinks we're all part of some vast government conspiracy."

"He sounds like a lost soul," Cashman said.

"It's a sad case. I just hope he stays out of trouble and takes care of himself, but I don't have much hope."

Doug hefted his briefcase. "Well, it was nice seeing you, Bernie, Amanda. I've got to get back to my office."

As soon as they'd said their good-byes and Doug was on his way, Bernie remembered *Prochaska*.

"This is a coincidence. I just testified in a case your father is defending. He's in Judge Belmont's courtroom. I think they're near the end."

"It's no coincidence. I'm on my way to see Dad. I'm doing a little work on the case with him."

"I should have guessed."

"It was nice seeing you again," Amanda told the criminalist.

"Same here," Cashman answered.

Amanda walked away, and Cashman watched her for a moment before continuing to the elevators that would take him to the main floor. From there, it was back to the crime lab and his continuing examination of the evidence in another case he knew he could solve.

14

AMANDA WALKED INTO THE COURT-
room moments after Judge Belmont bound
over Art Prochaska for trial and recessed for
the day. Frank was talking to his client, so
Amanda waited in the back of the courtroom.
Mike Greene packed up his attaché case
and started up the aisle. A look of surprise
crossed his face when he saw Amanda.
Then he smiled and walked over to her.

"How have you been?"

"Okay," Amanda answered, trying to hide
her discomfort.

"I haven't seen you in a while. Working
hard, or have you been away?"

Amanda laughed. "I can't remember my last vacation."

"Then it must be work," Mike said, because he wanted to keep talking to Amanda.

"I was very busy, then things slowed down. I've got a few drug cases, some DUIs. Nothing too exciting. What about you?"

"Well, there's this case and I've got two other homicides, but they might plead out."

"So you're not too busy either."

"Yeah, looks like neither of us is earning our keep."

"I heard Belmont bind over Prochaska," Amanda said.

Mike shrugged. "I've got a pretty strong case."

"Don't you feel bad about beating up my father?"

Mike grinned. "Frank can take care of himself. Besides, he told me that you two are going to be double-teaming me."

"I've been practicing my body slam all week."

When Mike finished laughing, he and Amanda realized that they had both run out of small talk. Mike wanted to know if Amanda was seeing anyone, but he didn't have the nerve to ask. The two attorneys shifted in place awkwardly.

"Well, I've got to get back to the office," Mike said after a few seconds of silence. "It was nice seeing you."

"Me too."

"I'll see you around," the prosecutor concluded. Then he was out the door, leaving Amanda feeling unsettled. To distract herself, she returned her attention to the front of the courtroom, where Frank was shaking hands with Prochaska. As soon as the jail guards slipped on the handcuffs and led him away, Amanda walked over to her father.

"Going back to the office?" she asked.

"Yeah. I saw you talking to Mike."

"We were just talking shop."

"You two haven't gone out for a while."

"I was seeing someone else but that's over."

"Do you think you and Mike might pick up again?" Frank asked, knowing that he had just entered a minefield.

"I don't even know if he's interested, Dad."

"He might be. He asked about you when we were waiting for court to begin."

"He was probably just making conversation."

"It didn't sound like it."

"Mike thinks he's got a pretty good shot at convicting Art Prochaska," she said, to change the topic. "What do you think?"

"Too early to tell. His evidence is circumstantial. There are no eyewitnesses, and there's nothing in the police reports to suggest that Art even knew the dead man."

"What do they have?" Amanda asked.

"The worst evidence for us is Art's fingerprint on a beer can that was on the night table in Ballard's room. The maids clean every day, so Mike can prove that the can was brought to the room after three in the afternoon. That puts him with Ballard sometime during that day.

"Then there are the bullets. Bernie Cashman testified that the bullets that killed Ballard are consistent with ammunition that was found in a closet during a search of Art's house."

"Any way to suppress the evidence?"

"The search looks pretty clean to me but you should take a look at it."

"Okay. Are you going to use Paul Baylor for the forensic work?"

"Yeah, but I don't expect much; finger-prints don't lie and they used neutron ac-tivation analysis to make the call on the bullets."

Amanda looked at her watch. "What are you doing for dinner?"

"I'm eating with you."

"Do you want to grab a bite at Signorelli's, that new Italian place on Twenty-first?"

"Sounds good. I've got about two hours of work in the office. We can leave around five-thirty."

Charlie LaRosa had already given Martin Breach a summary of the preliminary hear-ing, so he was prepared for Frank's call. Jaffe told Breach what he had learned about the government's case. Breach sounded calm on the phone, but he was seething inside. When he hung up, he looked across the desk at Henry Tedesco, who had heard the con-versation on the speaker phone.

"What do you think?" Breach asked, his anger barely under control.

"Seems like a good case for the state," Henry answered in his thick Irish brogue. Te-desco was one of the few men in Breach's employ who would tell him the truth. Breach ruled by terror, but he despised yes-men and prized Henry's honesty.

"Someone is fucking with us, Henry, and I want to know who it is."

"You think Art was set up?"

Martin leaned back and picked up a toothpick. He gathered his thoughts while he pried loose a piece of fried chicken that had gotten stuck between his teeth.

"Let's start with the fingerprint and them bullets," Breach said. "The fingerprints ain't Artie's and neither is the ammo that iced Ballard because Artie didn't kill him. So you got to find out who did."

"Any ideas? Anyplace you want me to start?"

"Yeah, two places. See what you can find out about that pimp Dorado. He'd love to have Artie out of the way. But it's the print and the bullets that really bother me."

Tedesco shrugged. "The obvious answer to the print is that whoever shot Ballard got a beer can that Art used and planted it on the end table."

"That was my first thought, but Art don't drink that brand and he swears that he can't remember touching the can."

Breach stared into space for a while, and

Tedesco let him think. Breach was one of the smartest people he'd ever met, and his ideas were always interesting.

"Henry, do you know any way of faking a fingerprint?"

"No, but I can find out if it can be done."

"Do that."

Breach spaced out again as he worked on his teeth with the toothpick. Henry waited patiently. Suddenly Breach sat up straight.

"Lab guys!" He looked at Tedesco. "Do you think Dorado could have gotten to one of the lab guys?"

Henry shrugged. "You can get to anyone if you try hard enough."

Breach jabbed the toothpick in Tedesco's direction. "Check out the lab guys. Find out if anyone is on Dorado's payroll." Then Breach muttered, "They better not be."

PART THREE
UNSPEAKABLE HORROR

15

MARTIN BREACH HAD GIVEN HENRY
Tedesco copies of the police reports in Art
Prochaska's case, and Henry had read them
carefully. Several reports of interviews with
the residents of the Continental Motel had
been written up right after the murder, but
there had been very little investigation of
any kind after the lab identified Prochaska's
thumbprint on the beer can. Tedesco concluded that Billie Brewster, the lead detective, was convinced of Art's guilt and was
focusing on Prochaska to the exclusion of
all other possible suspects. The evidence of
Art's guilt was very strong, but Henry knew

that Prochaska would never lie to Martin Breach; the two men were closer than brothers. If Art told Martin that he was innocent, he was innocent; and this meant that the real killer was probably feeling safe and very satisfied with himself.

Tedesco believed that his best chance of finding Ballard's killer was someone living at the Continental Motel. The police had not interviewed all of the residents on the evening of the killing, and most of the people who were interviewed claimed to know nothing that would help the police. Henry was well acquainted with people who lived in dives like the Continental. Many of them had been in trouble with the law or were in the United States illegally. These were people who, as a matter of principle, would not be honest with a policeman. And, of course, police officers had to follow rules when they interviewed a witness. Henry Tedesco had never had much respect for rules.

Henry talked to three people before he got a lead. Money and the threat of force loosened the tongue of a single mother who was hooking out of a room across the court from the one in which Vincent Ballard was murdered.

She told Henry about a conversation she'd had by the vending machine with one of the other residents the night after the killing.

Clarence Edwards and Edgar Lewis were sleeping soundly when Charlie LaRosa opened the door to their room with the master key he'd rented from the night manager for a hundred dollars. Edgar Lewis was dead to the world, but Clarence sat up, blinking sleep from his eyes, when Henry flipped on the lights.

Edwards was a skinny African-American with dreadlocks and tattoos, who had just served six months in a local jail for shoplifting after being convicted for the fourth time. Edwards stole only when he was out of work. He'd just gotten a job at a video store and was sharing the rent for the room with Edgar, whom he'd known since high school.

"What the fuck . . ." Clarence started to ask. Then he saw the guns and lost his bravado.

"Mr. Lewis or Mr. Edwards?" Henry asked pleasantly.

Clarence's mouth was dry, but he managed to answer the question. Edgar was waking up in the other bed.

"Would you and your friend please lie down, pull your blankets up to your necks and put your arms under the covers?" Henry asked.

"Who are these guys?" Edgar asked his friend. Henry nodded, and Charlie smacked Edgar across the face.

"We ask the questions, asshole," he explained. Edgar, who weighed 140 when he was eating right, was too dazed to do more than collapse on his bed.

"What you do that for?" Clarence demanded. Charlie took a step toward him, but Henry held up a hand and he stopped.

"My friend struck Mr. Lewis to let you know that we will use violence if we feel it's necessary. Now please lie down and cover yourself. If you do as we ask, no harm will come to you or your roommate and you might earn yourself some money."

As soon as Clarence and Edgar were under the blankets, Charlie tucked in their sheets and covers and used duct tape to seal them into bed.

"Comfy?" Henry asked as he pulled a chair next to Clarence. Clarence didn't respond. Henry smiled.

"A short time ago, your neighbor, Vincent Ballard, was murdered across the court. Do you remember that?"

Clarence looked nervous. Edgar glanced at his roomie for a brief second. Henry noticed.

"Clarence, we need to set some ground rules. If I ask you a question, you must answer it truthfully. Do you understand?"

"Yeah," Clarence answered in a surly tone. Henry sighed.

"I don't care much for your attitude, my lad. Let's see if we can make an adjustment in it." He took out a cigarette lighter and flicked on the flame. "Tell me, have you ever seen a person burn to death?"

"What!"

"It is truly horrible. The stench of burning flesh is revolting, and the screaming . . ." Henry shook his head. "Now, Clarence, if you don't start cooperating quickly I'm going to set you on fire. Taped into your bed as you are, you'll be unable to do much more than suffer. I imagine the pain will be intense. It is my hope that this example will make your friend more cooperative. But neither of you need to suffer if you'll just stop being recalcitrant. You do understand what that means, don't you?"

"Yes, sir," Clarence answered, though of the four men in the room only Henry could define the word.

"Good," Henry said, appreciating the "sir." "The quicker you answer my questions, the quicker we'll be gone. So, do you remember the evening of the murder?"

"Yeah, I do," Clarence answered.

"Your room is across the court from Mr. Ballard's room. Tell me what you saw."

"What happens to us if I say what I seen?"

"Not a thing. We'll let you go and you'll never see us again. And we won't tell the police about this." Henry smiled. "Not much good would come of that for any of us, would it?" Henry flipped a roll of money onto the bed. "You'll even get a little something for your time. So, you see, you have nothing to lose and everything to gain by being truthful. In fact, the only problem you'll have is if you aren't completely honest. If you lie and we let you go, we'll find you and that would not be good for you at all."

Clarence looked back and forth between the money and the cigarette lighter. The choice was a no-brainer.

"I didn't tell the cops nothing, but I can help you."

"Go ahead."

"I got up to take a piss. That's when I heard the music. It was loud. So I peeked through the blinds to see where it was coming from. That's when I seen 'em coming out."

"Who did you see?"

"This regular-size dude and this other guy. The one guy, I can't tell you too much about him. I didn't see his face. I didn't see the other guy's face either but he was big, like a pro wrestler. Like really huge. And that's all I can say, honest."

"This large gentleman—think hard—can you describe his face at all?"

Clarence closed his eyes. When he opened them, he shook his head. "All I can say is about his hair. It was real short, like a crew cut. I remember that. But they were both wearing coats and the collars were up."

Henry pointed at Charlie LaRosa. "Was the big man as large as my friend?"

Clarence studied the gangster. "He wasn't as tall but he was wider."

"Did you notice their car?"

"No. I went to piss and they were gone when I was done."

Henry turned to Edgar. "I didn't see nothing," he said quickly. "I was sleeping. Clarence just told me what he seen after the cops left."

Henry studied the two men for a moment. Then he flipped the lighter shut and nodded at LaRosa, who started to remove the tape that trapped the men in their beds.

"I hope I don't have to tell you to keep this little visit between us," he said, just before they left. Neither Clarence nor Edgar answered.

"Does the description Mr. Edwards gave mean anything to you?" Henry asked Charlie as they headed for their car.

"Felix Dorado's got a guy works for him, Reuben Corrales, who's a steroid freak. Dorado uses him for muscle and I think he was one of the guys guarding Juan Ruiz when we snatched him."

"Interesting. If Dorado figured out that Ballard ratted out Ruiz, he might have ordered our bodybuilder to carry out the hit as penance for losing Ruiz. What do you think?"

"That makes sense."

"See if you can find this gentleman, Charlie. Then we'll pay him a visit."

16

SHORTLY AFTER MIDNIGHT, A PASS-erby found the badly beaten manager of a North Portland liquor store sprawled on the floor behind his counter. Two robbers stoked on meth had pistol-whipped him after stealing liquor and money from the till. Before the EMTs took the manager to the hospital, he told the detectives that his assailants weren't wearing gloves.

Bernard Cashman and Mary Clark processed the crime scene and discovered fingerprints on the bottles the robbers had pawed through while selecting liquor to stuff into a gym bag. The thieves had also smashed a number of bottles during their rampage and had been kind enough to step in the rum, rye, and Bailey's Irish Cream that coated the floor. The liquor had moistened the mud on the bottom of one perp's sneakers, leaving a partial shoeprint for Mary Clark to find.

A light rain was falling when the forensic experts finished their work. Cashman's pickup was parked on a side street around the corner from the liquor store. He was putting his gear in the back when Mary walked up. She had been quiet all evening, and Cashman found this odd, since the normally cheerful criminalist liked to chat while working a crime scene.

"Got a minute?" Clark asked. She sounded nervous, and her lips were drawn into a grim line.

"Sure," Cashman answered with a smile. She wouldn't meet his eyes.

"This is really awkward for me, Bernie. I wanted to talk to you privately before I said anything."

"About what?" he answered, genuinely puzzled.

"A week ago, I reviewed a bunch of old cases to see if we could return the evidence to victims or relatives or, you know, destroy it."

Now Cashman was even more confused. Making recommendations about what to do with evidence from closed cases was a routine part of a criminalist's job. There was only a limited amount of storage space, and crime never took a holiday.

Clark looked up now and stared directly at her colleague. "One of the cases was *State v. Raymond Hayes*. You worked that case, didn't you?"

"Yes."

"That was the one where the print on the hammer was the crucial piece of evidence."

Cashman smiled proudly. "Steve Hooper told me that Hayes would never have pled if I hadn't found that print."

Clark paused, like a diver on a high board. Then she jumped.

"I don't think there was a print on that hammer, Bernie."

A queasy feeling spread through Cashman's gut. "What do you mean?" he answered calmly, broadcasting none of his concern.

"I know what you did. What I don't know is why."

"I honestly have no idea what you're talking about."

"You told the grand jury that Raymond Hayes left a fingerprint on that hammer, but you know that he didn't. I went through some of your other cases after I figured out what happened in *Hayes*. Two of them are really troubling me."

"Are you saying that I made mistakes in some of my cases?"

"It goes way beyond making a mistake."

Cashman looked bewildered. "You're suggesting . . . ?" The criminalist stopped. He looked appalled. "We've been colleagues and—I hope—friends, for years, Mary, so I'm going to chalk up your . . . Well, they are accusations. There's no other way to interpret them. I'm going to consider them a product of fatigue and forget that we had this conversation."

"I do consider you my friend, Bernie. That's why we're talking now, just the two of us. Do you think this is easy for me?"

"Mary, I don't know what you think you've discovered, but now isn't the time to discuss this. It's almost two in the morning. I'm wet and exhausted. I'm sure you are, too."

"We have to discuss it. I'm doing it now to

give you a chance to explain what happened before I talk to Carlos," she said, referring to Carlos Guzman, the head of the crime lab.

"Look, I appreciate the fact that you've come to me, but I'm not going to stand in the rain and defend myself from . . . Well, I don't really know what I'm defending myself from, do I? I'm going to have to see the files in these cases before I can explain why you're mistaken. So, let's get some rest. In the morning, show me the cases that disturb you. I know that there's a reasonable explanation because I have never done anything unethical. If you're still not convinced after we talk, tell Carlos your concerns. And, believe me, I won't hold it against you. I take my job very seriously and I welcome criticism."

Now it was Mary's turn to be confused. She had been certain that Bernie would be defensive or angry in the face of her accusations, but he was understanding, calm, and reasonable.

"What do you say, Mary? Can this wait until we've both gotten a good night's sleep?"

Clark still hesitated. Bernie smiled and held his hands out, palms up, so the raindrops bounced off them.

"Pretty please? I'm getting soaked."

Bernie was right. She was uncomfortable standing in the persistent drizzle. She would have been out on her feet if the adrenaline that had been produced when she got up the courage to confront Cashman weren't coursing through her veins. And it really wasn't fair to make Bernie defend himself before he'd seen what bothered her.

"Okay, Bernie. I'll wait. But you've got to explain everything to my satisfaction or I will go to Carlos."

"If I can't prove to you that there is no problem with every case you've studied, you should go to Carlos. Believe me, if I screwed up I'll take the hit rather than let an innocent man rot in jail."

The adrenaline wore off a few minutes after Mary Clark started for home, leaving her crushingly tired. Shortly after she drove onto the freeway, her eyelids closed for a second before jerking open when her car swerved. Fear straightened her in her seat and kept her alert for the rest of the drive.

Mary Clark had been married to a dentist for ten years before her hours and his dalliance with his dental assistant led to divorce. She lived in a converted farmhouse, which she'd gotten in the settlement. Gravel crunched under her tires when she pulled into the driveway. Mary had kept the porch light on when she left for the liquor store. She opened the door, and the alarm whined until she punched in the security code.

The criminalist hung her windbreaker on a coatrack before going into the kitchen for a snack. It was almost three, but she was starving. After gobbling down three Oreo cookies and a glass of milk, Mary turned on the alarm and trudged up the stairs to the second floor. She wanted to drop into bed, but she smelled of scotch, bourbon, and sweat, and her sheets would stink in the morning if she didn't take a quick shower.

While she brushed her teeth, Mary thought about Bernie's protestations of innocence. It was a criminalist's job to evaluate evidence objectively, and that was what she'd done as soon as her suspicions about the print on the hammer in the *Hayes* case had been aroused. She had worked from the hypothesis that Bernie had done nothing wrong. But now, in each case, she believed she had clear and convincing evidence of intentional wrongdoing.

If she was right, Bernie had just snowed

her. He'd played on the trust that had built up between them over the years, and she had been too tired and too overwhelmed with guilt to see it. She was a scientist and a damn good forensic expert. She was certain there was something wrong with the cases she'd reviewed, and she could not see how the errors could have been the product of a mistake. For a moment, Mary toyed with the idea of calling Carlos Guzman at home, but it was so late, and she needed sleep so she would be alert when she met with Cashman in the morning. Besides, no matter how sure she was, she owed it to Bernie to give him the chance to prove her wrong.

And what if she was wrong? She hoped that she hadn't destroyed their relationship with false accusations of ineptitude and outright criminal conduct. She was certain that there were problems with *Hayes* and the other cases, but her certainty had wavered after their conversation. Bernie seemed so sure of himself. She wanted to believe that he hadn't done what she suspected. Thank God, she hadn't rushed to Guzman with her suspicions. Maybe there was a good explanation for the fingerprints and the other things she'd found. There had to be. Bernard Cashman was one of the most respected criminalists in the state. He'd been her mentor when she started at the crime lab four years ago. More important, he was her friend, the person who consoled her when her mother died, the shoulder she'd cried on when her marriage was breaking up.

Mary finished taking off her makeup and stepped into the shower. The pounding water was steamy hot, and she almost fell asleep in the bathroom. After toweling off, she put on flannel pajamas and used her last ounce of energy to walk to her bed and crawl under the covers. Doubts still nagged at her, but she was too exhausted to entertain them for long, and soon she was asleep.

17

BERNARD CASHMAN APPEARED CALM while he was talking to Mary Clark, but inside he was furious. When he drove from the crime scene, he gripped the steering wheel so tightly that his knuckles turned white, and it took all of his self-control to keep his rage from turning into tire-screeching speed as he headed down I-205 toward the crime lab. Cashman could not believe what Mary was planning to do to him. He had never done anything to hurt her; he had always been kind and supportive, pushing her forward when she had doubts, cheerleading when she was successful. And this was how she repaid him. How dare she go snooping in his cases? How dare she interfere with his work? Did she have any conception of what was at stake?

Cashman parked in the rear of the lab, which was housed in a block-long, two-story building of gray metal and tinted glass only a few blocks from several suburban shopping malls. Well-tended lawns surrounded the building, and there was a small park with picnic tables on one side.

The evidence from the liquor-store robbery had been packed into several paper bags, which had been sealed at the crime scene. Cashman put them in his personal storage space, one of many in a secure area off the parking lot. In the morning, he would take the evidence inside the lab and log it into the main evidence vault before working on it. Now he had more pressing matters to take care of.

Cashman punched in a code on a keypad before swiping his key card to gain entry to the deserted building. He walked down several narrow corridors to the evidence locker, swiped his card to gain entry, and went to the area where closed files were kept. The evidence bag with the hammer was missing from the *State v. Hayes* file. He pulled the other cases that could have aroused Mary's suspicions. Nothing was missing, but the evidence of what he'd done was there, if you knew where to look.

Cashman and Mary Clark had desks that abutted in a large cubicle near the director's office. Each criminalist had a computer, black metal file holders, and personal in and out boxes. The desks weren't locked. Cashman searched Mary's desk but found neither the hammer nor any other evidence from cases he had worked. Where was the hammer? He would be ruined if she showed it to Carlos Guzman. He might even go to prison.

Cashman collapsed onto his desk chair. The moment he sat down, his eyes closed and he had to fight to open them. Sleep was a luxury he could not afford. He glanced at the clock. It was a little after two-thirty. Mary usually got to work around eight. What to do? What to do? He couldn't let her tell Carlos about the hammer. Take a deep breath and calm down, he told himself. Do what you do best, think! He had to approach the problem calmly. If he acted too quickly, he would be more likely to make a mistake, just like the one he had just learned he'd made in *Hayes*.

When Raymond Hayes murdered his mother, Cashman was new at the crime lab, and the respect of the detectives and his fellow criminalists was even more important to him than it was today. It was because of his need to be respected that Bernie first discovered he possessed powers to fight injustice and to right wrongs akin to the powers possessed by Superman, Captain Marvel, and the other superheroes in the comics he'd read as a kid. The young Bernie Cashman envied those superheroes. They were not prey to bullies, they were worshipped by others, and they shaped their own destiny— they were special. Until his epiphany, Bernard Cashman had never felt special.

As a child, Cashman was a painfully shy weakling, a target for schoolyard bullies. Cashman's father, a brutal, driven, self-made man, ignored his sickly son, whom he considered a disappointment. His overprotective mother coddled Bernard and refused to let him play with other children or exercise in any way, for fear that physical exertion would damage his health. Her incessant bragging about his intelligence embarrassed him, especially after he realized that there really wasn't anything outstanding about his mental powers. Oh, he was smart enough to master his schoolwork, but he soon discovered that he lacked the imagination that translated intelligence into genius. Someone else was always first in his class. Later in life, someone else always got the plum jobs. Cashman had accepted his mediocrity until the day he testified before the grand jury in the *Hayes* case.

In hindsight, Cashman could see that he'd made his mistake in *Hayes* because he'd acted too quickly, but he'd had no choice. He had worked the *Hayes* crime scene with Michael Kitay, a senior criminalist. Kitay, who was supposed to check the hammer for prints, suffered a heart attack at work and died at the hospital on the day before the grand jury in *Hayes* was convened. Cashman had been ordered to testify in Kitay's place. In the confusion, he assumed that Kitay had checked the hammer for prints, and he did not learn that the work had not been done until the morning of the grand jury, when he read through the reports that Kitay had prepared before he collapsed. When he looked for the physical evidence in the crime lab,

Cashman was told that the district attorney had taken possession of it that morning.

Cashman had intended to explain the problem to the prosecutor who was running the grand jury, but the DA was already in the grand-jury room when Cashman arrived at the courthouse. Then Steve Hooper had casually mentioned that the DA was counting on the criminalist to provide the forensic evidence that would link Raymond Hayes to the murder. The detective confided that the district attorney was worried that he would not get an indictment if forensic evidence did not connect Hayes to the crime. Cashman had not paid much attention to *Hayes*, because Kitay had taken the case for himself. He had no idea that finding a fingerprint belonging to Hayes on the hammer was crucial to the state's case until Hooper explained that Hayes had sworn he had never seen the blood-covered hammer before he had discovered it lying next to his mother's corpse, and had never touched it.

Cashman remembered feeling sick to his stomach as he took the oath. Within minutes, the deputy district attorney asked Cashman what the examination of the bloody hammer had revealed. If he testified that no one had examined the hammer for prints, he would let down the prosecutor and all of the policemen and detectives who had worked so hard on the case. Worse still, he would be responsible for a horrible murderer walking free. Cashman was in a panic. He imagined that he might even be fired if he let down the prosecutor. So, he testified that an examination of the handle of the hammer had revealed the fingerprints of Raymond Hayes. He convinced himself that his testimony wasn't perjury. When he was through testifying, Cashman planned to take the hammer to the lab and print it. He was sure that the print would be there. Everyone knew Raymond Hayes had killed his mother.

Cashman was excused after his testimony, and the DA walked with him to the anteroom where the next witness was waiting. When the door to the grand-jury room closed, and the jurors could not hear, the prosecutor had pumped Cashman's hand and said that Cashman's testimony had saved the state's case. Cashman asked if he might take the physical evidence back to the lab. To his horror, the DA had told him he was going to keep all of the physical evidence in his office until the trial was over. Cashman had returned to the lab in a daze and had hardly slept until the word reached him that Hayes had pleaded guilty because of his testimony about the print.

Everyone had treated Cashman like a hero when Hayes pleaded. It had been one of the greatest moments in his life. He had been terrified when he lied under oath, but after Hayes confessed to the murder, Cashman knew that he had done the right thing. Justice had been served, and Hayes's mother had been avenged. The hammer had stayed in evidence until after the execution, and Cashman had not seen it again. It never occurred to him that an examination of the hammer might reveal no prints, or the prints of another man. By pleading guilty, Hayes had admitted wielding it, so there had to be a print on the handle.

After the *Hayes* case, Cashman, like his superhero models, used his powers sparingly and wisely, choosing only the most heinous cases with the most evil villains. When the police were certain they knew the guilty party but didn't have enough evidence to convict, Cashman came to the rescue. Over the years, he had manufactured evidence in only a few cases, and he had felt good about it every time. When he had doubts about his mission, he would open the case file and view the victim's battered and defiled body, and his doubts would vanish. Now Mary, who had no idea of the good he'd done, wanted to destroy him. Worst of all, by exposing Cashman, Clark would be paving the way for appeals that would open the prison gates to murderers, rapists, and the other scum he'd put behind bars. She had to be stopped, but how? The moment he asked himself what he would have to do to stop Mary, it dawned on him that he wouldn't have a problem if Mary Clark did not exist.

Suddenly, Cashman was wide awake, his heart thudding in his chest. He liked Mary, he was very fond of her, but she was the only one who knew, she was the only person who could spoil everything. Cashman swallowed. What was he thinking? To take Mary out of the picture, he would have to . . . No. He shook his head. Such a thing was unthinkable.

Cashman swiveled his chair and leaned back. But what if—for the sake of argument—he could come up with a way to . . . remove Mary and avoid detection? The odds of success were certainly in his favor. He would be starting with a terrific advantage over the average criminal, because he could arrange to investigate Mary's death, thus giving himself the opportunity to point the finger away from himself and toward someone else.

An image of a deranged man dressed in orange flashed in Cashman's brain. He sat up in his seat. Jacob Cohen, the madman who lived in the vacant lot on Queen Anne and Hobart! What had Doug Weaver said? Cohen made a terrible impression in court; he was not believable. Weaver didn't think his client was dangerous, but what was he supposed to say? Hannah Graves and Steve Hooper obviously thought that Cohen was a danger to women. It wouldn't be wrong if someone like Cohen went to prison. Taking him off the street would be a good thing. He was a convicted sex offender and clearly insane. If he could stop the release of all those terrible people back into society while putting away a dangerous rapist, would that be wrong?

By two-thirty a.m., Cashman had worked out a plan and had analyzed it for flaws. He went to the evidence locker and found eight pubic hairs that had been seized from Cohen during the attempted rape case. Using tweezers, he transferred two of the hairs to a small vial. Then he replaced the two pubic hairs he had just taken with two similar pubic hairs from another old case. When he had collected the rest of the items he needed, he left the building.

Cashman learned quickly that it was one thing to fantasize about murder and another to actually kill a person. As soon as he began driving to Mary's house, his body betrayed him. Sweat beaded his brow, and his stomach rolled. Once, he felt so sick that he pulled over to the side of the road. As he sat with the door open, gulping in fresh air, he fought to block out all thoughts of Mary, but he couldn't and he almost turned back. Only the idea of the evil men he'd put behind bars walking free helped him to keep going. He did like Mary, but, he convinced himself, she was only one person. Dozens of innocents would be at risk if he didn't stop her.

At four-fifteen, Cashman parked in front of Mary's house. He had on the outfit he wore at crime scenes. His hand shook as he carried a large black bag and a rolled-up tarp to the front door, set them down on the porch, and rang the doorbell. There was no response after the first ring. A feeling of relief flooded him when he heard no sound inside the house after his second ring. Maybe Mary wasn't home. One part of Bernard Cashman hoped that fate had spared her from the terrible things he planned to do. Then a light went on in Mary's bedroom, and his stomach lurched. Moments later, Cashman heard footsteps on the stairs. Mary peered through the glass panes in the front door. Cashman steeled himself and forced a smile. Mary looked confused, but she turned off her alarm and opened the door wide. She looked even more confused when she noticed that Cashman was wearing Tyvex booties and latex gloves.

She was saying "Bernie" when Cashman gathered his courage and hit her as hard as he could in the solar plexus. Mary staggered backward into the house and collapsed in the entryway. He felt terrible as he slapped plastic cuffs on Mary's hands and ankles and taped her mouth shut, but this single act of violence freed him. He had committed assault, a felony offense punishable by prison. There was no going back now.

Cashman took a syringe out of his jacket pocket as Mary sucked in air through her nose. When she saw the syringe, Clark's eyes widened in fear and she struggled. Cashman stunned her with another body blow, then rolled up the sleeve of her pajama top and injected her. When she began to space out, Cashman patted Mary's shoulder.

"It's heroin from one of your cases," he told her in a calm, reassuring voice. "You'll find it quite pleasant."

It was vital to Cashman's plan that a forensic team would not find evidence of a struggle in Mary's home. When he was certain that she would be docile enough that he could stop holding her, the criminalist went outside and brought in the bag and the tarp, which he spread out on the floor. It wasn't difficult for Cashman to lift Mary onto the tarp. As soon as he was in college, away from his mother, Cashman had built up his body, and he was now in top physical shape. Before going up to her bedroom he pressed Mary's fingerprints onto the syringe and the glassine envelope in which the heroin had been stored. There was a wastepaper basket in Clark's bathroom, and he discarded the syringe and the envelope.

A few minutes later, Cashman returned to the entryway. He was carrying a set of old clothes, sweat socks, and a pair of sneakers he'd found in Mary's bedroom. He stripped off her pajamas. She moaned and rolled around sluggishly. The heroin had dulled her pain and made her listless. Mary's nudity embarrassed Cashman. He felt terrible about hurting her, but even worse about seeing her naked. After all, they were friends. But, he told himself again, he could not permit her to destroy his work. Cashman averted his eyes as much as possible when he slipped Clark's panties on her. He had to hug her and sit her up while he worked her into her bra and shirt. The scent of the soap she had used when she'd showered lingered on her skin, and her breasts pressed against him for a moment. There was a good deal of clothing between them, but he still felt intensely uncomfortable.

When Mary was dressed, Cashman rolled her in the tarp, slung her over his shoulder, took her to his truck, and placed her in the back as gently as possible. Part of him hoped that the heroin would dull her senses enough to stop her from being frightened. Cashman checked his watch. It was still dark. He returned to the house and began to search for the hammer and any other evidence that might incriminate him. His anxiety increased as minute after minute passed without discovering anything. He began to wonder if she'd secreted them somewhere else or if they were still at the lab and he'd missed them. After half an hour of fruitless searching, Cashman decided to stop. He needed the cover of darkness to transport Mary to his home.

Cashman lived in a two-story, red-shingle Craftsman with an unfinished basement on a quarter-acre of land in southwest Portland. His garage was toward the back of his house, at the end of a long driveway. Gretchen Studer, his neighbor on the garage side, was a nosy seventy-four-year-old widow, who slept at odd hours. He'd caught her on several occasions peeking at his house through the half-closed curtains in her second-floor bedroom. Cashman planned to park so the back of his pickup was even with the basement door. If Mrs. Studer was watching from her bedroom, it should look as if Cashman were bringing a rug into his house.

Fortunately, the Studer house was dark when Cashman parked the truck. By the time Cashman locked Mary Clark in his basement, it was almost five-thirty. He wanted desperately to sleep, but he had to get to work on time to keep up appearances, so he settled for a cold shower and several cups of coffee. Cashman was tempted to question Mary before he went to work, but he did not want to rush. He wanted her frightened enough to tell him what he needed to know, without having to cause her any more pain than was necessary. Lying in the dark would give her time to think.

18

CARLOS GUZMAN WAS A HEAVYSET man with a dark complexion, thick, black hair, and eyes the color of milk chocolate. He had a master's degree in forensic science and an undergraduate degree in criminal justice and had been promoted to head the crime lab after fifteen years on the job. He stopped Cashman as soon as Bernie arrived at the crime lab.

"You seen Mary?" Guzman asked. His voice was gravelly and he sounded a little like Edward G. Robinson in one of those black-and-white gangster movies from the forties. To keep in character, Guzman should have been puffing on a bad cigar, but smoking was not allowed in state office buildings.

"She's probably fast asleep," Bernie said. "We worked a liquor store robbery last night and we didn't finish up until the wee hours."

"Okay. Tell her to drop in when she shows up."

As soon as Guzman walked away, Cashman tried to remember if Mary had mentioned how many of his cases had concerned her. She had referred to *Hayes* by name, but he didn't think she'd told him how many cases she was looking into. Or maybe she had. Was it *Hayes* and two more? What really bothered him was his inability to find the hammer from the *Hayes* case in the crime lab or Mary's house.

Cashman checked his watch. He would drive by Jacob Cohen's lot during his lunch break to scope it out. Then he'd go home and give Mary more of the heroin he'd taken from two of her cases before returning to the lab. It was important that the toxicology results establish the presence of the opiate in Mary's system, for his plan to work.

After returning from his lunch break, Cashman would stay until five, his normal quitting time. After work, he would check out the lot again before driving to the bus stop closest to Mary's house. He would leave his truck in an inconspicuous spot near the bus stop and run to Mary's home to get her car. She lived only two miles from the bus line, and Cashman ran six to ten miles for exercise, so covering the distance would be no problem, and no one would take a second look at a jogger in Oregon. He would use Mary's car to transport her to Jacob's lot. Then he would take the bus to his car and drive the pickup home. Eventually, the corpse in the lot would be identified as Mary Clark and her car would be found nearby. When the lab discovered heroin in Mary's system and heroin missing from her cases, it would be only logical to conclude that she was a secret addict who had gone to Queen Anne Boulevard to buy dope.

After work, Cashman approached Jacob's lot from a back street and parked on Hobart under a large oak tree. Jacob's abandoned car was in the back of the lot, almost touching the wall of a four-story building. A bar occupied the street level, and low-rent apartments took up the other floors. The building that once stood in the lot had been destroyed in a fire. The ruins had been torn down, but no one wanted to rebuild in a high-crime area, and the large lot was now filled with trash and rubble.

It was raining hard. Only one intrepid hooker, desperate to raise money for a fix, was patrolling Queen Anne. Even without the rain, it was too early for much to be happening. A few pedestrians, huddled under umbrellas, hurried down the main drag. Later, a group of teenagers, oblivious of the weather, sauntered by, shouting insults at the waterlogged whore. No one walked down the side street where Cashman was parked.

The criminalist thought he saw movement in the abandoned car but wasn't certain until Jacob emerged, dressed in soiled jeans and a hooded sweatshirt, carrying a black plastic garbage bag. He hurried across the lot, his shoulders hunched against the heavy rain, until he reached a dumpster that stood near a side door to the bar. Cashman saw Jacob reach into the dumpster and figured he was scavenging for dinner. He watched for a few more minutes before driving home.

It was still raining when Cashman pulled into his driveway a little after seven. He ate dinner quickly before changing into an old long-sleeved T-shirt and jeans. Then he

slipped on latex gloves and put on a baseball cap to limit the transfer of any trace evidence to Mary's body. If he discovered any
evidence connecting him to Mary's murder
while working the crime scene, he would
dispose of it, but it was always wise to take
precautions.

Before opening the basement door,
Cashman grabbed a crowbar. Fear and guilt
flooded through him once again, but he
took a deep breath, turned on the light, and
walked down the stairs. Mary was cuffed,
gagged, and lying on the tarp. He had left
her in the dark without food or water all day
to heighten her fear. He didn't really want to
scare her, but it was essential that she tell
him where she'd hidden the hammer, and he
hoped that she would speak more freely if
she was terrified.

"Hello, Mary," Cashman said, squatting
so he could work loose the tape that gagged
her.

"Please, Bernie," she started to beg. Cashman steeled himself and slapped her.

"You put yourself in this position by snooping and I don't want to hear any whining. Do
you understand?"

Mary nodded. She bit her lip and tried unsuccessfully to stem the tears that flowed down her cheeks. The sight of those tears upset Cashman, but he remembered what was at stake and gathered the strength to go on.

"There's no reason to cry," Cashman said. "If you do as I say you won't suffer. Do you understand?"

Mary nodded again.

"What were you thinking?" Cashman asked with a brisk shake of his head. "Thank God I was able to stop you before you talked to Carlos. Don't you realize that your interference could have resulted in convictions being thrown out? Do you want the monsters I sent away back on the street?"

"I wasn't . . ."

Cashman slammed the crowbar down, breaking her collarbone. Mary screamed and turned white with pain. The shirt at her shoulder darkened with blood. Cashman felt terrible, but the sooner Mary talked the sooner he could end her suffering. She needed to know that he meant business.

"I'm sorry that I had to do that, but you must listen to me. No excuses and no lies."

Mary was turning her head from side to side and writhing with pain. Cashman waited patiently for her to collect herself.

"Where did you hide the hammer from the *Hayes* case, Mary?"

Clark was crying again. She shook her head.

"Please don't make me hurt you again. I feel terrible about this. If you help me find the hammer and tell me the names of the other cases you investigated, I'll let you live."

"I know you're going to kill me," she sobbed.

Cashman began to get angry. He had just told Mary that she was not to whine, and she wasn't answering his question. This was direct disobedience. He squeezed his eyes shut and gritted his teeth before slamming down the crowbar twice on Mary's face, breaking her nose and crushing her cheek. Blood spattered his T-shirt each time the crowbar made contact.

Mary blacked out, and Bernie felt tears well up in his eyes. He felt sick. Did she think he enjoyed this? Why did she have to be so stubborn? He sincerely hoped it wouldn't take too long to convince her that it would be easier to tell him the truth than to suffer.

"Are you ready to answer my questions now?" Cashman asked, but Mary didn't answer. She wasn't coming to. Cashman slapped her cheek, getting blood on his glove. She didn't react. He was sure that she was breathing, but she was not regaining consciousness. Cashman started to sweat. What if he'd hit her so hard that she stayed unconscious? How would he question her, how would he find the hammer? Cashman knelt down and shook Clark's shoulder.

"Mary, don't do this to me, wake up."

She didn't move. Cashman panicked. He slapped her face again and shook her again. She moaned but did not regain consciousness. Cashman stood up and took several deep breaths. He couldn't believe this was happening to him. The medical examiner would be able to tell if Mary had been moved after she died. Mary had to be alive when he took her to the lot, if the police were going to believe that she'd gone to Queen Anne to buy heroin and had been murdered by Jacob Cohen during an attempted rape.

Cashman checked his watch. He hadn't planned on moving Mary until two or three in the morning. He assumed that there would be too much activity around the lot until then.

But that might not be true in this downpour. What was he going to do? He could wait and hope that Mary regained enough consciousness to be questioned, but his plan would fail if she died while he was waiting.

Cashman made a decision. He would drive to the lot. If she woke up during the drive, he would question her about the hammer. If she was still unconscious when he got to the lot, he would kill her and take his chances. If the hammer stayed lost, he would be fine. Anyone who found it would still have to make the same deductions that Mary had, to realize that Raymond Hayes's prints had never been on the handle.

Bernie left Mary in the basement and went upstairs, where he put on a gray hooded sweatshirt similar to the one he'd seen Jacob wearing. If he had the sweatshirt and jeans on, people seeing him from a distance in this downpour might mistake him for Cohen. When he returned home, he would burn everything he wore to the lot.

Before going downstairs, Cashman opened the drawer of his night table and took out a .38 Special he had stolen from a crime scene two years ago. The gun had belonged to a pimp who had been stabbed twenty-seven times by a woman in his stable whom he'd abused one time too many. Cashman kept the gun for protection. He had never used it, but the lot was in a dangerous part of town, and he would feel safer knowing that he could defend himself.

When Cashman returned to the basement, he used a syringe to draw some of Mary's blood, which he put in a vial. Then he rolled Mary in the tarp and put her in the back of her car. During the drive to the lot, he strained to hear any sound that would tell him she was conscious, but she still had not regained consciousness when he parked under the oak tree across from the lot at ten o'clock.

Luck was with him. The rain had gotten worse, and there wasn't a soul around. Cashman carried Mary and his black bag to the center of the lot and threw his burdens down. He unwound the tarp and rolled Mary onto the rubble-strewn ground. Next, he took the crowbar and a very sharp carving knife out of the bag. It was essential that Mary not be identified for as long as possible. Cashman was on call this evening, and would be summoned to this lot to work the crime scene. He would never be allowed to do so if the victim was someone he knew. DNA might eventually prove that the corpse was Mary Clark, but it took time to complete a DNA test. By then, he would have concluded his work.

Cashman averted his eyes and began smashing Mary's face with the crowbar until it was unrecognizable. Next, he used the tip of the knife to remove her eyes. He thought he might throw up when he fished them out of their sockets and placed them in a black garbage bag similar to the one he'd seen Cohen carrying when he was scavenging for food in the bar dumpster. The desecration of Mary's body left him nauseated, and he stopped to catch his breath before going back to work. When Mary's teeth were destroyed to prevent identification by her dental work, he used the knife to cut off her hands to prevent fingerprint identification.

Next, Cashman ripped Mary's shirt and bra and stabbed her repeatedly. Mary was dead by now, but there was enough blood on her clothes and the ground for the medical examiner to conclude that she had been killed in the lot.

Every once in a while, Cashman cast a quick, anxious glance at Jacob's car and the surrounding streets, but luck was with him.

The rain was keeping Cohen and everyone else indoors.

Cashman was sweating and breathing heavily by the time he pulled Mary's jeans and panties down to her ankles to make it appear that she'd been the victim of an attempted rape. Before inflicting more damage, Cashman placed the two pubic hairs he'd taken from the evidence locker on Mary's leg, near her genitals, and smeared some of Mary's blood on them to hold them in place. Then he stabbed Mary in her abdomen and pubic area and cut her genitals. He tried not to look when the knife sliced in. He was sick and dizzy, but desperation drove him.

When he was satisfied that the murder looked like the work of a madman, Cashman pulled up one side of Mary's panties until they protected the pubic hairs he'd pasted to the body with Mary's blood. Then he laid the crowbar and knife on the ground near the corpse, hoping that Cohen would handle them. After gathering up the severed hands, he placed them in the garbage bag that held her eyes and put that bag in his black evidence bag. He would put the body parts in a dumpster close enough to the area to implicate Jacob, but not so close that an immediate connection to the murder would be made.

The rain had been pounding Cashman, and he was soaked to the skin. He stood up and cast one last look at the abandoned Buick that Cohen called home. As he peered into the darkness, he thought he saw movement in the car. Was Jacob watching him? Cashman grabbed the tarp, the garbage bag, and his black bag and walked from the lot while keeping an eye on the car. He did not relax until the lot was out of sight.

There were several dumpsters along the bus route. He got rid of the tarp in one of them, and the bag with the eyes and hands in another, which was several blocks away. A bus came by shortly after he disposed of his grisly collection. The driver was tired and gave him only a cursory look. Cashman kept his hood pulled down and stared at the floor of the bus as he headed to the rear. The bus was empty. He took a seat that faced in, so the best the driver would be able to see was his profile.

Cashman was bleary-eyed by the time he started his truck an hour later. He needed sleep desperately, but he knew he would have to wait. He had to call the police, but he couldn't do it from his home phone or his cell phone. When he was checking out the lot and the area around it, he had noticed a convenience store with a working pay phone. He drove to the store and waited until there was no one around the phone. When he was certain that he was unobserved, Cashman placed an anonymous call to 911 and reported seeing a man in a hooded sweatshirt attacking a woman in Jacob's lot.

The criminalist estimated that he had an hour before he would be summoned to the crime scene. By the time he pulled into his driveway, he was freezing, exhausted, and miserable. The minute he was in the door, Cashman stripped off his clothes, started coffee brewing in the pot in his bathroom, and took a scalding-hot shower. After his shower, he dressed in the clothes he would wear to the crime scene. He knew he should eat, but he was afraid he'd be sick, so he settled for dry toast and more coffee. He had just finished his two slices when the phone rang.

19

THERE WAS NO GLASS IN THE WIND-shield of the abandoned Buick that served as Jacob Cohen's home, so the front seat got soaked when it rained. Miraculously, there was still glass in the rear side windows, and Jacob had hung a sheet of opaque plastic over the back window, so the backseat was one of the few dry spots in the car. Jacob had crawled into the backseat when it got dark, but he knew better than to go to sleep until well after midnight. Someone could sneak up on him if he was asleep. It had happened more than once. Sometimes other homeless men stole from him, although, except for his books, he owned little that even the homeless would value. At other times neighborhood boys beat him for fun. If he was vigilant, he had a chance to run and they would just trash his car.

Even when Jacob wanted to sleep, sleep never came easily. There was the constant tension of living the way he did. Worse were the voices of the people he had killed. They whispered to him during the day, but they were much louder when he shut his eyes and tried to rest. Then there was God, who spoke to Jacob on rare occasions to remind him that he would burn in the fires of Hell for what he had done.

There were no street lamps on Jacob's side of Hobart, and rain and thick clouds blocked the moon. The darkness was almost impenetrable. If Jacob hadn't been alert, he would never have spotted the gray, shapeless mass that moved rapidly across the lot. Jacob leaned forward and stared into the night. In the absence of light, the apparition gave the impression of floating, but that couldn't be right.

When it was halfway across the lot, the mass shrank toward the ground and stayed there. Jacob guessed that the thing was kneeling. Then what Jacob guessed was an arm rose and fell several times. After that, the phantom worked busily at tasks that Jacob could not discern before scurrying across Hobart and heading west on Queen Anne.

Inertia kept Jacob in the car until the tumult in his mind drove him into the downpour. He had to know what had happened, even if he put himself in danger. Jacob crept forward slowly. He had no weapon, because he could not bear the thought of hurting anyone. Everyone believed that he'd assaulted that whore, but she had attacked him when he tried to warn one of her potential victims that congress with the Jezebel who haunted his corner would send his soul straight to perdition. Any injuries he'd inflicted on her were the result of his arms and legs flailing in self-defense.

Jacob began to make out a shape in the debris that covered the lot. At first he mistook it for a large rug or a full trash bag. Then he started to see details. He had been nervous when he left the safety of his car. Now fear was edging in. Was that hair? Was that an arm? Jacob began babbling Hebrew prayers under his breath as he inched closer. When he was near enough to see clearly, horror rooted him to the ground and caused him to stare soundlessly at the desecrated body.

Where hands should have been Jacob saw blood that had pooled around two jagged stumps. Where a face should have been, Jacob saw a raw, gelatinous mass. The eye sockets were empty. He dropped to his knees, put his face in his hands, and wept. How could someone do this and call himself a human being? Where was God when this abomination was occurring?

Sometimes Jacob talked to God, and sometimes God talked to him, but there were times when Jacob doubted that God existed and thought the doctors were right when they told him that the voices he heard were not real. Tonight, kneeling next to this wretched soul, he was troubled to his depth. No God would allow something like this to happen; no God would have permitted Jacob to exist after what he'd done. Jacob tried to shake himself loose of the idea of God, but the possibility that no Creator existed was too terrifying to hold on to for long. If God did not exist, Jacob would never be punished, and the one thing he knew for certain was that he deserved to suffer everlasting torment.

Jacob's thoughts drifted down to earth, and he saw the crowbar and knife lying next to the body. He reached out until his fingers were inches from the knife before stopping. Heat seemed to radiate from the blade; steam seemed to rise from it. He could see streaks of blood that remained on the surface despite the rain. Jacob grabbed the knife and pointed the tip toward Heaven. If there was a just God, lightning would strike the silver blade, course down the weapon, and skewer his heart, ending his suffering. But nothing happened.

The blade slipped from Jacob's fingers and his chin dropped to his chest. He began to sob. Sharp-edged pieces of concrete stabbed him through the material at his knees, but he was oblivious of the pain. Was the dead body a sign? If so, what did it mean? It occurred to him that he could turn the knife on himself. Was God demanding that he end his useless existence? He raised his eyes toward the sky and screamed, "What do You want from me?"

Steve Hooper was feeling lucky. Yesterday, a college basketball team he'd bet on had come back from ten down to beat the spread.

Tonight, he and his partner, Jack Vincenzo, had stopped for coffee, and on the way out of the restaurant, Hooper had won twenty-five bucks on a scratch-off ticket. Now, the dispatcher was talking about an anonymous report of an assault in an abandoned lot. But this was no ordinary lot. It was a lot that Hooper knew intimately, a lot he cruised every so often in hopes of catching its sole occupant doing something illegal so he could roust him and beat the shit out of him for resisting arrest.

So far, he'd had no luck. Usually, Jacob Cohen was either out scavenging for food or huddled in his car on the odd occasions that Hooper drove by, but tonight—if there really was criminal activity on Hobart and Queen Anne—he would have an excuse for creating a dialogue with his favorite pervert. And who knew where that might lead?

Hooper and Vincenzo had been out in the rain, looking for a witness in a homicide, and they were not far from the lot. Hooper radioed in that he'd take the call. He didn't ask for backup, because he didn't want any witnesses if he had the opportunity to fuck Cohen up. He wasn't worried about Vincenzo filing a complaint. Like Hooper, the thick-necked ex-MP had a loosey-goosey attitude toward the rights of the accused.

"That's Cohen's lot, isn't it?" Vincenzo asked as soon as Hooper got off the radio.

"The same. I knew it wouldn't be long before that asshole screwed up."

Hooper parked up the block from the lot, and he and Vincenzo approached on foot. If there was something to the call, he didn't want to alert Jacob to their presence. It was still raining, but the downpour was now just mist and drizzle. Hooper cursed the weather anyway. His suit was going to look like shit by the time he was through, and he'd have to send it out to be cleaned and pressed.

A wooden fence cut across the back of the lot. The detective peeked around it. Except for rats, nothing was moving. Hooper gave his eyes time to adjust to the dark before letting them roam across the rubble, looking for something unusual. He missed it the first time. On his second scan, he spotted someone kneeling next to a white, lumpy object.

"What's that?" Hooper asked his partner, pointing.

Vincenzo squinted into the darkness. He

used to have twenty-twenty vision, but recently he was wondering if he might not need glasses for reading.

"Cohen wears those hooded sweatshirts, doesn't he?" Vincenzo asked.

"Yeah."

"Whoever it is, he's kneeling next to . . . Man, it's hard to say, but that could be a person."

Hooper drew his weapon and edged onto the lot before moving in a crouch across the uneven ground. A rat, disturbed by the lawman's approach, scudded past an empty beer can, sending it spinning.

Jacob, who had been in a trance, had no idea how long he had been kneeling next to the body. The scrape of tin on rock was loud enough to break the spell. The hood of his sweatshirt swiveled toward Hooper.

"Freeze!" the detective shouted as he closed the distance. He hit Cohen on the side of the head, and Jacob went down. Vincenzo had his cuffs out. He wrestled Jacob onto his stomach, wrenched his arms behind his back, and secured his hands.

"Motherfucker," Vincenzo heard Hooper say, his voice barely above a whisper. Vincenzo had been oblivious of anything but Jacob while he was subduing him. He turned toward the body.

"Holy shit," Vincenzo said reverently.

Both detectives were too stunned to feel anything but awe. They had both seen a lot of violence, but this was way over on the high end of the bell curve. Then a dark rage seized Vincenzo and he started to raise his fist. Hooper caught his partner's arm.

"No, Jack. We're going to do everything by the book tonight."

Vincenzo glared at Hooper, who shook his head. He was as outraged as Vincenzo by the violence that had been inflicted on the poor woman who lay at his feet, but his anger was under control.

"No smart-ass defense attorney is going to get one inch out of us, Jack. We will be choirboys here, fucking choirboys. We don't touch him, we don't question him unless he says it's okay, and we don't search his shithole of a car without a warrant." Hooper stared into Jacob's eyes. "This fucker is not walking."

Vincenzo's arm dropped. He knew his partner was right. If he hit Cohen, he'd be trading a possible dismissal for a moment of satisfaction.

"Mr. Cohen," Hooper said, his voice tight with hate, "I'm going to read you your *Miranda* rights. Please stop me if you don't understand what I'm saying. I want to be sure that you fully understand your constitutional rights."

Jacob didn't move and he didn't speak. The voices were whispering to him again, and he couldn't understand a word of what Hooper was saying.

Bernard Cashman parked across from the lot and sat in the dark for a moment. Sweat beaded his brow, his heart was beating rapidly, and his mouth was dry. This was the big test, and he didn't feel up to it. His brain felt like mush, his muscles ached from fatigue, and simply keeping awake required almost all of his energy. He tried to remember the last time he'd had any sleep, but that simple calculation was almost too much for him.

Cashman forced himself out of the pickup and walked to the rear to get his gear. He felt as if he were moving through a thick fog. Adrenaline and caffeine were the only things keeping him awake. When he was through working the crime scene and everything was under control, he would crash, but until then he had to stay sharp, and he wasn't certain that he could pull it off.

The criminalist had just locked the truck when Ron Toomey drove up. Toomey, a tall, lanky redhead, had been working at the crime lab for three years. Cashman had been teamed with him before and found him competent if unimaginative.

The rain had stopped, but it was still damp and cold, and a stiff wind was blowing. Cashman hunched his shoulders and ducked his head as he walked over to his fellow criminalist.

"What are you doing here?" he asked while Toomey was collecting his gear.

"Carlos sent me over."

"Where's Mary? Isn't she on call tonight?"

"She was a no-show at work and she didn't answer her phone."

"Is she sick?" Cashman asked.

"Beats me." Toomey looked up at the sky and shook his head. "I wish Mary had picked another night to fink out."

Cashman followed Toomey as he trudged across the lot. A tarp had been erected over the body to protect it and the crime scene.

Cashman hoped that the rain hadn't washed away evidence that would implicate Jacob Cohen.

"What have we got?" Toomey asked Steve Hooper, who was supervising several uniformed officers.

"Hey, Ron, Bernie," Hooper answered as he pointed at the body. "Looks like a rape-murder." He nodded toward a marked car that was parked next to the curb on Hobart. "Perp's in the back. We got him cuffed and I got a man with him. You want to go over him for evidence we can do it at the jail after he's booked in."

"Have you searched him?" Cashman asked.

"Just a pat-down for weapons. There's a crowbar and a knife on the ground next to the vic. I haven't touched them. The perp lives in that abandoned car. A search warrant is on the way. You can go through the car as soon as it gets here."

"You seem pretty certain you've got your man," Cashman said, keeping his voice neutral.

"No question. We found him right next to the body and I know this fucker. He hates women. You'll see that when you take a good look at the corpse." Hooper shook his head in disgust. "This guy is really sick."

"Why don't you take away the tarp," Toomey said. Hooper signaled two of the uniforms. Cashman took out his camera and started taking pictures of the scene as soon as the tarp had been removed. Then he photographed the body.

As soon as Cashman was finished taking pictures, they bagged the crowbar and knife. Then Toomey and Cashman knelt by the corpse.

"This is bad," Toomey muttered. He studied the face, and Cashman held his breath. Toomey frowned but didn't say anything. Cashman exhaled. Toomey hadn't recognized the victim as a coworker and neither had Hooper or Vincenzo, who knew Mary. They probably hadn't stared at her for too long. Cashman had done such a good job destroying Mary's features that even someone used to working with homicide victims would not want to look at her face more than was necessary.

While Toomey and Cashman worked the crime scene, news vans from two television stations parked on Queen Anne. The police were keeping the gawkers on the sidewalk, and a TV reporter was interviewing some of them. Cashman looked over his shoulder and saw Hooper walking toward the reporters. He returned his attention to Mary, examining his handiwork with a professional eye.

"Bingo," Toomey said.

"What do you have?" Cashman asked.

"Two pubic hairs. They're plastered to her thigh with blood."

Cashman suppressed a smile as he watched Toomey use tweezers to remove the hairs and place them in an envelope. At Cohen's trial, Toomey would testify that he had found the hairs and matched them to the defendant.

The search warrant arrived while the criminalists were still working around the body. Cashman saw Jack Vincenzo walking it over after taking it from the uniformed officer who had transported it to the scene. He stood up.

"We've got the warrant for the car," Vincenzo told them.

"I'll take the car," Cashman said to Toomey, keeping his tone casual. "You finish up here."

Vincenzo led him across the lot to the

Buick, which balanced on the rims, canting downward on the driver's side. Cashman took out a flashlight and played it over the inside. On the front seat was a black plastic garbage bag secured with a red cardboard-and-wire tie. Rain beaded the outside of the bag. Cashman photographed the interior of the car. Then he handed the camera to Vincenzo and climbed into the front seat.

Cashman untwisted the tie. The bag was filled with crumpled clothes. He checked on Vincenzo. The detective was standing up straight. His head was over the roof of the Buick and he couldn't see what Cashman was doing inside the car. Cashman fished around in the garbage bag until he found two T-shirts. He stuffed one shirt inside the other. After sneaking another look at the detective, the criminalist took the vial with Mary's blood and splashed it on the front of the outside shirt. If he hadn't stuffed one shirt inside the other, the blood would have soaked through to the back of the shirt and a clever criminalist would realize that no one was wearing it when the blood was spattered on the front. It wasn't unusual for homeless people to wear layers of clothing, especially in cold weather, so finding blood on the front of the inside shirt shouldn't arouse suspicion. After emptying the vial of blood and putting it back in his pocket, Cashman mashed the top shirt together in a way someone would who had stripped off the shirt, crumpled it up, and tossed it in the garbage bag.

"Jack," he shouted, after stuffing the T-shirts back into the bag.

Vincenzo ducked down. Cashman pointed at the shirts. "Give me the camera."

While Vincenzo watched, Cashman documented the discovery of the T-shirts. When he was through, he handed the camera back to Vincenzo, took the T-shirts out of the garbage bag, and put them in an evidence bag.

There were two more garbage bags in the back of the Buick. Cashman crawled into the backseat and went through them. One contained food. The other contained books. Most of them were religious. There were the Old and New Testaments, a Koran, books about Eastern religions. Some of the books were literature. There were Dostoyevsky's *Brothers Karamazov*, Herman Hesse's *Siddhartha*, and works by Sartre and Camus. Cashman saw nothing that he could use to tighten the noose around Cohen's neck.

Toomey was done with his work about the time that Cashman finished up. They talked to Hooper and Vincenzo. Then Cashman turned the T-shirts over to Toomey. He told Toomey how he'd had very little sleep in the past few days and asked him to log in the evidence. As soon as Toomey walked away, Cashman climbed into the cab of his pickup and breathed a sigh of relief.

Mary Clark was dead. Jacob Cohen was in custody, charged with her murder, and the case against him was airtight. Cashman had committed the perfect crime. Best of all, the murderers and rapists he'd taken off the street would remain behind bars. Cashman smiled. The people of Oregon were safer because he had acted decisively to protect them. He would drive home content and sleep the sleep of the just.

20

AMANDA HAD NOTHING ON HER CAL-
endar until an eleven o'clock hearing that
she'd already prepared for, so she didn't set
her alarm when she went to bed. Even so,
she woke up shortly after six, her usual time.
After a fruitless attempt to get back to sleep,
she did twenty minutes of calisthenics, ate a
healthy breakfast of cold cereal and berries,
then set out for the office on foot under a
sky streaked with drab gray clouds.

The weekend was coming up, and Amanda
had nothing to do. She thought about calling one of her girlfriends, but most of them
were married or seeing someone. It was one

thing to double-date and another to be a fifth wheel.

While Amanda waited for the light at Burnside, she thought about her brief meeting with Mike Greene at Art Prochaska's preliminary hearing. Was Mike really interested in seeing her again? The few dates that Amanda had been on with Mike had taken place during a terrible period in her life, when she was recovering from the trauma of her escape from the Surgeon, a serial killer who had kidnapped her so he could torture her to death. Her nerves had been scraped raw, and Mike had treated her with kid gloves. Knowing what she'd been through, he had never pushed her to have sex. Amanda had been grateful for the consideration Mike had shown her, but their time together was more like time spent with a good friend than a lover. Then Amanda had ended the relationship abruptly, without giving Mike an explanation. It had not been fair to him, but Amanda was so stressed out that she wasn't thinking clearly or acting appropriately. It had not been her finest hour.

Amanda had dated Toby soon after she'd dealt with the psychological impact of another terrifying incident and was eager to resume a normal life. She flashed back to the night a team of killers had invaded her father's house. Frank had almost died, and she'd been forced to kill a man. It was Mike who had comforted her that evening. She remembered the compassion on his face and the tenderness with which he held her as she sobbed against his chest.

After the home invasion, she'd kept everyone at arm's length. Then, one day, she'd decided to stop feeling sorry for herself. Vigorous exercise had been an important part of Amanda's life since she'd started swimming competitively as a little girl, but she had let herself go while she was dealing with her trauma. The day she went back to the Y to start working out again, Toby was coaching the masters team. They'd met before, during one of Amanda's workouts, and the day she'd returned to the pool they'd talked briefly on the deck. The next week, they had their first date.

Mike had called to see how she was doing while she was recovering from the effects of the home invasion, but he had not suggested that they get together. She believed that he was reluctant to get involved again because of the way she'd broken up with him. It had been abrupt and cruel, and her only excuse was the severe mental stress she'd been under at the time. When he finally got up the nerve to ask her out during a chance meeting at the courthouse, she was already seeing Toby. Mike had put up a brave front, but Amanda could tell that she'd hurt him.

If Mike did ask her out, Amanda knew that she should turn him down unless she was ready for a serious relationship. But he probably wasn't interested anymore. Mike had not spoken to her since the prelim. Her shoulders slumped. Hell, no one had called her. She wondered if anyone ever would call or if she'd end up one of those driven career women who worked eighteen-hour days to keep from thinking about their barren personal lives.

Suddenly, Amanda burst out laughing. What a fool she was. She was only thirty-three, her relationship with Toby had been over less than a month and already she was consigning herself to life in a convent. There were plenty of men out there and plenty of time to meet them. "Ditch the self-pity and grow up," she told herself. Either she would find someone or she wouldn't. She was a survivor. She'd had to kill to survive, and she'd almost died twice. She didn't need a man to feel good about herself. Still, in the back of her mind was a fear of growing old alone, of not finding that one true love who made your life different, who made you soar. The "love of your life" that her father had found when he married her mother.

Amanda squared her shoulders and stuffed the negative thoughts deep down until they almost disappeared. She was not going to play this game. A cutting wind was blowing in from the river. Amanda turned up her jacket collar and forged on. It was going to be a cold and depressing day, but she was not going to be depressed.

When Amanda was a few blocks from her office, she bought a grande café latte at the Nordstrom coffee bar, for warmth. She took a sip and planned her day. She would handle her hearing at eleven, work out in the pool at the Y at noon, then work up the jury instructions for a burglary case that was going to trial in a few weeks. All in all, it would be an uneventful day, but a day without excitement was good once in a while.

Jacob Cohen's parents were waiting for Amanda in the reception room at Jaffe, Katz,

Lehane, and Brindisi. As soon as Amanda opened the hall door, the rabbi stood up, and Amanda knew that she was going to have to scrap her plans.

Solomon and Valerie Cohen did not look like the stereotypical rabbi and rabbi's wife. Solomon, who wore Armani suits and Hermès ties, could easily be mistaken for a banker or an attorney at a white-shoe law firm. He was just over six feet tall, with blue eyes, a square jaw, and styled black hair through which were threaded streaks of aristocratic gray. The rabbi still moved like the athlete he'd been in high school, where he'd been a varsity basketball player.

Valerie Cohen, who had grown up in one of Portland's wealthiest households, was tall, blond, and tanned, and would have looked right at home on the cover of *Town & Country*. She had created a minor scandal when she broke off her engagement to a member of her country-club set to marry Solomon, whom she'd met at a party when he was home on a break from his rabbinical studies.

"Amanda, we need to talk to you," the rabbi said. "Can you spare some time?"

Amanda told the receptionist to hold her

calls before leading the couple to her office. As soon as they were seated, Valerie clasped her hands tightly in her lap, and the rabbi laid one of his large hands over hers.

"I apologize for coming in without an appointment but . . . You know we have a son?"

Amanda nodded.

"His name is Jacob and he's been arrested."

The rabbi spoke haltingly. His features were drawn, and it was obvious that he was under a great strain.

"What's the charge?" Amanda asked.

"It's all too much," Valerie said. She started to cry.

"A member of our congregation works in the district attorney's office. He called me last night. He said that Jacob is charged with murder and that there's a strong case against him. He urged us to hire a lawyer."

"I'll be glad to help if I can. What else do you know about the charges?"

"I don't know much, but before we get into that there's something we have to know," Rabbi Cohen said. His wife looked wretched. "If we hire you, you can't let Jacob know that we're paying your fee. You'll have to tell him that you're court-appointed if he asks. Can you do that? Will it be a problem?"

Amanda's brow furrowed. "Why won't Jacob let you help him?" she asked.

Solomon looked like someone in great pain. "Valerie and I love Jacob. We've never done a thing to hurt him, but . . . How much do you know about our son?"

"Not much," Amanda said. She had known Rabbi Cohen forever. He was her rabbi and he'd presided over her bat mitzvah. But she knew very little about the Cohens' son, whom she'd seen at temple when he was young and had not seen there in many years.

"Our son has lived a very sad life," Valerie said. "Several years ago, something terrible happened and many people died because of something Jacob did. His guilt unbalanced him and he's never recovered."

"What happened? What did Jacob do?"

"Jacob was rebellious as a boy," Valerie said, avoiding the question. "He ran away from home several times and was in trouble in school—nothing criminal—truancy mostly, disruptive behavior. He had a lot of difficulty making friends. We hoped that would change when he went to college, but he refused to apply. You can imagine how this upset us."

"Actually, he did get a very good job, even though he didn't go to college," the rabbi said in the same tone he'd used when he told Amanda that Jacob had been charged with murder. "He was hired as an air traffic controller. You have to be good at math and spatial relations. Jacob has a high IQ. He really applied himself. It takes several years of training before you're allowed to work the board at an airport and he stuck it out. After six years, he was given a position at O'Hare in Chicago."

"Jacob's troubles began when he met that woman," Valerie said bitterly. "We knew it was a bad match. She wasn't educated, she was common, and she wasn't Jewish. We don't even know where they met, and he wouldn't talk about her background. When we tried to discuss her he became very hostile."

Valerie paused. Solomon squeezed her hand, and she continued.

"Jacob has always been difficult where religion is involved. When he was young he claimed he was an atheist. It was a constant battle to get him to go to services. We think he denied his heritage to hurt us, though I don't know why. We tried to be good parents. It's just . . . He was always so angry.

"Jacob insisted on marrying this woman and he refused to be married by a rabbi. Solomon was furious. There were angry words spoken. After that, Jacob cut us out of his life. He wouldn't return our calls and his wife wouldn't talk to us. She claimed she was honoring Jacob's wishes."

"You said that something terrible happened," Amanda pressed.

"His wife told the doctors that Jacob caught her with a man and she told him that she was going to leave him, she was filing for divorce. He went to work the day she left him. He shouldn't have; he was too upset. He must have become distracted. Jacob made a mistake." Cohen's left hand curled into a fist. "Two planes collided." Valerie was crying again. "Hundreds died," he said, his voice shaking. "No one survived.

"Jacob had a nervous breakdown. His wife didn't know what to do, so she called us. We flew out immediately. It was terrible. He was in the mental ward at the county hospital. They had to sedate him. The doctor said that he was babbling biblical verses, blaming women and the CIA for the crash."

"We put him in an excellent private hospital in Portland," Valerie said. "He had the best care, but it didn't help, and our relations with him grew worse. He saw us as jailers; he said we were conspiring with the government to keep him drugged and locked away. He refused to admit that he was responsible for the crash. He said that his wife had conspired with the CIA to make the planes crash so he would be blamed and locked away, leaving her free to live with this other man."

"His ramblings made no sense," the rabbi said. He sounded defeated. "No matter what the doctors tried he would not stop claiming that his wife was in league with the devil."

"Do you know the medical diagnosis for Jacob's mental problems?" Amanda asked.

"The doctor said that he's a paranoid schizophrenic," Valerie answered. "They told us that this would explain his being a loner, not making friends. Supposedly the disease can stay hidden until a person reaches college age. Then it can come out if there is a triggering event, like his troubles with his wife or the crash. That's what the doctors told us."

Valerie paused. She looked ashamed of

her son. Amanda hoped that wasn't true. Schizophrenia was no one's fault.

"How did he get out of the hospital?" Amanda asked.

"Medication," the rabbi said. "The doctors figured out a dosage that kept his delusions in check. After a year of progress, the decision was made to treat him as an outpatient. It was a disaster."

"Not at first," Valerie said. "We thought he was going to make it when he was released." She wrung her hands. "We were so full of hope. He had his own apartment and he was hired as a clerk in a convenience store. The manager took a chance on him. And it worked for a while. But he stopped taking his medication. We didn't know until it was too late. He disappeared and started living in that lot. We didn't find out where he was until he was arrested for attacking a prostitute."

"We tried to help him when we heard. We said that we would hire a lawyer for him. He wouldn't talk to us. He denied we were his parents. The court appointed an attorney. He tried to help Jacob, but Jacob is his own worst enemy. He was convicted of attempted rape and sent to prison."

Amanda suddenly remembered her meeting with Doug Weaver in the courthouse corridor.

"Was your son recently acquitted of a charge of failing to register as a sex offender?"

"Yes. How did you know?"

Amanda told the rabbi and his wife about her conversation with Doug Weaver.

"It sounds like Doug did a terrific job," Amanda said. "Why haven't you asked him to represent Jacob?"

"We checked on Mr. Weaver," the rabbi said. "He did do a good job for Jacob, but that was a simple case. Jacob will face the death penalty. Mr. Weaver has not been very successful in murder cases."

"One of his clients was executed," Valerie said.

"Jacob is too important to us to take a chance on Mr. Weaver," Rabbi Cohen said. "You and your father are the best. Jacob needs the best. Please help him. If . . . if he has done something terrible he did it because he couldn't help himself. He needs help; he needs psychiatric care, not prison."

"Okay, but I have to warn you that I may not be able to do any better than Doug."

"We feel more comfortable with your firm," Valerie said. "Mr. Weaver just doesn't inspire confidence."

"Jacob's case is going to be very expensive."

Valerie looked Amanda in the eye. "Jacob is our son. We will do whatever is necessary to see that he gets the best defense and the best care."

"I'll need a one-hundred-thousand-dollar retainer," Amanda said, "but the actual cost of Jacob's defense will be higher. I won't know how much higher until I decide how much time the case will take, the experts we'll need, co-counsel, et cetera."

Valerie Cohen opened her purse and took out a checkbook. Amanda buzzed her secretary and told her to bring in a retainer agreement.

When the Cohens left, Amanda thought about how hard it must be to raise a son like Jacob. The Cohens were concerned parents who had tried their best, but Jacob had not turned out well despite their best efforts. That, sadly, was not uncommon. She'd represented enough young people charged with crimes to know that much.

Amanda had no idea what it was like to be a parent, but she thought that it must be a very hard job, probably the hardest job a person could have. Every child was born with infinite promise, and every parent was filled with infinite hope at the moment of birth. Then things went wrong. You could see why if a child was a crack baby or the parents were abusive, but how did you explain what happened in loving households when a child became a criminal or an addict or a runaway? How did parents recover from a broken heart? Did they ever? The Cohens were suffering. Most probably, their suffering would never end, but Amanda would try to ease it by seeing that Jacob received fair treatment in court no matter what he'd done.

21

AMANDA JAFFE PLANNED ON VIS-
iting Jacob Cohen at the jail after she finished her eleven o'clock hearing. The clock
on her computer told her that she had time
to get a latte before the hearing if she left
right away. She looked out of her window at
the dark clouds drifting over the West Hills.
They looked threatening, but there was no
rain predicted for today. She didn't trust the
prediction, so she packed a small umbrella
in her attaché case and headed for the coffee shop, which was catty-corner from the
courthouse.

It was brisk out, but Amanda was preoccupied by thoughts of the legal argument she was going to make. She was asking for discovery of a policeman's notes, and the DA was arguing that the discovery statutes did not require the officer to turn them over to the defense. The facts were unique, and Amanda was not certain that she would win. She was thinking about a recent court of appeals case that contained language useful to both sides when she got in line to order her latte. She had just paid when she spotted Mike Greene sitting by himself at a back corner table, studying a position on a wallet chess set that he often carried in an inside suit pocket. Mike was a rated expert who had played on the USC chess team as an undergraduate and still competed on occasion. He kept a chess set on the credenza in his office and was known to work on his game when he had spare time.

Mike looked up from the chess position and saw Amanda watching him. He looked surprised at first. Then he broke into a grin and beckoned her over. Amanda realized that there was no way she could turn down the invitation without being incredibly rude, so she grabbed her latte and sat down across from the prosecutor.

Mike nodded at the attaché. "Going to court?"

"I've got an eleven o'clock hearing in front of Peterson, a discovery motion. It's an interesting issue. It was discussed in a footnote in *State v. Lorca*, but the court didn't resolve the problem. It'll make for an interesting appellate issue if I lose the case." Amanda pointed at the chess set. "What are you doing?"

"I'm playing in a small tournament this weekend and I'm working on my openings. I'm really rusty. All the young kids are using computers to learn the latest wrinkle these days and I'm afraid I'll get my butt kicked by some ten-year-old if I don't put in some time preparing."

Mike hesitated, then gathered his courage. "What are you doing this weekend?"

Amanda was embarrassed by the fact that she had no plans. "I was just retained on the *Cohen* case, so I'll probably be at the office."

"You're not going to be at the office on Saturday night, are you?"

"Uh, no, why?"

"There's a French thriller at Cinema 21 that's supposed to be pretty intense. I was thinking of going."

"What about the chess tournament?"

"We don't play at night. The games start early on Saturday morning. The second round begins around noon. I'll be through by four. We could grab an early dinner and catch the show."

There were often surprises in trials, and experienced trial lawyers knew how to hide their emotions from the jury so as not to prejudice their clients. Given their history, Amanda was certain that Mike was as nervous as she was, but anyone watching their conversation would never have known that Mike's and Amanda's hearts were thudding.

"What do you say, Jaffe?" Mike asked, smiling as if he could read her mind. "The film's supposed to be good, you can pick the restaurant, and I promise to get you home before your father's curfew."

Amanda broke out laughing. Mike had a good sense of humor, and she did enjoy being with him. If she hadn't been such a wreck emotionally when they were dating, maybe . . .

"Okay," she heard herself say. "Basta's is right down the street from the theater. I'll make a reservation."

Amanda glanced at the clock. "Oops. I've

got to run," she said, taking another quick sip of her latte before replacing the lid and grabbing her attaché. "See you Saturday."

Doug Weaver's law office was on the outskirts of downtown Portland, on the third floor of a five-story building that was crumbling from neglect. The better offices in the building looked out on the freeway. Doug had a view of a brick wall. The airshaft between the buildings was too narrow to let in sunshine on sunny days, but rain streaked his window when it stormed, and made the sunless days even bleaker.

It had not always been this way. After law school, Doug had been hired as an associate at a respected medium-size firm that represented businesses. Doug's work centered on drafting and reviewing contracts. It had not taken him long to realize that he was not enjoying himself. The money was good, but the work was deadly dull, and the prospects for doing anything exciting were slim. Doug had come away from law school with an interest in criminal defense, but Karen had argued that he should take the job with the biggest paycheck. When he asked the partners if he could take on some criminal court appointments to get trial experience, they had explained that they couldn't spare his billable hours and, anyway, lawyers at their firm rarely went to court.

When Doug told Karen that he was thinking of quitting the firm, his wife adamantly opposed the move. She had a definite idea about the lifestyle she wanted to live, and Doug's salary factored into her plans. Doug's desire to leave his firm was the cause of constant friction in a marriage that was failing badly. He had given in for another painful year, to try to salvage their relationship. Finally, he had put his foot down by quitting without discussing his decision with his wife. How the marriage lasted a few more years after that was still a mystery.

Doug liked being on his own and handling the type of cases that excited him. His income went down dramatically the first year, but he'd been retained on several good cases in his second, and had started to make a decent living, though nowhere near what he'd been making before. Doug drank heavily when he was at the firm, to cope with the stress at work and home. As his practice improved, his drinking decreased. Then Raymond Hayes was sentenced to death. Losing the case and the problems in his marriage sent Doug into a downward spiral. He fell off the wagon and lost several good clients. When he couldn't afford the rent on his midtown office anymore, he'd moved to his current place, which is where he was practicing when the receptionist told him that Amanda Jaffe was in the waiting room.

"What brings you to my neck of the woods?" Doug asked when the receptionist showed Amanda into his office. He thought Amanda looked frazzled.

"I have a problem you might be able to solve. Remember Jacob Cohen?"

"How could I forget?"

"I take it you haven't read the paper today or watched the news?"

"Don't tell me he's back in trouble?"

"Big trouble. He's charged with murder."

Doug felt sick as he remembered Jacob's confession and Hannah Graves's warning.

"This morning his parents retained me to represent him."

Now he fought to hide his disappointment. He'd done a great job for Jacob—won an impossible case—and the Cohens hadn't even interviewed him.

"I've just come from the jail. Jacob wants you to be his lawyer. He was very adamant on this point."

Doug could not help smiling. "Let me guess. He explained, using quotes from the Bible, that you are going to burn in Hell for eternity because you are female."

Amanda nodded. "Pretty nasty Bible quotes, at that."

"And you're here because . . . ?" Doug asked, hoping against hope that Amanda was going to ask him to team up with her.

"I called Rabbi Cohen and explained the problem. He's aware of Jacob's hatred of women, but he still wants me on board. I want you to convince Jacob to keep me as his lawyer. I told the rabbi that Jacob trusts you and I always have a second chair when I try a death case. Are you interested?"

"I'm definitely interested. But what happens if I can't convince Jacob to keep you as his lawyer?"

"You did a hell of a job winning Jacob's failure-to-register case, and you have a lot of experience handling capital cases. If Jacob rejects my help, I'll recommend that the Cohens retain you to represent Jacob."

The offer terrified Doug and gave him hope

at the same time, and—for a moment —he wasn't sure yet whether fear or hope would rule the day. Fear of failure kept him from jumping at the chance to be part of a high-profile case. He didn't know what he would do if Jacob Cohen was executed because of a mistake he made.

But what if he pulled it off? What if he helped save Jacob Cohen from a lethal injection, maybe even assisted in winning an acquittal? Would that make up for what he'd done to Raymond? No, he could never be absolved of that sin. But wouldn't he be giving himself back some of the pride he'd once had in himself and his work if he could give Jacob his life?

And there was the money. This was a capital case. His fee would be substantial. He would be able to pay off a lot of his debt and meet his other obligations. Hopefully, the publicity from the case would generate new business. If everything went well—if Cohen was acquitted or received a life sentence—he wouldn't be a loser anymore. Doug was tired of the pointed way his colleagues avoided talking about State v. Hayes when he was around. He'd bet that they talked about it plenty when he wasn't there. He didn't know whether they blamed him for the execution or felt sorry for him; either attitude was intolerable. A win in *Cohen* would help him regain the respect of his peers and his self-respect.

Doug knew that he had to do something with his life or he was just going to continue to sink under the weight of his own self-pity. He had to take a chance to save himself. It suddenly became clear to him that he would be turning his back on his future if he turned down Jacob's case.

22

KATE ROSS, THE IN-HOUSE INVESTI-gator at Jaffe, Katz, Lehane, and Brindisi, was five-seven and looked fit in a pair of tight jeans, a white man-tailored shirt, and a navy blue blazer. Kate, whose dark complexion, large brown eyes, and curly black hair made her seem vaguely Middle Eastern, had been recruited right out of Caltech into the computer crimes division of the Portland Police Bureau. When she'd grown bored sitting behind a desk, she had wangled a transfer to the narcotics squad. Her career was on the upswing until she was made the scapegoat in a police shooting and was forced to resign.

Kate's special talents with computers and detection had landed her a job as an investigator for Reed, Briggs, Stephens, Stottlemeyer, and Compton, Portland's largest law firm. While working there, Kate had talked Amanda Jaffe into representing Daniel Ames, the newest Reed, Briggs associate, when he was framed for the murder of a senior partner. After the two women cleared him, Kate and Daniel had come to work at Amanda's firm. Now they were living together.

The day she read the police reports in Art Prochaska's case, Kate Ross purchased a look at the "confidential" guest register of the Continental Motel from the Pakistani night clerk. After making a list of people who had been present on the night that Vincent Ballard was murdered, she had started interviewing the residents still living at the motel. Only a few of the people on the list were in the first night, so she'd returned to the motel several times to try to catch the other guests.

Unit 115 was on the ground floor across the court from Vincent Ballard's room. No one had been in during the other times Kate had visited, but tonight she got lucky. After she knocked twice, the door to the room was opened a few inches by a chubby, hard-used African-American woman who, Kate guessed, was probably in her early twenties. The woman was wearing a bright red tube top and a short, tight skirt. Her feet were bare, but Kate spotted flashy platform shoes next to a leg of the bed. The woman's hair was done in cornrows. Kate bet that a wig would cover them when the woman left the room.

"Marsha Hastings?" Kate asked.

"Yeah," the woman answered, eyeing Kate with suspicion.

Kate showed her credentials. "I'm a private investigator and I'd like to talk to you. I won't take up much of your time."

"Talk about what?"

"I understand that you were living here when one of the residents who lived across the court was murdered."

"I told the police I don't know nothing about that. I wasn't here when he got killed."

Kate let her shoulders sag and looked disappointed. "I'm really coming up empty tonight," she sighed. "My boss was certain that someone would collect the reward."

"What reward?" Hastings asked, suddenly much more interested.

"I'm authorized to pay cash for reliable information, but no one seems to have seen or heard anything. Thank you for your time."

"Wait a second," Hastings said as Kate turned to leave. "I wasn't here, but I know something might help you. Who you say you working for?"

Kate handed Hastings her business card. "I'm employed by Frank Jaffe of the law firm of Jaffe, Katz, Lehane, and Brindisi. We represent the man who was arrested for the murder."

Hastings opened the door wide enough for Kate to squeeze through. The shades were drawn, but a lamp on a night table and a TV provided some light. Kate could smell tomato soup. A Campbell's can was standing on the dresser next to a pot that was balanced on a hot plate. A girl of five or six, dressed in pajamas, was sitting on the floor in front of the TV. A bowl of soup sat on the floor in front of her. Next to it was a plate covered with Ritz crackers. The girl cast a quick, uninterested glance at Kate, then shifted her eyes back to the set.

"That's Desdemona. Don't pay her no mind. So, what I have to do to win this reward?"

"We're interested in anyone who may have

seen or heard anything about the murder that would help prove our client's innocence."

"Okay, well, like I said, I wasn't here, but I talked to someone who seen something. He didn't tell me much, but I can tell you what he said."

"Who did you talk to?"

"Uh-uh. I tell you that before you pay me and you don't need me no more."

Kate smiled. "I'm not going to stiff you. Look, here's ten dollars for your time. If your information is good there'll be more."

"Ten bucks ain't much," Hastings sniffed. "The other man paid me a hell of a lot more."

"What other man?"

"A few days ago two men come by doing what you're doing, asking people here about the murder."

"Were these men with the police?"

Hastings laughed. "Not likely."

"Did they say who they were working for?"

"Nah, and I didn't ask. They was scary."

"Can you describe them?"

"Do I get some extra money for this?"

Kate handed Hastings a twenty.

"One fella was big. He looked rough, like

a gangster. The one did all the talking was a skinny guy. Looked like a mouse with these big teeth sticking out. And he talked like the leprechaun in those horror movies."

"He was Irish?"

"That's what I said."

"Can you tell me any more about these men? Did they tell you their names?" Kate asked.

Hastings shook her head. "I didn't want to be around them any more than I had to."

"What did you tell these men about the killing?"

"That's a whole 'nother subject. You got to pay me for that."

Kate gave Hastings another twenty.

"I was out by the machine for a Coke the afternoon after that man got killed, and Clarence was getting one too."

"What's Clarence's last name?" Kate asked, looking at her list.

"Never got it. I just seen him once or twice and he say his name is Clarence. He lived with another boy named Edgar."

A Clarence Edwards and an Edgar Lewis had been living at the motel on the evening of the killing, but they'd moved out a few days later.

"Okay. What happened with Clarence?"

"He told me he seen the guys that done it."

"Clarence saw the killers?"

"That's what he said."

"I've read the police reports. If we're talking about Clarence Edwards, he didn't tell the police a thing."

"Yeah, well, he wouldn't. Clarence has been inside."

"He's an ex-con?"

"So he says. He was sort of mysterious about it, wouldn't tell me what he done. But he had prison tats and he said he done federal time." She shrugged. "He could have been lying."

"Did Clarence describe the killers to you?"

"You gonna give me more money for this?"

"Let's hear what you have to say first."

Hastings hesitated. "I'm being truthful here."

"I believe you."

"Clarence said there was two guys. One, he didn't have no good impression of—just regular size—but he said the other guy was really big, like a pro wrestler."

This wasn't what Kate wanted to hear. Art Prochaska was really big.

"Did he say anything else about the big guy?"

Hastings's features scrunched up as she concentrated. Then she broke out in a smile.

"The hair, he said the big guy had short black hair."

Kate's pulse accelerated. Art Prochaska was bald. If Clarence Edwards had told the truth to Marsha Hastings, and Hastings wasn't making up everything she'd said, Kate might have gotten her first break in the case.

Kate spoke to the other residents on the list, but none of them provided additional information. Before driving home, she called Frank on her cell phone and told him what Hastings had said.

"Do you think she's telling the truth?"

"Yes. But she's just relating what Clarence Edwards told her. He could have lied to impress her."

"And Edwards is gone?"

"Yeah, the day after she gave his name to the two men."

"From her description, the man with the brogue could be Henry Tedesco."

"If it was Henry, then Martin Breach is running his own investigation."

"I'm not surprised. Martin doesn't care about much, but he would do anything for Art."

"What do you want me to do?" Kate asked.

"See if you can find Edwards."

23

STEVE HOOPER PARKED IN A LOT adjacent to the Oregon State Medical Examiner's Office; a two-story brick building that had once been a Scandinavian funeral home. At the front desk, he asked for Dr. Sally Grace, the assistant ME who was going to perform the autopsy on the woman found in the lot at Queen Anne and Hobart.

A few minutes after the receptionist buzzed her, a slender woman with frizzy black hair walked up to the front desk.

"Hey, Steve, are you ready to rumble?"

Hooper smiled. He liked Sally. She was smart and competent and had a great sense of humor. The detective nodded toward a corridor that led to the back of the building.

"Is my date waiting?"

"She is. Come on back."

The detective followed Dr. Grace to the rear of the building.

"When you said you wanted to come over for the autopsy, I called the lab and had them rush the tox report," Dr. Grace said while they put on blue water-impermeable gowns, masks, goggles, and heavy black rubber aprons. "They found heroin."

"That's what I figured when I saw the tracks. She was probably an addict or a whore looking to score."

"That's a deduction I'll leave to you Sherlock Holmes types. However, I did notice something you might want to think about. You probably didn't pick up on it at the scene because it was dark and her arm was covered with blood."

The ME led the detective into the autopsy room. The naked body of the dead woman lay on one of the two stainless-steel autopsy tables that stood on either side of the room. She had been cleaned up, but there was no way to disguise the horrible assault she had suffered. Hooper, who had seen it all, grimaced when he got a good look at the corpse. Dr. Grace pointed at the needle marks on the victim's arm.

"These tracks are relatively fresh and I didn't find puncture marks on any other parts of her body."

"So?"

"I'd guess she started to use recently. I'm also not that certain about her being the type of hooker who would hang around Queen Anne. Her hands were missing but her feet were intact. The perp didn't remove her sneakers and socks. See here?"

Dr. Grace, always respectful of the dead, gently lifted the victim's right foot. Hooper leaned down. He didn't get it at first. Then he frowned.

"The toes, right?"

"That and the calluses."

Hooper studied the foot again. He was confused. "She doesn't have any calluses."

"Exactly," Dr. Grace said, beaming. "This woman took very good care of her feet, or had someone do it for her, which would cost." Dr. Grace pointed at the dead woman's toes. "You're looking at a French pedicure. There are two types of polish on her toenails—clear polish on most of the nail and off-white on the tips. The nails haven't grown much after they were polished, so the pedicure is recent."

The ME showed Hooper the soles of the victim's feet. "I'm guessing that someone used a pumice stone on her heels, probably the same person who gave her the pedicure."

"What are you telling me?"

Dr. Grace shrugged. "It's just odd. Down-and-out addicts spend their money on a fix, not a pedicure."

"Maybe she wasn't down and out. Maybe she's rich and she started experimenting. She gets hooked and runs out of smack, so she goes looking for more in the wrong neighborhood."

"That's a good explanation. But something else bothers me. Cutting off the hands, bashing in the face, and destroying her teeth—that's something you do to conceal the victim's identity."

Hooper smiled and shook his head. "Jacob Cohen hates women, really hates them. He was trying to obliterate this poor woman. If he had his way, he'd get rid of every female on the planet."

Hooper pointed at the dead woman's

face. There were empty sockets where the eyes had been gouged out, fractured cheekbones could be seen where the crowbar had come down hard enough and often enough to smash through flesh, the nose was completely flattened, and the jaw was unhinged.

"That's the act of a madman and Jacob Cohen is a violent lunatic."

"I've never met the gentleman."

"Hopefully, you never will. He's already served prison time for trying to rape a prostitute in the same lot."

"Well, there was no rape here. The killer mutilated the victim's genitals but I found no evidence of sexual activity during my initial examination."

"She was probably dead before he could try anything. I can't imagine him being turned on after he did this."

Hooper shook his head in disgust. "This is an act of pure rage, Sally, and Cohen purely hates females. And don't forget, we've got his prints on the knife and I found him next to the body."

"Like I said, I just work here. You're the detective."

"Hey, it doesn't take a detective to solve this one, but thanks for the info. I'll pass it on to the DA. If you thought of this stuff, so will the defense attorney. It doesn't pay to get caught napping."

Dr. Grace flipped on her goggles and pulled up her mask. Then she picked up an electric saw and prepared to start the autopsy.

"Shall we?" she asked.

"Be my guest," Hooper replied.

24

THE JAIL GUARD LET DOUG WEAVER into the contact-visit room at the Justice Center jail, then closed the door to the corridor behind him. Doug sat down and pulled out the discovery packet Kate Ross had picked up from the district attorney's office that morning. When Doug learned that Hannah Graves was handling Jacob's murder case, he asked Amanda to have Kate get the discovery, because he didn't want to see the deputy district attorney until it was absolutely necessary. Doug was certain that the next time they met, Graves would say, "I told you so," or gloat silently, and he would not be able to muster a rejoinder, especially now that he'd seen the autopsy and crime scene photographs. Doug was no stranger to gruesome pictures, but the horror inflicted on the woman in the lot went beyond anything he had ever seen.

Very little in the police reports, lab reports, or autopsy report helped the defense. Detectives Hooper and Vincenzo had arrested Jacob next to the body. Two T-shirts had been found in the abandoned car where Jacob lived. The lab had matched the blood on them to the victim. There had been no sperm found on the victim, and no sign of forced sex; but two of Jacob's pubic hairs had been found in the victim's blood on the victim's thigh, and her genitals had been mutilated.

Jane Doe had been stabbed and beaten. A knife and a crowbar, both showing traces of the victim's blood, had been found next to the body. The lab had not found Jacob's fingerprints on the crowbar, but they were all over the knife. The only good news was that Jacob had not confessed. According to the detectives, he had barely spoken at all, and when he did open his mouth, he spoke Hebrew.

Doug was rereading the autopsy report when the electronic locks snapped on the door that opened into the corridor leading to the cell block. Doug looked up as two guards escorted Jacob into the room. The first time they'd met at the jail, Jacob had reminded Doug of a wild animal on high alert. This afternoon, he moved listlessly. His shoulders slumped, he dragged his feet across the floor, and he did not look at Doug.

"What's wrong with him?" Doug asked the guards.

"I have no idea," answered one of the guards with an indifferent shrug.

"He's not doped up, is he?"

"You have to ask the nurses."

The guards helped Jacob into the chair on the other side of the table. He slumped down on the seat as soon as they let go of his arms. His eyes were bloodshot from a lack of sleep, and there were dark circles under them. His wild, unkempt hair was the only thing that reminded Doug of the mad energy he'd grown to expect from his client.

"Jacob, are you okay?" Doug asked as soon as the guards left.

His client's head rose slowly until he was

looking at Doug. When he spoke, he sounded frightened.

"I saw him."

"Saw who?"

"The devil."

"Where?" Doug asked, forcing himself to make the question sound sincere, because he was anxious to keep Jacob talking.

"He's gray, like a shadow."

"Where did you see the devil, Jacob?"

"In my lot. He smote that woman, then he flew away."

"You saw someone kill the woman in your lot?"

Jacob nodded. Doug pulled his pad closer and poised his pen over it.

"Tell me what happened. Tell me everything you saw," he said, relieved that they had a dialogue going.

"I was in the back of my car. It was very dark, so I couldn't be sure, at first. There was just something floating across the ground, like a wraith or a phantom. Then he . . . he destroyed her." Jacob had been speaking as much to himself as to Doug, but his eyes suddenly focused on his lawyer. "She must have been truly tainted to deserve such punishment. She must have been a true daughter of

Sodom." He shook his head and whispered, "I've never seen so much blood."

Jacob's head sagged and his hands began worrying each other.

"Jacob," Doug said. When he didn't answer, Doug repeated his name. Jacob managed to raise his head.

"I want you to think very hard, okay?"

His client did not acknowledge the question, and Doug wasn't certain that Jacob had heard him, but he forged on.

"Don't answer quickly, okay? Just think for a moment. I know you believe that you saw the devil—and you may have—but there's another possibility I want you to consider. Could the thing you saw have been a human being—a man or a woman? You said it was dark. According to the police reports it was raining and the cloud cover was blocking the moon. It would have been pitch-black in your lot. Think about it. Could you have seen a person and just thought you saw the devil. People do terrible things at times, Jacob. They create horror that is worthy of the devil."

"A person can't float or fly," Jacob said.

"No, but someone might seem to on a very dark night if the person was dressed in dark clothing." Doug held up his hand. "Don't answer me now. Just think about what you saw. I'm not saying that you didn't see the devil. I just want you to open your mind to other possibilities, okay?"

Jacob nodded.

"Good. Now I have a few more things to say to you. If you want me, I'm going to be your lawyer again and I'm going to work as hard to help you this time as I did the first time, when we won. So, do you want me to represent you in this case?"

"You set me free," Jacob said. "You didn't let them put me back there."

"That's right, Jacob. I protected you and I'm going to try to protect you again. It's going to be harder this time, but we're going to fight together, okay?"

Jacob nodded.

"Jacob, do you trust me?"

"Yes."

"Do you trust me to do what's right for you?"

Jacob nodded.

"I'm going to ask you a favor and I want you to think before you answer. And I want you to promise me that you will not get upset or excited. Will you promise?"

Jacob looked suspicious. "What do you want?"

"Another lawyer came to visit you yesterday. Her name is Amanda Jaffe."

Jacob started to tense up.

"You just promised me that you wouldn't get upset or excited."

"She's one of them."

"No, she's not. She's someone I trust very much and she is a brilliant attorney who I need to help me win your case. She's an expert at research and she's one of the best trial lawyers in the state."

Jacob glared at Weaver but held his tongue. Doug saw that as progress.

"Look, Jacob, either you trust me or you don't. Think about what I've done for you. No one thought I could win that case and set you free, but I did win. And I want to win this case, especially now that you've told me that you didn't murder this woman. But I need help. A death penalty case is too big for one lawyer to handle. And the lawyer who can help me the best—can best help you— is Amanda. Trust me on this. Tell me I can bring her on board. It's really important."

Jacob closed his eyes, and Doug prayed while he waited for his client's answer. He could handle Jacob's case without Amanda; he could bring in another lawyer, like Marge Cross, to second-chair. But the odds on a good result would go way up with Amanda Jaffe as part of Jacob's team.

Finally, Jacob nodded and Doug smiled with relief. "Good decision," he assured his client. "You won't regret this. Now, let's get back to your case. You just told me that someone, who you think may have been the devil, murdered that woman in your lot. But you did touch the knife?"

"Yes."

"How did that happen?"

Jacob's eyes dropped and he pressed his hands against the sides of his head.

"God has given me so many trials. I was tired of it all, tired of living like an animal, tired of the voices in my head."

Tears formed in Jacob's eyes. "So much suffering, so much pain. I thought, maybe, this was a sign. That God was telling me that it was all right to end it."

Jacob sighed. "I know I'm going to Hell when I die, but it couldn't be worse than . . ." His head dropped. "I thought the blood, her suffering, was a sign."

"You were going to kill yourself?"

Jacob looked up. "I'm already dead. It would have been easy."

"Then why did you stop?"

Jacob shook his head. "I don't know, I don't know."

Jacob closed his eyes, and Doug took a moment to think. If Jacob was to be believed, he was a witness to a murder and not the murderer, but the evidence said that he was lying—or so crazy that he had convinced himself that the devil had murdered Jane Doe so he wouldn't have to accept responsibility for what he'd done.

"Let's go back a bit, okay?" Doug said. "You're in your car and you see someone or something go across the lot, right?"

Jacob nodded.

"What did you see this thing do next?"

"It dropped down, like it was kneeling or praying."

"Okay."

Jacob squeezed his eyes shut and clenched his fists. Doug could see how hard he was trying. His eyes snapped open.

"A hand came up and down. He was striking her. He did that a lot. Sometimes, he would pause. Then he would do it again."

"That sounds right. The woman was

stabbed many times and she was hit with a crowbar, too. That would be consistent with what you saw. What happened next?"

"I was afraid. I didn't want to go out there, even when it was gone."

"You saw the man leave?"

Jacob nodded.

"The detectives found you next to the body. How did you get there?"

"I had to see. I was afraid, but I had to see."

"So you went over to find out what had happened?"

"Yes."

"Did you go right away?"

"No, I was afraid. I stayed in my car for a while."

"Do you have any idea how long?"

"No, but he had disappeared."

"The killer?"

Jacob nodded.

"Okay. So, after a while, you went over to the body."

"When I saw her . . . My brain was on fire. I don't remember everything clearly."

"You told me that you picked up the knife."

Jacob nodded.

"Did you touch her with the knife, even accidentally?"

"No."

"What about the crowbar, did you touch that?"

"No, just the knife."

"Jacob, the police have found some physical evidence that connects you to the murder. I need to know if you have an explanation for what they discovered, okay?"

"Okay."

"Here's the evidence against you. First, the detectives found you next to the body, which you've explained. Second, your prints were on the knife, and you've told me how that happened. Now, they also searched your car. There were some plastic bags that you were using for your clothes and books. There was one in the front seat, and the criminalist who looked through it found two T-shirts with blood on them that matched the victim's blood. Can you tell me how her blood got on the shirts?"

Jacob looked confused. "The shirts were in my car?"

Doug found the photograph of the shirts Cashman had taken inside the car. Jacob stared at the photograph for a few moments.

"Are these yours?" Doug asked.

"Yes, but I wasn't wearing them when that woman was killed and there wasn't any blood on them when I took them off."

"Do you have any idea how the victim's blood got on your shirts?"

"No."

"Did anyone go to your car after the woman was killed and before the police came?"

"I didn't see anyone, but they could have." He stared into space as he remembered how he had felt kneeling next to the battered, blood-soaked corpse. "My mind left me, at times. I didn't even feel the rain."

"Did you change clothes after you went over to the body? Could you have done that and not remembered?"

"No. When they took me to jail I was wearing the same clothes I had on when I went to look. The police will have them. You can see them. I don't know anything about the blood."

"You're saying that you didn't leave the body from the time you discovered it to the time the police arrived?"

Jacob nodded.

"Did you get a good look at the body?" Doug asked.

Jacob ran his tongue over his lips and nodded again.

"The police report states that the killer removed the victim's hands and eyes," Doug said, trying to describe the desecration as delicately as possible. "Did you see the hands or eyeballs?"

Jacob's brow furrowed. He shook his head. "I don't remember seeing them."

"They weren't on the ground near the body?"

"They could have been. I didn't look around. Mostly, I prayed."

Doug decided to move on.

"Okay. Let's talk about the last piece of evidence. And I don't want to embarrass you, but murder is the most serious charge there is and this was a torture murder, so the DA is probably going to ask for the death penalty. You understand that, don't you?"

Jacob nodded.

"I wish there was some delicate way to put this, but I want to save your life, I don't want you to die. So you've got to be one hundred percent honest with me. If you don't tell me the truth and I believe what you tell me, I'll use what you tell me to make decisions. I could do something stupid that could really hurt you. Do you understand what I'm getting at?"

"I won't lie."

"Good. The dead woman was partially undressed."

Jacob turned bright red and twisted in his seat.

"There's no evidence of sexual assault, no semen," Doug said quickly, "but the police did find something near the woman's genitals that implicates you."

Jacob turned away and began mumbling to himself. It was difficult to understand him but Doug thought he was repeating some of the biblical quotes about fallen women, which he'd heard before.

"Jacob, please, this is important. The police found two of your pubic hairs attached to the woman's thigh with her blood."

Jacob clamped his hands over his ears.

"I know this is embarrassing, Jacob—I know how you feel about women—but we've got to talk about this. I need to know if you . . . if you took down your pants and touched that woman."

Jacob shook his head from side to side and began rocking on the chair.

Doug took a deep breath and leaned

back. Everything had gone so well until he had mentioned sex. Now he'd lost him.

"Please, Jacob. The district attorney is going to tell the jury that the only way those hairs could end up where they did is if you were lying naked on top of that woman. If you didn't, you have to tell me how they got on her thighs, in her blood."

25

BERNARD CASHMAN WAS FASCI-
nated by the criminal mind. Driving home
from a particularly gruesome crime scene,
he would often wonder how the person who
created it felt the morning after. The criminalist had read true-crime books about serial
killers like Ted Bundy, had watched television interviews with incarcerated murderers,
and had read police interrogations of killers
he had helped bring to justice. He knew that
there were murderers who were consumed
by guilt and actually confessed to ease their
conscience. Some killers appeared to be totally unaffected by what they had done, while

others were bothered by their deeds but were able to live with them. On occasion, Cashman had thought about how he would hold up if he killed someone. Now he knew.

Bernie had felt terrible when Mary was his captive, and hurting her had made him sick. Like most criminalists, Cashman was able to distance himself from the violence he saw at a crime scene, but he had not been able to do that while he was killing and disfiguring Mary. Yet to his astonishment, he got past his bad feelings quickly.

Cashman believed that he was able to sleep soundly and to purge himself of any guilt he had felt initially because, unlike someone like Bundy, he was not really a murderer. True, he had killed Mary, but he had acted for the greater good. Soldiers killed people in battle, and no one thought that they were murderers. Soldiers felt that they were doing the right thing when they killed, because they were defending their country. While he regretted having to take the life of someone he knew and liked, Cashman believed he had been defending the citizens of Oregon when he killed Mary.

Several days after Mary's disappearance, Bernie was in a positively cheerful mood when Carlos Guzman walked up. Cashman was finishing up a fingerprint comparison in the liquor-store robbery case he had worked with Mary Clark on the evening she'd accused him of lying about the print in *Hayes*.

"Any luck?" Guzman asked.

"I hit the jackpot. I used AFIS the day after the robbery," Cashman said, referring to the automated fingerprint identification system, "but it couldn't come up with a match. But I just got the prints of two men who were arrested last night for another liquor-store robbery with a similar MO." Cashman grinned. "I've identified enough points of comparison to tie both of them to the first case."

"Great work, Bernie."

"Thanks."

Guzman started to leave, but Cashman stopped him. He had waited a reasonable amount of time to discuss Mary Clark with his superior. It would only be natural for Mary's colleagues to be concerned about her unexplained absence, and Bernie wanted to make sure that everything he did was consistent with the actions of an innocent person. Besides, the analysis of the evidence was finished, and it all pointed to Jacob Cohen. Cashman had heard through the grapevine that the detectives and Hannah Graves were convinced Cohen had murdered the unidentified woman in the vacant lot. No harm could come to him now if authorities discovered Jane Doe's identity.

"I'm concerned about Mary Clark," Cashman said. "She hasn't been in for several days. Have you heard anything from her?"

Guzman frowned. "I'm worried, too. I've left a few messages on her answering machine and on her cell but she hasn't returned my calls."

"I can't get through to her, either. Do you think something's wrong? It's not like Mary to just take off like this without telling anyone where she's going. She's very responsible."

"When was the last time you saw her or spoke to her?" Guzman asked.

"We worked this case—the liquor-store robbery. It was early morning, two, two-thirty. I spoke to her right before we left. She said that she was going home."

"So that's what, two days ago?"

"Three. I hope there's nothing wrong."

"Me, too."

Guzman couldn't stop thinking about Mary Clark after he left Cashman. As soon as he got back to his office, he picked up his phone and dialed one of the sergeants at central precinct who attended his church and was an occasional golfing partner.

"Fritz, Carlos Guzman here. I've got a favor to ask."

"Shoot."

"Do you know Mary Clark?"

"She's one of your people, right?"

"Yeah."

"I know who she is. Why?"

"She worked a crime scene with Bernie Cashman a few nights ago, and no one has seen her or talked to her since. I've left several messages on her answering machine and cell phone, but she hasn't returned them."

"You want me to send a car out to her place?"

"That's what I was thinking. She's not the type to get sick or go somewhere without letting us know."

"Consider it done," the sergeant said.

An hour later, Sergeant Fritz Auslander received a call from Philip Moreland, the officer he'd sent to Mary Clark's house.

"What's up, Phil?" Auslander asked.

"I'm uncomfortable with this, Sarge," Mo-

reland said. "There was no car in the driveway. I rang the bell and knocked on the door
and no one answered. Then I tried the knob.
The door wasn't locked. I opened it and yelled
that I was a cop. No answer. Then I noticed
that she has an expensive alarm system, but
it was off. It doesn't make sense that someone who'd pay that much for a house alarm
wouldn't put it on and would leave the front
door unlocked when she left the house."

"Did you talk to the neighbors?"

"Not yet, but I was thinking that she could
be in the house, hurt. Do you want me to go
in? I wasn't sure I could do it without a warrant."

"We're not looking for criminal activity.
Maybe she had a heart attack or something.
Go on in and get back to me."

When Moreland called back twenty minutes later he sounded nervous.

"No one's home, and it doesn't look like she
was going anywhere. Her toothbrush, hair-
brush—stuff like that—are still in the bathroom. I checked her drawers and closet.
They seemed full, and I saw a set of luggage.
There's no sign of a struggle, either. Everything is neat and in place."

Moreland hesitated, and Sergeant Auslander sensed that there was something else the officer wanted to say.

"What aren't you telling me, Phil?"

"There's a wastebasket in the bathroom. I could see a syringe in plain view. It's sitting on top of some balled-up tissues. And there are two glassine envelopes like you keep heroin in. I got as close as I could without touching anything. There are traces of some kind of powder in the envelopes."

Sergeant Auslander was quiet for a minute. Moreland waited.

"Look," the sergeant said, "get her plates from DMV and run them. Put out an APB for the car. Maybe she was in an accident. Check the hospitals."

"Will do. What about the stuff in the basket?"

"Leave it. Let me do some thinking, and call me if you get something on the car."

"I'll get back to you, Sarge."

As soon as Moreland was off the line, Auslander called Carlos Guzman and told him what the officer had found.

"You think Mary is using heroin?" Guzman asked. He sounded incredulous.

"I don't know what to think. I don't know the woman. But—if I were you—I'd go through the narcotics cases she handled recently to see if any of the evidence is missing."

Guzman swore.

"Hey," Auslander said, "it's never easy. One of my first partners had a habit. The precinct was like a funeral home the day they busted him. But you've got to look."

"You're right," Guzman said with a sigh. "This could turn into one motherfucker of a day."

26

GARY BRINKMAN HAD BEEN A BIT of a bookworm in high school and college, where he'd earned a degree in computer science. The idea of competing in a sport never crossed his mind until his doctor told him that lack of exercise was affecting his health. He still might have remained overweight and physically challenged if he hadn't started dating Wendy Franz, a fellow engineer at Intel, who had gone through college on a track scholarship. After his doctor's appointment, Wendy insisted that he start a regimen to lose weight and get in shape. Gary started running and dieting.

The farther he ran, the slimmer he got. Running soon became an addiction that Wendy heartily supported. Gary transformed himself from an overweight computer geek into a slim, muscular long-distance runner with a goal of completing the Portland Marathon.

The forested paths of the Wildwood Trail ran for more than twenty miles through Portland's park system. On a cool, clear Saturday, Gary and Wendy were pacing their way through a twelve-mile workout when Wendy slipped on a rock that had rolled down the steep, brush-covered hillside towering above the trail. She pitched sideways and rolled halfway down the lower slope, where a tree trunk arrested her fall. Gary scrambled down the hill.

"Are you all right?" he asked his girlfriend, who was gripping her side and scrunching up her face in pain.

Gary knelt beside Wendy and helped her into a sitting position. It was while she was sitting up that she saw something in the thick foliage in front of her.

"Wendy, are you okay?" Gary repeated.

Wendy pointed toward the thick underbrush.

"Is that . . . ?" she asked, unable to complete the sentence.

Gary looked where she was pointing. He stood up and walked over, bending from the waist as he got closer.

"Holy shit," he whispered when he realized that he was looking at a human hand.

Zeke Forbus swore loudly as he stumbled down the steep hillside for several feet before arresting his slide. As soon as he caught his breath, he started edging down the hill again toward the body.

"Why can't these fucking felons murder their victims in a sports bar, someplace nice?" Forbus bitched. "Why do we have to go to dumps that smell like cat piss or the fucking woods all the time?"

"Maybe we should make that a condition for leniency," Billie Brewster answered. "A perp can reduce his sentence by five years, say, if he kills the victim where we can get a beer and a decent burger."

"Goddamn it," Forbus swore again as the hillside gave way, spraying dirt and small rocks in his wake.

Just below them, a criminalist and Dr. Sally Grace were kneeling by the body, while above them, on the trail, the runners who had discovered it waited under the watchful eye of a uniformed officer.

"So, Sally, what have we got?" Brewster asked as soon as she skidded to a stop near the bushes where the body had been hidden.

"A dead guy," the ME answered as she stood up.

"I told you she was brilliant, didn't I?" Brewster said to Forbus, who was brushing dirt and leaves off his clothing. "Care to share any more technical information with those of us who didn't go to medical school?"

"What's left of him doesn't look good. Animals got at him but I'm guessing heroin messed him up first. I saw a lot of needle marks. And he wasn't killed here."

"So he was killed by someone?" Brewster asked. "We're not dealing with an OD or a heart attack?"

Dr. Grace shook her head. "He was shot in the back of the head."

"Can I take a look?" Brewster asked.

"Be my guest."

The ME stepped aside and Brewster did a deep knee-bend to get down close to the corpse. Forbus stood behind her and looked over her shoulder. Most of the dead man's face was gone. Forbus frowned.

"You find any ID?" Forbus asked.

"His name is Juan Ruiz," the criminalist told Forbus, handing him an evidence bag containing a wallet. Forbus had on latex gloves, but he still handled the wallet gingerly.

"Juan Ruiz," he muttered as soon as he saw the picture on the dead man's driver's license. "Yeah, Ruiz. I knew I knew him." Forbus looked at Brewster. "We questioned him about that Dominquez killing about a month ago."

"He works for Felix Dorado, right?" Brewster said.

"Which means we look at Martin Breach's men for this," Forbus answered.

Brewster turned to Dr. Grace. "As soon as you do the autopsy, let me know if you find any bullet fragments. I'd be curious to know how they compare with the slugs that killed Vincent Ballard."

PART FOUR
SCIENCE
FICTION

27

WHEN THE JAFFES NEEDED A FOREN-sic expert, they used Paul Baylor, a slender African-American who had worked at the Oregon state crime lab for ten years before going out on his own. Paul had been willing to meet at Jaffe, Katz, Lehane, and Brindisi, but Frank liked to get out of the office when he could, so he and Amanda drove to Oregon Forensic Investigations.

"So, how did your date with Mike go?" Frank asked as he turned into the entrance of an industrial park near the Columbia River.

"How did you know I went out with Mike?" Amanda asked, a little put off by the question. She loved her father dearly, but he did have a tendency to stick his nose into her personal affairs.

"His secretary mentioned it when I was at the DA's office this morning."

Amanda was relieved that Mike hadn't blabbed to her father, but she didn't appreciate her social life being a topic of gossip at the DA's office. She had to admit, though, that she'd had a good time. The movie was better than expected, and she'd enjoyed their dinner conversation. If she was going to be totally honest with herself, she would admit that she'd been sorry when the evening ended at her front door.

"It was just dinner and a movie, Dad." Amanda said as they drove down a street flanked by warehouses.

"Do you know the Cohens well?" she asked, to distract her father.

Frank shrugged. "The rabbi and I have talked after services and at a couple of men's club meetings and I've seen him and Valerie at parties, but I'm not a close friend, more of an acquaintance. Why?"

"I'm looking into the possibility of a mental defense, and I was wondering if you had any insight into Jacob or the family."

"It's common knowledge that Jacob has serious problems. I know something happened when he was living in Chicago and he went to the penitentiary for attempted rape. The rabbi set up an appointment to see me when Jacob was arrested. Then he canceled. I never knew why."

"If you hear anything you think will help, let me know, okay?"

"Will do."

Frank parked in an open space in front of an unremarkable concrete building. A ramp led to a walkway that passed in front of an export-import business and a construction firm and ended at Oregon Forensic Investigations. The door opened into a small anteroom furnished with two chairs that flanked a table covered with old copies of *Scientific American* and *BusinessWeek*. In one wall of the reception area were a door and a sliding glass window. Baylor's secretary was sitting at a desk on the other side of the glass window, preparing a report for a client. Amanda gave the secretary her name. Moments later, Paul Baylor walked out, wearing a herringbone jacket, an open-collar blue dress shirt, and freshly pressed tan slacks.

"It's been a while," Baylor said with a smile

as he ushered his clients into a cramped office furnished with an inexpensive desk, mismatched chairs, and a bookcase stuffed with scientific journals and case files. The office was for meeting with clients and writing reports. Paul's real work was conducted in a large lab behind the office.

Frank, Amanda, and the forensic expert made small talk for a few minutes before getting down to business. There was a legal pad on the desk. Baylor picked up a pen.

"Tell me what you've got for me."

"Ladies first," Frank said.

"Have you read about the Jane Doe who was murdered in the lot on Hobart and Queen Anne?" Amanda asked Baylor.

"There was something on the evening news a few days back. A rabbi's son was arrested, right?"

"Jacob Cohen. He's my client. Jacob is a paranoid schizophrenic with a history of sexual assault. He was living in an abandoned car in the lot where the murder occurred. The detectives found him kneeling next to the body. The woman was beaten and stabbed. He admits he handled the knife."

Baylor looked confused. "What is it you want me to do?"

"My client swears that someone else killed the woman."

"Did he identify the killer?"

"Uh, yes. He believes that the murderer is Mephistopheles."

Baylor gaped at Amanda for a second. Then he laughed. "The devil?"

Amanda nodded. "The red guy with the horns."

"And you want me to look for trace evidence of what—brimstone?"

"You find brimstone, and I guarantee I can get the DA to drop the case," Amanda said.

"It shouldn't be a problem," Baylor said. "I've got a specific test for brimstone. If it's there, I'll find it. Is there anything else you want me to look for—pitchfork marks, tail tracks?"

Amanda smiled. Then she got serious.

"Actually, there are some things that bother me. Jacob is very insistent that he didn't commit the murder."

"How many of your clients admit they're guilty?" Baylor asked, flashing Amanda an indulgent smile.

"Not many, but my co-counsel, Doug Weaver, has represented him before. He says that Jacob is so crazy that he doesn't think he can lie. It's hard to explain, but he's very serious about everything."

"You think he's innocent?" Baylor pressed.

Amanda sighed. "No. I think he's delusional. He probably murdered the woman and convinced himself that the devil did it so he wouldn't have to face the truth, but I wouldn't be doing my job if I didn't have you double-check the lab's work. The cops found two T-shirts in Jacob's car with the victim's blood on them. Jacob admits that they're his shirts but he says that he wasn't wearing them when the victim was killed and he says that he has no idea how the blood got on them. I'd like you to make certain that it is the victim's blood on his shirts.

"Then there is something else that I found odd. The woman was stabbed repeatedly and bludgeoned with a crowbar. Both weapons were found next to the body. Jacob admits handling the knife but he says that he never touched the crowbar. The crime lab found Jacob's prints all over the knife, but there are no prints on the crowbar."

"Who worked on the case for the state?" Baylor asked.

"Ron Toomey and Bernie Cashman."

"They're solid," Baylor said.

"I know, but everyone makes mistakes, though I doubt it in this case."

"You have the reports for me?" Baylor asked. Amanda handed him a thick manila envelope. Baylor took it and placed it to one side.

"I'll arrange to look at the evidence. If I need to perform tests here, can you get me a court order so I can bring the stuff over?"

"Write me an affidavit and I'll make a motion to the judge."

"Good." He turned to Frank. "Tell me your troubles."

"Art Prochaska has been indicted for the murder of a junkie named Vincent Ballard. The guy was executed at the Continental Motel with two shots to the back of the head."

"Was there anything special about Ballard?"

"Not that I can tell. He used to be rich, made his money in one of those dot-com start-ups. But it went under when the bubble burst in the nineties. Ballard had developed a habit back when he could afford it. After he went broke he went downhill fast.

He'd been scratching out a living doing temp computer work. From what we've learned, his habit was really bad toward the end."

"That doesn't sound like the type of person that Martin Breach would have Art hit."

"I agree. And Art is adamant that he's been set up."

"Why do the cops think Prochaska did it?"

"Art's fingerprints were found on a beer can in the victim's room. The can wasn't in the room when the maids cleaned, so there's a small time frame when it could have been put there. Art swears that he was never in the room and that he never touched the can.

"Also, the bullets that killed the victim are consistent with bullets found in Art's house, but Art says he didn't shoot Ballard."

"Who are the criminalists on the case?"

"Bernie Cashman and Mary Clark."

"Okay. I'll take a look at the ballistics stuff and the fingerprints and I'll get back to you."

28

CARLOS GUZMAN WAS WORKING AT his desk when the receptionist told him that Sergeant Auslander was on line two.

"What's up, Fritz?"

"We found Mary Clark's car."

"Where?"

"It was parked at the end of Hobart near the vacant lot where that Jane Doe was murdered a few nights ago. Do they have an ID for the victim yet?"

"Jesus, you're not suggesting . . . ?"

"Word is the victim was a user. What happened when you looked through Clark's files?"

"This is just between us, Fritz."

"Sure."

"There was heroin missing from several cases. Internal Affairs is looking into it."

"That's too bad. Don't take it personally. And, if you want my advice, I'd take a look at the Jane Doe."

As soon as Guzman hung up, he remembered something and dialed an extension in the district attorney's office.

"Hannah Graves."

"This is Carlos Guzman at the lab."

"Hi. What can I do for you?"

"You're handling the Jacob Cohen case, right? The murder in the lot?"

"Yes."

"Did you try Cohen's attempted rape case with the prostitute?"

"That was mine too."

"Who testified in court about the lab work in that case?"

"Mary Clark. Ron Toomey did some stuff but we stipulated to that. Mary was the witness. Why?"

"This isn't public knowledge yet, but Mary has been missing for several days. I had a policeman check her house. She's usually very responsible. I thought she might be inside. Maybe she had a heart attack or was seriously injured. Mary wasn't at her home, but the officer saw a syringe and what he thought was heroin in a wastepaper basket in her bathroom."

"Did he touch it?"

"No. He was there to see if Mary was hurt. Anyway, I checked to see if heroin was missing from any of the cases Mary was working on. It was. Then I got a call about Mary's car. They found it on the same block as the vacant lot where Jacob Cohen killed the Jane Doe."

"And you think . . . ?"

"What if Mary developed a habit and she needed a fix? She knows where she can get heroin on the street. So she goes to Queen Anne and Hobart and Cohen sees her and remembers that she testified against him."

Guzman waited patiently while Graves digested what he'd told her.

"Thanks, Carlos," Graves said after a few moments. "You may have made my day. We thought Cohen killed the victim because he's nuts, but you've just given me a hell of a motive. Has anyone gone to view the Jane Doe since you found out about the car?"

"No. I'm going to the ME's office as soon as I get off the phone with you."

"Let me know as soon as you know if the dead woman is Mary Clark. This could be a huge break."

Hannah Graves sounded very excited, but Guzman could not share her enthusiasm. If he was right, Mary had died a horrible death.

"Hey, Billie, I fished the bullet fragments out of Juan Ruiz's skull," Sally Grace said as soon as the detective picked up the phone.

"I'll have someone from the lab pick up the fragments and check them against the bullets in Prochaska's case. If I can get Prochaska for a second homicide I owe you a cold one."

"And dinner. I'm not a cheap date."

The women talked for a few more minutes before Dr. Grace hung up. She had another autopsy to perform, and she was getting ready to leave her office when the receptionist told her that Carlos Guzman and two detectives were in the reception area and wanted to talk to her. Moments later, Guzman, Steve Hooper, and Jack Vincenzo trooped into her office.

"That was fast," Dr. Grace said.

"What do you mean?" Guzman sounded puzzled.

"Isn't this about the bullets I took out of Juan Ruiz's head?" the ME asked.

"No, Sally, that's not why I'm here." He sounded grim "This is about the Jane Doe from the lot at Queen Anne and Hobart. Do you still have the body?"

"Yes."

"We'd like to look at it."

Dr. Grace picked up the phone and asked to have the body of Jane Doe brought to the autopsy room. Then she led the men to the back of the building. It was normal for the people she brought to her work area to talk, to relieve the tension of being in the presence of the dead; but this time no one said a word during the short walk from her office.

The body was wheeled in moments after they arrived. The men gathered around the corpse. Guzman took a deep breath, then turned pale when Sally exposed the victim's face. Hooper swore.

"What do you think?" Vincenzo asked.

Guzman was appalled by the damage that had been done to the victim's face, but he forced himself to look. He fixed Mary Clark's face in his mind, then mentally rearranged the face of the corpse as if it were a jigsaw puzzle. When he was satisfied, Guzman nodded.

"It's her," he said, then turned away from the body and faced Sally. She thought he might be on the verge of tears.

"Do you know this woman?" she asked.

"I'm pretty certain she's Mary Clark, one of the criminalists from the crime lab."

Dr. Grace had met Mary. She stepped forward and stared intently at the battered face.

"Oh, my God," she whispered.

Bernard Cashman, Carlos Guzman, and Steve Hooper followed Patrolman Philip Moreland up the stairs to Mary Clark's bedroom. Below, criminalists and detectives were swarming around the house, looking for clues to her murder. Cashman suppressed a smile, knowing that there were none to be found.

"It's in here," Moreland said as he pointed into the bathroom that adjoined Mary's bedroom. The policeman stepped aside and Cashman, his boss, and the detective walked over to the wastepaper basket. The syringe and the glassine envelopes Cashman had planted were resting on top of some crumpled tissues.

"Thanks, Phil. We won't need you anymore," Guzman said.

Moreland walked downstairs, leaving the three men standing in the door to the bathroom. Guzman stared at the evidence of Mary Clark's fall from grace and shook his head sadly.

"I never saw this coming," he said as Cashman photographed the bathroom and the basket. The men were silent as Cashman removed the evidence and bagged it. When he was through, Guzman sighed.

"Poor Mary," he said.

"Don't beat yourself up, Carlos," Cashman told his boss. "None of us suspected that she had a habit."

"I feel bad about not recognizing her when we found the body," Hooper told them.

"You shouldn't," Cashman said. "Ron and I worked with her every day and we didn't know it was her."

Hooper shook his head. "Her face was so fucked up I just didn't want to look."

The men were quiet, standing around the wastepaper basket as if it were Mary's coffin. Then Hooper clenched his fist.

"That pervert is going to pay."

"I'm sure he will, Steve," Cashman said. "You caught him with the body, Ron's tied him to the pubic hairs, the blood on the T-shirt connects him to Mary, and his prints are all over the knife. You have a very solid case."

"Weaver and Jaffe are probably going to try an insanity defense to keep Cohen off death row."

"That is a worry, but either way he'll pay," Cashman said. "Sometimes I wonder if having to spend the rest of your life locked in a cage isn't worse than a death sentence."

"An eye for an eye, Bernie," Hooper answered angrily. "That's what I believe in. Killing scum like Cohen is garbage disposal."

Bernie wanted Hooper and Guzman to leave so he could search for the hammer. He handed Hooper the bag with the syringe and the glassine envelopes.

"Can you take these downstairs and get them logged in? I want to finish up here."

"Sure thing," Hooper said as he grabbed the bag.

"We'll get out of your way and let you get to work," Guzman said. He shook his head sadly. "I just had to see it for myself."

Guzman and Hooper headed for the stairs. As soon as they were out of sight,

Bernie turned slowly, looking for any place he had missed when he searched the bedroom on the evening he abducted Mary. He had been rushed that night but now, under the guise of conducting a thorough crime-scene investigation, he could spend all the time he wanted looking for the hammer from the *Hayes* case.

Cashman went through every drawer in the room and every inch of space in the closet. He even looked under the bed. Then he searched Mary's bathroom. Nothing. He moved down the hall to the guest bedroom. When he was through in there, he searched the hall closets. He was growing desperate. If another criminalist found the hammer before he did, it could be disastrous.

An hour later, Cashman was convinced that the hammer was not on the second floor. That left the ground floor and the attic. Several people were combing the ground floor, but no one had started in the attic. A door at the end of the second-floor hall opened onto a narrow flight of stairs. Cashman was sweating from nerves and his stomach was in a knot as he climbed them.

"Bernie," a voice from the bottom of the stairs called.

Cashman froze. Had they found the hammer? Mary had hidden it, and everyone would want to know why. It wouldn't take them long to wonder if her reason for hiding the weapon was somehow connected with Bernard Cashman, the criminalist who had miraculously cracked the *Hayes* case by finding a fingerprint on the handle.

"Yes," Cashman answered.

"Carlos wants everyone downstairs."

"What for?" he asked anxiously.

"He wants to find out what we've got so far."

"I haven't finished with the attic."

"You can do that later. He wants you now."

Cashman swore to himself. There was no way to avoid the meeting. He turned and headed downstairs, praying that he would have a chance to search the attic later.

29

WHEN HENRY TEDESCO WALKED INTO Martin Breach's office at the Jungle Club, Breach was wearing a black satin shirt, gold chains, and tan double-knit slacks. Henry's boss was bent over, using chopsticks on Thai takeout so spicy that Henry could see sweat beading the patches of scalp showing under Breach's comb-over.

"What have you got for me, Henry?" he asked as he slurped up a reddish yellow curry made with coconut milk.

"You remember wondering if someone from the crime lab was on Felix Dorado's payroll?"

Breach nodded.

"Have you read about the unidentified woman who was murdered in that vacant lot on Queen Anne?"

"Yeah?"

"The police identified her. She's Mary Clark, a forensic specialist from the Oregon state crime lab who worked on the murder at the Continental Motel. Now here's the interesting part. She had a smack habit."

Breach stopped eating. "You think this bitch was paid to frame Artie?"

"You know what they say about smoke and fire."

"A heroin addict," Breach muttered to himself. "That fucker Dorado must have got to her."

"Once he found out she was an addict he'd own her."

"I want you to visit Frank. Tell him. Maybe he can do something with it—suppress the evidence, something like that."

"I learned something else that will be even more useful."

Tedesco told Breach what Clarence Edwards had said to Marsha Hastings about the two men he'd seen leaving Vincent Ballard's motel room on the night of the murder.

"We need to turn Frank on to Edwards," Breach said.

"That may be a problem. He disappeared the day after we spoke. I have men looking for him but I think he left the state."

"Is the whore still living at the Continental?"

"Yes, but that may not help Art," Tedesco said. "If I understand my law properly, Mr. Jaffe won't be able to get the description into evidence."

"Yeah, right, hearsay," said Breach, who was as knowledgeable about criminal law as many attorneys. "The whore would be testifying to what this Clarence told her, but she didn't see nothing herself."

"We might not need Edwards or the Hastings woman. I may have a line on one of the shooters."

Breach smiled. "That would be good."

Tedesco nodded agreement. "If we can find him we may be able to convince him to unburden his conscience."

"No question about that, no question about that," Martin Breach said as he licked his lips in anticipation.

30

DOUG WEAVER HAD PRACTICED
law almost as long as Amanda had; he'd tried
six death-penalty cases and he'd argued in
the Oregon Supreme Court on four occasions, but he was still nervous about working with an attorney who was looked upon
as a star in the legal firmament.

Amanda had scheduled a brainstorming
session at her office. Doug usually dressed
down for a skull session with other lawyers.
For this meeting, he wore a suit, shined his
shoes, and arrived ten minutes early. More
important, he had not had a drink since

Amanda had asked him to co-counsel Jacob's case.

Moments after he told the receptionist his name, a woman walked into the waiting area and introduced herself as Kate Ross, the firm's investigator.

"Amanda's still tied up with a client. She sent me to apologize. We've commandeered the conference room. You can wait in there. It shouldn't be too long."

A long table made of dark polished wood stretched across the center of the conference room. Bookshelves packed with law books and statutes filled the wall on one side of the table, and a blackboard took up most of the wall at the end of the table opposite the door.

"There are soft drinks in the kitchen and we've got coffee and tea," Kate said, pointing at a credenza that stretched along the wall opposite the bookshelves. Arrayed on the credenza were silver trays with fruit and assorted pastries, urns full of coffee and hot water, a hand-carved wooden box holding an assortment of teas, a matched set of china cups, saucers and plates, a box of expensive silverware, and several bottles of water.

"Coffee would be great," Doug told her.

"Okay. I'll be back when Amanda is ready." Kate pointed to a telephone on the credenza. "Buzz me if you need anything."

The investigator left, and Doug noticed two thick three-ring binders on one side of the table. A label that read STATE V. COHEN and another label, reading AMANDA JAFFE, were affixed to one cover. Kate Ross's name was on the other. Lying next to the binder were a legal pad, a pen, and two sharpened pencils. Doug's case reports were collected in manila folders with handwritten labels. He vowed to create a folder like Jaffe's as soon as their meeting was over.

It was warm in the conference room, and Doug thought about taking off his jacket, but he kept it on, because he wanted Amanda to think that he was all business. He filled a cup with black coffee and took his case files out of his briefcase. Separate files contained the police reports, lab reports, and autopsy report in the case. Another section held Doug's confidential notes of his interview with Jacob Cohen and other internal documents that he had copied for Amanda but which would not be turned over to the DA. A manila envelope was filled with pictures of the crime scene and the autopsy photographs. He shuddered when he remembered the close-up of Jane Doe's face. It had reminded Doug of one of those Picasso paintings, where the facial features are present but flattened and rear-ranged. Without the eyes and with the dam-age done to the cheeks, mouth, and nose, the poor woman barely looked human.

Suddenly, the door opened and Amanda and Kate walked in.

"Hey, Doug," Amanda said, greeting Weaver as if he were an old friend. Amanda filled a cup with coffee and snatched a crois-sant off the pastry tray. Kate took a bottle of water and some fruit.

"Kate and I have read through the file and we've formed certain impressions," Amanda said when they were seated. "If it's okay with you, though, we'd like to get your take on the case first. That way we won't influence you and we'll see if we're on the same wave-length."

Doug would have preferred to hear Aman-da's ideas first, in case his were off the mark. He didn't want to look foolish. But he agreed to Amanda's suggestion.

"I have to admit the state's got a solid case here," he said, "but I did read things in the reports that raised questions. What surprised me was how many of the questions were cleared up if I assumed that Jacob didn't kill Jane Doe."

"What troubled you?" Amanda asked.

"Okay, well, I'm having a problem understanding what happened with the crowbar. There were multiple stab wounds and the victim was hit with the crowbar a lot. Jacob admits handling the knife, and the lab found his prints all over it, but why aren't his fingerprints on the crowbar? I mean, the easy answer is that he wiped off the crowbar, but why wipe off the crowbar and not wipe off the knife?"

Doug paused to see if Kate and Amanda were with him. When Amanda nodded, he continued.

"Of course, the solution to the problem is simple if someone else killed Doe. The killer wipes his prints off both weapons and leaves them near the body, where Jacob finds them. He grabs the knife, like he said, but doesn't touch the crowbar."

"We've been thinking along the same lines," Amanda said. Doug smiled like a student who'd just received a gold star from his favorite teacher. "What else have you got?"

"I thought back over my interview with Jacob after reading the autopsy report and the police reports. Something didn't make sense. Jacob says that he never left the lot between seeing the murder and the cops arriving. So, how did Jane Doe's eyes and hands get out of the lot?"

"The answer to that is obvious," Kate said. "Cohen lied."

Doug nodded. "That's one possibility. But—if he's telling the truth—either he had an accomplice, which isn't likely, or the real killer took the hands and eyes away. Think about it—why would Jacob want to dispose of the hands and eyes?"

"Because he's crazy," Kate answered. "At least, that's what Hannah Graves will say."

"Or he doesn't want anyone to figure out who she is," Amanda added.

"That doesn't work, Amanda," Doug said. "If Jacob didn't want anyone to know Jane Doe was connected to him, why take the trouble to get rid of the eyes and hands but leave her body in the lot?"

"Good point," Amanda conceded. "What are your thoughts about the bloody T-shirts that were found in the garbage bag in Jacob's car?"

"That's a stumper," Doug admitted, "but there is something that worries me about it. When he was arrested, Jacob was wearing a sweatshirt and a T-shirt. The police report says that there wasn't any blood on either of them. It was cold and raining all evening. Jacob would have been wearing the sweatshirt over his T-shirt, so how did the blood get on the T-shirts that were found in his car and not get on the sweatshirt?"

"That's easy," answered Kate, who Doug realized had been designated to play the devil's advocate. "The vic comes into the lot while Jacob is in his car wearing only the T-shirts. Maybe he was changing clothes. Anyway, he runs out and kills her. Then he sees the blood on his shirts, so he goes back to the car, strips off the bloody T-shirts and puts them in the garbage bag before putting on the clothes in which he was arrested."

"That fits the evidence, but it doesn't make a lot of sense," Doug responded. "It was cold and nasty that night. He's not going to run out in the rain in a T-shirt. He's going to put on the sweatshirt first.

"But let's assume you're right. What did he do after he changed his clothes? Doe was really worked over. If he did any damage after he returned to the body there would be blood on the sweatshirt."

"I admit there's a problem for the state here," Amanda said, "but, given the other evidence, I don't see a jury acquitting because Cohen was wearing a T-shirt and sweatshirt with no blood on them when he was arrested."

"That's true, but everything makes sense if Mr. Cohen is innocent and the killer put the bloody shirts in the garbage bag."

Amanda looked unhappy. "There are a number of problems with that theory, Doug. Cohen admits that the shirts are his, so the killer had to take them from the car, get blood on them and put them back. When did the killer do that? The ME concluded that Jane Doe was killed in the lot, so the shirts had to be planted after the murder and before the cops arrived."

"Jacob could have been so distracted after he found the body that he didn't notice the murderer going to the car and planting the evidence," Doug said.

"Okay, but when did the killer get the shirt? He didn't do it while Cohen was in the car, so he had to take it from the car after Cohen went to the body. Then he had to run over to the body while Cohen was there and get blood on the shirts without Cohen seeing him. Cohen thinks the devil is the killer. The devil could make himself invisible and do that, but I can't think of any human who could.

"Cohen also said that he waited for a long time before he built up enough courage to see what had happened. Why would the killer wait around in the rain all that time and then go to the car and risk discovery?"

"Those are good questions," Doug said. "I'm afraid I don't have any answers for you."

"Yeah, well, neither do we," Amanda said, sounding frustrated. "And there is the most damaging piece of evidence—the pubic hairs. How did they get on the victim's thigh, secured to her leg by her own blood? If Cohen is innocent, someone had to figure out a way of getting his pubic hairs, which means that there was an elaborate plan to frame Cohen for this murder. What possible motive would anyone have to do that?"

Before Doug could answer, Frank Jaffe walked in.

"Working on Jacob Cohen's case?" he asked.

"Yeah. Doug, this is my father, Frank Jaffe."

"Pleased to meet you," Frank said, nodding in Doug's direction. "I'm sorry to interrupt, but Henry Tedesco just dropped by and gave me some information about your case that might be important. They've identified the Jane Doe. She's Mary Clark, a criminalist at the crime lab."

"That's not good," Doug said.

"Why does that make a difference?" Kate asked, confused by Weaver's reaction.

"When I met with Jerry Cochran about Cohen's attempted rape case he let me go through the file. Mary Clark testified in court against Jacob at his trial for assault and attempted rape."

"Didn't Clark do some of the lab work in Prochaska's case?" Amanda asked.

Frank nodded. "That's why Henry was here. It turns out that she was a heroin addict. The lab found traces of heroin in her blood, and heroin that was stolen from the crime lab was found in her house. The police think that Clark went to the lot to buy drugs. Henry suggested that someone who had a grudge against Art and Martin may have found out about Clark's habit and blackmailed her into framing Art. Martin thinks that we should double-check the lab work in Art's case."

"Paul's doing that, isn't he?" Kate asked.

"Yes, and we should tell him about this new development."

"How did they figure out that Clark is the victim?" Amanda asked.

"When she didn't show up at work for several days, a cop went to her house. She and her car were gone. The car was found near the lot and someone connected the dots."

"Thanks for the info, Dad."

"My pleasure. I'll leave you to your work. Nice meeting you, Doug."

"This is all we need," Weaver said as soon as Frank left. "Now Graves can prove opportunity, means, *and* motive. We had a good argument that Jacob was insane when it looked like Jane Doe's murder was a random killing. Graves can counter our assertion that Jacob was too crazy to know what he was doing by showing that he knew the victim and had a motive to kill her."

The brainstorming session went on for another hour. Before it ended, they agreed that Kate would work up a list of lay and expert witnesses for the penalty phase. Doug volunteered to put together a set of penalty-phase jury instructions and research legal issues that pertained to the specialized field of death-penalty sentencing. The assignment would be easy for Doug, who had prepared jury instructions and memos on sentencing issues in his other cases and would only have to bring himself up to date on the latest case law.

When Doug left Amanda's office, he was feeling upbeat. She had gone out of her way to be friendly, and she had treated him as an equal. She also seemed pleased with his analysis of the case. The only negative feelings Doug carried away had to do with the hurdles they would have to overcome to save Jacob Cohen's life.

31

"MIKE GREENE IS HOLDING ON three," the receptionist told Frank.

"What's up?" Frank asked as soon as he picked up.

"I'm afraid I'm the bearer of bad tidings, Frank. The body of Juan Ruiz, a small-time drug dealer who works for Felix Dorado, was discovered in the woods a few days ago. He'd been shot in the back of the head, execution-style, just like Vincent Ballard. We compared the bullets that killed Ruiz with the bullets that were found in Art Prochaska's closet. They're a perfect match. And it gets worse for your client. The lab conducted a ballistics test on the gun we found in Prochaska's house. There's no doubt that it fired the bullets that killed Ruiz."

"I take it that you're going to charge Art with this murder, too."

"I'm afraid so. I'll be going to the grand jury tomorrow. I'll call you when I have an indictment and we can set the arraignment."

Frank hung up and swiveled his chair so he could look out at the West Hills. The dark clouds that hovered over them fit his mood perfectly. Until Mike's call, Frank believed he had a fighting chance to win Art's case. No witness put Prochaska—who was not easy to miss—at the Continental. Cashman would testify that bullets like those found in Art's closet had killed Ballard, but he couldn't swear that the bullets actually came from the box found in the closet, and he had testified at the preliminary hearing that Art's Glock had not fired those bullets. Any advantage Frank had would disappear if a judge let Mike introduce evidence of a second similar murder committed with bullets like those found in Art's house and fired from Art's gun.

Normally, a prosecutor could not tell a jury about a crime that was not charged in the indictment, but there were exceptions to the rule. One exception allowed the state to introduce evidence of crimes so similar that the natural inference would be that the person who committed one had most probably committed the other. Mike would argue that Ballard and Ruiz were drug addicts executed in the same manner by bullets from the same batch. Frank wasn't sure that it would be error for a judge to allow the introduction of evidence from the Ruiz murder in the trial of the Ballard homicide, and he bet that Mike was researching the case law on the admissibility of evidence of other crimes at this very moment.

A knock on his door distracted Frank. "Got a minute?" Kate Ross asked her boss.

"Is your meeting over?"

"Yeah, we just broke up."

"I was going to buzz you anyway. I just received a disturbing call from Mike Greene."

Frank told Kate about the new development in Art Prochaska's case.

"That sucks," she said when he finished.

"That it does." Frank shook his head in frustration. "Damn. I thought we got a break when you told me what you found out at the motel, but we may have to start thinking about a deal. Now, why did you want to see me?"

"I wanted to know if Tedesco gave you an address for Clarence Edwards or the names of the men who came out of Ballard's room."

"No. I did ask him about the Continental but he got very cagey. He wouldn't even admit he was there. But I'm not worried. If Martin finds the men who killed Ballard we'll know. He'd do anything to save Art. How's Amanda's case going?"

"Not great. I'm meeting Paul Baylor at the crime lab this afternoon to look at the evidence in the *Prochaska* and *Cohen* cases. I'll let you know if anything exciting happens."

Amanda and Frank had gotten court orders that permitted Paul Baylor to take several pieces of evidence from the Oregon state crime lab to his private lab for testing. Kate and Paul had arrived at the state crime lab at three, and it was almost five by the time Paul collected the items he wanted to inspect and completed the paperwork.

"Where is Mary Clark's car?" Paul asked Carlos Guzman just before he was ready to leave.

"Out back," Guzman said, his face showing the sadness he still felt every time Mary's name was mentioned.

"I feel bad about Mary, too," Paul said. "I just can't believe she was using heroin."

"You're not the only one. Everyone here is still in a state of shock. I'm just glad we got the bastard who killed her," Guzman said, forgetting that Kate and Paul might not agree with him, "but it won't bring her back." Guzman sighed. "You want to see the car?"

"If we could," Paul said.

Guzman fished the keys out of the case file. Then he looked up at the clock.

"Damn, I don't have anyone to babysit you, right now. We had a crime wave this afternoon. Everyone's out at scenes or working on rush jobs."

"Don't make me come back, Carlos," Paul pleaded.

"All right, I'll go out with you. I can use the fresh air."

Guzman led Kate and Paul down several hallways and outside to the back lot.

"This shouldn't take too long," Paul told the lab chief. "Your guys didn't find anything connecting Cohen to the car when they went through it. No prints, no blood. I'm just double-checking to be thorough."

Guzman paced around while Paul checked the interior of Clark's car and looked under the hood.

"Find any smoking guns?" Guzman asked as Paul wandered around to the back of the car.

"I'm not telling you," Paul answered with a smile as he opened the trunk. Kate peered over Paul's shoulder and saw a rumpled plaid blanket, a baseball cap, and other objects that Mary had tossed in. Paul pushed them aside and lifted up the mat covering the well that held the spare tire and the jack. The tire was screwed into the base of the trunk. Paul looked at the tire briefly and was about to lower the mat when Kate stopped him.

"Hold up a sec. Do me a favor and unscrew the tire, will you? I want to make sure there's nothing under there."

"Like what?" Paul asked.

"Clark was stealing dope from the lab. Maybe she hid it in the tire well."

Paul unscrewed the bolt that held down the tire and lifted the tire out of the trunk. At first, Kate thought there was nothing in the tire well. Then she realized that there was something lying there. Kate studied the object while Paul rested the tire against the fender.

"Get a picture of this, will you?" Kate asked Baylor.

"What did you find?" Guzman asked as Paul took a digital camera out of the bag he'd brought to the lab.

"Whoever put it in there wrapped it in cloth that's so dark it blends into the shadows," Kate said.

As soon as he finished shooting the package, Paul slipped on a pair of latex gloves, lifted the object out of the car, and unwrapped the black cloth, revealing an evidence bag containing a hammer. Kate looked through the clear plastic. She noticed brown smears on the hammer, which she recognized as dried blood.

"Why would Clark hide this evidence bag?" Kate asked the lab chief.

"I have no idea," Guzman said as he stared at the surprise package.

"That's a coincidence," Kate said.

"What is?"

She pointed at the label with the case name, which was attached to the evidence bag. "This is from the *Raymond Hayes* case, the guy who was executed. His attorney,

Doug Weaver, and Amanda are co-counsel in Jacob Cohen's case. I just met him today."

Paul turned to Guzman. "Was heroin involved in *Hayes*?"

"Not that I know of." Guzman frowned. "A day or so before Mary disappeared I asked her to go through some closed cases to see if we could destroy or return evidence. *Hayes* was one of them."

"I'll call Doug when we get back," Kate said. "Maybe he knows about a tie-in between *Hayes* and Mary Clark." She pointed at the hammer. "What do you want to do with this, Paul?"

"I can't see how it has anything to do with Clark's murder, but I'd like to go over it, just to be certain." He looked at Guzman. "Can I take this with me?"

"I'm not going to turn it over until our lab looks at it and Hannah Graves says it's okay."

"Carlos is right," Paul said. "His people should get the first look. If the DA objects, Amanda can go to court for another order."

32

"HEY, BERNIE," CARLOS GUZMAN said. "Just getting in?"

"There must have been a full moon last night. All the crazies were running amok. There was a pileup on I-5. I worked the crash site until ten. Then, just as I was getting ready to go home, I got called to the double homicide at the Cock and Bull tavern. I didn't crawl into bed until three."

"So you haven't heard about the hammer?"

Cashman's pulse went from zero to two hundred in a nanosecond, but his expression didn't change.

"What hammer?"

"The damnedest thing happened yesterday afternoon."

Guzman told Cashman about the discovery that Paul Baylor and Kate Ross had made in the tire well of Mary Clark's car.

"*Hayes* was your case, right?" Guzman said.

"Yes."

"Did Mary work on it?"

"That was me and Mike Kitay."

"That's right, before his heart attack." Guzman shook his head sadly. "Mike was a great guy."

"He helped me out a lot when I started."

"Can you think of any reason why Mary would take evidence from *Hayes* and hide it?"

"No. That's bizarre. I can't even remember her talking about the case."

"Tell me if you remember anything, okay?"

"Sure. Where's the hammer now?" Cashman asked nonchalantly.

"Hannah Graves decided to give the evidence to Paul Baylor so the defense could examine it. She figured that the judge would give it to them anyway."

"So Paul's got it?"

"Yeah, I couriered it over as soon as we were through with it and Hannah gave me the okay. Well, I've got to go. There's a crisis in the drug lab."

Guzman headed down the hall, and Cashman went to his work area, walking slowly to avoid suspicion. As soon as he got to his desk, he called Oregon Forensic Investigations and pretended to be a potential client. Baylor's secretary told Cashman that her boss would be in court all day and wasn't expected back until after five, which meant that Baylor hadn't had a chance yet to examine the hammer.

Cashman leaned back and closed his eyes. He had a pounding headache. Baylor was very smart. Cashman had no doubt that he would figure out what was wrong with the hammer as soon as he had the time to inspect it and the evidence bag at his leisure. If Baylor got near the hammer, Cashman's career would be over.

The rest of the day crawled along at an excruciatingly slow pace. As soon as he could get away from the lab without arousing suspicion, Cashman drove to the industrial park where Baylor had his office. He parked his car several blocks away. There were very few people walking on the streets, and he was able to work his way to the side of a warehouse with a good view of the front of Paul's building without being seen. Cashman checked his watch. It was a little before five, and Baylor's reserved parking space was empty. Cashman hid in the shadows and waited.

Paul Baylor had been on the stand until court recessed at five o'clock. Then the attorney for whom he was working insisted on holding a postmortem in a bar near the courthouse. Considering what he was being paid, Paul felt that he couldn't refuse. By the time he was able to beg off and return to Oregon Forensic, his secretary had gone home and the businesses on either side had closed up for the night.

It took an effort for Baylor to trudge up the ramp to his office. He had a slight headache from court and a soft buzz from the alcohol he'd imbibed while conferring with his client. There were lights on the walkway, but they were dim and none of them were over his office door. Baylor bent down to find the keyhole. He missed the first time and swore. In his exhausted state, it took all of his concentration to perform this simple task.

Baylor didn't bother to turn on the lights in the reception area, because the numbers on the keypad for the alarm were illuminated. He punched in his code and was about to go to his office when a man rushed across the room. Baylor was so shocked that he didn't raise his arm when the intruder swung a weighted sap at his head. The pain from the blow was blinding. Baylor's knees buckled. The second blow dropped him to the floor. The third blow knocked him unconscious.

Amanda paused in the entrance to Paul's hospital room and stared. The top of Baylor's head was wrapped in gauze and he had two black eyes.

"It's not as bad as it looks," Paul said, contorting his face into what was supposed to be a smile but ended up as a grimace when a bolt of pain hit him.

"Why don't I believe you?" Amanda said.

"Okay, it's almost as bad as it looks. I've got a concussion but there's no permanent damage. I'm only in tonight for observation."

"What happened?" Amanda asked as she

cleared some pillows off a chair and moved it to the side of Paul's bed.

"Someone broke into my lab last night after I got back from court."

"Did you get a good look at him?"

Paul shook his head. "He was wearing a ski mask and he rushed me so fast that I was down and out before I knew what happened."

"It sounds like you're lucky to be alive."

"If he wanted to kill me he could have. But I didn't ask you to come to the hospital so you could tell me how sorry you feel for me—although the concern is appreciated. I think this was more than just a random burglary. I looked through my office and the lab while I waited for the police. The thief took some drugs I was testing, my laptop, stuff you'd expect a junkie to take. But he also grabbed an item you wouldn't expect an addict to steal—the hammer we found in the tire well of Mary Clark's car."

"The hammer? That doesn't make sense. Was it with something valuable? Maybe the thief was in a hurry and scooped it up with some things he thought he could sell."

"That's not what happened. A courier from the crime lab brought over the hammer while

I was in court. I called in for messages during the lunch break and my secretary told me it had been delivered. She said that she put it on my desk in the office on top of the mail. The laptop and other things the thief took from my office were on the other side of the desk and the rest of my mail wasn't touched."

"So you didn't have a chance to inspect the hammer?"

"No. I was going to look at it in the morning."

"What do you think is going on?"

"I have no idea. Maybe this guy was just a thief and he took the hammer for some weird reason of his own. But it's too big a coincidence to just write off. Mary went to a lot of trouble to make sure no one would find that hammer. Then we find it and it's the subject of a random theft? I don't buy it."

33

REUBEN CORRALES HAD BEEN RE-
lieved when Felix Dorado eased up on him
after he offed Vincent Ballard, but he knew
that his status could change instantly. Felix
was quick to anger and sometimes it was
hard to figure out why he was pissed off. But
for the time being, Reuben felt that he was
out of the doghouse. Since the murder, Felix had even let him off babysitting the street
dealers and made him one of his bodyguards.

Tonight, Felix was clubbing, and Reuben
had been sent to the bar to order a round
for Dorado, Pablo Herrera, and the four *pu-*

tas they had brought with them. The women were hanging all over Dorado and his lieutenant, laughing at any stupid joke Felix made as if it were the funniest thing they'd ever heard, and letting Dorado and Herrera grope them, without complaint. It made Reuben jealous and horny, so he focused his full attention on the total knockout who pushed next to him at the bar, grazing his hip with hers and smiling to show a luscious mouth full of pearl-white teeth straight out of some toothpaste commercial.

"Sorry, this place is so crowded."

"No problem," Reuben said, stepping back to give her more space.

The broad was stacked, and her long dark hair was loose and sensuous. He caught her eyeing his biceps and decided to take a shot.

"You're new here," Reuben said. "I ain't seen you before."

"My name is Jenny. I just moved to Portland." She flashed her smile again. "I don't know anyone."

"Now you know me. I'm Reuben. Reuben Corrales. Where you move from?"

"LA. I was dancing in a club down there but I had some trouble with the manager." She shrugged, and her hair bounced. "You know how it is."

Reuben nodded, savoring a vision of Jenny, naked, swinging around a pole with her hair flying and her fantastic breasts bobbing to a rock-and-roll beat.

"You here alone?" Jenny asked.

"No." He pointed toward the booth in which Dorado, Herrera, and the women were squeezed together. "I'm with them."

The woman looked disappointed. "So you got a girlfriend."

"Oh, no," Reuben said quickly. "The women are with those two guys. I'm bodyguarding."

The woman let her eyes drift over his chest and shoulders. "That's easy to believe," she said. "You must be a serious lifter."

Reuben blushed. "I've been in contests."

"Your arms look like boulders." Jenny let her eyes drop a bit, acting coy and shy. "Could I touch one? I've never been with someone with a build like yours."

Reuben smiled and flexed his right biceps. "Sure. Go ahead."

"My God. I can't even get my hand around it." She giggled. "How did you get a build like this?"

Reuben explained how a serious body-builder develops his physique, and the woman hung on his every word. She also moved closer while he was talking until their crotches were almost touching. Reuben was painfully aware that his biceps weren't the only part of his anatomy that was as hard as a rock.

"Reuben," the woman whispered as her hand grazed Corrales's erection. "There's another part of you I'd like to touch."

"Oh, yeah?" Corrales said, his voice suddenly husky and his temperature up several degrees.

"You look flushed," she said. "Why don't we go outside and get some air?"

Corrales cast a nervous glance at the booth. The drinks he'd ordered had arrived, and there were three other bodyguards anyway. Felix wasn't going to miss him.

"It is a little hot in here," Reuben agreed.

Jenny put her tongue in his ear, then whispered, "It may get a lot hotter."

Reuben led the woman to the club's back entrance and stepped through the steel door into the back alley. His lust had narrowed his focus to a spot just below his belt line, and he didn't notice the men who were standing beside the door until one of them stroked a Louisville Slugger across his shin. Reuben collapsed in agony and didn't feel the needle slip in. A moment later, he was unconscious. Jenny put the syringe in her purse as she walked out of the back alley to a waiting car. A second car pulled up beside the unconscious weight lifter. Henry Tedesco popped open the trunk, and Charlie LaRosa and another huge man lifted Reuben and dumped him in.

34

AMANDA, PAUL BAYLOR, AND KATE had already gathered in the conference room at Jaffe, Katz, Lehane, and Brindisi when Doug Weaver wheeled in a dolly with the *Raymond Hayes* files.

"Thanks for bringing those over," Amanda said.

"No problem." Doug looked at Paul. "How are you feeling?"

"Pissed off," Baylor answered. "I really want to find the bastard who did this."

"I don't blame you," Doug said as he un-hooked the bungee cord that held the two banker's boxes in place. When he dumped the files out onto the table, Doug noticed a stack of photographs that Baylor had taken at the crime lab. The picture on top showed the trunk of Mary Clark's car.

"Is that where you found the hammer?"

"Yes," Kate said.

Doug studied the picture. "This is really weird," he said. "Why would Clark do this? Ray is dead and the case is closed. She wasn't even involved. Bernard Cashman was the forensic expert who worked it up. Are you certain that it was Clark who hid the hammer in the trunk? Couldn't it have been someone else?"

"There's no doubt that Mary handled the evidence bag," Baylor said. "They dusted it for prints and hers are all over it."

The next photograph was a close-up that Paul had taken when the evidence bag had been removed from the trunk. The hammer was clearly visible through the plastic.

"It's strange seeing the hammer after all this time," Doug said. "I didn't pay much attention to it during the case."

Amanda looked at him oddly. "Wasn't it the key piece of evidence?"

"Yes, and I was going to have an expert take a look at it until Ray decided to plead guilty."

"You never had the state's findings double-checked by an expert?" Baylor asked, trying to hide his amazement.

Doug colored, embarrassed by criticism he probably deserved.

"I didn't think it was necessary if we were pleading guilty," he explained. "I stipulated that the hammer was the murder weapon in the penalty phase. There wasn't any doubt about that. The police found it next to the body and Mrs. Hayes's blood was all over it."

"Could you tell us about the *Hayes* case?" Amanda asked. She could see how bad Weaver felt and she wanted to give him a chance to talk about something other than his failure to get the hammer tested.

"There's not much to tell. It wasn't that complicated. Ray grew up on a farm in eastern Oregon. When his dad died his mom tried to make a go of it, but she was along in years and they didn't have much money. Ray wasn't a big help either. He was a hard worker but not very bright. The shrink I used thought that he wasn't mentally handicapped but he was very low normal.

"Eventually, Ray's mother sold the farm and they made enough to move to Portland. Ray worked at a gas station until he screwed up and got fired. Then he worked in a supermarket as a box boy, but that didn't work out either. He was unemployed when his mom was killed."

"He did kill her, right?" Kate asked.

Doug looked upset again. "I'm pretty certain he did, but right before he died Ray said he didn't kill his mother."

Weaver's voice caught. His features crumpled for a moment, and Amanda thought he might cry.

"Sorry," Doug said.

"That's okay," Kate said. She knew what it was like to see someone die and know that you were responsible. When she was on the police force, she'd shot a twelve-year-old boy to death. It didn't make any difference that the kid was an assassin hired by a gang to kill a snitch because a juvenile couldn't be tried as an adult and could literally get away with murder. Justified or not, Kate knew that the cost of being responsible for the loss of a human life was a piece of your soul.

"A neighbor called the cops when she heard screams coming from Ray's house,"

Doug said when he regained his composure. "The police caught Ray running away.

"The first time I talked to Ray he told me that he was asleep in his room when his mother's screams awakened him. He said he found her dead in the entryway and heard someone running out the back door. He claimed that he was chasing a man when the police stopped him."

"Did you believe him?" Kate asked.

"I wasn't sure what to believe. No one saw anyone else going in or out of the house, but none of the neighbors paid attention until the cops came."

"Did the police find evidence that there had been anyone but Ray and his mom at home?" Amanda asked.

"No, but that doesn't mean that there wasn't someone else there. Mrs. Hayes had just come back from shopping. Her shopping bags were in the hallway and the door was open. A clerk at the local market told the detectives that he'd given her forty-three dollars in change. Mrs. Hayes's purse was found near her body. It was open and her wallet was on the floor. There weren't any bills in it. Her diamond wedding ring was also missing.

"I thought maybe someone saw her get the cash and followed her home, but there weren't any witnesses to support the theory. The cops never found the money or the ring, but Ray had enough time to hide it before the police arrested him. Not many officers were involved in the search of the neighborhood and they didn't look for long."

"If Ray said he was innocent, why did he plead guilty?"

"I told him he should."

Doug paused to see if anyone would condemn him. When no one said anything, he continued.

"See, Ray did make a short statement to the police before they took him downtown. They gave him the *Miranda* warnings after they cuffed him and they asked him if he'd killed his mom. He swore he didn't hurt her, so they asked him about the hammer. He said he'd never noticed it, which was possible if he ran outside after someone. The cop who arrested him tried to clarify what he meant, so he asked Ray if he held the hammer. Ray said he never touched it. When Cashman found Ray's prints on the handle of the hammer, they had him.

"I knew we'd get killed at trial. Ray is so

slow that he would have been destroyed if he took the stand. I tried to get Poe to offer Ray life if he pled but he refused. He said that Ray deserved to die for what he'd done. Maybe I should have gone to trial but it seemed so hopeless. I gambled that the jury would be lenient if they knew Ray had accepted responsibility by pleading guilty. It was Ray's only brush with the law. So I convinced him to plead."

"Did he protest?" Amanda asked.

"Not really, which is another reason I think he really did kill his mother. All he said was that he trusted me and would do what I thought was best. But I miscalculated." Doug closed his eyes for a minute. "Martin was brilliant and I wasn't. He knew how to push the jurors' buttons. By the time he was through he made it sound totally unreasonable to let Ray live."

"But you think he did it?" Kate persisted.

Doug paused. Then he nodded. "Most of the time I do, but sometimes . . ." He shook his head. "He was so serene when he died. I don't know how anyone could do what they say he did and be so at peace with himself."

"What happened to the hammer after the trial?" Kate asked.

"I assume it was part of the evidence that was sent to the Supreme Court when the case went up on automatic review. When the appeals were exhausted the evidence was probably returned to the crime lab."

"Carlos said he'd assigned Mary to look through a number of old cases to see if they could destroy or return the evidence," Baylor reminded Kate.

"That's right. She probably came across it when she was doing the review," Kate said.

"Which still doesn't explain why she would take a hammer from a closed case to which she had no connection," Amanda said.

Kate looked at the packed boxes and sighed. "It looks like I'm going to be here late trying to find the answer to that question."

35

FRANK JAFFE WAS JERKED OUT OF a sound sleep by the jangling of his phone. He tried to ignore the ringing, but the caller was persistent. When Frank rolled toward the phone, the clock on his nightstand read 2:06.

"Who is this?" he asked, making no attempt to hide his annoyance.

"Call the cops and meet them at the vacant house on Forty-second and Trafalgar. There's only one on the block. A present is waiting for you: Rueben Corrales and Luis Castro—the two men who killed Vincent Ballard—and the gun they used to kill him.

Tell the cops that a parolee named Clarence Edwards was living at the Continental Motel on the night Ballard was murdered. He saw Corrales and Castro leaving Ballard's room."

"How . . . ?" Frank started to ask as the line went dead. He hadn't recognized the voice, but he didn't have to be Albert Einstein to figure out that Martin Breach was behind the call. That meant Henry Tedesco had found Ballard's killers.

Frank dialed Mike Greene's home number. Mike wasn't any happier than Frank to have his sleep disturbed, but he was awake instantly when Jaffe told him why he was calling. As soon as he hung up, Frank splashed water on his face; pulled on a pair of jeans, a flannel shirt, and sneakers; and headed for Forty-second and Trafalgar.

Forty-second and Trafalgar crossed in one of Portland's least desirable neighborhoods. There were more weeds than grass in most yards and plenty of BEWARE OF THE DOG signs. Frank had no trouble finding the vacant house, because there was an ambulance parked at the curb next to two marked cars.

A chill wind and temperatures in the thirties had not stopped a crowd from gathering. Two uniformed officers were blocking access to the house and keeping the rubberneckers at bay. Frank was getting out of his car when one of the uniforms walked over.

"You'll have to move, sir. This is a crime scene."

"I know. I'm Frank Jaffe. I got the tip about the two men and called Mike Greene from the district attorney's office."

"Mr. Greene isn't here yet. You'll have to wait until he arrives."

"Are the two men alive?" Frank asked.

"You'll have to ask the DA for that information."

Frank was about to press the officer when Mike parked behind him.

"This gentleman says he wants to go inside," the officer said as soon as he'd checked Mike's ID.

"It's okay," Greene said. "What did you find in the house?"

"The front door was open when we got here but the lights were off inside. The two men were lying on the kitchen floor with gags in their mouths. They'd been handcuffed together. The keys to the handcuffs were on the kitchen table. They've both been roughed up but the EMTs checked them and said there aren't any serious injuries."

"Do we know who they are?" Mike asked.

"They had their wallets on them. One guy's a bodybuilder name of Reuben Corrales. The other guy is Luis Castro. They've both done time and they're known associates of Felix Dorado."

"Did you find a gun?" Frank asked.

The officer looked at Mike. He nodded.

"Yes, sir, it was with the keys. A guy from the crime lab photographed and bagged it like you asked and it's on the way to the lab."

"Are the men in any condition to be interviewed?" Mike asked.

"Yeah, but I don't know if you'll get anything out of them. They did answer the medic's questions but they clammed up when the detectives got here."

Mike turned to Frank. "You can come in but don't say anything. I'll do the talking."

"That's fine with me," Frank said.

"Then let's go meet these gentlemen."

A chain-link fence surrounded a lawn that had not been cared for in a while. As Mike opened the gate, two EMTs walked out of the house. Mike had a brief conversation with them before walking up a slate path to the front door of a dilapidated bungalow. A criminalist was busy snapping pictures of a front room that was bare of furniture. When Mike opened the door, the wind blew dust balls across the floor with the force of a slap shot.

A policeman was standing near the kitchen sink, guarding two men who were seated on rusted bridge chairs at a cheap table in the kitchen. One of the men was as big as a refrigerator. The second man was five-ten and wiry. They'd been staring morosely at the tabletop but they looked up when Mike and Frank walked in.

Also seated at the table was Zeke Forbus. His partner, Billie Brewster, was leaning against the wall. Brewster signaled Mike and Frank to step out of the room, and she followed them into the living room.

"What's happening?" Mike asked.

"Nothing much," the detective answered. "I told Zeke to have a go at them. I thought two Hispanics were more likely to open up to a good old boy than they would to a woman. But he hasn't got shit from them."

"Okay," Mike said. "Let me take a crack."

"Be my guest."

"Hi," Mike said, taking one of the unoccupied chairs at the table. He flipped open his wallet to show them his identification. "I'm Mike Greene with the Multnomah County District Attorney's Office. How are you feeling?"

"I'm not saying anything without a lawyer," Luis Castro said.

"That's your privilege, Mr. Castro, but my take on this is that you and Mr. Corrales are victims of kidnapping and assault, and I'll need your help to catch the people who did this to you."

The men didn't say anything.

"Look, I know you have records and I know you work for Felix Dorado."

Corrales looked up, surprised, before dropping his eyes back to the table. Mike decided to focus on the weight lifter.

"You probably think that I don't really care about what happened to you because you're an ex-con who works for a drug dealer. But I take my job seriously, Mr. Corrales. If we find the men who did this I'll go after them as hard as I would if they'd kidnapped a priest. You can believe that."

Corrales continued to stare at the table.

Mike tried to get the men talking for a few more minutes before giving up. Frank had been watching the interrogation from a corner of the room. Mike, Frank, and the two detectives walked out to the front lawn, where Corrales and Castro wouldn't hear them.

"That went well," Brewster said.

"What did you expect?" Mike answered with a tired smile. "They're professional criminals. To these boys there's no difference between ratting out Dorado or the person who kidnapped them. A snitch is a snitch. Right now, they're probably thinking that they'll take care of it themselves."

"They'd think again if you could make a case that they murdered Vincent Ballard," Frank said to Greene.

"You mean if the gun comes back as the murder weapon?"

Frank nodded.

"I hope you're not counting on a dismissal in *Prochaska* if the ballistics test comes out positive, because that won't happen," Mike told Frank. "I wasn't lying back there. I see Corrales and Castro as kidnapping victims and I'll bet Martin Breach is behind this. I'm also pretty sure that the gun will come back as the murder weapon, but all that says to me is that Prochaska killed Ballard and Breach had the weapon planted, hoping we'd cut Prochaska loose and arrest two of Dorado's men. I'm not going to help Martin Breach in his war with Felix Dorado, Frank. Without something else tying Corrales and Castro to Ballard's murder, I'll have to release them."

"There's an eyewitness who may be able to put Castro and Corrales at the Continental," Frank said.

Brewster's eyes widened. "How long have you known this?" she asked.

"Kate talked to a resident at the Continental. She didn't see anything, but Clarence Edwards, who was renting a room across from Ballard, told her he saw two men—one with a bodybuilder's physique—leaving Ballard's room on the evening of the murder.

"Tonight, the anonymous caller told me that Edwards might be able to make Corrales and Castro. Kate's been trying to track down Edwards. He's on parole. You can work through his parole officer to find him."

Mike looked upset. "You shouldn't have held back on this, Frank. What were you going to do, spring him on me at trial?"

"No. If Edwards panned out I'd have given you discovery, but right now I have no idea where to find Edwards or what he'll say."

Mike went quiet, and Frank let him work out what he wanted to do. It was cold outside, but no one noticed.

"Okay," Mike said. "Here's the deal. If the gun we found checks out as the murder weapon I'll hold Corrales and Castro as long as I can, but I won't be able to hold them for long. A first-grader could convince any judge in the courthouse to release these guys based on what I have now. If the gun is good I'll probably be able to beat a false arrest charge, but even that will be close."

"Will you look for Edwards?"

"I'll call his PO first thing in the morning."

"Thanks, Mike."

"I'm just doing my job, Frank, which is to get the man who killed Vincent Ballard. I don't care if it's Prochaska or Corrales. I do care that I get the right one."

36

WHILE HE WAITED ON HIS SIDE OF the cramped noncontact visiting room for the guards to bring Jacob, Solomon Cohen thought about the ways in which his relationship with his son had tested his faith in God. Solomon and Valerie had lived through Jacob's battles with the demons in his mind, his marriage outside the faith, and his incarceration for a vile crime, attempted rape. Now the police were saying that he had committed not just murder—which would have been terrible under any circumstances—but an atrocity.

The rabbi thought back to the baby Jacob,

so beautiful, so sweet. When had it gone wrong and how much were he and Valerie to blame? Parents were under so much pressure. You had to think about everything you did and said, because you were never certain what effect your words or actions might have on a young mind.

The rabbi could not understand how a just God could punish His servant in the cruelest way possible. Solomon would have gladly traded his life for Jacob's peace of mind. It was always easier for a parent to suffer pain than to watch his child in torment. Solomon could have taken the easy way out and accepted Jacob's troubles as a test from God, but he did not believe that God would be so cruel—though history had provided plenty of evidence to the contrary. When all was said and done, Rabbi Cohen had no idea why he and his wife—good, loving parents—had a son who was so sorely afflicted that he could do what the police believed he had done to that poor woman.

At Doug's urging, Jacob had agreed to talk to his father. Solomon wanted this meeting—he had longed for reconciliation during the long, painful years when Jacob rejected him and Valerie completely—but he was very worried that he would do or say something that would lead to a further estrangement. The rabbi wished that Valerie had come in with him, but he didn't want to overwhelm his son. Jacob's mother was in the reception area. If all went well, the rabbi would ask Jacob if he would like to talk to her.

A door opened, and a guard brought Jacob into an identical narrow space on the other side of the thick glass. He was terribly thin. His head was down, and his shoulders were stooped. He did not make eye contact with his father.

The guard guided Jacob onto a stool and told him to use the telephone affixed to the wall on his side of the glass. As soon as Jacob held the phone to his ear, the rabbi spoke.

"How are you? Are they treating you well? Are you getting enough to eat? Are you . . ."

The rabbi realized that he was running on without giving Jacob a chance to answer, so he stopped.

"They keep me in isolation so no one can hurt me," Jacob answered quietly. It was odd hearing his voice after all these years. Solomon had almost forgotten how it sounded.

"And the food, is it okay? I've heard that jail food isn't so good."

Jacob shrugged. "I don't mind. I was eating out of garbage cans, so anything would be an improvement."

Solomon wondered if Jacob had just made a joke. It was hard to tell, because Jacob would not look at him. But there had been an inflection in his son's voice.

"We like Mr. Weaver and Miss Jaffe. What do you think of them?" the rabbi asked.

"They're very kind. They try to protect me. I like them."

"I'm glad."

Jacob didn't say anything else, and Solomon couldn't think of anything else to talk about. He'd been instructed not to discuss the case, and he had no idea what interested Jacob these days. They'd had a shared interest in the Portland Trail Blazers basketball team when Jacob was younger. Valerie had no interest in sports, so Solomon and Jacob had gone to the games without her. They would always eat at a restaurant of Jacob's choosing before the game. The experience of spending time alone with his son had been incredibly rewarding for the rabbi. He wondered how Jacob remembered those times.

"Is there anything your mother or I can do for you?" the rabbi asked.

"Not really."

"Would you like me to bring you some books? I can ask Mr. Weaver if that's okay. Is there anything you'd like to read?"

Jacob looked directly at his father for the first time.

"I had books in my car. I would like to read those books." He sounded excited. "Would you see if you could get me some of my books? I don't think the jailers will find them objectionable. Many of them are about God and religion."

"Does religion interest you?"

Jacob nodded. "I often wonder why I am so beset by trials and why God has deserted me."

Solomon was stunned that Jacob was troubled by the same grim thoughts that worried him.

"Have you drawn any conclusions?"

Jacob smiled sadly. "I think that God believes I am a bad person because I killed all of those people. I think he's making me suffer for what I've done."

Solomon felt tears well up in his eyes. He pressed his palm against the glass. He and

Jacob had pressed their palms together to show solidarity, when his son was little. It was their special handshake.

"You're not bad, Jacob. You made a mistake. The consequences were terrible but you never wanted anyone to be hurt. I don't believe that God would make you suffer for something you didn't intend."

"I'd like to believe you but too much has happened to me. Not only has God punished me for an act I didn't intend; he has punished me over and over for things I didn't do. There has to be a reason for that."

"You mother and I don't believe you hurt that woman. We want you to know that."

"Thank you," Jacob said. Then he pressed his palm against the glass so it covered his father's hand.

"I know I've been a terrible son. Please forgive me."

Solomon was too choked up to answer. Suddenly Jacob gulped down air as he tried to fight back tears.

"I'd like to go now," he said.

"Can we visit you again?"

Jacob thought for a moment. Solomon held his breath.

"I'd like that," Jacob said, and the rabbi exhaled.

Jacob signaled for the guard, and Rabbi Cohen watched as his son was led back to his cell. When the door closed behind Jacob, Solomon had one regret: he hadn't told Jacob he loved him. There had been a moment when he had thought about saying the words, but he'd been afraid that Jacob would say nothing or say something hurtful. In the end, he'd decided not to risk rejection when the visit was going so well. Perhaps he would tell Jacob the next time.

As Solomon walked to the waiting area to tell Valerie about the meeting, he thought about what had happened. The meeting had been short, but it had gone well. He did not let himself become excited or hopeful. After a psychiatrist friend put a name to Jacob's mental disorder, Solomon had read everything he could about paranoid schizophrenia. The world inside Jacob's mind was not Solomon's or Valerie's world. It was a land of dreams and nightmares. The angels and devils that dwelled there could whisper in Jacob's ear at any moment. In today's meeting, angels had guided his son, but Solomon knew that Jacob's personal demons could warp his view of his parents at any time and destroy any good feelings that had come out of the rabbi's visit.

Valerie looked up expectantly when Solomon appeared. He decided to tell her how well the meeting had gone and hide his fears and misgivings.

37

"GOOD MORNING, ART," FRANK Jaffe said when the guards let his client into the contact-visit room. "There's been a development in your case. I don't want you to get your hopes up, but I might have good news for you by the end of the day."

Prochaska sat calmly, his hands folded on the table, seemingly oblivious of the horrible fate that awaited him if his lawyer did not win his case. Frank suspected that some of his serene demeanor stemmed from inside knowledge about the kidnapping of Reuben Corrales and Luis Castro.

"A few nights ago, I was awakened by an

anonymous caller who told me that I could find the two men who murdered Vincent Ballard and the gun they used in a vacant house at Forty-second and Trafalgar. I called the DA and he sent some officers to the house."

"Did you find the guys?" Prochaska asked. Frank searched his client's face for any sign of irony, but he saw nothing to make him think that Prochaska was mocking him.

"Yes, Art, we did. We found a bodybuilder named Reuben Corrales and another man, named Luis Castro, tied up in the kitchen. They'd been abducted and worked over by persons unknown. There was a gun in the kitchen, too. A ballistics test proved that it fired the shots that killed Ballard."

Prochaska smiled. "That's great, Frank. When do I get out?"

"It's not that simple. There's still the indictment charging you with the murder of Juan Ruiz." Art did not react. "Then there's the fact that Corrales and Castro work for Felix Dorado, who is rumored to be in a war to take over Portland's drug trade from Martin."

"That would give them a reason to frame me, wouldn't it?"

"Well, yes, Art. But it also gives Martin a

reason to frame them. Mike Greene thinks that Martin planted the gun to get you off. So, right now, whoever kidnapped Corrales and Castro hasn't helped your case."

"You said there was good news," Art said, unfazed by Mike Greene's stubborn refusal to cut him loose.

"There may be. The anonymous caller told me that there's an eyewitness named Clarence Edwards who saw Corrales and Castro leaving Ballard's room on the night of the murder. Kate gave me the same information. Two days ago, Edwards was arrested in California on a warrant issued by his parole officer for leaving the state without permission. Mike Greene is going to interview him this morning and have him view Corrales and Castro in a lineup. If he picks them out as the men he saw at the motel there's a good chance you might get out of here."

"I'm sure he'll say it was them, since it wasn't me."

"Mike wants you in the lineup, too."

Art frowned. "Why does he want to do that?"

"To see if Edwards picks you instead of Corrales. It's a gamble, Art. I have to tell you that our case will be damn near impossible to win if Edwards picks you. But Greene will have to dismiss if Edwards picks Corrales."

"What do you think I should do?"

Frank looked into Prochaska's eyes. "If you're innocent—if you were nowhere near that motel when Ballard was killed and you had nothing to do with the murder—you might want to take the chance. But you should refuse if you killed Ballard."

Prochaska smiled. "I told you I didn't do it, Frank. I wasn't lying."

For some strange reason, Frank believed Prochaska.

Clarence Edwards and Edgar Lewis had packed up and run the moment Henry Tedesco and Charlie LaRosa left their motel room. Edwards had experienced nightmares in which he was being burned alive ever since. Now he was back in custody, twisting nervously in an intentionally uncomfortable chair in a stuffy interrogation room at the Justice Center, where he had been left alone with his thoughts for almost an hour. He was hungry and thirsty and scared and positive that the man who looked like a rat was going to barbecue him sometime soon.

The door opened and Mike Greene and Billie Brewster walked in.

"What's going on here, man?" Clarence demanded.

"Good morning, Mr. Edwards," Mike said.

"I want my lawyer."

Brewster stood against the wall and Mike sat opposite Edwards at the table. He placed a thick file on the table and patted it.

"This is yours, Mr. Edwards. It's a record of your life of crime. As a result of your attempt to flee from the responsibilities of your parole, it's thicker than it was last month. It will get fatter still if you give me any shit, because I'll walk out of here without offering you a way out of the mess you made for yourself."

"I didn't make no mess. I was fleeing for my life."

"Do you want to explain that to me?" Mike asked.

Clarence imagined how he would feel if he was strapped into a bed and set on fire. He folded his arms across his chest, looked at the floor.

"I ain't saying nothing without a lawyer," he mumbled.

It was clear that Clarence was very scared. Mike would love to know why.

"Here's the deal, Mr. Edwards. If you still want an attorney when I'm finished telling it to you I'll see you get to make your call. But I think you're going to want to cooperate with me when you hear what I have to say. If you accept my offer and are completely truthful you will not be prosecuted for your parole violation and you will be released from custody."

"What do I have to do?"

"First, you have to answer some questions."

"Like what?"

Mike told Clarence the date of Vincent Ballard's murder and asked him where he was living on that day. The DA knew that Edwards was staying at the motel, and he wanted to start the questioning with a softball, but Clarence didn't see this as an easy question. Any question about Ballard's murder terrified him. If he admitted that he was at the Continental, he was certain he was going to be asked what he saw, and he didn't know how the rat-faced man wanted him to answer. But, the DA would have the motel records, and they would show where he was living. Clarence saw no profit in lying.

"Probably the Continental Motel," Edwards told Greene.

"Okay. Now you know that a man named Vincent Ballard was shot to death in a room across the courtyard from your room?"

"Yeah."

"You could see his room from yours, right?"

"I guess."

"We've interviewed guests of the motel and we know you told one of them about something you saw that night. I'd like you to tell me what that was," the prosecutor said.

This was the moment of truth. So far, Clarence had not committed himself, but he knew that he would be up to his ears in the Ballard murder investigation if he admitted seeing the two men leave the motel room. He might even have to testify in court with the rat-faced man in the room. The problem was that he'd be back in jail for a parole violation—and probably get his parole revoked—if he didn't give the DA something useful.

Clarence was no dummy. He hadn't graduated from high school, but he'd developed plenty of street smarts since he'd left home at sixteen. One thing you learned on the street was how to play people. Sometimes it meant the difference between getting beaten or killed and surviving. Clarence decided to play Mike Greene.

"If I tell you what I seen, what's in it for me?" he asked, stalling for time so he could work on his plan.

"Every time you give me an honest answer you're one step closer to freedom."

"Well, I did see something. If I tell you, I want out of here."

"It's not that simple, Clarence. You tell me what you know. If you're honest with me you'll be home free."

Clarence pretended to be thinking, but he already knew what he was going to do.

"I got up to take a leak and heard this music coming from across the court. It was loud, too loud for that time of night."

"What time was that?"

"All I know is it was real late."

"Okay, what did you see?"

"Two men. One guy was normal. I can't help you too much there. But the other guy was real big, like he pumped iron or used steroids. I got a better look at him, but it wasn't great."

"Do you think you could pick out either man in a lineup?"

"The little one, probably not. The big guy, yeah, I might be able to do that, but I can't promise. It was dark, I was sleepy and I just had a quick peek."

"I'd like to have you try, anyway."

"What do you mean?"

"I'd like you to view a lineup."

Alarm bells went off. Clarence hadn't realized that the cops had arrested anyone. He thought he could just give vague answers and the DA would let him split.

"When?"

"Now."

"I don't know, man. This is heavy shit. I wouldn't feel right knowing someone was executed because I fingered him."

"Clarence, I have no ax to grind. I want complete honesty. If you're certain, pick someone. If you're not certain, definitely do not pick someone. It won't affect our deal."

Clarence thought long and hard and decided that he could eat his cake and have it too. He wanted to smile, but he fixed Mike Greene with a look that said he was a good citizen who wanted to do his duty.

"Okay," Clarence said, "I'll take a look-see."

After Mike assured him that the men on the other side of the thick glass could not see him, Clarence Edwards walked up to it and peered through. Luis Castro was second from the right in the first group. Frank Jaffe, Billie Brewster, and Mike Greene watched Edwards with an intensity commensurate with the stakes involved in the police procedure. After staring at the lineup for almost a minute, Edwards stepped away from the glass and shook his head.

"I can't say anyone in there is the shorter guy. I never did get a good look at him."

The defense attorney and the DA exhaled.

"Okay," Mike said, "you did your best."

Greene had not expected Edwards to identify the smaller man, after what he'd told them. This had been a test to see if Edwards would finger someone just to get out of jail. The DA leaned down and spoke into a microphone, asking for the next group. Moments later, six men who looked like a pro football line shuffled onto a stage across from the room in which Frank, Brewster, Mike, and

Clarence Edwards were watching them. Art Prochaska was second from the left and Reuben Corrales was the last man on the right.

As soon as Corrales walked onto the stage, Clarence knew that this was the man he'd seen outside Vincent Ballard's room, but he let his gaze linger on the bodybuilder for only a moment. Clarence's mouth was dry and his heart was beating fast. He pretended to study each of the huge men carefully, but he had already decided that it was safer to say that he didn't recognize anyone in the lineup. That way he wouldn't have to go to court. To make it seem that he was trying, Clarence asked to have the men step forward and turn to the side. Then he asked to have Corrales and another man step out again. After a few more minutes, he turned to Mike Greene.

"I can't say for sure that it's any of them. I mean, that guy on the end could be him," he said, pointing at Corrales so it would seem as though he was being honest if Corrales was ever arrested, "but I'm not going to swear under oath about the man."

Frank tried not to show how disappointed he was, but at least Edwards had not selected Prochaska. Mike thanked Edwards and had an officer take him back to his cell, after assuring him that he appreciated his effort and promising to talk to his parole officer in the morning.

"We're back to square one," Mike said as soon as Edwards was out of the room.

"He picked Corrales as the person who most looked like the man he saw at the Continental, Mike. Dorado is trying to frame Art and you're helping him."

"You're conveniently forgetting that Prochaska's prints were found on the beer can on Ballard's night table."

Frank didn't show it, but the discovery of the gun that had killed Ballard and the arrest of two men who fit Clarence Edwards's description of the men at the Continental had made him forget about the thumbprint—the most damning evidence against his client. He talked with Mike a little longer, but all the time they were talking, part of his brain was trying to reconcile his belief that Arthur Wayne Prochaska was innocent with the presence in Ballard's motel room of evidence that Prochaska had been in the room where Ballard had been brutally murdered. His last hope was Paul Baylor. If the forensic expert didn't find some way to challenge the print, Art was dead.

"Have you had a chance to go over the forensic evidence in the *Prochaska* case?" Frank asked as soon as Baylor picked up the phone.

"I reviewed the ballistics match and the fingerprint evidence this morning."

"What did you find?"

"Nothing that's going to help you. I looked at the readouts from the neutron activation analysis that was conducted at the Reed reactor. The bullet that killed Ballard matches the bullet from Prochaska's closet."

"What about the print on the beer can?"

"The print isn't on the can anymore, of course. Cashman lifted it with fingerprint tape and put it on a card for comparison and preservation. But he took a photograph of the can with the print before he did the lift. I compared the print in the photograph with Prochaska's fingerprints, and they match. I also compared the print on the card with Prochaska's prints, and they match."

"Damn. Art swears he was never in that room."

"Someone could have taken the beer can

after Art touched it and planted it," Baylor suggested.

"I thought of that. Art doesn't drink that brand and he can't remember holding a can of that beer. He's pretty positive about that."

"Either he's lying or he forgot that he held the can, but his prints are definitely on it."

Frank hung up and stared out of the window. He didn't see anything in the sky that would help him win Art Prochaska's case, but he kept looking, because everything on planet Earth was killing him.

38

DOUG WEAVER WAS HAVING AN-
other nightmare, but this one was different.
Instead of being at the penitentiary on the
day of Raymond Hayes's execution, he was
in the woods, trapped in a blizzard. Doug
struggled through the knee-high drifts, trip-
ping forward, pausing to wipe the snow off
his glasses.

In his dream, the wind chill drove the temperature below zero. Each breath of frozen
air seared his lungs. He was weak, but he
was compelled to struggle on in order to
save Ray, who was always just out of reach.
Doug caught glimpses of him through the

trees when the wind let up. He called out, but Ray didn't hear him.

Doug knew that neither of them would last long in the storm, but he also knew, without understanding how, that there was a way out if he could just discover it. It had something to do with the snow, which was like a fine powder. Doug was getting desperate. He tried to spin in a circle to search for a path to safety, but the snow was falling more rapidly, and he could not see through it. He screamed harder for help, and he was screaming when he sat up in bed with the full realization that he knew what was wrong with the hammer and the evidence bag. It had been so obvious that no one had seen what was literally right in front of everyone's eyes.

His first insight was followed by two more: Raymond Hayes was dead because Doug was an incompetent hack who had been too lazy to have Bernard Cashman's work double-checked, and Cashman had murdered Ray as surely as if he had shot him.

Doug felt numb. He wandered into the kitchen in the dark. There was enough light from the moon to see the cabinet where he kept his liquor. He sat at the kitchen table and poured his first glass of scotch since agreeing to work on Jacob's murder case. By the time he finished his second glass, he was sobbing quietly. What had happened to his life? Where had all the promise gone? His future had seemed so shiny after law school. All that was left now was loneliness, guilt, and failure.

Anger at Cashman replaced self-pity halfway through his third glass of scotch, and Doug began thinking of ways to avenge Ray. He looked at the kitchen clock and tried to read the time. The alcohol had affected him, and it was a struggle to make out the position of the hands of the clock in the dark. He finally decided that it was a little before two.

If Doug had been sober and had thought a little longer, he would have understood how foolish he would be to confront Cashman, but Doug was so angry and intoxicated that he was not thinking straight. He turned on the light and found his phone book. Cashman was not listed. He looked up the number for the state crime lab, and dialed it. After several rings, an automated directory gave him a number of choices. Doug pressed O.

"I know it's late," Doug said when the night operator answered, "but it's urgent that

I speak to Bernard Cashman, one of your criminalists, about a case he's working on."

"I can't give out Mr. Cashman's home number," the operator said. "You can call back in the morning when he's in."

"This can't wait. Can you call him and tell him it's Doug Weaver and I have to talk to him about the hammer in the *Hayes* case? I'm certain he'll take the call."

When the operator put him on hold, Doug started to have second thoughts. Maybe he should wait until morning. He could tell Amanda what he'd figured out, and they could go to the district attorney. He had almost decided to hang up when the operator told him that Mr. Cashman would not accept his call. Doug breathed a sigh of relief and hung up the phone. He'd been a fool to act so rashly. He should run his theory by Paul Baylor, anyway. Doug himself was no scientist. Maybe he was wrong. He'd go back to bed and try to sleep. He wanted to be fresh in the morning.

Before he went back to the bedroom, Doug made one more call, to Amanda Jaffe's office. A recorded menu told him her voice-mail extension. He pressed her number, and Amanda's voice asked him to leave a message.

"Amanda, this is Doug Weaver. I'm calling in the middle of the night. I know you're not in, but I've got to see you first thing in the morning. I just had a nightmare. I was in the woods in a terrible snowstorm and Raymond Hayes was just out of reach. In the dream, the snow was so dense that I couldn't see anything, but there was something weird about the snow. It wasn't made up of thick flakes. It had the consistency of powder. That's when I figured it out. I know what's wrong with the hammer. I . . ."

Doug had call waiting on his phone, and he heard an insistent beep on the line.

"Someone's calling me on my other line. I'll tell you what I figured out in the morning. It's about Bernie Cashman. Have Paul Baylor there."

He heard the annoying beep again, and pressed FLASH to switch to the other call.

"Doug Weaver?" a voice asked.

"Yes. Who's this?"

"Bernie Cashman. You just called me. I was pretty groggy from being woken up. That's why I didn't take your call. But I couldn't get back to sleep. I kept thinking that the call must be important if you phoned at this hour."

Doug didn't know what to say.

"Are you there?" Cashman asked. He didn't sound upset or scared. He sounded calm, like someone with a clear conscience.

"Yes, I . . . Well, I represented Raymond Hayes," Weaver mumbled while he tried to get his thoughts together.

"I know. You told the operator that this was about the hammer in Mr. Hayes's case."

"I know you lied about finding Ray's print on the hammer," Doug blurted out.

"I don't know what to say." Cashman sounded shocked.

"I can prove it," Doug said.

"I doubt that, since I did find Mr. Hayes's print. Are you forgetting that your client admitted the murder?"

Doug was almost overcome with guilt. He wanted to explain how he'd persuaded Ray to plead, but he was not going to let Cashman distract him.

"I'm going to the district attorney in the morning. I'll tell him what I know and you can explain yourself to him."

"If you were planning on going to the district attorney, why did you call me?"

"I . . . I was going to give you a chance to

explain why you did it, why you murdered Ray."

"I had nothing to do with the death of Mr. Hayes. The state executed your client. I know you attended the execution. It must have been difficult for you to watch him die, but I had nothing to do with it."

"We'll let the prosecutor decide that. I don't think I should talk to you anymore."

"Look, why don't I come to the district attorney's office tomorrow? I'll be glad to answer any questions you have, in his presence, to show you that I'm innocent of whatever it is you think I've done."

Now Doug was completely confused. "You'd come to see the DA?" he repeated.

"Of course. I have absolutely nothing to hide. When would you like me to be at his office?"

"I . . . I'm not sure. I'll have to talk to some people in the morning."

"Fine. Call me at the lab when you have a time. It takes me about twenty minutes to drive downtown."

Doug hung up. His heart was racing. Cashman sounded so sincere. Could he be wrong? Weaver knew that he wouldn't be able to get back to sleep, and he needed another drink desperately. He filled his glass and took a sip. Soon after that, Doug's eyes grew heavy, and he slumped forward, resting his head on his arms.

"Wake up, Mr. Weaver."

A hand shook Doug's shoulder. He raised his head and stared blearily at Bernard Cashman, who was standing in his kitchen wearing a Seattle Mariners baseball cap, latex gloves, and Tyvex booties, and holding a gun.

Adrenaline cleared the cobwebs immediately, and Doug threw himself backward, almost upsetting his chair.

"Careful, Mr. Weaver," Cashman said. "Take deep breaths. I want you to calm down."

"How . . . ?"

Cashman smiled. "You learn many things while investigating crime. The finer points of breaking and entering, for instance."

The criminalist pointed at the bottle of scotch. "Pour yourself a full glass and drink it down. It will help you to relax."

"I've had a lot to drink, I . . ."

"That wasn't a request, Doug, it was an

order." Cashman waved the muzzle of the gun at the bottle. "Fill the glass and drink it down."

Weaver did as he was told.

"Good. Now drink another glass and we can get down to business."

Doug was still intoxicated from the scotch he'd drunk earlier, and two drinks in rapid succession made him very woozy.

"Tell me what you think you know about the hammer," Cashman said.

Doug hesitated.

"Do you want me to shoot you, Doug? I won't shoot to kill, because I want you to talk to me. But I will shoot you in parts of your body that will cause you to feel horrible pain. Now, please tell me what you think you figured out about the fingerprint on the hammer."

Doug was no hero, so he told the criminalist what he thought had happened. Cashman nodded.

"You're very clever and quite correct. Who have you told about your epiphany?"

Doug knew that he had to lie about his call to Amanda's voice mail.

"I left a message at the DA's office. I said I had proof that you lied about the fingerprint. If anything happens to me the police will know it was you."

Cashman frowned. This was not what he wanted to hear, but it made sense. Weaver had told him that he was going to the district attorney's office in the morning. If Weaver had left a message implicating him, he was in trouble. He studied Doug for any sign that he was lying. Doug was a poor poker player, and being drunk made it even harder for him to bluff.

"Did you call anyone else after you phoned the DA?" Cashman asked.

"No. It was late. I didn't want to wake up anyone."

"I don't believe you, Doug. I think you made a call, but I don't think it was to the district attorney."

Doug swallowed. "It was. They'll get it in the morning. If you hurt me they'll know who did it."

"You're a lousy liar, Doug. Now tell me who you really called, and you'd better be honest this time."

Doug looked into Cashman's eyes and saw placid pools devoid of emotion. Images of Mary Clark's mutilated body filled Doug's thoughts, and he accepted the fact that he was going to die. The knowledge gave him the freedom to act. He grabbed the scotch bottle and lunged to his feet, upsetting the table. The move surprised Cashman. He stumbled backward to avoid being struck by the table. Weaver swung the bottle. It came close enough to Cashman's face that he could feel air brush by him. He shot Doug in the chest as Doug was raising the bottle for a second strike. The lawyer followed through anyway and connected with Cashman's shoulder. The impact jarred the bottle out of Doug's grasp, and it shattered on the floor. He lunged at Cashman and wrapped his arms around him. The two men staggered backward, crashing into the refrigerator. Cashman kneed Weaver in the groin. Weaver's grip loosened. Cashman threw Weaver aside and shot him in the stomach. Weaver's knees buckled, and he slumped to the floor. Cashman shot him again.

So this is how it's going to end, Doug thought.

Cashman was in a frenzy. He knelt by Doug's head and pressed the gun between Doug's eyes.

"Who have you told about the hammer?" Cashman demanded desperately.

Weaver wished Karen could see him now. He felt proud of himself, because he had died fighting, and he also felt giddy with the knowledge that he had not betrayed Ray a second time. An old schoolyard taunt came back to him.

"That's for me to know and you to find out," he said just before he died.

Rage swept through Cashman. He stood up and pulled back his leg to kick the dead man, but the rational part of his brain reined him in. He was wearing protective booties, but any contact between him and Weaver's body could leave trace evidence. Cashman remembered that they had touched while they fought. He knelt down and examined Weaver from head to toe. When he was satisfied that he had not deposited any hairs or fibers on the dead lawyer during the struggle, he scanned the kitchen for any evidence he might have left.

Suddenly, he remembered the shots. There had been three of them, and someone might have heard. The police could be on their way. If neighbors heard the shots, they could be watching the house. Cashman turned off the kitchen light and peeked through the blinds. There were lights on in the house next door. Cashman went to the back door. He saw no lights in the homes behind Weaver's. The criminalist ducked out the door and raced through the small back-yard. There was no fence, but there was a hedge. He squeezed through it and ran to his truck, which he'd parked several blocks away. He had been smart to hurry. A police car passed him on the way to Weaver's house shortly after he pulled away from the curb.

As he drove home, Cashman thought about the unfairness of life. Here he was, trying to do the right thing, and his efforts were turning into a nightmare. First, he'd had to deal with Mary. Now Doug Weaver had tried to spoil everything. Where would it end?

Cashman willed himself to calm down and think. Was his situation really that bad? If the night operator learned that Weaver had been murdered, she would probably contact the police and tell them about Weaver's call, but she would also tell the police that Cashman had refused to accept it. He'd made his call to Weaver from a pay phone, so it couldn't be traced to him, and there shouldn't be any evidence in Weaver's house that would lead to him.

Weaver had figured out Cashman's lie about Raymond Hayes's fingerprint, but Cashman didn't know if he'd told his suspicions to anyone else. And, if he had, there was no proof of what he'd done now that he'd gotten rid of the hammer and the evidence bag. All he had to do was stand firm when he was questioned. Deny, deny, deny. How could they prove he was lying? If they produced the photograph that Paul Baylor had snapped when he took the evidence bag from Mary's car, Cashman would say that the powder was on the side you couldn't see, or suggest that Mary had put the hammer in a new evidence bag before hiding it in her trunk. They might suspect that he was lying, but they would never be able to prove it.

Cashman exhaled. Everything would work out for the best, because he was smarter than everyone else, always one step ahead of the pack—no, make that several steps ahead.

39

AMANDA HAD A MEETING WITH A
client scheduled for eight and didn't play
Doug Weaver's voice-mail message until nine.
She listened to it twice. Doug's speech was
slurred, and it sounded as if he'd been drinking. His talk about a dream and a snowstorm
strengthened that impression. But he also
sounded as if he believed that he'd cracked
the mystery surrounding the hammer.

Doug had said that he'd see her first thing
in the morning, but he had not been in the
waiting room when she saw her client out,
and there were no messages from him in her
slot. Amanda dialed his office.

"Doug Weaver, please."

There was silence for a moment.

"Is this Doug Weaver's law office?" Amanda asked, wondering if she'd dialed a wrong number.

"Who's calling?" the receptionist said. She sounded as though she was fighting back tears.

"Amanda Jaffe. We're working on a case together."

"Oh, Miss Jaffe, you can't talk to Mr. Weaver. He passed away."

"He what?"

"Mr. Weaver is dead."

"Oh, my God! What happened?"

Now the receptionist was crying. "Someone broke into his house last night and shot him," she managed. "It's so terrible."

Amanda was stunned.

"Do the police know who killed Doug?" she asked.

"I don't know. There were two detectives here when the office opened. They searched Mr. Weaver's office, but they didn't tell me anything, except that he was dead."

"Are the detectives there now?"

"No."

Amanda talked to the receptionist about Doug a little while longer. When she hung up, she felt disoriented and had to take deep breaths to get her equilibrium back. When she was calmer, she listened to Weaver's call again, then phoned Paul Baylor.

When his phone rang, Paul Baylor was in his lab, testing a sample of cocaine that had been seized during a routine traffic stop. The executive who had been driving the Mercedes swore that the powder wasn't cocaine. His lawyer was certain that the executive was in denial, and Paul's test results supported that theory.

"Doug Weaver was murdered last night," Amanda said as soon as the forensic expert picked up the receiver.

"What happened?" Baylor asked, stunned by the news.

"I don't know much. I got my information from the receptionist at his office. A detective told her that someone broke into his house and shot him."

"That's awful."

"I didn't call just to tell you about the murder, Paul. When I came in this morning, there was a voice mail from Doug. He called late last night to tell me that he knew what was wrong with the hammer."

"He figured it out?"

"He said he did, but he was interrupted by another call before he explained anything. I wrote down what he said. Let me read it to you. I couldn't make any sense out of it. Maybe you can."

Baylor was quiet when Amanda finished. He asked Amanda to read the message to him again.

"Hang on, will you," Baylor said when she was through.

Paul went into his office and spread the photographs of the hammer in the evidence bag across his desk. Doug hadn't seen the hammer or the evidence bag, so his deductions had to have been made from these photographs.

"I don't see a damn thing," Baylor muttered. Then he froze. That was it. Doug hadn't seen anything, either. He grabbed the phone.

"I'm an idiot," Baylor said, barely able to contain his excitement. "It's the powder."

"I don't understand."

Amanda felt a chill pass through her as

Baylor explained his theory. Then she felt sick. Amanda asked Paul to come to her office immediately, and hung up.

Paul hadn't known Doug Weaver long, but he seemed like a nice guy. Now he was dead—murdered—and Baylor was certain that the killing had not been the result of a random burglary gone wrong any more than the theft of the hammer from his lab had been. The odds were pretty damn good that Doug Weaver was dead because he had been smart enough to figure out why Mary Clark had taken a hammer from the evidence locker at the state crime lab.

Paul Baylor was a man of science— thoughtful, objective, and unemotional in most situations. But he wasn't any of that now. At this moment, Paul Baylor was very angry, and he vowed to channel that anger into the energy he would need to make the person who attacked him and murdered Doug Weaver pay, not only for his crimes but for the harm he'd done to the reputation of every criminalist in Oregon.

When Baylor walked into the conference room, he found Amanda and Kate Ross waiting.

"Tell Kate what you told me," Amanda said.

Baylor handed Kate a photograph. It showed the hammer in the evidence bag just after it had been removed from the tire well of Mary Clark's car.

"Doug never saw the hammer and the evidence bag after we took it out of the car," Baylor said, "but he did see this photograph. So, I'm guessing that he figured out everything from what he saw in the picture."

Kate studied the photograph for a few moments before shaking her head.

"I don't get it."

"Do you remember Doug asking if someone other than Mary could have stolen the hammer and put it in the tire well?" Baylor asked.

Kate nodded.

"I told him that we knew that Mary took the hammer because the bag had been dusted for fingerprints and hers were all over the plastic. To raise prints, Cashman had to dust the hammer with black fingerprint powder. Some of the powder should have rubbed off on the plastic when the hammer was placed in the bag, but I don't remember seeing any powder on the hammer or the bag when we found it in Mary's car. What about you?"

"No. I'm pretty sure there wasn't any."

"There was powdery snow in Doug's dream," Amanda said. "I think Doug's subconscious was reminding him that there should have been fingerprint powder on the hammer and the bag. He must have remembered that he hadn't seen any in the photograph."

Kate's brow furrowed. "Are you suggesting that Cashman lied about finding Hayes's print on the handle?"

"If there was no powder on the hammer, that's a real possibility," Baylor said, "but I don't know how to prove it without the hammer and the bag."

"Cashman is one of the most respected criminalists in the state," Kate said.

"Yes, he is," Paul agreed. "I never would have expected something like this from Bernie, but he wouldn't be the first forensic expert to go bad. There have been several cases across the country where people working in crime labs have faked evidence or given false testimony in court. The most famous is a former head serologist of the West Virginia state police crime lab. The West Virginia Supreme Court called his actions shocking and accused him of corrupting the legal system. And there was a criminalist at the Oklahoma City police lab. A man was executed for rape and murder after she testified, but her colleagues reviewed the evidence slides in the case and found no sperm on the critical slide. So, it's not unheard of for something like this to happen."

Everyone was silent for a moment while they tried to look at the *Cohen* case in light of this new information. Amanda had come to some conclusions of her own, and she wanted to see what the others came up with. Kate was the first to break the silence.

"If Cashman lied about the print, he had a motive to attack Paul and steal the hammer."

"It gets worse, Kate," Amanda said. "I've been trying to get around it, but I still keep coming to the conclusion that there's a good chance that Bernie murdered Mary Clark to keep her from talking to Carlos Guzman."

"I don't know," Kate said, but Amanda could tell that her friend wasn't rejecting the idea completely. Once you accepted the possibility that Cashman had faked the results in the *Hayes* case and attacked Paul to steal the evidence of his wrongdoing, it didn't take much imagination to picture the criminalist committing more violent crimes.

"Let's assume that Bernie lied when he told the grand jury that he discovered Hayes's print on the hammer," Amanda said. "Hayes is executed, the case is closed, and Cashman is safe. Then fate intervenes. Carlos Guzman asks Mary to look through a bunch of closed cases to see if evidence from them can be returned or destroyed. One of the cases is *Hayes*. She sees that there isn't any fingerprint powder on the hammer or the evidence bag and she gets suspicious. But Bernie is so well respected by everyone—Mary included—that she doesn't go straight to Guzman. Instead, she confronts him and he kills her. Then he frames Jacob for the murder.

"Think about it, Kate. Where were we hung up with Jacob's case? One of our biggest problems was how the bloody T-shirts got in Jacob's car. Who found the T-shirts?"

"Damn," Kate said.

"The killer didn't wait around until Jacob left his car to plant them," Amanda said. "He just walked up to the car as bold as brass while he was investigating the killing for the state of Oregon and smeared the shirts with some blood he'd taken from Clark."

For a moment, it looked as though Kate was going to agree with Amanda. Then she frowned.

"Your theory only works if Cashman was planning to frame Jacob before he killed Clark. He'd have to have known about Jacob and his mental problems, his hatred of women. He'd have to know where Jacob was living.

"And don't forget the pubic hairs. If Cashman framed Jacob, he had to get Cohen's pubic hairs before he murdered Clark so he could plant them on her thigh. How would he do that?"

"Cashman would have access to Cohen's pubic hairs if there were some in the crime lab evidence locker in the file of his attempted rape case," Baylor said.

"And Cashman did know about Jacob," Amanda said.

She told everyone that she'd heard Doug tell Cashman where Jacob lived and his past history with women, after Jacob's acquittal.

"What good is this theorizing?" Kate said. "The hammer and the evidence bag are gone. That photograph isn't enough to prove that Cashman faked evidence in *Hayes*."

"No," Amanda said, "but we might be

able to prove that he faked evidence in other cases. Paul, do you still have the evidence in Art Prochaska's case at your office?"

"I haven't sent it back to the crime lab yet."

"Good. I want you to look at it again. Assume it was faked. See what you come up with. And while you're at it, can you check the evidence in Jacob's attempted rape case to see if there were any pubic hairs preserved in the file, and if any are missing?"

"I might need a court order to see the old file."

"Call me if you do. Kate, I want you to look into other cases where Cashman was the criminalist. Maybe you can find an attorney who thought there was something fishy about his testimony or findings."

"Will do," the investigator said.

"And Kate," Amanda said, "I want you to make a few copies of Doug's voice-mail message. It was probably his last call, and it mentions a possible suspect. That makes it evidence in a criminal investigation, and I have to turn a copy over to the police."

"I hope we're wrong about this," Baylor said. "Can you imagine the chaos one crooked criminalist can cause? No juror will ever believe a criminalist's testimony again if it becomes public knowledge that criminalists fake evidence or lie under oath about it."

"Let's worry about that later. Right now, all I care about is nailing Cashman."

"This is the proverbial can of worms," Baylor said.

"This is a whole warehouse full of worms. And I'm not just talking about the consequences to the justice system if it turns out that Cashman has been lying in court about forensic evidence. If we're right, Cashman attacked you, and he killed Doug Weaver and Mary Clark because they were threatening to expose him. That means that we could all be in danger if he finds out that we're on to him."

40

IT WAS DIFFICULT FOR AMANDA TO concentrate on her work after the meeting with Paul and Kate, and time crawled as she waited for news. Frank was in Houston, handling the pretrial motions in a multi-defendant white-collar fraud case. Amanda knew her father. He would grab a quick dinner after court and work all evening with the other defense attorneys. She would have loved to talk over Jacob's case with him, but she knew better than to take up his time when he was in the middle of complex litigation that would demand his full attention.

Paul called a little after three with bad

news. Carlos Guzman had let him look at the file in Jacob's attempted rape case. All eight pubic hairs listed on the inventory for the file were present. Paul said he would tell her if he found anything when he went over the evidence in Prochaska's case.

Amanda was disappointed, but she was still convinced that her theory about Cashman was correct. She spent the next hour going over everything she could remember about Cohen's case to see if she could think of a new avenue of investigation. When she glanced at her clock, it was after four. Suddenly, she remembered that she was going out with Mike Greene this evening. It would be nice if her evening out helped her forget Jacob's case, but she didn't hold out much hope.

A friend with a season subscription and a conflicting engagement had given Mike Greene two tickets to the Portland Arts and Lectures series. The speaker had won last year's Pulitzer Prize for her fictional account of a first-generation Asian-American woman growing up in the Midwest. After the lecture, Mike and Amanda had dinner in the Pearl, at an Italian restaurant a few blocks from Amanda's condo.

Mike thought that Amanda seemed distracted all evening, and he was sure of it after watching her eat. Amanda was usually an enthusiastic dinner companion. Tonight, she picked at her meal and turned down dessert—a sure sign that something was wrong.

Mike chalked up Amanda's mood to the ambivalence she felt about their relationship. Mike was afraid to tell Amanda how he felt about her, because he didn't know how she would react. They had started dating when she was in the grip of post-traumatic stress disorder caused by her encounter with the Surgeon. It wasn't the best way to begin a relationship, and he was afraid that the problems she had during the time they were seeing each other would always color the way she thought about him. He had been walking on eggs since Amanda had agreed to go out with him again.

After they finished eating, Mike walked Amanda to her condo and was pleasantly surprised when she invited him in for an after-dinner drink. He settled on the couch while Amanda took a bottle of ice wine out of the freezer and poured them each a glass. After Mike took a sip, he read the label and saw that it came from a local vineyard.

"This is delicious. I'm going to get a few bottles."

"I thought you'd like it," Amanda said, but she wasn't smiling and she looked very tense.

Mike decided to take a chance. "Is something bothering you?"

Amanda hesitated. She wanted to talk to Mike about Cashman, but he was the prosecutor who was representing the state in *Prochaska*.

"Does it have to do with us?" Mike asked, trying hard to mask his anxiety.

Amanda shook her head. "No, Mike. I've really enjoyed going out with you again."

Mike's shoulders, which had hunched from tension, sagged with relief, but Amanda was too preoccupied to notice.

"Then what's going on?" Mike asked.

Now was the moment to ask for Mike's help, but Amanda hesitated. She was certain that Mike would help her if she asked, because he cared for her; but if she didn't care for him, she would be using him.

Amanda thought about Toby Brooks. They'd had fun together, and great sex at times, but she had never felt a real connection with Toby after the initial thrill of their first few dates had worn off. She had always felt a connection with Mike. She didn't have to dress up or playact for Mike. He'd seen her at her worst and he still cared. She could be natural with Mike. The bottom line was that she could get along without him, but she didn't want to. She wanted him in her life; she wanted him with her forever.

"Something's happened in one of my cases," Amanda said.

"Do you want to talk about it? I'm a pretty good listener," Mike said.

"I don't know. It might put you in a funny position."

"Why is that?"

"It involves a case you're handling."

"Why don't you start talking? If I think we're getting into dangerous territory I'll tell you."

Amanda made a decision. Mike was one of the smartest people she knew, and he'd be coming at the problem fresh. Maybe she was wrong about Cashman. There were no pubic hairs missing from the old file, and they couldn't be one hundred percent certain that there was no fingerprint powder on the hammer, now that it was gone. Mike might be able to point out where she'd gone off track. And if he agreed with her, it would help to have a prosecutor on her side.

"I'll be right back," Amanda said.

She found her cassette player and placed it on the coffee table in front of Mike.

"You know who Doug Weaver is, right?"

"Yeah," Mike answered with a sad shake of his head. "I heard about it this morning."

"And you know Doug and I were co-counseling the *Jacob Cohen* case?"

Mike nodded.

"Doug left this voice-mail message for me late last night. It was probably the last call he made before he was killed."

"Have you given a copy to the police?"

"Kate ran one over this afternoon. I already talked to the detective who's working the case."

"Good."

"I want you to hear the call."

Mike's brow furrowed as he listened to Doug's voice-mail message. He shook his head after Amanda replayed it at his request.

"This doesn't mean a thing to me, but I'm guessing it does to you."

Amanda gave him a rough outline of Hannah Graves's case against Jacob Cohen.

"It sounds like your boy's goose is cooked," Mike said.

"I don't think he's guilty."

"Are Weaver's murder and this tape connected to *Cohen*?"

Amanda nodded. "I think there's a possibility that Bernard Cashman murdered Mary Clark and framed Jacob."

Mike's eyes went wide. "You're shitting me, right?"

"I wish I was."

Amanda told Mike about the hammer Kate Ross and Paul Baylor had found in Mary Clark's car and about the conclusions they'd drawn. The deputy DA was totally focused during Amanda's recitation. When she finished, Mike didn't look convinced.

"You realize you don't have a shred of evidence that Cashman is guilty of any of this. You don't have the hammer; you don't have any proof that Cashman attacked Paul Baylor or Mary Clark or Doug Weaver."

"Doug specifically mentions Cashman on the tape," Amanda said, trying not to sound desperate.

"How could I get that tape into evidence? It's hearsay. And even if the jury heard the tape, Weaver doesn't say a thing about

Cashman that any reasonable juror could conclude is an accusation of guilt. What he does say is that he's had a spooky nightmare about snow. Last time I looked, dreams weren't admissible to prove guilt."

"I know he did it, Mike."

"Hey, I know lots of people who've committed crimes and are walking around because we don't have the evidence to arrest them. And Cashman isn't one of them. I'm sorry. I just don't buy this."

"Would you pursue Cashman if we could prove that he fixed other cases?"

"Do you have a specific case in mind?"

"Paul Baylor is taking a look at the evidence in the Vincent Ballard murder."

Mike shook his head. "Prochaska's guilty as sin, Amanda. We've got him cold."

"That's only because Cashman says that he found Art's thumbprint on a beer can in the murdered man's motel room and because he says that the bullet that killed Ballard matches a bullet from Art's closet. If Cashman lied about the evidence you have no case."

"Frank had Paul Baylor double-check that evidence, didn't he?"

"You know I can't answer that."

"That's what I thought."

"If I tell you something will you swear you won't use it?"

"Damn it, Amanda, I don't like this."

"Do you think I'd ever do anything to hurt you or compromise one of your cases?"

Mike was in love with Amanda. When you loved someone, you trusted her. The fact that she trusted him enough to confide in him meant a lot to Mike.

"Go ahead," he said.

"Art swears that he was never in Ballard's room, and Frank believes him."

Mike laughed. "If Prochaska swears he's innocent that's enough for me. He's the most honest homicidal drug dealer I know."

"I'm dead serious, Mike. Art is a homicidal maniac and a drug dealer, but he trusts my dad. If he murdered Ballard he wouldn't admit it, but I don't think he'd be as adamant about his innocence as Frank says he is."

Mike softened. He could see that Amanda was upset and he regretted being sarcastic.

"I just don't buy your theory. Bernie is one of the best criminalists we have and I've never heard a whisper of suspicion about his results."

"You were at that house the other night

when they found the gun that was used to shoot Vincent Ballard. Dad told me that the ballistics test is positive."

"We both know that Martin Breach planted the gun," Mike said.

"What if he didn't? What if Corrales and Castro murdered Ballard with that gun?"

"Have you talked to Hannah Graves about this yet?"

"I can't," Amanda said. "Doug told me she's really got it in for Jacob, and you know how she is. Both Doug Weaver and I humiliated her in trials recently. She's not going to listen to anything I've got to say.

"You could talk to Carlos Guzman in confidence," Amanda added. "Ask him if he's ever had any concerns about Cashman's results."

"Not based on what you've given me. Planting that kind of doubt about Bernie could destroy his career."

"Think of the consequences if I'm right. There's more at stake here than Cashman's career. If Raymond Hayes was innocent, Cashman murdered him. Do you want Jacob Cohen and Art Prochaska on death row for something they didn't do?"

"Jesus, Amanda, Cashman has testified in

hundreds of cases. Every one of them would have to be reviewed if he was found to have falsified the results in even one case."

"They *should* be reviewed if he's faked results in even one case. Look, Mike, I want to be wrong as much as I want to be right, but I can't stand by and do nothing."

Mike took a deep breath and exhaled. "I don't want you to think that I'm not taking what you've told me seriously."

"I know I'm asking a lot. Will you think about what I've said?"

Mike was in turmoil. He wanted to help Amanda, but she was asking him to try to dig up dirt on a criminalist who was respected by everyone in the state. Still, Amanda was scrupulously honest, and she would never use him to gain an acquittal for a client.

"Okay," Mike answered reluctantly, "I'll go to Guzman and ask him if he's ever had any problem with Bernie. But I know what he's going to say."

Amanda smiled with relief. "You're a good guy, Mike. You mean a lot to me."

Mike's heart pounded and it took all of his self-control to keep his composure.

"You know how important you are to me, Amanda."

"Yes, I do." Amanda looked down. "I don't know how you put up with me. I've been a real shit to you at times."

Mike took a deep breath, then plunged in headfirst. "I put up with you because I love you."

The words hung in the air between them. No one moved for what seemed an eternity to Mike. Then Amanda put her wineglass on the table and stood up.

"I don't want you to go home tonight."

Mike wasn't certain he'd heard Amanda correctly.

"Will you stay the night?" she asked.

Mike didn't answer right away. When he did, he sounded frightened but determined.

"Amanda, I want to make love to you more than anything on this Earth, but you really hurt me before. I can't go through that again. If you go to bed with me it's got to be because you love me as much as I love you."

"You know when I broke up with you it wasn't you. I was really messed up from what happened with the Surgeon. And it's taken a long time for me to get over that and to realize how much you mean to me. I do love you, Mike. I wouldn't have asked you to stay if I didn't love you. Now, are we going to get into a deep philosophical discussion or are you going to take me to bed?"

Mike broke into a grin. Several very witty answers to that question occurred to him but he had enough sense not to use any of them. Instead, he stood up and took Amanda in his arms.

PART FIVE
POETIC
JUSTICE

41

WHEN STEVE HOOPER WALKED INTO
Bernard Cashman's office, the criminalist was
working on a report and whistling a happy
tune.

"Got a minute, Bernie?" the detective
asked.

Cashman looked up and smiled. "For you,
any time."

The detective grabbed the chair from the
desk next to Cashman's and settled his bulk
in it. It had belonged to Mary Clark. If Hooper
realized whose chair he was sitting in, he did
not show it.

"What's up?" Cashman asked.

"I'm working the murder of that lawyer, Doug Weaver."

"I've been expecting someone to contact me," Cashman said, faking a sad smile.

"Did you know him well?"

"I've testified in a few of his cases. He was Raymond Hayes's attorney, remember?"

"Yeah, I saw him at the execution. He seemed decent."

"That was my impression."

"I understand he called you the night he was killed."

"Not exactly," answered Cashman, who had rehearsed his answers to the questions he was certain he would be asked. "An operator called me. It was the middle of the night."

"I've talked to her."

"Then you know that I never spoke to Weaver. I only talked to the operator. She said that Weaver wanted to speak to me about the hammer in the *Hayes* case. I'd been in a deep sleep and I was exhausted so I didn't take the call. I thought he'd ring back in the morning."

"Do you have any idea why he'd want to talk to you about the hammer?"

"I haven't a clue, but something weird has

been going on with it. You know that Mary Clark took the hammer from the evidence locker and hid it in her car? And then a thief stole the hammer along with some other stuff from Paul Baylor's lab."

"I know all about that. Hannah had me look into it."

"What have you come up with?"

"Not a thing. It could be a coincidence. Still, Clark taking the hammer and hiding it, then it's stolen and Weaver calls you about the hammer right before he's murdered. It makes you think."

"I agree completely," Cashman said. "I've given the matter a lot of thought, but I haven't come up with anything useful. You don't think this business with the hammer and Weaver's death is going to help Cohen's case, do you?"

"No way. Cohen is a dead man."

"Good. I was worried."

Cashman paused and forced himself to appear solemn and thoughtful like a man carrying a heavy burden. He looked directly at Hooper and hunched forward while folding his hands in his lap.

"Steve, do you think it would have made a difference if I'd taken Weaver's call?"

"No, I don't."

Cashman shook his head sadly. "Sometimes I wonder if I could have prevented Weaver's death if I'd talked to him."

"That's bullshit, Bernie. It was the middle of the night. I wouldn't have taken the call. And what would you have done, anyway? Even if you heard someone breaking in while you were on the phone with Weaver, he lived miles away."

"No, you're right, but I just have this feeling that I could have made a difference. I know it isn't logical."

"Don't beat yourself up about it."

Cashman sighed. "I'll try not to, but . . ."

"No 'buts.' Put this behind you."

Cashman nodded, as if he was going to take Hooper's advice very seriously. The detective pulled a cassette player out of his pocket and laid it on Cashman's desk.

"What's that?" the criminalist asked.

"This is a voice-mail message that Weaver left for Amanda Jaffe on the evening he was killed. Tell me what you think."

Cashman listened intently to see if anything on the tape gave him away. He was greatly relieved when the tape ended.

"I don't know what to say. I can't make

heads or tails out of the dream he had. He does mention me. I assume he was going to suggest that he and Jaffe talk to me about whatever he wanted to discuss when he tried to get through to me. Other than that . . ."

"The reference to snow doesn't mean anything to you?"

"No. What do you make of this, Steve? Do you have any idea why Weaver called me and Jaffe?"

"Not yet."

"What does Amanda think?"

"If she's got a theory she hasn't shared it with me." Hooper stood up. "I've taken enough of your time. If anything occurs to you, give me a call, okay?"

"Of course. I have a personal interest in this case. Will you keep me in the loop?"

"Definitely."

As soon as Hooper left, Cashman allowed himself a self-congratulatory smile. He believed that he had passed this latest test in the investigation with flying colors. He was still smiling when Carlos Guzman and Paul Baylor walked by his office in the direction of the evidence locker. It was the second time in the past few days that Baylor had been nosing around. During a casual conversation with the lab director, Bernie had found out that Baylor had looked at Jacob Cohen's attempted rape case. Cashman had been tense for a day or two, but nothing seemed to have come of Baylor's inquiry. Now Baylor was back, and Cashman was beginning to regret that he had not taken care of the forensic expert permanently when he had the chance.

Cashman paused to marvel at the casual way he thought about taking a life. A few weeks ago, the mere thought had made him physically ill, but he'd grown used to the idea and—he had to admit—he did feel more powerful since he'd freed himself from the natural repulsion most people experienced when they thought about killing a fellow human being. Of course, Cashman did not consider the killing of Doug Weaver or Mary Clark to be an expression of a depraved or criminal desire. He had killed the lawyer and the forensic expert for good reasons. That was what made him different from monsters like Ted Bundy or Jeffrey Dahmer.

There was no question that he had changed since the unfortunate incidents with Mary Clark and Doug Weaver. Killing Clark and Weaver had made him feel so self-confident. He believed that he could do anything and handle any situation. Cashman could see how he had evolved from an insecure boy filled with self-doubt. Now, he thought of himself as a superior man. What would his fellow employees at the lab say if they knew his secret?

Guzman and Baylor disappeared from view and Cashman sighed. He was being silly. There was no need to worry about Paul Baylor. Baylor couldn't hurt him. No one could hurt him.

42

AMANDA JAFFE STARED AT THE PA-perwork that covered the table in the conference room. Spread out before her were police reports, lab reports, autopsy reports, and the reports from Kate Ross and Paul Baylor. She had read them and reread them in the hope that a word or a phrase would ignite an idea she could use to save Jacob Cohen from death row, but there was nothing useful. Amanda took a sip of her latte and rested her bleary eyes for a moment. As soon as they were closed, she thought about Mike Greene.

A week had passed since Amanda had

slept with Mike, and it had been one of the best weeks of her life. They had been together almost every night, and Amanda had to admit that making love had never been more satisfying. With Toby, sex had often been an athletic event. There were times when Amanda thought Toby expected her to raise a placard with a point total after each encounter. Sex with Mike was different and thoroughly enjoyable. They had both been nervous the first time, but there had been no clumsy groping and no anxious stops and starts once they were in bed together. When they were both exhausted, Amanda had fallen asleep contented, and she had experienced that feeling of contentment each time they made love. It had been difficult to concentrate at work, because Amanda found her thoughts filled with images of sex, and that was not good. She needed to focus on the *Cohen* case, which was not going nearly as well as her personal life.

Mike had managed to talk to Carlos Guzman about Cashman, and the lab director had told him that the forensic expert's competence and honesty had never been questioned. Mike had even asked around his office and had not come up with a single complaint about the criminalist. To the contrary, his fellow DAs felt lucky when Cashman worked on their cases.

Neither Kate Ross nor Paul Baylor had made any progress in proving that Bernie had framed Jacob, and Amanda had no other strategy for gaining an acquittal. Once they were in the penalty phase, she knew that the odds of saving Jacob's life were not good.

Art Prochaska's chances were also grim, and the threat of a death sentence was even more immediate, since Prochaska was scheduled to go to trial in a week.

A knock on the door brought Amanda out of her reverie. Kate sat down across from her. In her hand was a sheaf of papers, and on her face was a big smile.

"I've got the fucker," the investigator proclaimed as she handed the papers to her boss.

As Amanda shuffled through the papers, her grim expression gave way to a grin.

"You are amazing," Amanda said when she was finished. "How did you think of this?"

"I was reading through the transcript of the prelim in *Prochaska* and it dawned on me that no one ever questions the academic credentials of a witness. A guy says he was summa at Harvard and everyone just nods. But we think Cashman is a liar, and it occurred to me that if he lied about something big, like Hayes's fingerprint, he might have lied about his academic achievements, so I did a little digging into his academic history."

"Aren't there privacy issues? How did you get this stuff?"

Kate had graduated from Caltech with a degree in computer science and was an expert hacker. She shook her head.

"You don't want to know, and don't even think of trying to get what I just handed you into evidence in a court of law. However, since you are a genius, you would probably have thought about checking Cashman's credentials yourself. Then you would probably tell your father about your brilliant idea and suggest that he ask some nice judge for a subpoena to secure copies of Cashman's academic record to use at Art Prochaska's trial."

"Right you are," Amanda said as she handed the papers back to Kate. "And I would have done all this without ever seeing these papers that you never gave me."

"Or telling Frank where the idea really came

from," Kate answered. "He's old school and I think he thinks that there's not much difference between computer hacking and armed robbery."

43

CARLOS GUZMAN HAD ESCORTED Paul Baylor to the evidence room, waited while he took the pubic hairs from Jacob Cohen's attempted-rape file, then led him to a lab with a microscope and left him alone. Twenty minutes later, Baylor massaged his eyelids for a moment before fixing another hair to a slide and placing it under the lens. A triumphant smile spread across his face. He knew the moment he saw the fifth hair from Jacob's file that it was different from the others. He had the bastard.

Then the smile faded. Paul could prove that at least one of the pubic hairs in Jacob's file was different from the others, but he was a long way from proving that it was Bernard Cashman who had taken the hairs from the file. And what about the evidence in Art Prochaska's case?

Baylor sighed, his triumph of a moment ago forgotten. He had looked at the readouts of the neutron activation analysis until he was bleary-eyed, and his conclusion was always the same: the sample from the bullet that had killed Vincent Ballard was consistent with the sample taken from the bullet found in Prochaska's closet. And then there was that damn thumbprint. How could . . . ?

Baylor froze as he remembered a story he'd heard a few years ago at a convention for forensic scientists. He'd been at the bar in his hotel with a group of criminalists from back East, and one of them had told the story. They'd all laughed at how dumb some people could be. What was the name of the criminalist who had gone to prison—Harvey, Hasty? He couldn't remember, but he did remember that Harvey, or Hasty, had been caught in the most bizarre way.

The subject of the story wanted to go to work for the CIA. The CIA interviewer had pointed out that the criminalist had sworn to obey the law while working for his state law enforcement agency, but CIA operatives were sometimes asked to break the law of the country in which they were working. The interviewer wanted to know if that would be a problem. The criminalist, thinking that it would help him get the job, bragged that breaking the law would be no problem for him. He then told the interviewer how he had faked fingerprints in a case to ensure the conviction of a defendant. The CIA had turned the information over to the FBI, and the injustice was eventually corrected. But it wasn't this aspect of the case that excited Baylor. It was the method the criminalist had used to fake the print that had Baylor's heart pounding.

It took all of Baylor's self-control to keep him from racing back to his lab to reexamine the fingerprint card, but he calmed down long enough to examine the rest of the hairs in Jacob's file and to dust the file to see if he could find Cashman's prints on it. When he finished his work, Paul thanked Carlos Guzman and drove back to his lab.

As soon as he was through the door, Baylor found the evidence card with Prochaska's thumbprint that Cashman claimed to have lifted from the beer can in Vincent Ballard's motel room. He removed a small section of the card with a hole punch. Then he placed the section in his electron microscope and scanned it. Every element has its own X-ray signature and frequency. The electron microscope identified the X-ray signature of every element present on the sample he'd taken from the card.

"Yes!" Paul shouted when his suspicions were confirmed. He punched his fist in the air with the enthusiasm shown by Tiger Woods when he won the Masters. He'd made the breakthrough that would break Cashman. His satisfaction would be complete when he figured out how the bastard had faked the ballistics test, but he already had an idea how that illusion had been created.

Paul took a deep breath. When he was calm, he dialed Amanda Jaffe's number.

"What's up, Paul?" Amanda asked.

"I made a breakthrough in *Cohen*," he said excitedly. "Remember I told you that I checked to see if there were any pubic hairs missing from Jacob's attempted-rape file?"

"Yes. You said there were eight hairs listed on the inventory and eight in the file."

"There are eight, but only six are Cohen's. I tried to think of what I would do if I were going to frame Jacob. I'd use the hairs in the file but I'd have to assume that a smart defense attorney might figure out that the file was the source."

"Cashman put someone else's hair in the file!"

"Bingo! I went back to the crime lab and examined the hairs. Two of them aren't Cohen's."

Amanda thought of something. "Paul, the last time anyone saw Clark was when she and Cashman worked that liquor store robbery, wasn't it?"

"Right."

"So Mary was probably killed within twenty-four hours of finishing her work."

"That fits with the estimate of time of death in the autopsy report," Baylor agreed.

"If Clark confronted Cashman after they finished working the crime scene and he killed her soon after, he'd have to have gotten the pubic hairs quickly. So he probably took the substitute hairs from another file at the lab. I'm willing to bet that we'd find a file with two missing hairs if we searched the files in the evidence locker."

"I agree," Baylor said.

Amanda was quiet for a moment. Then she frowned.

"We still can't prove that Cashman took the hairs unless he was incredibly stupid and handled the file without gloves."

"I dusted the file for prints. His aren't on it."

"Damn. Well that's great work, anyway, Paul. Don't let up. You figured out how Cashman faked the pubic hairs. You'll get the rest."

Baylor paused for a dramatic heartbeat. Then, when he could stand it no longer, he said, "I know how Cashman faked the thumbprint."

44

"THIS IS DEPRESSING," FRANK Jaffe said to Amanda, as they walked down the nearly empty fifth-floor corridor toward Judge Arthur Belmont's courtroom on the morning of the first day of testimony in Art Prochaska's case.

"What's depressing?" Amanda asked.

"Oregon did away with the death penalty in 1964. When it came back in the eighties, there were mobs of reporters and spectators crowding these halls whenever someone was on trial in a capital case. I couldn't walk two steps without a reporter jamming a microphone in my face or being blinded by the lights from television cameras. But we've gotten so used to state-sanctioned executions that everybody takes these capital cases for granted nowadays."

Amanda looked around the quiet courthouse corridor, where the people she passed in the hall were preoccupied with their own problems and uninterested in whether a middle-aged gangster had murdered a lonely junkie. Her father was right. It looked as though the only person interested in Art's case was Martin Breach, who got up from a bench and walked over to the lawyers.

"How are things looking, Frank?"

"You can't predict what will happen in a trial, but I'm feeling good about our case."

"Did you come up with something about that fingerprint?" Breach asked.

"Yes, I did."

"Did one of the lab guys set up Artie?"

The question was asked without emotion, but Frank could sense rage swimming below Breach's calm surface like a great white shark cruising beneath the placid waters off a beach filled with vacationers.

"Sit in on the trial when the state's forensic expert testifies this afternoon and you may be pleasantly surprised," Frank said with a reassuring smile.

"You don't think it will hurt Artie to have me in court?" Martin asked anxiously.

"Not today, Martin, not today."

Bernard Cashman had studied the composition of the jury in the *Prochaska* case before choosing his wardrobe. An hour before court, he'd still not decided which suit and tie to wear. Most of the jurors were from the lower and middle classes, so he didn't want to look too well dressed: but there was a retired doctor, and also a housewife who was married to a wealthy architect. They might not give full credit to the testimony of a witness who dressed down too much. In the end, he selected a conservative suit that he'd purchased at an upscale department store, instead of one of the suits that he'd had hand-tailored in London on a recent trip, and a solid navy blue tie. He felt that the outfit was understated but tasteful.

Mike Greene summoned Cashman to the witness stand an hour after court resumed in the afternoon. Cashman had treated himself to a light lunch at one of the better downtown restaurants, but had not ordered wine. Even though he was not worried, he wanted to be clear-headed for Frank Jaffe's cross-examination. Cashman had testified against Jaffe's clients before, with success, and Frank had not laid a glove on him at the preliminary hearing, but it was better to be safe than sorry. He couldn't imagine what the attorney had learned since the preliminary hearing that he could use to call into question the evidence that would lead to Art Prochaska's well-earned conviction. True, the defendant had probably not killed Vincent Ballard, but he had gotten away with murder and numerous other serious crimes in the past. This time, he would not be so lucky.

As Cashman strode down the center aisle of the courtroom, he spotted Martin Breach and several of his associates. Breach fixed the criminalist with an intimidating stare that unnerved Cashman for a moment, but he forgot about the mob boss as soon as he was through the bar of the court and standing in front of the witness box, ready to take the oath.

Cashman's hair had been styled the day before, and his beard and mustache were neatly trimmed. After being sworn, he dazzled the jury with his smile, then humbly related his academic credentials and work experience in the pleasing baritone that was so effective with jurors. After these preliminaries, Mike Greene asked Cashman to explain the investigation that he had conducted at the Continental Motel. Then Cashman explained how he had discovered the thumbprint of the defendant, Arthur Wayne Prochaska, on a beer can that had been sitting on the night table in Vincent Ballard's room and why he had concluded that the bullets that had caused Mr. Ballard's death were consistent with bullets discovered in a box of bullets found by the police during a search of the defendant's closet. By the time Mike Greene finished his direct examination of the witness, the jurors were nodding after every statement Cashman made, and he was certain they were convinced beyond a reasonable doubt that Prochaska was guilty as charged.

"Your witness, Mr. Jaffe," Judge Belmont said.

"Mr. Cashman," Frank said, "you testified that you graduated from the University of Oklahoma with a degree in chemistry, did you not?"

"That's correct."

Amanda handed Frank a document. It was hard for Cashman to tell from his seat across the courtroom what it was. Frank studied the document for a moment before turning back toward the witness.

"Would you please tell the jurors the name of the professor who taught the first chemistry class you took in college?"

Cashman chuckled. "That was many years ago. I'm afraid I can't remember his— or her—name."

"Can you tell the jurors the name of any professor who taught you chemistry?"

Cashman shrugged. "I simply don't recall any of them."

"There would have been several, wouldn't there, if you were a chemistry major?"

"Well, yes."

Frank took another look at the document he was holding.

"Let me give you an easier task. Would you please tell the jury the title of three classes you took in your major while at the University of Oklahoma?"

Cashman shifted in his seat. "Let's see. There was introduction to chemistry, of course, and organic chemistry, and I believe one of them was called advanced chemistry."

"Those sound about right, but I'm having a problem."

Frank stood and strolled across the space between the defense table and the witness box. On the way, he handed a thin packet of papers to Mike Greene and the bailiff. When he reached Cashman, he handed him an identical packet.

"For the record, Your Honor, I've just handed the district attorney and Mr. Cashman copies of Mr. Cashman's undergraduate transcript from the University of Oklahoma and his transcript from graduate school at the City University of New York. I'd like them marked as exhibits."

"Any objection, Mr. Greene?" Judge Belmont asked.

"No, Your Honor."

"Very well," the judge ruled.

"Can I have copies of these documents given to the jurors?" Frank asked.

"No objection," Mike said.

Amanda handed a stack of copies to the bailiff, who distributed the transcripts to the jurors.

"Maybe you can help us out, Mr. Cashman," Frank said after each juror had a copy. "My eyesight's a lot worse since I've gotten older, so maybe I missed them, but other than intro to chemistry—in which I believe you received a grade of C—I can't find another chemistry course listed on that transcript. Could you point them out to the jurors?"

"They're not on here. The college must have sent you someone else's transcript. I remember getting an A in my introductory chemistry class."

"I see. This is all a big mistake?"

"Well, obviously."

"Just for the record, before I move on, what major did the Bernard Cashman who is listed on this transcript have?"

Cashman pretended to study the document. "It appears to be secondary education."

"Not chemistry?"

"No."

Frank looked at the second transcript. "It looks like the City University of New York screwed up, too. This is supposed to be the transcript of someone named Bernard Cashman, but it shows that this fellow never finished his master's degree, and it looks like it was in the education department, too—not forensic science."

Cashman did not respond.

"You'd better call up those schools when court is over and get this straightened out, so you won't be embarrassed the next time you testify," Frank said.

Cashman was seething inside, and he vowed to make Jaffe pay. Not right away, when suspicion would fall on him, but later—maybe years later—when waiting would make revenge all the sweeter. Jaffe was laughing at him now, but he would see who had the last laugh.

Frank glanced at Amanda, who handed him a folder that Paul Baylor had put together.

"I'd like to ask you a few questions about the thumbprint you found on the beer can in Vincent Ballard's room. You said that you dusted the can with black fingerprint powder."

"Yes," answered Cashman, who was relieved that there would be no more questions about his academic record.

"Then you used tape to lift the print, which was highlighted by that black fingerprint powder, and transfer it to an evidence card so it could be preserved as evidence?"

"That's correct."

Frank scratched his head. When he turned toward the jury, he looked puzzled.

"Can you explain to the jury and to me why there are traces of copy toner, like you'd use in a Xerox machine, on the evidence card with Mr. Prochaska's print?"

Cashman felt faint. "There isn't any copy toner on the card," he stated with as much authority as he could muster.

"Gee, that's not what my expert and Ron Toomey, one of your coworkers at the crime lab, told me," Frank said.

"I . . . I don't know what you're talking about."

Cashman looked toward Mike Greene, desperate for him to object, but Greene was leaning back in his chair, studying him, stone-faced. Martin Breach was sitting a few rows behind the prosecutor. His eyes lasered in on Cashman. The expert's stomach rolled and he forced himself to look away.

Frank turned toward the judge. "With your permission, Your Honor, I would like to interrupt Mr. Cashman's testimony and put on Paul Baylor, the defense forensic expert."

"That's highly irregular, Mr. Jaffe. The state hasn't rested yet."

Mike Greene stood up. "In the interests of justice, Your Honor, the state has no objection."

Greene walked to the bench and handed the judge a document. "This is a stipulation between the parties arrived at yesterday afternoon to the effect that Ronald Toomey, an expert at the Oregon State Crime Laboratory, if called to testify would agree with Mr. Baylor's scientific conclusions regarding the ballistics tests and fingerprint analysis conducted by Bernard Cashman. Mr. Toomey's reports are attached to the stipulation."

Cashman glared at Greene. If the stipulation was entered into yesterday, he'd been set up.

The judge read the stipulation and Toomey's report before turning to the witness.

"Mr. Cashman, I think it would be best if you stepped down."

"Your Honor, could you please order Mr. Cashman to stay in court?" Greene asked.

While the deputy district attorney was talking, Paul Baylor entered the courtroom, and two police officers slipped into seats in the last row, next to the door. Judge Belmont noticed the policemen and ordered Cashman to take a seat in the front row of the spectator section.

"Mr. Baylor," Frank said after his expert had been sworn and had told the jury about his academic credentials and work history, "did I ask you to review the conclusions of the state crime lab in Mr. Prochaska's case?"

"Yes."

"Were there two specific pieces of evidence on which I wanted you to concentrate?"

"Yes, the thumbprint Mr. Cashman claimed to have found on a beer can that was located on a night table at the crime scene and the ballistics tests conducted on the bullets that caused Mr. Ballard's death and bullets found in Mr. Prochaska's home."

"Now that you've finished your tests, do you agree or disagree with Mr. Cashman's conclusion that Mr. Prochaska's thumbprint was on the beer can?"

"It's my conclusion that there is no way to tell whose print was on that can."

"Why is that?"

"If there was a print on the can, Mr. Cashman destroyed it."

"But Mr. Prochaska's print is on the evidence card, is it not?"

"Yes, but the print did not come from the can. The print was faked."

"Please explain what Mr. Cashman did."

Paul Baylor turned toward the jurors, who were leaning forward, eager to hear what he had to say.

"Mr. Cashman had me going at first. There was a match when I compared Mr. Prochaska's prints with the evidence card he created. When I blew up the crime scene photograph of the print on the can I made the match again. Then I got an idea, and I tested the fingerprint card. There were chemicals on the card that were consistent with copy toner.

"Here's how Mr. Cashman faked the print," Baylor said. "While at the crime scene, Mr. Cashman took one photograph of the can to show where he found it in the motel room and a close-up of the can. Someone's print may have been on the can, but after Mr. Cashman applied the tape to the area he had dusted, any print would disappear from the metal surface, leaving a blank space. So no one can go back and check the beer can to see what print—if any—was on it.

"Next, Mr. Cashman found a fingerprint card with Mr. Prochaska's prints in the police files. Then he scanned a picture of the beer can and Mr. Prochaska's prints into a computer. Once that was done, he cropped the fingerprint he wanted to the size it would be if it was found on the beer can and he overlaid it onto a picture of the can, making it look like Mr. Prochaska's print was on the can before he made the lift. That way, anyone who blew up the photo of the beer can taken at the scene would find a match with Prochaska's prints."

"Have you asked a computer expert to verify your conclusion?"

"Yes. His report is attached to mine."

"Go on," Frank said.

"Faking the evidence card was just as easy and equally clever. Mr. Cashman made a photocopy of Mr. Prochaska's prints from his real fingerprint card and lifted the print he claimed to have found on the beer can from the photocopy. Then he transferred that print to a blank evidence card. If I hadn't tested the card and found copy toner, he would have gotten away with it."

"So, what you're saying is that it is impossible to tell if there was ever a fingerprint on the beer can?"

"Yes. If there was a print, Mr. Cashman removed it."

"Assuming that there was a print on the can, is it possible to say who made it?"

"No."

"What about the ballistics evidence that shows a match between the bullets taken from Mr. Ballard's head and the bullets found in Mr. Prochaska's home?"

Baylor looked directly at Cashman before he answered. Cashman's features were frozen into a mask of hate.

"That was equally clever and incredibly simple. The people at the nuclear reactor did conduct neutron activation analysis of two samples, but neither of them came from the bullet that killed Vincent Ballard. These samples are very small and both of them came from one of the bullets that were found in Mr. Prochaska's closet. We ran a second test on a sample from the bullet that did kill Mr. Ballard and one of the bullets from Mr. Prochaska's closet and they don't match."

"No further questions," Frank said.

The jurors were whispering to one another, and Judge Belmont looked stunned.

"Do you have any questions for the witness, Mr. Greene?" the judge asked.

"No, Your Honor, but I would like Mr. Cashman taken into custody. At a minimum, he has committed perjury concerning his credentials and his test results, and the charges may be more severe. There is an ongoing investigation on which I cannot comment."

Cashman leaped to his feet. "This is outrageous!" he shouted. "I've done nothing wrong."

"Mr. Cashman," the judge said, "please don't make any statements until you've spoken to an attorney. You're in court. Everything you say is being recorded and can be used against you."

Cashman started to open his mouth but thought better of it. The policemen who had been sitting in the back of the courtroom had moved next to Cashman while Greene and the judge were speaking. Cashman noticed them and turned pale.

"You may take Mr. Cashman into custody," the judge instructed the officers.

Cashman straightened his cuffs and submitted to being searched with as much dignity as he could muster. As he was being handcuffed, Cashman turned his head and saw Martin Breach watching him. As soon as their eyes met, the mob boss formed a pistol with his thumb and finger. He pointed it at Cashman and smiled. Cashman looked away quickly, but he could not get that chilling image out of his mind.

As soon as the criminalist was out of the courtroom, Mike Greene addressed the court.

"Your Honor, in light of Mr. Baylor's testimony, which Mr. Toomey agrees with completely, coupled with the very real possibility that Mr. Cashman has perjured himself about his qualifications and the results of the tests that incriminated the defendant, I find myself in the position of having to move for a dismissal of the murder charge in this case.

"Mr. Prochaska has also been charged with being an ex-convict in possession of a firearm in the indictment in this case, and with the murder of Juan Ruiz in a separate indictment. The ex-con charge is based on the fact that a firearm was found during a search of Mr. Prochaska's home. The Ruiz murder charge is based on ballistics tests conducted on the weapon found in Mr. Prochaska's home. The search warrant that allowed the police to search Mr. Prochaska's home was based on Mr. Cashman's affidavit, in which he swore that he found a fingerprint belonging to the defendant on an item discovered in Mr. Ballard's motel room. The state believes that the statements in the affidavit were intentionally false. Therefore, we have no choice but to move for a dismissal of the two charges: murder and ex-convict in possession of a firearm."

"Quite frankly, Mr. Greene, I am shocked by what I've heard in court today," Judge Belmont said. "This is an incredibly serious matter—two murder charges—but I would be derelict in my duty to the justice system if I did not grant your motion."

The judge turned toward the defendant. "I am dismissing all of the charges against you, Mr. Prochaska. You'll be taken back to the jail for processing and released."

As soon as Judge Belmont left the bench, Prochaska grinned at Frank.

"Man, you're good. Not only did you get me off but you put that liar in jail. What's going to happen to him?"

"It's too early to tell, Art. There's an investigation going on right now and Mr. Cashman could be facing murder charges before this is over."

"Wouldn't that be a shame," Art mused, but he was thinking that it would be better if Bernard Cashman were not behind bars, where it would be harder for Art to get at him.

Mike walked over to Frank as the guards took Prochaska back to the jail.

"That was good work," the prosecutor said.

"I had nothing to do with it." Frank smiled at Amanda. "Thank my brilliant daughter. It was her idea to check on Cashman's academic record. And Paul was no slouch either."

"I'm just embarrassed that it took me so long to figure out something that was so simple," Paul said.

"Slow but steady wins the race," Frank said.

"That's not a comment on my intellectual abilities, is it?" Baylor asked.

Frank laughed, and Mike and Amanda smiled. After a little more chatter, Paul and Frank left.

"How are you feeling?" Amanda asked Mike as he gathered up his things.

"Like shit. Prochaska may have been innocent in the Ballard case but I'm certain he killed Juan Ruiz. Now, thanks to Cashman, he's getting away with murder. And I can't begin to think of the mess we're going to have when we start reviewing Cashman's cases."

"You'll feel a lot better when they free the innocent men from prison who were framed by Cashman."

45

MIKE GREENE STOOD UP WHEN
Bernard Cashman and his attorney, Alec De-
Haan, were shown into the conference room
in the district attorney's office. Cashman had
been released on bail yesterday afternoon
and had slept in his own bed last night. He
was dressed in an expensive hand-tailored
suit and appeared to be his usual jaunty self,
but after a night and part of a day in jail, the
sparkle in the criminalist's eyes had been replaced by a wary look.

Mike nodded at Cashman and said "Good
morning, Alec" to Cashman's portly, balding attorney. If Cashman had hired DeHaan,

who was very good and very expensive, he knew he was in serious trouble.

"Have a seat," Mike said, indicating two chairs on the other side of the table.

Sitting with Mike were Carlos Guzman, Steve Hooper, and Billie Brewster. All of the law enforcement officers looked grim. De-Haan knew them. He nodded in their direction.

"I see you've got the troops with you," De-Haan said.

"We're all very interested in your client," Mike said.

"Obviously, or you wouldn't have arrested him. But there has to be a reason for this meeting. Care to tell me why we're here?"

"We know that Bernie faked evidence in one murder case and we suspect that he has faked evidence in several other cases. As we speak, the lab is doing an audit of every case in which Bernie has been involved."

"That's ridiculous," Cashman blurted out. "I stand by my results in every case I've handled. I'm human, so I may have made a mistake or two during my career, but fake evidence results—never! And why would I want to frame Prochaska? I don't even know the man."

DeHaan laid a hand on his client's forearm. "This is not the time, Bernie. Remember what we discussed earlier? Let me do the talking in here."

Cashman shut up and settled for glaring at Mike.

"My client does have a good point. Why do you think he would frame someone he doesn't know?"

"That has us all puzzled," Mike said. "We can't figure out why he would fake the results in *Prochaska* and *Cohen*."

"*Cohen*?" Cashman blurted out. "You're saying that there's something wrong with that case, too?"

"You know Ron Toomey, don't you?" Mike asked DeHaan.

The lawyer nodded.

"He and your client were the criminalists who worked Mary Clark's crime scene. Two pubic hairs belonging to Jacob Cohen were found on her thigh."

Cashman leaned over and whispered in DeHaan's ear.

"As I understand it," DeHaan said, "Mr. Cashman had nothing to do with the discovery of the hairs. Ron examined the body."

"That's right, but we checked the evidence

locker. There were supposed to be eight of Cohen's pubic hairs in a file from an old case in which he was accused of attempted rape. The number of hairs in the evidence locker matches the number on the receipt, but two of them aren't Cohen's. It looks like someone removed two of his hairs and put them on Mary Clark's corpse to make it look like Cohen tried to rape her. Then those hairs were replaced with hairs from somewhere else—probably another case file. We're checking on that now."

DeHaan conferred in whispers with his client.

"Mr. Cashman doesn't know anything about these hairs. Mr. Toomey discovered them. As I understand it, Mr. Cashman never touched them."

"That may be true, but it is faked evidence in another case in which he was involved."

"You still haven't explained what his motive would be for rigging the cases of men he's never met."

"We're looking into that," Carlos Guzman said. "In the meantime, he's suspended from his duties in the crime lab and Mike intends to prosecute him for perjury."

"That's not fair, Carlos," Cashman said. "I have important work to do."

"Someone will fill in for you until we straighten this out."

Cashman searched the room for a friendly face and settled on Detective Hooper.

"Steve, tell them I'd never do this. We've worked together on a lot of cases. Have you ever questioned my results?"

Hooper had to force himself to meet Cashman's stare. When he spoke he sounded embarrassed.

"I've always respected you, Bernie, but . . ." The detective shrugged. "There's a lot for you to explain and it doesn't look good. I think there are even some questions about the fingerprint on the hammer in the *Raymond Hayes* case."

Fear shot through Cashman until he remembered that the hammer and the evidence bag were gone and no one could prove he'd done anything wrong.

"We both want to get the bad guys, Bernie, but faking evidence, that's going too far."

"Prochaska is evil, Steve."

"Well, yeah, I suppose so, but what about the guy who really killed Ballard? He's just as bad and he's going to walk because of what you did. Everybody is pretty upset, Bernie. I don't want to even think about the possibility that Hayes was innocent. We'd appreciate it if you could clear this up for us."

"There's nothing to clear up. You know Hayes killed his mother. I haven't done anything wrong. There's been a mistake."

DeHaan laid a cautioning hand on Cashman's forearm, and his client stopped speaking.

"You asked for this meeting for a reason, Mike," DeHaan said. "What is it?"

"I might be willing to make a deal on the perjury case if Bernie tells us the names of the cases in which he's falsified evidence or given false testimony."

Cashman leaned over and whispered heatedly in his lawyer's ear. DeHaan whispered something in reply. Cashman leaned back and glared at Greene.

"My client is adamant that he has never intentionally falsified evidence in a case, but I'd be derelict in my duty if I didn't listen to your offer. Right now, however, Mr. Cashman is upset and I think it would be better if the two of us finished this discussion in your office."

"That's fine with me. Why don't you see Bernie out? I'll tell the receptionist to bring you back to my office when you're ready."

Cashman started for the door. Then he stopped and turned back toward the prosecutor.

"I'd appreciate it if you addressed me as Mr. Cashman from now on, Mr. Greene. My friends call me Bernie. I no longer consider you a friend."

"So, what do you think?" Mike asked everyone as soon as the door closed behind Cashman and DeHaan.

"I think we've got Bernie dead to rights on perjury and obstruction of justice and whatever else you can come up with in connection with the Vincent Ballard murder, but I don't see a case against him for anything else," Billie Brewster said.

"I agree," Hooper chimed in. "I know you think he might have killed Mary Clark, but Cohen's still my bet, even with the pubic hairs. Hannah agrees. And there's no proof that the hairs that were found on Clark's thigh came from the evidence locker. I know it would be a big coincidence, but Cohen could have left them when he tried to rape

Clark. There could be another explanation for the two odd hairs that were found in Cohen's old case file."

"Hannah could probably get a conviction in *Cohen*, but there's a hell of a lot of evidence pointing at Bernie," Mike said.

"Not evidence," Hooper corrected, "conjecture. For him to be the killer he'd have to have lied about the print on the hammer, and we can't prove that with the hammer missing. So you've got no motive and no other evidence against Bernie for the Clark murder."

"He's right," Guzman said. "Unless we find something wrong with some more of Bernie's cases, the Ballard case will turn out to be an isolated incident."

"You're not thinking of keeping him on?" Mike asked, alarmed.

"No, even one instance of perjury and falsifying evidence is too serious," Guzman answered. "But there's a big difference between lying in a trial and killing two people."

"You're right," Mike conceded. He checked his watch. "Alec is probably waiting for me. I'll let you know if Bernie decides to come clean about other cases."

"If there are other cases," Hooper added.

* * *

Cashman drove home from the district attorney's office in a daze. How could they suspend him after all he'd done for the police, the prosecutors, and the people of this state? He was a hero; he'd saved the lives of people who could have been the victims of some of Oregon's most vicious criminals. He didn't deserve this.

Cashman put any thoughts of going to jail out of his mind. That was simply not possible. He worried most that he would be fired for fabricating evidence and lying in court. If that happened, no other forensic laboratory in the country would hire him. What would he do then?

When he entered college, he did plan to major in some area of science, but he had not done well in chemistry or the other science classes he'd taken. That's when he decided to be a science teacher. But the idea of being a teacher never excited him. Then, when he was in graduate school, he had noticed an opening for a forensic scientist at the crime lab in Colorado and he had falsified his transcripts. Things would have gone badly for him if he'd been caught, but he'd made such a good impression at his interview that no one had questioned his credentials or checked with his schools. After his first job, no one had asked about his school credentials again.

Cashman guessed that it would be just as easy to take on a new identity and falsify his résumé again, but that would mean working somewhere else. He liked working at the Oregon state crime lab. He was respected there. He didn't want to go anywhere else.

Cashman willed himself to calm down. As he saw it, he had five potential problems: the *Cohen* and *Prochaska* cases, the assault on Paul Baylor, and the disposal of Weaver and Clark. Bernie knew that the police might call what he'd done to Clark and Weaver murder, but he could not bring himself to label his actions in this way. Taking the lives of Clark and Weaver had been necessary to preserve the greater good, but he was objective enough to know that others might not see his actions in this light. His greatest fear was that he would be charged with murder, but when he thought about the possibility, he really didn't see that happening.

There was no evidence that he'd shot Doug Weaver—or was there? There was a piece of evidence that could pose a problem. The .38 he'd used to shoot Weaver was still in his home. In the excitement of his escape from Weaver's house, he'd forgotten to get rid of it. Then he'd put it in his nightstand. He'd planned to dispose of it, but he had not gotten around to it yet. Okay, he'd get rid of the gun. How to do that, though? Cashman thought back to the meeting. Greene was definitely trying to get him to panic. That was it! He'd bet he was under surveillance right now. They were counting on him panicking and running to get rid of the weapon. They knew they didn't have the evidence for a search warrant for his house, but if he was caught taking the murder weapon out of his house . . . Well, he wasn't going to fall for that.

And there was another reason why he couldn't get rid of the gun right away. He needed it for protection until he could get another weapon. Cashman shivered involuntarily when he remembered the way Martin Breach had looked at him. He knew all about Breach. The man was ruthless and insane—a maniac with a penchant for torture and mayhem. No, he needed the gun for now, but he vowed to get another as soon as possible.

What about Mary Clark? They knew about the pubic hairs, but there was no way they could prove he took them. As far as he could figure it, there was no way they could charge him with Clark's murder. And if there were evidence that he had assaulted Paul Baylor, he would be sitting in a jail cell.

So he was safe from the most serious charges. That left criminal charges connected with the manufacture of evidence. He was in trouble there. They couldn't get him for the *Raymond Hayes* case now that he'd gotten rid of the hammer and the evidence bag, and he didn't think they would be able to prove that he was responsible for planting any of the evidence in the *Cohen* case, but he couldn't see a way to explain the thumbprint or the ballistics evidence in *Prochaska*.

A thought occurred to Cashman. He smiled. What if he admitted his sins and repented? He could say that he knew Prochaska was a dangerous criminal, and got carried away. Alec DeHaan could argue that he had succumbed to the pressures of the job. Maybe he had mental problems, depression, something like that. Could they fire him if he faked the evidence because of a mental disorder? Wasn't that covered by the Federal Disabilities Act? Yes, that was it. He would deny everything else and say that what he did in *Prochaska* was the product of temporary insanity. That would take care of everything.

As soon as he was home, Bernie poured himself a glass of twenty-five-year-old scotch and sipped it while he prepared a dinner of coquilles St. Jacques. The scallops he'd purchased at his favorite fish market were exceedingly tender, and the wine he chose to accompany them was exquisite. By the time he finished dinner, Cashman was certain that what had happened during the *Prochaska* trial was only a temporary setback. His world was in disarray now, but he was certain that his life would be back on an even keel very soon.

46

MARTIN BREACH HAD A BIG GRIN on his face when Art Prochaska walked into his office in the Jungle Club. He stood up, walked around his desk, and hugged his friend. Henry Tedesco watched the homecoming from a sofa at the side of the room.

"Welcome back, Artie," Tedesco said, his Irish brogue making the greeting sound like poetry.

"It's great to be out of that jail," Prochaska said to Breach. "Thanks for having Charlie pick me up."

"What? Did you think I was going to have you take a fucking taxi?"

Art smiled. He knew Martin would never let him take a taxi, but he felt that he should thank him anyway. Charlie had driven him home, where Maxine had showered with him, helped him get rid of weeks of sexual tension, and fed him a heaping plate of bacon, eggs, and toast. While he was eating, Maxine told Art that Martin wanted to see him about some business when he was ready.

When Art was seated and Martin was back behind his desk, Breach offered Tedesco and Prochaska Cuban cigars from one of several boxes he had smuggled into Miami along with his narcotics shipments. Art lit up, but Tedesco declined. Martin pointed his cigar at Prochaska.

"Frank tells me this fuck Cashman set you up."

"It looks that way."

"That's not nice. If the Jaffes hadn't caught on to this prick, bad things could have happened to you."

"I knew Frank would do right by me," Art said.

"That don't change the fact that this fuckhead faked evidence to frame you."

"No, it don't," Art agreed.

"What are we going to do about this guy?"

Art shrugged. "It looks like we don't have to do anything. Frank told me the cops think he killed two people. It'll do him good to do time. I got friends in OSP who'll look him up once he's there."

Breach shook his head. "That might not work. Frank told me that everyone thinks Cashman killed the broad in the lot and that lawyer, but he doesn't think they can prove it. Worst he's probably going to get is some time for fucking with the evidence, but that won't amount to much and it won't be hard time. With Alec DeHaan as his lawyer he'll probably cut a deal and he won't do time at all."

Prochaska's brow furrowed as he thought about what Breach had just said. Tedesco could almost see wheels turning.

"That ain't right," Art said when he had mulled over the situation.

"My thought exactly," Breach agreed. "I was thinking maybe Charlie should pay Cashman a visit, maybe take him somewhere so we could explain why what he done was bad. Maybe give him an attitude adjustment."

Prochaska smiled. "That's a good idea, Marty."

"I'm glad you agree, Artie."

47

"COME ON, COME ON," CHARLIE LaRosa whispered to Teddy Balski, a cat burglar who worked for Martin Breach. Balski, who was crouched next to the lock on the side door of Bernard Cashman's house, looked over his shoulder.

"You want to do this?" he asked, making no attempt to hide his annoyance.

"I don't like standing around out here where anyone can see us," answered LaRosa, who had been looking around nervously while Balski jimmied the lock. It was three-thirty a.m. and there were no lights on in the homes of Cashman's neighbors, but it would take only one citizen with an urge for a late-night snack to screw up their operation.

"There," Balski said.

LaRosa opened the door. Cashman's state-of-the-art alarm system issued a plaintive whine for less than three seconds, because Martin Breach had bribed an employee of the security company to give him Cashman's code and the location of the keypads.

"Cashman's bedroom should be at the top of the stairs," LaRosa whispered as the men moved through the kitchen into the entryway at the front of the house. He had memorized the floor plan of Cashman's house, which Breach had also purchased.

LaRosa and Balski crept up the stairs stealthily. They planned to knock Cashman out and take him to the warehouse that Breach used for torture and interrogations. Normally, Charlie didn't have any feelings about his assignments, but he liked Art and he hoped that Cashman put up a fight so he could hurt him. It was one thing to go down for something you did, but framing a guy for something he hadn't done, well, that wasn't right.

When they reached the top of the stairs,

LaRosa signaled Balski to step back. Then he opened the door quietly and walked into the dark bedroom. He had taken a step when he saw a flash of light. Then he died.

It was a good thing that Bernard Cashman had been so worked up that he could not sleep, or he might not have heard the brief whine his alarm emitted before Charlie LaRosa punched in the security code. Moments later, he was crouched at the side of his bed, .38 Special in hand.

Employees of the crime lab were also police officers, and Cashman had excelled on the shooting range. Now that he'd killed twice, he was not troubled by the thought of taking another life. True, he was frightened by the knowledge that someone had broken into his home, but his fear was tempered by the anticipation of punishing the burglars for daring to invade his property.

The door to his bedroom opened. Moonlight backlit a large, black shape. Cashman aimed at the center of the silhouette and fired. Then he aimed a second shot at the intruder's head. The burglar staggered backward and fell. Someone else issued a startled cry. Cashman rushed to the door and pumped two shots into Teddy Balski, who stared at Cashman for a second before tumbling backward down the stairs.

Cashman descended the stairs slowly, his gun leading the way, until he was standing over Balski, whose ragged breathing told Bernie that he was still alive. Cashman aimed between Balski's eyes and fired another shot just as he heard the sirens.

Cashman froze. Someone had called the police. From the sound of the sirens, they would be at his house in minutes. Did he have anything to worry about? No. These men were burglars, there were two of them, and they had broken into his bedroom in the middle of the night. If ever a homeowner had a right to use lethal force to defend himself, it was under circumstances such as this. Cashman was breathing a sigh of relief when he heard the police car skid to a halt in front of his house. He was about to open the door for the officers when a thought paralyzed him.

The gun! He had shot the intruders with the .38 Special he'd used to kill Douglas Weaver. Normally, no one would think of running a ballistics check to see if his gun was the murder weapon in Weaver's case, but he was a suspect in Weaver's murder and someone was bound to think of testing his gun. What was he to do?

A pounding on his front door distracted Cashman.

"Open up, police," a man shouted.

"I'm coming," Cashman yelled back as his mind raced to find a solution to his dilemma. "Don't shoot. I live here. I'm a policeman, too."

Suddenly, Cashman thought of a plan.

"I'm holding a gun," he shouted through the door. "I'm putting it down on the floor."

Cashman opened the door and stood back with his hands up. Two policemen stood on his front porch. They were young, they were extremely tense, and they were pointing weapons at him.

"It's okay. They're dead," Cashman assured the officers. "Two men broke into my house. I shot them. There's no danger."

"Please keep your hands up, sir, and identify yourself," said a tall, thickly built redhead, who Cashman figured was in his late twenties.

"I'm Bernard Cashman, a forensic expert at the Oregon state crime lab. I own this house. I'm glad you're here. I'm scared to death." Cashman pointed at the .38, which he'd tossed on the floor. "That's their gun. You'll need it for evidence."

"Can you show me some ID, Mr. Cashman?"

"Certainly. My wallet is in my bedroom. You'll have to come up, anyway. One of the men is on the stairs and the other is in front of my bedroom door on the landing."

On the way to Cashman's bedroom, the officers checked Balski and LaRosa for signs of life. When the criminalist had satisfied the officers that he was who he claimed to be, the redhead took him downstairs to the kitchen, to wait for the experts from the crime lab and the detectives.

Cashman put up water for chamomile tea, which would calm his nerves, and a pot of coffee for the police and forensic scientists. While he ground the coffee beans, Cashman sighed deeply and pretended to be distraught.

"I know they broke into my house and I shot them in self-defense. God knows what they would have done to me if I hadn't gotten the gun. But I feel—I don't know—I guess 'guilty' is the appropriate word."

"That's common in shooting situations,

Mr. Cashman," the officer assured him. "You know you can get counseling. Most cops who kill someone in the line of duty feel bad about it, even when the dead guy deserves to be shot."

"Thanks for your reassurance. Maybe I will look into getting counseling. By the way, how did you manage to get here so fast?"

"Your neighbor, a Mrs. Studer, had trouble sleeping, too. She looked out her bedroom window and saw the two men jimmying your lock and called 911."

"Ah, Mrs. Studer," Bernie said just as the teakettle began to whistle.

I must remember to thank the nosy bitch, he thought to himself.

"You're in deep shit, Bernie," Billie Brewster told Cashman when she walked into his kitchen.

"Why do you say that?" answered Cashman, who had been sipping his tea while his compatriots from the lab rummaged through his home, dusting for prints, taking pictures, and doing everything he was used to doing in other people's homes.

"You got any coffee?" Brewster asked. She'd been awakened from a sound sleep and had raced over without stopping for a cup of java at the local 7-Eleven as soon as she learned in whose home the double shooting had occurred.

Cashman pointed at the counter. "I put up a pot for the team," he said. "It's a Peruvian roast."

"They put caffeine in the coffee in Peru?"

"I never drink decaf," Cashman answered, offended by the question.

"Good, because you're going to have to stay alert. Do you know who you just shot?"

"No." Cashman drank his tea. "It was dark and everything happened very fast. The squad car drove up minutes after I shot them. Since then I've mostly been in here."

Brewster walked to the counter where Cashman had thoughtfully set out coffee mugs, sugar, and cream.

"What did happen?" she asked, taking a sip of strong, black coffee.

"I gave a statement to the first officer on the scene."

"Humor me."

"Of course. Forgive me. I know how these things go. It's just that I've never been a victim before."

Brewster worked on her coffee while Cashman told her about the shooting.

"I was having trouble sleeping and I heard my alarm go off briefly."

"It stopped?"

Cashman nodded.

"That means they had your alarm code."

"I guess they must have."

For some reason, it had not occurred to Cashman that the burglars must have had his alarm code. The idea made him very nervous.

"So you heard the whine," Brewster said. "Then what happened?"

"Naturally, I was scared to death. I hid behind my bedroom door. When the door opened I attacked the intruder out of desperation. I must have startled him because he staggered backward onto the second-floor landing. He was holding a gun, and it flew out of his hands while he was going backward. I grabbed it and shot him. There was another man and I shot him, too."

Brewster nodded. "You say the guy on the landing was holding the gun, then he dropped it and you picked it up and shot him with it?"

"Yes."

"Did you know that he had another gun in his jacket?"

"A second gun?"

"Yes."

"No, I didn't know that."

"Sort of strange to be packing two guns?"

Cashman shrugged. "I don't think that's so strange. He's an armed burglar. He's obviously into guns. You still haven't answered my question. Why did you say I was 'in deep shit' when you entered the kitchen?"

"You've pissed off some very serious people, Bernie. The guy at the top of the stairs is Charlie LaRosa, one of Martin Breach's enforcers."

Cashman blanched.

"You should have thought twice before framing anyone in Breach's organization, let alone Art Prochaska, Breach's only friend in his sick and corrupt world."

"I didn't . . ."

Brewster held up her hand. "What you did in court is for the DA. I don't want to discuss that case. But it looks like Martin Breach isn't waiting for the courts to decide this one."

"Can you arrest him?"

"Not unless he confesses or we find written instructions in LaRosa's pocket from Breach ordering him to kill you."

"You've got to protect me."

"You know we don't have witness protection. That's the feds. And anyway, you're not a witness. You're a defendant."

"There must be something you can do. You can't stand by and let Breach murder me."

"I don't have a single piece of evidence that implicates Martin Breach in this burglary. For all I know, LaRosa and Prochaska were tight and LaRosa decided to kill you on his own."

"We both know what happened here."

"No, we don't."

"How am I going to protect myself?"

"I can't answer that, but you can't leave the jurisdiction. That's a condition of your bail."

Cashman's self-confidence had deserted him. He was terrified. Breach would be furious when he learned that Cashman had killed two of his men in addition to framing his best friend. If he stayed in Oregon, it was only a matter of time before Breach got him.

Brewster stood up and stretched. Then she drained her mug.

"Thanks for the coffee, Bernie. I've got to get back to work. One piece of advice, though. If I were you I'd work out a deal with Mike where I got protection for coming clean. That might be your best, and only, hope for staying alive."

48

MIKE GREENE SAW FEAR IN BER-
nard Cashman's eyes when he followed his
lawyer into the conference room at the district attorney's office. Steve Hooper and Billie
Brewster flanked Mike, but instead of looking
grim, as they had looked at the first meeting,
they seemed relaxed and confident.

"You know what happened at Mr. Cashman's house two nights ago?" Alec DeHaan
asked as soon as he and his client were
seated.

"I've read all the reports, and Billie briefed
me," Mike answered.

"What are you doing about Martin Breach?" DeHaan demanded.

Mike shrugged. "There's nothing we can do. We can't question the burglars, because they're dead; and no one has come up with a shred of evidence connecting Breach to the crime."

"You know Breach sent those men," De-Haan insisted.

"I don't know any such thing, Alec."

DeHaan looked upset. "Mr. Cashman and I have been talking. We feel that his life is in danger. He might be willing to discuss a deal along the lines you suggested, if it included protection from Martin Breach."

Mike didn't respond at once. Instead, he stared at Cashman until Cashman looked away.

"My office is no longer interested in the deal I proposed, Alec. We're way beyond deals at this point."

Mike pushed a document across the table. While DeHaan was reading it, Mike turned to the criminalist.

"Mr. Cashman, this morning the grand jury indicted you for the murder of Doug Weaver."

"What?" Cashman exclaimed.

"Don't say a word, Bernie," DeHaan cautioned his client. Then he asked Mike, "What's going on here?"

The prosecutor addressed his answer to Cashman. "We've got you, Bernie. You finally screwed up."

"Don't say a word," DeHaan repeated.

"He doesn't have to, Alec. I'll lay it out for both of you. We ran a ballistics check on the gun Bernie used to shoot Charlie LaRosa and Theodore Balski. It's the same gun he used to murder Doug Weaver."

"That's not Mr. Cashman's gun," DeHaan said. "If you really read the police reports, you'd know that the gun belonged to Charlie LaRosa. LaRosa dropped it when my client fought with him."

"We don't believe your client's story. LaRosa had another gun on him, and only your client's fingerprints were on the .38."

"LaRosa is an ex-con, a dangerous criminal," DeHaan said. "Are you shocked that someone like that would bring two guns with him when he's committing armed robbery?"

"What about the fingerprints?"

"LaRosa and Balski were both wearing gloves. That's why LaRosa's prints aren't on the gun. My client held the weapon when he shot LaRosa. That's why his fingerprints are all over the .38."

Mike waited a beat. Then he smiled. "I don't mean the fingerprints on the gun. Your client did a great job explaining why his are on the .38 and LaRosa's aren't."

"Then what are you talking about?" De-Haan demanded.

"According to Mr. Cashman, Charlie LaRosa was holding the .38 when he walked into Mr. Cashman's bedroom. Mr. Cashman says that he surprised LaRosa, who dropped the gun when he staggered backward onto the second-floor landing."

"Where is this going?" DeHaan said.

"Bear with me. As your client told it, the gun is on the floor, he picks it up, shoots LaRosa, shoots Balski, the cops come seconds later, he drops the weapon on the floor near the door, tells the officers what he did with the gun, they come in the house and take custody of the weapon. Is that about right?"

"That's what's in the reports."

"Then your client has a problem. His fingerprints are on the cartridge casings of the bullets that were left in the gun, and there's no way that could have happened unless he loaded the weapon, which—according to his own statements—he did not do."

DeHaan's mouth opened, then closed again. Mike shifted his gaze to Cashman, who was pale and wide-eyed. Steve Hooper stood up, and Billie Brewster followed him around the table.

"Mr. Cashman, you are under arrest for the murder of Douglas Weaver," Hooper said. "I am now going to give you your *Miranda* rights. If you don't understand any of these rights, please tell me and I will repeat them for you."

Cashman looked shell-shocked as Hooper read him his rights from a laminated card to be certain of not making a mistake. Then Cashman was cuffed and led away.

"I'll be up to talk to you at the jail," De-Haan said. "Don't discuss your case with anyone."

DeHaan's shoulders slumped as soon as the door closed.

"You really think he murdered Weaver?" the lawyer asked.

"I think he killed Weaver and Mary Clark, and I think he attacked Paul Baylor and stole the hammer from the *Hayes* case. And I'll indict him for the murder of Raymond Hayes if we ever find the hammer. Now that would make an interesting legal issue for the Supreme Court. Is it murder to lie about evidence in a capital case that leads to the execution of an innocent man? I'd sure like to argue that one, but I'll settle for putting Bernie on death row for Weaver's murder."

Suddenly, DeHaan looked exhausted.

"He does have a way to escape the death penalty, Alec. We're certain that Hayes isn't the only person Bernie framed. If he'll plead to aggravated murder with no parole and tell us of all the cases he fixed, I'll try to convince Jack not to pursue the death penalty. Get back to me soon. This may be Bernie's only chance to live."

"Do you think he'll take the deal?" Amanda asked Mike Greene over dinner at her apartment that evening.

"I don't know. Cashman is a strange duck. I'd have to have a PhD in psychology to have any chance of figuring out what makes him tick."

"I hope he does, so you can find out who else he's framed. It makes me sick to think that there are innocent men rotting in prison."

"We may not need a deal to figure out what cases were made with tainted evidence. We found a scrapbook when we executed the search warrant in Cashman's house. It has clippings of some of Cashman's cases. Guzman is checking what Cashman did in every case in the book. If we're lucky we'll catch the cases where he framed the defendants."

"That would be terrific."

Amanda and Mike ate in silence for a few moments. Then Amanda had a thought.

"You know, it's sort of poetic justice, the way you caught Bernie."

"What do you mean?"

"It was the gun he used to kill Doug that did him in. Doug avenged Raymond Hayes. He's really the one who nailed Bernie. It's just sad that he had to die to do it."

"I'm sad about everything to do with this mess. Mary Clark was a very nice person, and Raymond Hayes dying . . . And think about the damage to the system. How will jurors believe the next forensic scientist who gives testimony? You have one rotten apple like Cashman and everything can fall apart."

"The system has survived worse than this. Cheer up. The vast majority of criminalists are honest, decent people. There might be some initial damage but everything will get back to normal eventually."

"You're probably right," Mike said, but Amanda wasn't certain he really believed that.

"You're much too morose this evening. Think about Jacob Cohen. He'll be out of jail tomorrow."

"I guess that's one good result," Mike answered grudgingly.

"Think about the fact that you get to grouse about the case to me over a nice dinner."

Mike smiled.

"You can also focus on what's going to happen after this nice dinner," Amanda said. Then she batted her eyes at her dinner companion and ran her tongue slowly and lasciviously across her lips.

"Oh, no," Mike moaned. "You don't expect me to have sex with you?"

"Perish the thought."

"Okay, then. I just wanted to make sure that you weren't trying to hustle me into bed."

"Not a chance. I was thinking more of the rug in front of my fireplace."

49

HANNAH GRAVES AND MIKE GREENE walked out of Judge Belmont's chambers and sat at the counsel table closest to the jury box. Graves looked angry. Amanda Jaffe followed the prosecutors into the courtroom. She spotted Rabbi Cohen and his wife, Valerie, sitting with the other spectators and flashed a brief smile at them before sitting next to Jacob.

Shortly after the lawyers were seated, Judge Belmont took the bench, and his bailiff called Jacob's case.

"For the record," Judge Belmont said, "I have just met in chambers with District Attorneys Hannah Graves and Michael Greene, representatives of the state of Oregon; and Amanda Jaffe, representing defendant, Jacob Cohen. Mr. Cohen is charged with several crimes, the most serious being murder.

"It is my understanding from our discussion in chambers that the state wishes to dismiss the charges against the defendant in the interests of justice. Is that correct?"

Hannah Graves was furious at having to dismiss against Cohen, who she still stubbornly believed was guilty, and Mike had volunteered to speak for the district attorney's office.

"That is correct, Your Honor. As you are well aware, there have been several developments concerning the evidence in this matter and the state feels that it cannot proceed against Mr. Cohen given the current posture of the case."

In chambers, Mike had told Judge Belmont about the problem with the pubic hairs and the government's suspicion that Bernard Cashman had murdered Mary Clark to keep her from talking to Carlos Guzman about the hammer in the *Raymond Hayes* case. All parties had agreed that this information should not be put on the record because of the ongoing investigation into all of Cashman's cases.

"Very well," the judge said. "I will dismiss all of the charges against Mr. Cohen. He will be released from jail as soon as he's processed out. If there is nothing further, court will be adjourned."

As soon as the judge was off the bench, Hannah Graves walked out of the courtroom without saying a word. Mike smiled at Amanda and followed Graves into the hall. He knew that Amanda would have to talk with her client and his parents. He would be seeing her that evening, anyway.

Amanda had told Jacob that his case was going to be dismissed that morning. He had been suspicious and confused by the rapid turn of events, and Amanda had the feeling that he would not believe he was free until he was back on the street.

"It's all over, Jacob," Amanda assured anymore."

"She does," Jacob said, nodding in the direction that the departing prosecutor had taken.

Amanda smiled. "That's true, but Hannah is the only one. Jack Stamm, the head DA, authorized the dismissal himself, so you don't have to worry about being charged again."

Rabbi Cohen and his wife walked over to Amanda and their son. Jacob looked down at the floor, but he didn't do anything else to reject his parents.

"We can't tell you how grateful we are," Solomon said as he shook Amanda's hand.

"You saved our son," Valerie added.

"Actually, Doug Weaver saved Jacob. He figured out that Cashman lied about the print on the hammer when we were all stumped and I'm guessing that he gave up his life rather than tell Cashman that he'd left me a message, because Cashman never came after me. Doug was a very brave man."

The rabbi nodded, and his wife looked sad. "There's been so much tragedy because of that man."

"Well," Amanda said, "it's over now."

Then she turned to Jacob. "Have you given any thought to what we talked about?" Amanda asked. He had been taking medication and had been greatly improved the last two times Amanda had met with him.

Jacob nodded. "I'll go to the hospital," he said quietly, still not looking at his parents.

"I visited it with your folks. It's a very good

hospital. The grounds are beautiful, and your room will be very nice. It will be much better than sleeping in that lot. You'll be safe."

Jacob didn't respond.

"Jacob's parole officer gave his okay. He'll be released in an hour or so and you can drive him over," she told Solomon. Then she addressed her client.

"Is that okay, Jacob? Can your mother and father drive you? They really want to."

Jacob looked up from the floor. "Okay," he answered softly.

Valerie reached out slowly and tentatively until her hand rested on Jacob's forearm. He didn't flinch or resist.

"We love you, Jacob. We never thought that you did what they said. We want to help you any way we can. That's what parents are for—to love you and help you, especially when times are hard."

Jacob nodded.

"I've got to take Mr. Cohen upstairs," the guard said.

"Okay," Amanda said. "Your folks will be waiting for you."

Jacob started to walk away. Then he stopped and turned toward Amanda.

"Thank you," he said.

Amanda smiled. "It's been my pleasure."

As soon as Jacob was out of the courtroom, Rabbi Cohen released the breath he'd been holding in.

"He seems better," Valerie said.

"He does," Solomon agreed, but Amanda could hear the reservation in his voice. They all knew that Jacob would never be completely cured. Their hope was that he would get well enough to lead the most normal existence he was capable of.

"I hope that the hospital works out," Amanda said.

"We all do."

The Cohens walked away and Amanda felt her chest swell with pride. She felt very good about saving Jacob and about continuing to fight for him even when it seemed certain that he had killed Mary Clark. There were a lot of bad days when you were defending bad people you knew were guilty, but a case like Jacob's made it all worthwhile.

EPILOGUE

BERNIE HELD OUT TO THE BITTER end, but he finally took the deal. They insisted that he had framed innocent men, and they wanted to know why. He was willing to have Alec DeHaan give Carlos Guzman a list of cases in which he had given false testimony or rigged the evidence, but he refused to explain why he'd chosen the men he'd sent to prison. Cashman knew that they were monsters, and he felt no duty to explain. In his eyes, he was a martyr who was sacrificing his life and career to a worthy cause that the morons and mediocrities who now controlled his life would never understand.

It didn't take more than a few days in jail for Bernie to regret his decision, but it was too late to take back what he'd done. What wore on him was the boredom; the absolute certainty that tomorrow would be exactly like yesterday, and the day after tomorrow would be more of the same. And the food was atrocious and inedible. How was he going to put up with the food?

On the third day after his plea and sentencing, he was still in the Justice Center jail, awaiting transport to the penitentiary, when a guard came to escort him to a noncontact room for a visit. Alec DeHaan made a practice of meeting with him in a contact room. He could not imagine who else would visit him—certainly not those ungrateful cretins from the crime lab. They had deserted him. To think that he had believed they were his friends.

"Knock when your visit is up," the guard told Cashman as he opened the door to the narrow room. When Cashman stepped inside, his mouth opened and he stared at his visitor.

Martin Breach smiled at Cashman and gestured toward the telephone receiver that hung from the wall. If Cashman had not been bored out of his skull, he would have screamed for the guard, but he knew that Breach could not get to him through the bulletproof glass, and he was curious why the man who wanted to kill him was paying him a visit. When he picked up the receiver, he was holding on to the possibility that Breach was here to tell him that he was going to forgive and forget.

"How did you get in here?" Cashman asked.

"I could tell you," Breach answered with a chilling smile, "but I'd have to kill you."

Cashman lost his color, and Breach chuckled.

"Just kidding," he said. "Actually, killing you is the farthest thought from my mind, Bernie. I was rooting for you to get life. See—and I hope you don't mind me waxing philosophical—I don't believe that religious mumbo jumbo about an afterlife. I think this is all you get and when you die it's like sleep, only there's no dreams and you don't wake up.

"If I'm right, death ain't so bad, no worse than a dreamless sleep. So you could say that dying puts an end to suffering, which is why I never wanted you to die. If you was executed you would have gotten away with trying to frame Artie and I want you to pay for what you done."

Cashman wanted to say something, but

he was paralyzed with fear. Breach could see that, and he smiled.

"I'm guessing you're scared because of my reputation. Well, you should be. You can see how easy it was for me to arrange for this visit. I also arranged to have any trace of it disappear. You can scream your head off about me being here, but you'll never be able to prove it.

"So why am I here? I'm here to tell you that no matter where you go I'll find out. My contacts are that good. And as soon as I find out where you are I'll arrange to have you punished. The people will be different, their methods will be diverse, but you will suffer big-time for the rest of your life for what you did to my best friend."

Breach got up and put his hand on the knob that opened the door to freedom, but he paused before he left.

"People will be waiting for you, Bernie, and they have instructions to make sure that you survive every beating so that you can move on to your next encounter with pain. I wish you a long life."

The door closed behind Martin Breach. Cashman stared through the glass for a moment. Then he began to sob.

ACKNOWLEDGMENTS

I GOT THE IDEA FOR *PROOF POSI-tive* several years ago, when I started seeing news articles about criminalists in state and federal crime labs around the country who were intentionally falsifying evidence or giving false testimony in court to get convictions. As someone who practiced criminal law for twenty-five years and who questioned the conclusions but never the honesty of the forensic scientists who testified against my clients, I found these articles disturbing. Fortunately, the vast majority of the men and women who work in the nation's crime labs are honest and hardworking. It is a shame that their reputation has been tarnished by a few very bad apples.

Three upstanding and dedicated forensic experts helped make this book realistic. On occasion, I have taken literary license with crime-scene procedure. Please don't blame these men for this. They told me the way it's supposed to work. I just didn't always follow their advice. I am very grateful to Brian Ostrom for teaching me about crime-scene procedure and for spending countless hours reviewing my manuscript for errors. I am indebted to Brent Turvey for reviewing my manuscript, for teaching me very clever ways to falsify evidence, and for writing "Forensic Fraud: A Study of 42 Cases," *Journal of Behavioral Profiling*, April 2003, vol. 4, no. 1. Finally, I want to thank Jim Pex for reviewing the manuscript and pointing out my errors.

For the prologue, I leaned heavily on Dave Groom's chilling account of the execution of Jerry Moore, which he recounted in "The Executioner's Face Is Always Hidden," in the June 1997 issue of *The Oregon Defense Attorney*, a publication of the Oregon Criminal Defense Lawyers' Association. Much of the best prose in my prologue was taken from Dave's account, because I could not improve on it.

I also want to thank Scott Miles for the information provided in "A Gideon Moment," *The Champion*, the magazine of the National Association of Criminal Defense Attorneys.

Others who assisted with the research for this book are Bridget Steyskal, Pat Callahan, Nancy Laundry, and Emily Lindsey.

I want to thank Jean Naggar, my agent, and everyone at the agency for their continued support, but I want to especially thank Jennifer Weltz for her brilliant idea.

Kudos to Jill Schwartzman, my intrepid editor—thanks for all your hard work. Thanks to Christine Boyd for coming up with the title for this book, and thanks to the marketing and publicity departments for all the work they put into all of my books. Actually, I am indebted to everyone at HarperCollins for the way they have championed my writing.

As always, I want to thank the home team: my son, Daniel, and his delightful wife, Chris; my daughter, Ami, and her husband-to-be, Andy Rome; and my muse, my fabulous wife, Doreen. You are the best.